THE DEMI

'You can't help getting caught .... smartly paced story . . . well conceived and well executed' *SFX*

'An amazingly quick and enjoyable read' *British Fantasy Society*

'Explosively creative barely defines *The Demi-Monde: Winter*. It blew me away' James Rollins

'As labyrinthine and darkly witty as its predecessor . . . Rees's abundant imagination and punning, neologism-strewn prose carries [*The Demi-Monde: Spring*] off with aplomb' *Daily Mail*

'Elegantly constructed, skilfully written, and absolutely impossible to stop reading' *Booklist*

'The writing is state of the art . . . exquisitely worked out and told at a cracking pace . . . Welcome to holo-hell' Stephen Baxter

'Incredibly entertaining' *The Times*

'Rees makes the book work: the world he's created is a psychopathic nightmare' *Guardian*

'Part *Matrix*, part *Escape from New York*, with a dash of film noir and a whole host of imagination . . . Beautifully written [with] a serious kick ass plot' *Falcata Times*

'A fast paced fantasy [that is] very intelligent . . . ensures all fans will be on tenterhooks' *SciFiNow*

'If you're looking for a unique and ambitious blend of Cyberpunk, Steampunk, Historical, Dystopian, SF, Fantasy madness, you have to check this out' *Zoessteampunkreviews.com*

'This is a quartet that aficionados of both SF and steampunk will want to read and having read it they will probably feel duty-bound to inform their friends. And so they should. [We are] hugely looking forward to the conclusion' *Concatenation*

Also by Rod Rees

THE DEMI-MONDE:
Winter
Spring
Summer

THE
DEMI-MONDE
FALL

ROD REES

Jo Fletcher
BOOKS

First published in Great Britain in 2013 by Jo Fletcher Books
This edition published in Great Britain in 2014 by

Jo Fletcher Books
an imprint of Quercus
55 Baker Street
7th Floor, South Block
London
W1U 8EW

A CIP catalogue reference for this book is available
from the British Library

ISBN 978 1 84916 510 5 (PB)
ISBN 978 1 84916 661 4 (EBOOK)

10 9 8 7 6 5 4 3 2

Typeset by Ellipsis Books Limited, Glasgow
Printed and bound in Great Britain by Clays Ltd, St Ives plc

Contents

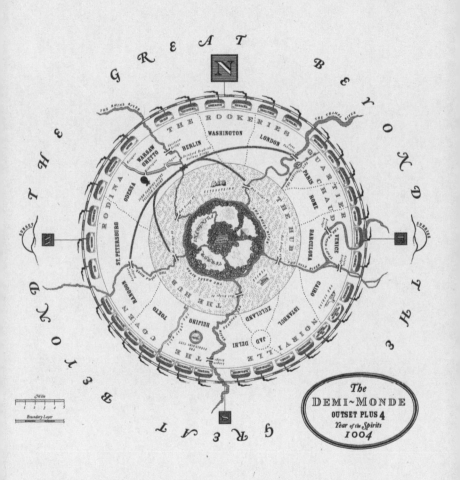

The Most Secret   Order of Grigori

1 February 2019

I am pleased to report that all aspects of the Final
Solution are now in place and ready for execution on the
30th April this year. Moreover, I am able to advise the
Grand Council that Ella Thomas, who since her arrival in the
Demi-Monde has manifested the most virulent and powerful of
Lilithian tendencies, has been assassinated and with her
death a profound enemy of the Grigori and a major obstacle
preventing the success of the Final Solution eliminated. Now
the only opponent of any note still active in the Demi-Monde
is Norma Williams, her last act being to disrupt the
'Victory in the Coven' rally sponsored by Reinhard Heydrich,
and held on the last day of Summer. The Grand Council should
note that measures have been taken to minimise the impact of
her intervention on the attitude of the ForthRight
population regarding their attending the Ceremony of
Purification and that I have ensured that my agents in the
one remaining Portal giving access from the Demi-Monde to
the Real World have been alerted. It is impossible for Norma
Williams to escape from the Demi-Monde and return to the
Real World.

Thus all is set fair for the execution of the Final Solution.

Recognising that such an ambitious undertaking as the Demi-
Monde - the most sophisticated virtual world ever conceived
- would be extraordinarily difficult to conceal - especially
as it involved the clandestine accessing of confidential DNA
data relating to Fragiles - we chose to disguise the
Demi-Monde's true purpose by persuading the US military to
adopt the simulation as a training ground for their
neoFights.

The true purpose of the Demi-Monde is fourfold:

- To digitally replicate a coterie of individuals identified
as possessing the MAOA-Grigori gene, who, given the
appropriate stimulus (notably regarding their appetite for

continued over...

blood and their exposure to Cavoritic radiation), are capable of having this latent Grigori aspect resuscitated;

– To digitally replicate a critical mass of the element Cavorite (aka Mantle-ite) in the Demi-Monde, this in the form of the Great Pyramid located in the region known as Terror Incognita. As the Grand Council will be aware, despite our best efforts, it has proven impossible to fabricate viable quantities of Cavorite here in the Real World and certainly nothing like the quantity necessary to achieve activation of the MAOA-Grigori gene (this being equal in magnitude to the Cavoritic radiation experienced during the meteor strike of 1795);

– To digitally recreate a number of the more talented scientists from history to work in the Heydrich Institute for Natural Sciences in the Demi-Monde's virtual Berlin to help the Real World scientists develop noöPINC, the latest iteration of our Personal Implanted nanoComputer. NoöPINC is a cyborg-virus, that is a virus with nanocybernetic structures incorporated into its makeup. The virus itself a development of the unsuccessful 1947 Plague – is Fragile-specific and hence is harmless to Grigori or those possessing an activated MAOA-Grigori gene. The Grand Council may rest assured that there will be no repeat of the unfortunate events of 1947 when the Plague mutated to an extent that it presented a lethal danger not only to Fragiles but also to Grigori;

– To entice the daughter of the President of the United States into the Demi-Monde in order that her Real World body might be inhabited by her cyber-doppelgänger, Aaliz Heydrich. This was achieved and Miss Heydrich has proven herself very accomplished with regard to promoting the faux-religious organisation the Fun/Funs. Six million members of the Fun/Funs will be attending the Gathering on the 30th April, when their Grigorian aspect, nurtured in their doppelgängers ('Dupes') active in the Demi-Monde, will be energised.

All four of these ambitions have been or are in the process of being achieved. In three short months the breeding stock of the Grigori will have been enhanced by the six-million-strong nuGrigori created with the assistance of the Demi-Monde; all Untermenschen (notably the Jews, the blacks and the Asiatic races) that contaminate the genus Homo will have been eradicated; and the purified Fragiles will have been culled and the rump remaining reduced to

continued over...

dutiful serfs by the use of noöPINC. After eight thousand years of hiding in the shadows the Grigori stand on the brink of taking their rightful place as the Master Race.

I remain Your Humble Servant,

Professor Septimus Bole

Prologue

The office of Sir Broderick Bole, ParaDigm House, Whitehall, London
The Real World: 15 February 1947

Operation Downfall was the codename given to the disastrous American-led invasion of Japan which began in October 1946. The operation was ultimately abandoned when US servicemen contracted a hitherto dormant infection that became known to the world as the Plague of '47. The surrender of Japan was ultimately realised by the use of atomic weapons against the cities of Hiroshima and Nagasaki, the bombs dropped by Vickers-ParaDigm Valiant aircraft of the RAF on the 15th December, 1946.

History of the Second World War, 1939–1946: Dwight D.
Eisenhower, ParaDigm Publications

Bole hated Fragiles, the corollary being he loathed Frank Kenton with a passion.

'I never knew it got so darned cold in England, Broderick,' said Kenton, warming his backside in a rather exaggerated fashion in front of the large fire that was keeping Bole's office the warmest room in Whitehall.

'It's *Sir* Broderick, actually, Mr Kenton,' Bole corrected, who detested anyone, let alone an American barbarian like Kenton, omitting his title. With an effort of will he kept his temper in check and his hands from Kenton's throat. He needed the Fragile. 'But you are quite right: this winter is one of the worst in living memory.'

'Well, I guess that's the problem with the weather, it's so darned unpredictable.'

Bole said nothing, though he was tempted to tell Kenton that the Bole Institute for the Advancement of History *had* predicted that the winter of 1946/1947 would be a bad one. And now the winter was here and the Institute's forecast confirmed, the difficulties caused by the abnormal cold were such that even the euphoria generated by the defeat of Japan had been dampened. Since the beginning of February Britain had been in the grip of snow, snow and more snow. Roads had been made impassable, railway lines had cracked and power stations had shut down. Even before the Winter of '47 had run its course, with February not even over, the tabloids had already christened it 'The Great Winter'.

Bole's American visitor had obviously massaged sufficient warmth into his buttocks to allow him to begin the meeting. Kenton sat down in Bole's guest chair and made to light a cigarette.

'I'd rather you didn't,' said Bole tersely.

'Didn't what?' asked Kenton.

'Smoke.'

'Really? Why not? Doctors say it's good for you: the nicotine stimulates the nervous system.'

'I doubt whether such stimulation can compensate for the inhalation of the noxious cocktail of toxins contained in cigarette smoke. This being the case, I would prefer it if you refrained. I do not wish to be a passive participant in your unhealthy habits.'

Reluctantly Frank Kenton returned the cigarette to the pack.

Bole shot his heavily starched cuffs, arranged his legal pad and fountain pen a little more exactly before him, and began. 'You must forgive me for asking, Mr Kenton, but which department do you represent? Since the demise of the OSS, the actual make-up of American intelligence organisations has become a trifle confused.'

Kenton gave a rueful grin, which made him look even younger than he was. The dossier the Intelligence Bureau had prepared said he was thirty-four but in truth the combination of sandy red hair, freckles, horn-rimmed spectacles and bow tie gave him the appearance of an adolescent out on his first job interview. He certainly didn't look like the high-flyer of American counter-intelligence he was reputed to be.

Nor the racist he most certainly was, but then Kenton kept his rather extreme opinions regarding 'race contamination' to himself, presumably on the basis that if his secret affiliation to the Ku Klux Klan became known it would put something of a crimp on his career prospects.

'Well, ya know, Brod . . . Sir Broderick, my position is sorta . . . ill-defined,' Kenton answered as he wrung his hands, made uncomfortable by not having a cigarette to fiddle with. 'I sorta float around, doing whatever I'm asked to do. But for pay and rations I'm part of the Strategic Services Unit.'

'And your current responsibilities?'

'I'm attached to General MacArthur's staff. I act for the general on matters pertaining to the occupation of Japan.'

'Then you seem a long way from the centre of those operations, Mr Kenton.'

'The general asked me to come to London to liaise with Para-Digm Rx regarding the problems we're experiencing in Japan. The disease situation is getting kinda serious. We're hoping, Sir Broderick, what with you being majority stockholder in Para-Digm Rx and all, that you might be able to put a little pepper on ParaDigm's tail. It is, after all, the largest pharmaceutical company in the world: if anyone can help, it's ParaDigm.'

Bole nodded and then took the opportunity to take up the

coal tongs and heap more coal onto the fire. He wanted Kenton's nicotine dependency to really kick in before the negotiations went much further. 'Tell me a little of the background to this disease,' he said as he stoked the fire.

'As you know, Operation Downfall began with the invasion of Kyushu on the third of October '46 . . . as soon as the typhoon season was over. Kyushu was intended to be the staging post for the assault on the main island, Honshu. The land operations were pretty confusing for a while: the Nips were well dug in and there were more of them than our intelligence had predicted. It was Okinawa writ large: a real bloodbath. The consequence was that casualties ran high and the hospital ships attached to the invasion fleet were run ragged, so it took a while for the medical staff to identify that a good proportion of those invalided off the beaches had contracted a fever. They'd got what we now call the "Jap Jitters".'

'Describe it.'

'As best we can tell it's some form of filovirus, though the symptoms seem to suggest it's closely akin to the bubonic plague in that it attacks the lymphatic system.'

'Incubation period?'

'Four to five weeks.'

'The vector?'

'We're not sure but the smart money is on fleas.'

'Contagious?'

'Very. Those with the disease have had to be strenuously quarantined.'

'How many fatalities from the Plague thus far?'

Kenton shuffled on his chair. Bole knew that the information he'd asked for was something the US Army had been desperately trying to keep under wraps, something most certainly not for public consumption. 'To date, a little over one hundred thousand members of our armed forces have died from the Jitters.

The mortality rate is running at around eighty per cent. That's why we evacuated Kyushu.'

And also why ParaDigm – prompted by Sir Broderick's unborn son, Thaddeus – had been obliged to use atomic weapons to persuade the Japanese to surrender, but regarding this, Bole remained silent.

'I understand the disease has a racial bias.'

'That's correct, Sir Broderick. Negroes are particularly susceptible: black GIs have been dropping like flies.'

As it had been intended they should drop, and the other UnderMentionable scum – most notably the Jews – with them. What Bole hadn't expected was how quickly the Plague had mutated, to such an extent that it now threatened the Grigori themselves. Which was why ParaDigm was making its vaccines available to the Fragiles: the Plague had the potential to cull the wrong subspecie of the genus *Homo*.

'Treatment?'

'None.'

'And now it has a foothold on the west coast of the United States.'

Kenton eyed Bole suspiciously. 'How do you come to that conclusion, Sir Broderick?'

'Mr Kenton, my department was not named the Intelligence Bureau on a whim, it being expert in acquiring, analysing and drawing conclusions from . . . intelligence. The Jap Jitters, as you so charmingly call this disease, has, according to this intelligence, now been reported in Seattle, where as of yesterday forty-seven people were held in the containment wing of the Seattle General Hospital. Presumably the disease was brought to Seattle by the crews of vessels returning to the navy dockyards from Japanese waters. There are also outbreaks reported in San Francisco and San Diego. My understanding is that the US government is considering the imposition of martial law in these areas and the enforcement of a *cordon sanitaire* stretching along the Sierra Nevada designed to protect the Midwest from the spread of the infection.'

Kenton sighed in a despairing sort of way. He suddenly looked tired and his shoulders sagged as though weighed down by the responsibilities he was carrying. 'You are remarkably well informed, Sir Broderick, I was led to believe that that information had been assigned the very highest security classification. As you'll appreciate, the last thing we want is the civilian population in the USA panicking.' Kenton took a deep breath. 'But you are quite correct, the situation is . . . grave. The disease has reached the USA and we are struggling to contain it. That's why I'm here. We need the help of ParaDigm Rx.'

Bole pushed a piece of paper across the desk to Kenton. 'This is a transcript of an article carried in the *London Gazette* of the twelfth of January 1931. It describes a plague gripping the island of Zanzibar, which lies just off the coast of Tanganyika.'

Kenton read the piece and then looked up at Bole. 'You believe the Jap Jitters is the Zanzibar Plague?'

Bole nodded. 'The virologists at ParaDigm Rx have compared the two pathogens and have confirmed them to be very closely related. The Zanzibar Plague was, just like your Jitters, a highly infectious haemorrhagic filovirus. Where your American medical experts are in error is that there is no intermediate carrier: the Plague is pneumatic, transmitted directly, person to person, and it is this which makes it so deadly. Death itself comes from necrosis of the internal organs – they literally melt – and, as might be expected, is hugely painful.' Bole paused for a moment, as though collecting his thoughts. 'The Zanzibar Plague, Mr Kenton, is one of the most deadly diseases ever encountered by man. It is not a pleasant way to die.'

'While, Sir Broderick, I am intrigued by this historical coincidence, I am at a loss to see how it might assist my country.'

'As Zanzibar is a protectorate within the British Empire, Para-Digm Rx was asked to search for a vaccine that would prevent the spread of the disease.'

'You were successful?'

A nod from Bole. 'We were successful.'

'This is wonderful news, Sir Broderick, wonderful news. How quickly can ParaDigm Rx make the vaccine available?'

'The first batch of fifty thousand doses could be shipped by the end of February, with a further two million doses being shipped each month thereafter.'

Kenton was quiet for a moment. He was probably, Bole supposed, comparing the prognosis of the American epidemiologists regarding the spread of the Plague through the USA with Bole's delivery forecast. The two, as Bole knew, were incompatible. To Frank Kenton's credit he kept a straight face and tried to play a weak hand with as much panache as he was able. Unfortunately, Bole had already seen his cards.

'Is there any way in which production could be raised?' Kenton asked.

'What quantity of vaccine do you require, Mr Kenton, and against how strict a timetable would it need to be delivered?'

'At least seventy million doses, ideally supplied within three months.'

Bole contained a smile: this was exactly the quantity he had anticipated being requested and was exactly the quantity he had stockpiled in the ParaDigm Rx warehouses in Yorkshire. He gave his head a theatrical shake. 'To do that, Mr Kenton, would require a Herculean effort.'

'But it can be done.'

'Yes, but at a cost.'

'What cost?'

'Twenty pounds a dose.'

'Merciful heavens! Twenty pounds! That's over eighty bucks a shot! That's usurious. That'll cost the US nearly six billion dollars!'

'That is if seventy million doses are adequate for your purposes,' Bole observed. 'The prognosis of the Intelligence Bureau, based on the disease's rate of infection, is that half the population of the USA will die within the three-month period you cite. And before you ask: no, it is impossible to supply more than seventy million doses of the vaccine within the three-month deadline.'

And by supplying less than half the needed doses, eighty million Americans will die and the US economy will be crippled, Bole added silently. Whilst the Plague hadn't acted in quite the way predicted, it could at least be used to weaken the British Empire's most formidable economic and political rival.

'But six billion dollars!'

'That's one way of looking at it, Mr Kenton, the other is that you are valuing the lives of American citizens at a rate of eighty dollars each, which seems to me to be quite a bargain.'

Kenton shook his head. 'The President . . . Congress will never wear it. For the love of God, Sir Broderick, Britain and America are meant to be allies . . .' For a moment he seemed stunned by the enormity of the numbers. 'Surely the cost can be cut?'

'If you want such a huge quantity of vaccine shipped against such an incredibly tight timetable then you must expect it to be an expensive exercise.' Bole shrugged. 'But if the terms are unacceptable you are perfectly at liberty to go elsewhere.'

'You know darn well there isn't any "elsewhere". You're blackmailing us.'

'I would appreciate it if you could be a tad less emotional, Mr Kenton. Emotion impairs clear thinking and from what I can see from the Surgeon General's report to the President clear thinking is now of the essence.'

Bole was delighted to see Kenton's eyes widen. It was obviously beyond his comprehension how the Intelligence Bureau could have got access to such a top-secret document so quickly.

'According to the Surgeon General, by the end of the year there won't be much of a USA left to blackmail. What was his prognosis? Ah, yes, I remember: of the one hundred and fifty million American citizens currently extant, if the Plague is left unchecked this number will be reduced to just thirty million. Time to buy stocks in morticians I think, Mr Kenton.'

'This is no laughing matter.'

'I never laugh, Mr Kenton. I am taking this matter very seriously and that is why, despite the enormous difficulties ParaDigm Rx has to overcome, it *will* supply the seventy million doses within three months and hence save seventy million American lives.' Bole took a sip of his honeyed water. 'Of course, the supply of the vaccine is just one of the challenges you will be facing.'

'I don't follow.'

'You will need to tell those American citizens denied the vaccine – the *untreated* eighty million – that they are being condemned to death.'

Bole could tell by Kenton's reaction that this was something that hadn't occurred to the man. 'There'll be panic.'

'Which could be avoided.'

'How?'

'It is not for me to dictate US domestic policy, but it might be possible for ParaDigm Rx to provide you with a quantity of placebo vaccines – imitation vaccines – containing nothing but purified water. These will be useless in fighting the Plague, of course, but it will give some comfort to the recipients and help avert panic. Everybody will *think* they are being vaccinated even though, in reality, less than half the population will have been protected.'

'But how to choose who gets the real vaccine and who gets the fake?'

'Oh, I am sure a good Christian like you will be able to choose those Americans who most deserve to be protected from the Plague. Salvation, as I understand it, is only given to the righteous.'

And the white.

Book One

Book One

Part One:
Percy Shelley

'GOD HAS SPOKEN TO ME' SAYS KENTON.

AMERICA'S POTTY EX-PRESIDENT

EX-PRESIDENT Frank Kenton confirmed last night what many had long suspected: not only is he a crypto-fascist and a racist but he's also nutty as a fruitcake!

Addressing an audience of 100,000 admirers in the Los Angeles' Coliseum last night, Kenton announced that he had received a visitation from God in the form of an angel named Vera who had given him eleven orbs 'which glowed green with a heavenly light'! God, it seemed, has instructed Kenton to lead those who have accepted God's Word – the people Kenton called 'Believers' – back to righteousness and to prepare them for Revelation. Kenton named himself the Last Prophet, claiming his coming fulfils the Elijah prophecies of Malachi 4:5-6.

But worse was to come, with Kenton telling the packed audience that the final cataclysmic struggle between good and evil, between God and Satan, has already commenced, that the world has entered the Time of Tribulation which will culminate in the End of Days. Fortunately, according to Kenton, Satan will be vanquished and we can look forward to the second coming of the Messiah who will lead us to Revelation, when Believers will be 'born anew'.

MARILYN MONROE JUST LOVES BEING EXILED TO BRITAIN.

1:01

London, the Rookeries
The Demi-Monde: 90th Day of Summer, 1005

Following the successful landing of the Column of Loci on Terror Incognita, the final arrangements for the Ceremony of Purification to be held on the 90th day of Fall are to be enacted. This will involve:

- The notification of those six million citizens of the Forth-Right who were recipients of the Victory in the Coven medal that they should attend the Ceremony ('the Attendees'). They should be advised that failure to accept this honour will be deemed a Crime against the Forth-Right and they will be punished accordingly. Responsibility: Comrade Commissar Heinrich Himmler
- The arrangement of all logistical aspects of transporting the Attendees to Terror Incognita and of housing/feeding them whilst there. Responsibility: Comrade Commissar Antoine-Henri Jomini
- The ForthRight Navy to achieve River Supremacy for one week prior to the Ceremony in order to facilitate the use of barges to transport the Attendees across the Wheel River. Responsibility: Comrade Admiral William Teach
- The cryptos employed by the Checkya in NoirVille to use black propaganda (notably the promulgation of *The Protocols of the Sages of nuJuism and of the Most Ancient and*

All-Seeing Order of Kohanim) to encourage NoirVille to declare war on the JAD, this to ensure that the NoirVillian HimPis are 'otherwise engaged' during the Ceremony. Responsibility: Comrade Commissar Francis Walsingham

- The arrest of the Normalist leader and dissident Norma Williams. Responsibility: Comrade General Roman von Ungern-Sternberg

Extract from the minutes of the emergency PolitBuro meeting held under the guidance of the Great Leader on the 1st day of Fall, 1005

'Queek, *mon chéri, fais beaucoup de* bang, banging.'

Burlesque Bandstand was only too happy to oblige. He pushed Norma out of harm's way behind him and then, standing side by side, he and Odette started blasting the Checkya agents who were racing to cut off their escape route out of the Crystal Palace. They were fortunate that the big blond bugger who had thrown the gas canisters seemed to know his business and was using his pistol to good effect, but even with his help, Burlesque knew it would be nip and tuck whether they came out of this alive. There were a lot of the bastards shooting at them, and in the end it was only thanks to the hordes of screaming, running, panicking people milling around that they managed to elude their pursuers and to shove their way along a corridor, through the stage door and into the street.

Outside there was even more chaos, with thousands of men, women and children flooding out of the Crystal Palace as they tried to escape the fighting inside. The one piece of good luck was that the curly-haired item who Norma had slapped – Percy Shelley, Burlesque thought she had said his name was – seemed to have a getaway planned. 'This way, Comwades! I have a steamer waiting just thwee stweets away.'

Reluctant though he was to follow the man – men who couldn't pronounce their 'r's were not, in his opinion, to be trusted – Burlesque had no other option, so he took a tight hold on Norma's arm and, with Odette's help, they bullied their way through the press of people. A few minutes later the six of them – the big blond bugger seemed to have a woman in tow – were scrambling aboard a getaway steamer that was standing puffing and panting down a side street.

Once he had seated himself, Shelley adjusted the pince-nez perched atop his long nose, then spoke. 'We must move quickly, Comwades,' he said, seemingly irritated by having to raise his voice to compete with the noise of the steamer's pistons as the driver opened up the vehicle's boiler. 'I suspect that once order has been we-established and Heydwich wealises that you have escaped then a hue and cwy will be waised. We're not far fwom the docks, and once there, I am sure Comwade Moynahan's bottomless wallet will secure us six berths on a barge heading for NoirVille.'

Burlesque decided that he'd had enough of all this fucking around with blokes he didn't know giving him orders. He shoved the muzzle of his revolver up against the side of Shelley's head. 'Just 'ang on a mo', matey. We ain't goin' anywheres till I know just 'oo the fuck you are.'

Shelley hesitated as though not quite sure whether he should be taking Burlesque's threats seriously. 'I say, Comwade, this is hardly sporting behaviour, 'specially when a chap ain't even heeled.'

His protest did him no good and to emphasise how seriously she and Burlesque took 'sporting behaviour' Odette pushed her pistol into his groin. '*Et, monsieur*, pleeze, do not of the movements mostly sudden make otherwise I will blow away your . . . 'ow you say, *zizi, mon chéri*?'

'Willy,' suggested Burlesque.

'*Bon!* If you make the moves *rapide*, monsieur, you will go through life *sans votre* willy. *Comprenez?*'

Shelley certainly seemed to *comprenez*. 'Wouldn't dweam of it, Comwade, what with a gweat many of the fairwer sex mightily enamoured of that particular piece of artillewy. But all this thweatening ain't necessawy, don't cha know? We are members of the Normalist movement sent to wescue Norma Williams.'

'Norma don't need no rescuing, mate. Me an' Odette will do all the fuckin' rescuing—'

'It's okay, Burlesque,' said Norma quietly, 'I think these people are friends.' She gave Shelley a sidelong look. 'Friends after a fashion, that is. We can go now, Percy,' and a relieved-looking Shelley rapped the silver pommel of his ebony cane on the ceiling of the steamer and the driver eased it out into the traffic.

Burlesque had to marvel at Norma's powers of recovery: with the exception of her red eyes – *blood*shot if he wasn't mistaken, which he supposed was to be expected given that she was a Daemon – she'd quite shaken off the effects of the gas attack and had regained her composure. There was a certainty about her that Burlesque found strangely reassuring, but then, he supposed, he *was* in the presence of the Messiah.

Norma turned to the big blond bugger lounging in the corner of the steamer. 'You say you're with the US Army, Corporal Moynahan?'

He nodded. 'That's correct, Miss Williams, I'm a proud member of the Fighting Fifth, the best combat regiment in the whole of the Real World. My platoon has been searching for you for almost nine months. You sure as hell have been a tricky dame to track, Miss Williams.' He pushed a hand out in Norma's direction which, after a moment's hesitation, she shook.

'Well, you've found me now so I guess it's better late than never. I've been waiting a long time for the cavalry to arrive to take me home.' Norma nodded to the really quite dishy girl sitting next to Moynahan. 'Aren't you going to introduce me to your friend, Corporal?'

'This is Miss Maria Steele . . . or more officially, Sister Maria of the exiled Sacred and All-Seeing Convent of Visual Virgins.'

'You're an auralist?' Burlesque wasn't very keen on auralists. The word was they could read a bloke's aura and from that tell what he was thinking . . . though with a bird as good-looking as Maria this wouldn't be too much of a stretch. One look at her and blokes would only be thinking one thing: what'd she look like with her kit off?

'I am indeed an auralist, sir, and I am pleased to use my talents to assist in the extraction of the Messiah from the clutches of Heydrich.'

Norma nodded her appreciation.

'Mr Percy Shelley, I've a feeling you already know,' continued Moynahan.

'Yeah, I know Percy Bysshe Shelley,' Norma said, glaring angrily at the man.

'Please, Norma, do not judge me too harshly,' replied Shelley. 'I did what I did to pwotect you. I would never, ever, do anything that would endanger you.'

Norma eyed him suspiciously. 'Okay, we'll keep this conversation on hold, Percy, but you better believe that I'll be watching you like a hawk.'

'Before we go any further, Norma,' continued Shelley, 'I'd be much obliged if you'd ask your chums to stop pointing their pistols at my gwoin. They're making me a tad nervous.'

Norma laughed. 'It's okay, Burlesque . . . Odette . . . I think we can put the guns away.'

'Thou art Burlesque Bandstand and Odette Aroca?' gasped Sister Maria.

As was her wont whenever there was a pretty girl involved,

Odette stuck her oar in. '*Oui, je suis Odette Aroca et c'est mon homme, Burlesque Bandstand.*'

The pretty girl smiled and replied in French. '*Pardon, Mademoiselle Aroca, je ne vous ai pas reconnue. On ne vous reconnaît pas du tout sur vos photos qui sont exposées sur les couvertures des magazines à sensation.*' ('I'm sorry, Mademoiselle Aroca, I did not recognise you. You do not look like the pictures shown of you on the covers of the penny dreadfuls.')

'Wot? Wot's this tart saying?' Burlesque hated it when the conversation descended into Frog.

Norma interpreted. 'She's saying that you don't look much like the pictures shown on the covers of penny dreadfuls.'

'Wot pictures?'

Here Sister Maria brought a well-thumbed paperback out of her bag. '*These* pictures. Thou and Mademoiselle Odette art legendary freedom fighters, Monsieur Bandstand, and the stories of thy adventures, bestsellers. I am especially enamoured of the tale which relates how thou causèd the Awful Tower to come crashing down on the head of Beria, that most terrible of men.'

'Gor, look at that, Odette, me and yous is famous.' The cover of the book showed a man and a woman – a very *slim* man and a woman, which Burlesque ascribed to artistic licence – each brandishing a devil-may-care look and a brace of pistols. 'Well, it don't look a lot like me, but the artist got me titfer right,' and he tapped the bowler hat that was perched on the back of his head. He handed the book to Odette, who studied the cover and then scowled.

'*Merde!* This is, 'ow you say, Burlesque, the mostly fucking terrible. My 'air, it 'as none ov the waves for which I am mostly famous. *Quand je trouve l'artiste, je lui arracherai les couilles!*' ('When I find the artist I'll rip his bollocks off!')

'Oh, it ain't that bad, me darling. 'E's caught your charms

right, ain't 'e? I like the way they're peeking out from under your ripped dress. Real sexy.'

'Look, when you two have finished admiring yourselves, maybe we can get back to the business at hand,' Norma scolded. 'Perhaps, now everyone has been introduced, you could tell me what's your plan, Corporal?'

'I think it would be better if you call me Dean, Miss Williams.'

'Very well, Dean it is.'

'Okey-dokey. And with your permission I'll call you Norma.' A nod from the girl. 'My orders, Norma, are to get you hotfoot back to the JAD so you can use the Portal to return to the Real World. Problem is that I think this is going to be a mite tougher now that we've put a burr up Heydrich's ass. Everyone and his father's going to be out looking for a girl who looks like Aaliz Heydrich.'

'Portal? Wot's a Portal?' asked Burlesque.

Moynahan glanced towards Norma, who signalled him to continue. 'It's a means by which Daemons can move between the Real World – your Spirit World – and the Demi-Monde. Originally there was a Portal in each of the Sectors of the Demi-Monde but now there's only one left . . . the one in the JAD, which is where I'm intent on taking Norma.'

'Then the quicker we get to the docks the better. I think the Checkya will already be looking for me. And in the mean time, Dean, why don't you tell me how you and your pals came to be at the Crystal Palace tonight?'

London, the Rookeries
The Demi-Monde: 85th Day of Summer, 1005

The assassination of Comrade-Commissar Beria and the success of the Normalist movement gave a fillip to opponents of Heydrich's rule within the ForthRight. But their increasing agitation was matched by a crackdown on dissidents by the Checkya, who moved to neuter protests by seeding *agents provocateurs* into the ranks of anti-Heydrich organisations. Such were the numbers of cryptos mobilised by the Checkya that the Summer of 1005 is remembered as the 'Season of Suspicion', the time when it was impossible to trust *anybody*.

The Fall of the ForthRight:
Percy Bysshe Shelley, FreeWill Press

FIVE DAYS EARLIER . . .
Percy Bysshe Shelley was not built to be a fugitive. He had not been ordained by Fate to live alone as an isolated thing. He was a gregarious man. He liked carousing. He liked the finer things in life. All these were denied a fugitive. As a fugitive he had to regularly shift rooms, which entailed his laundry not being done properly; had to eschew his favourite restaurants, tailors and barbers; and had to forgo the pleasures of communing with the more accommodating women of his acquaintance. But the most trying aspect of this new life was that he was unable to

publish his poetry, and thus he went through his days troubled by the consideration that nothing wilted faster than laurels that were being rested upon. Soon he would be forgotten, and this was the unkindest cut of all. Shelley hated the thought of being deposited on the dung heap of history.

Life as a fugitive was, in a word, beastly. So beastly that now, after almost three Seasons of ducking and diving, he was utterly disenchanted with the whole sorry experience. But disenchanted or not, the problem remained that the Checkya were indefatigable in their efforts to apprehend him and hence, if he did not wish to spend the rest of his life chained to a wall in Wewelsburg Castle, he had to duck and dive with alacrity. Since his contretemps with Comrade Crowley, he was one of the most wanted men in the Demi-Monde, with a thousand-guinea reward on his head. This being the case, it was better to be free and on the flee than captured and on the rack.

There were times, though, when even the threat of incarceration wasn't enough to overcome the tedium and spiritual degradation associated with wearing unremarkable clothes, eating in second-class restaurants and sleeping on the couches of reluctant friends and less-than-enthusiastic admirers. At such times Shelley threw caution to the wind, would don his very best – if sadly ill-pressed – evening suit, and sally forth for a night of dissipation and debauchery. Which was why tonight he found himself in the best box in the Canterbury Theatre with a jolly doxy on his arm and a rather superior bottle of pink champagne cooling in an ice bucket.

'Swell 'ere, innit, George?' commented his companion, a trollop by the name of Delores.

It took an instant for Shelley to realise that the girl was addressing him. He had used so many aliases of late that he was damned if he could keep track of them. Then he remembered: his current *nom erroné* was George Rowley, the name of the scoundrel who had had him expelled from university. His hope was that by using this sobriquet and rogering Delores in as unconventional a manner as his imagination could conjure, he would ruin Rowley's reputation as a devout UnFunDaMentalist.

'It is indeed, Comwade Delowes.' He waved a careless hand to encompass the crowds of ne'er-do-wells and nonentities who sat in the stalls stretching below him. 'Gathered here tonight are the most weviled members of our Sector's population: the idle, the stupid and the vicious. But it behoves us to wemember that this wiff-waff, given an education and a change of clothes, could be pwesidents, genewals, empwesses . . . even pwiests if they were degenewate enough, there is such little diffewence between the awistocwacy and these miscweants. Those of the cwiminal class have their own codes of honour, their own argot, their own uniform and their own mowals . . . just as their supposed betters do.' Shelley took a sip of his champagne. 'Indeed, my obliging little stwumpet, I would suggest that the one thing necessawy to be both an awistocwat and a cwiminal is the espousing of an amowal attitude towards your fellow man.'

Delores laughed. 'Gor, George, you toffs dun 'alf talk funny. Iffn I didn't know better I'd 'ave you down as a versifier or some such.'

Now *that* comment came as something of a straightener and Shelley determined he'd have to be a damned sight more considered in his speechifying if he wished to continue to be a free man. With this in mind he sat further back into his chair in order that he was more completely shrouded in the shadows that bedecked the box and raised his opera glasses to make a thorough study of the audience, searching their faces for clues that might alert him to the presence of Checkya agents. His perusal came to a sudden halt when his gaze settled upon a girl sitting in the box on the opposite side of the theatre.

It couldn't be!

Though the girl's features were half hidden by a veil and his sight of her was somewhat obscured by her two beefy companions, he was certain it was Norma. The way she held her head with just a touch of arrogance, the strength of the chin that peeped so enticingly out from beneath the veil, and the gestures she made with her delicate, artistic hands . . . these were the things that no artifice could mask.

It was her!

Norma Williams . . . his Delightful Daemon . . . the most Blithe of all the Spirits . . . his True Love. In that instant his mind drifted back to those heady days when she had first come to the Demi-Monde, of his being enraptured by her independent spirit and spritely beauty, of their madcap escapades. Yes . . . and his efforts to keep her out of the clutches of Crowley which had led to him being branded an Enemy of the People.

A love thought lost but now retrieved . . . So astonished was Shelley by this wonderment that before he quite knew what he was about he had leapt to his feet, knocking over the champagne in the process.

The squawk from Delores brought him out of his trance. ''Ere, George, wot's wrong wiv yous? That's expensive bubbly you's tipping on the floor.'

Shelley laughed. 'What of it? Tonight, I have dwunken deep of joy and will taste no other wine.'

'Is yous all right, George? Gor, you looks as iffn you've seen a ghost.'

'Not a ghost . . . an angel. An angel who will twansport me on gossamer wings to a heaven here in the Demi-Monde.' He delved into his pocket and tossed a few guineas into Delores' lap. 'This will weward you for your inconvenience, Comwade Delowes. Now I must away: I have an assignation with perfection.'

Delores was not impressed. 'Yous can't leave like this, George. I thought yous and me were gonna be bouncing the mattress later.'

'Think of this as an escape, my dear, think of it as Fate pwesewing you from an evening of such sordidness that I doubt even your cowwoded soul would wecover.'

He moved to open the door of the box and then stopped when he felt the cold certainty of a derringer pressed against his neck.

'I would be obliged, Mr Shelley,' said the soft voice, tinged with a Yank accent, 'if you would resume your seat. Even as we speak Checkya agents are en route to arrest you.'

Slowly Shelley turned his head. The dull expression had gone from Delores' face, replaced by one of steely determination: looking at the girl, Shelley had no doubt that if push came to shove she would have no hesitation in plugging him.

'My dear Delowes, disappointed though you undoubtedly are that you will not be pleasured by Percy's pintle, there is no weason for you to wesort to menaces. I ain't at me best when I am scwewing at gunpoint.'

'Enough, Shelley! I am Special Branch agent Bella Boyd, assigned to the task force charged with bringing Enemy of the People Percy Bysshe Shelley to book.' She pressed the muzzle of the derringer more fiercely into his neck. 'I am aware, Mr Shelley, of your espousal of the creed of non-violence that is Normalism, but please understand that I suffer no such scruples. If you fail to resume your seat I will shoot you down like the cur you are.'

Bella Boyd was perfectly correct, Shelley did have an aversion to violence, but unfortunately his aversion to spending the rest of his life hanging by his bollocks from a meathook was even greater. 'Ah, Miss Boyd, I pity you and your ilk; so keen to wound with sharpened swords or, as in this case, with bwutal bullets. Yes, I will sit . . .'

Despite his somewhat peripatetic lifestyle of late, Shelley had still managed to indulge his passion for gymnastics and hence his body was in prime fettle. He moved quickly and with the agility of a dancer, pirouetting away from the pistol whilst simultaneously smashing an elbow into Miss Boyd's face. She hit the floor like a sack of potatoes. Reaching down, he prised the derringer from her hand and then glanced around to check the scuffle had not alarmed any in the audience. It seemed it had not.

He was out of the box and into the corridor beyond in a trice, fate having ensured that his departure was timed to perfection. Even as he looked about, trying to establish which direction led to the exit, he heard a shout from his left.

'There! There's the scallywag. That's Shelley.'

Shelley took to his heels, racing along, dodging between the latecomers scuttling to take their seats before the curtain went up, barging into hapless waiters carrying bottles and glasses . . .

Then he had an inspiration. 'Fire! Fire!' he bellowed and as though by magic the corridor was suddenly full of panicked theatre-goers desperate to establish if their lives were in danger. This swarm of perplexed people was sufficient to form a very effective barricade between him and the pursuing Checkya, so much so that – breathless and horribly dishevelled though he was – Shelley emerged from the theatre still a free man.

1:03

Cairo, NoirVille
The Demi-Monde: 85th Day of Summer, 1005

The teachings of HimPerialism are enshrined in the HIM Book, the most sacred book in the NoirVille religious corpus, which contains the inerrant and infallible Word of ABBA. The text of the HIM Book was translated by the great mage and scholar Arthur Aristotle from Pre-Folk manuscripts destroyed during the Great War of 512.

A Fool's Guide to HimPerialism: Selim the Grim,
Bust Your Conk Publications

The way Corporal Jake Massie of the 5th US Combat Training Regiment saw it, the mission had been a total waste of fucking time . . . a *dangerous* waste of fucking time.

The intelligence they'd received that Norma Williams was active in the Quartier Chaud had been just so much baloney. By the time he'd gotten to Paris the girl was long gone and now the word was she had been kidnapped by the Empress Wu and taken to the Coven. Soldier though he was, Massie had decided to give the Coven the go-by. No way was he going to Wu-ville. Wu-ville was bad fucking news for guys who had an affection for their nuts. Anyway, he was low on money, low on inclination and to cap it all he had a fucking lowbrow in tow. Yeah, his orders might be that he should 'seek, secure and protect Norma Williams in order that she might be returned safely and expeditiously to the Real World' but he was fucked if he would do that at the risk of spending the rest of his natural being sucked dry by a blood-hungry Dupe or castrated by a LessBien. And wandering around the Demi-Monde with a Neanderthal like Tommy Holder as his wingman was a sure-fire way of making one – or possibly both – of those happen.

NeoFight 3rd Class Tommy Holder was a walking fucking disaster area.

Which was the main reason Massie had had them make their move back to the JAD during the day, slipping out of Barcelona just after dawn. Holder got confused in the dark – presumably that was when the solar battery working his one and only brain cell went into shutdown mode – and began muttering about the night being Satan's time and other religious shit. So a dawn escape it had been: they'd stolen a rowboat, sculled across the Nile and then dodged through the crowded, stinking backstreets of Cairo in the direction signposted 'Safety'. It had been a good decision: the way Massie saw it, it was better to be lost in the heaving mass of virtual humanity pushing and shoving its way along Saliba Street than trying to skulk down the deserted street at night. Skulking got you noticed by the HimPeril, the NoirVillian secret police. So, like pieces of human flotsam, Massie and Holder allowed themselves to be borne along by the crowd, trying as best they could to keep to the shadows.

It was tough going and, even after over three hundred days' service in the Demi-Monde, Massie was still stunned by the febrile, desperate energy of this part of Cairo and by its poverty. Most of the people living and working here were the fellahin dispossessed when the nuJus had taken over the JAD, sold down the financial river by their fellow Shades. These were the poor bastards untouched by the pixie dust of riches brought to town by NoirVille's burgeoning blood trade. They were a forgotten class of people: the 'never hads' . . . the 'never would haves'.

And the streets were as noisy as they were depressing. Every one of the crowd of people who swirled around Massie and Holder seemed to be shouting, singing, screaming, crying, cursing or, in the case of one lunatic, banging on a drum. Even the ABBA-generated familiarisation cyber-constructs they had had to study before entering the Demi-Monde hadn't prepared him for this level of madness.

But somehow they made it through the maze of narrow streets and alleys and, three hours south of noon, the pair of them found themselves standing in the lee of a doorway with just the Khan al-Kalili souk separating them from Checkpoint Bravo, the second major gateway through the JAD wall – the twenty-foot-high concrete wall that circled the nuJu homeland, sealing it from the rest of NoirVille. And once through there, they were only half a mile from the sanctuary of the Portal.

So close . . . but so very far.

The problem was that the souk was watched and guarded by the HimPeril, who would spot them for certain. Sure it was market day and sure the plaza was abuzz with people but most of them were Shades and he and Holder were white.

Very white.

Even as he watched, he saw a trio of the black-uniformed HimPeril agents strutting between the market stalls, swinging their steel batons in an arrogant, casual manner and shouldering aside any poor bastard who got in their way. Instinctively Massie checked the M-29 he had slung under his coat.

'When we gonna make our move, Corporal?' whispered Holder.

'When I'm fucking ready,' Massie snarled back, 'and don't call me "Corporal". It's a sure way of tipping off the Dupes that we ain't kosher. You gotta try not to act so fucking stupid, Holder, otherwise you're gonna get us both fucked over.'

Holder flinched back as though he'd been slapped and immediately Massie cursed himself for overreacting. But Holder *was* stupid; fuck, he could barely read and write and as a consequence hadn't properly grasped how much fucking danger they were in. His big, dopey blue eyes blinked back embarrassed tears. They were funny eyes, staring out at the world with an odd mixture of imbecility and pent-up violence.

'Okay, Holder, take it easy, just try and remember that we're operating undercover. This is a plain-clothes operation.'

He almost laughed. In the Demi-Monde 'plain clothes' necessitated him wearing a ridiculous stovepipe hat and thunder-and-lightning red-and-blue-striped trousers with a matching frock-coat. He looked a complete prick, but then so did every other man in Cairo.

'Just keep quiet. We're only a couple of blocks away from the Portal. All we've got to do is get through the Wall and we're home free.'

Holder looked at him with the dumb-fuck expression that Massie had come to hate. As Massie saw it, the US Army must be really fucking desperate if it had been reduced to accepting fuckwits like Tommy Holder into its ranks.

But the real problem Massie had was that Holder was both stupid *and* nervous. After the run-ins they'd had with the Signori di Notte in Venice, Holder had the jumps real bad, so bad that the guy had started praying to himself and in the Demi-Monde that wasn't a great idea.

Massie smiled ruefully to himself: maybe he should start praying too. Holder wasn't the only one shitting himself. He had the shakes too and he was meant to be the guy with all the battle-mileage. But then the Demi-Monde was scary enough to give anyone the frights, even pros like him. He hated the fucking Demi-Monde. He hated the fucking Dupes and the weird way they dressed and acted. He hated their weird fucking religions. But most of all he hated being continually worried that they'd spot that he was a Daemon. If that happened then the shit would really hit the fan.

Silently, Massie berated himself for being such a wuss. Maybe he was just going stir-crazed, maybe he'd been holed up in the Demi-Monde for too long. Being spotted as a Daemon was a stupid thing to be worried about. There was no way the Dupes could suss he was a Daemon, not unless he got cut or he bumped into a Visual Virgin.

'Fucking zadnik Hamites,' he heard Holder mutter.

'What's that, Holder?'

'Fucking homosexual niggers,' the boy said in a louder voice and then nodded towards the people swarming around the marketplace. 'All these black bastards are unclean in the sight of the Lord. Ham, Cain's son, violated his grandfather, Noah, when Noah lay naked and drunk in his tent, and in punishment God caused his skin to turn from white to black. That is the origin of the black races . . . and that is why all Hamites are cursed by God . . . why they all indulge in obscenities of the flesh.'

'You don't really believe that shit, do you, Holder?'

Holder glanced towards his corporal and frowned. 'Yeah. The Bible is the inerrant word of God, so it's got to be true. That's what the Last Prophet said.'

Massie shook his head. This was getting surreal. Here he was standing in a fucked-up virtual world debating the Bible with a religious fascist – a Believer – possessing the IQ of a turnip. The Last Prophet, Frank Kenton, had a lot to answer for.

Frank-fucking-Kenton. The fucking fanatic who, back in '47, had convinced himself and most of what was left of the electorate that the Plague had been visited upon America as punishment by God for the country's dissolute and sinful ways. And once elected, President Kenton and the rest of the Klan who had followed him into the White House had imposed sixty years of religious bigotry, censorship, intolerance and guilt about sex on the USA. Sure, the Kentonite ReDeemed Republicans had been booted out of office in the elections of 2014, but there were still a lot of people who believed in the fundamentalist shit that Kenton had spouted and Holder was obviously one of them.

'Well, fuck what the Last Prophet said, just keep your voice down. The last thing we want is to draw attention to ourselves. Okay, Holder, time to rock and roll, and if we get challenged by any of the Brothers, just stay mute and let me do the talking. Stay cool, Holder, just stay cool.'

With Holder at his heels, Massie pushed out of the shadowed doorway and strode across the sunlit plaza, the cobbles glinting from the wash of recent rain. It was lucky he was such a big man and was able to bully his way through the press of people swarming through the plaza, elbowing past the burqa-swathed woeMen haggling over yams and chickens, ignoring the entreaties of the peanut vendors squatting next to their piles of nuts and sweets, ducking away from the snake-charmers and the HimPerialist fakirs, flinching back from the stench of the boys selling odd-smelling sweetmeats and the perfumed sheMen clustering excitedly around the stall selling dyes and cosmetics. The one good thing was that it seemed impossible for the HimPeril to spot them in this maelstrom of humanity.

But they did.

He and Holder were only fifty yards away from Checkpoint Bravo when there was a shouted challenge. 'Hey, yo' dere, yo' Blank boys. Ah's wanna see yo's papers.'

There were three HimPeril agents, big guys carrying steel batons and a grudge against Blanks.

'Where's yo' going, man?' asked the biggest agent as he came to a halt in front of Massie.

'Going to the JAD. Fixing on having ourselves a little R and R.'

'Hmm, hmm, dat's nice, dat is. Ah likes it when Blanks make wiv de exit powder, it sorta raises the tone ob NoirVille when dere are fewer whiteniks in de place. Trouble is, ah gets to thinkin' yo's might be nuJu badniks looking to get back to yo' pigsty.' His tone hardened. 'Okay, lemme see yo's papers and suchlike.'

Massie did as he was asked and nodded to Holder to do the same. As the boy handed the papers to the HimPeril agent, his hand was shaking.

'Yo' look like yo's shittin' yo'self, white boy,' observed the agent. 'Yo' bin doing sumting ungodly. Yo' bin a *baaad* mother?'

Holder shook his head and then looked imploringly towards Massie.

'Yeah, an' de way yo' keep makin' dem puppy eyes at yo' Man here, ah'm thinking yo' might be a sheMan.' The agent stretched out a hand to caress Holder's cheek. 'Yo' sure look like a sheMan wot wiv yo' skin bin so smooth and tender.' He winked at Holder and gave him a smile. 'So's how 'bout yo's and me making wiv a little ob de private Man2naM action?'

By NoirVillian standards it was just a little innocent flirting but, as was his wont, Holder overreacted.

'Get thee behind me, you black pervert . . . you spawn of Satan.'

'Wha' yo' say?'

'I said, fuck off, you black bastard.'

The Shade looked at Holder as though he couldn't quite believe what he was hearing and then a smile wrapped itself over his face. 'Man, yo's one Blank who's wanting to commune with ABBA real urgent.' And with that he smashed his fist into Holder's face.

A blow like that would have felled most men, but Holder wasn't most men. He was big and powerful and his nervous system so primitive that it was incapable of communicating messages from his jaw to his brain, messages to the effect that said brain should be shutting down for a while. But the one thing the piece of muscle that masqueraded as his brain could do efficiently was to signal that it was pissed off. An angry Holder hauled out the M-29 he had hidden under his coat and started blasting away.

Amongst the things the US military used the Demi-Monde for was to test a number of its newer weapons, and one of the most successful of these was the sloBurst ammunition Holder had loaded in his rifle. The sloBurst was a dumdum for the twenty-first century, designed to explode just a nanosecond after impact. As such, the sloBurst was lethal against soft targets, and as soft targets went, the NoirVillians crowding the market square were up there with the best of them.

The boy let rip with a full magazine, blowing the HimPeril agents and a whole swathe of shoppers to dog meat. In seconds the pungent aroma of the marketplace had been augmented with the stench of vaporised SAE. As the assault rifle clicked on empty, thirty busted bodies were lying in a circle around Holder and the rest of the crowd had been reduced to a screaming, panic-stricken mob. Seeing his chance to make a getaway, Massie grabbed Holder by the shoulder and dragged him in the direction of the gate leading to the JAD.

1:04

The JAD, NoirVille
The Demi-Monde: 85th Day of Summer, 1005

TO SISTER MARIA C/O THE SACRED AND ALL-SEEING
CONVENT OF VISUAL VIRGINS IN THE JAD PO BOX
11/48 + + + GREETINGS + + + WOULD INFORM YOU THAT
WORD HAS REACHED ME THAT PERCY SHELLEY HAS
LOCATED NORMA WILLIAMS IN LONDON + + + WOULD
REQUEST ADVICE AS TO ACTION TO BE FOLLOWED + + +
VILLIERS

PAR OISEAU

**PigeonGram sent by George Villiers on the 86th day
of Summer, 1005**

Corporal 1st Class Dean Moynahan was bored. Not with the Demi-Monde . . . he liked the Demi-Monde because – paradoxically – it seemed more real than the Real World . . . the Demi-Monde had a vibrancy and an urgency about it that was absent in the Real World.

No, what was boring Moynahan was having to man the shitty first-floor room overlooking the entrance to the Portal that Captain Simmons – prick that he was – insisted on calling 'Observation Post #1'. What Moynahan was meant to be observing he wasn't too sure, but orders – in this case, 'look out for any atypical Dupe behaviour' – were orders. It seemed that the firefight that had gone down in the Khan al-Kalili souk just an hour ago had got the good captain spooked. And that was why Moynahan was sitting by the window, smoking a cigarette – the Demi-Monde wasn't big on health and safety regulations –

working on his distance-learning course in linguistics and watching the crowds of JADniks streaming past along the cobbled streets below.

He took another glance up and down Bar-Ilan Street but as far as he could see none of the nuJu men were doing anything remotely 'atypical', just going about their very typical business like they did on any other typical day. They were all sporting typical kippahs and broad-brimmed hats and wandering around in their typical zoot suits or sitting at the zinc-topped tables in the cafés that lined the street enjoying a typically bracing cup of café au gore. None of them seemed to be taking an undue interest in the Portal, but that was hardly surprising given that it was hidden inside a nondescript warehouse set in a nondescript terrace running along a nondescript street across from the nondescript house where Moynahan was sitting.

Moynahan yawned and tried to stretch the sleep out of his body. And it was a big body too: he measured six-three in his stocking feet and weighed in at two hundred pounds, all of it honed muscle.

He stopped yawning.

There was a flash of red in the street below and that, if he wasn't very much mistaken, was the red of the robe of a Visual Virgin. He blinked and rubbed his eyes. He had never seen a VV before and he didn't want to make a mistake. VVs – according to the briefing sheets pinned to the notice board in the Portal – were 'a real and present danger'. With the Lady IMmanual having become such a big deal in Venice, most of the VVs had decamped to the JAD, which was bad news for Real Worlders trying to keep a low profile in the JAD. Word had it that a Visual Virgin could spot a Real Worlder easy as blinking. Real Worlders had atypical auras.

Satisfied that he wasn't seeing things, he hit the panic button which connected the Observation Post with the Portal across the street, ringing the warning bell that told the rest of the platoon to keep out of sight and away from the windows.

'Hey, Sergeant,' Moynahan yelled, as he reached for his M-29, 'I think we might have ourselves a situation.'

Sergeant Sol Edelstein reluctantly opened an eye and used it to give Moynahan a quizzical look. 'What you hollering about, Moynahan?'

'There's a VV down there in the street, snooping around.'

Edelstein was over by the window like a shot, though he made damned sure that most of his bulk was hidden behind the threadbare curtains. 'Where?' And Moynahan pointed to the end of the street.

The VV was a trim, tall and imperious piece dressed in the diaphanous red robe that was synonymous with the Virgins and wearing a red half-veil that hid most of what Moynahan suspected was a very beautiful face.

'What do you reckon she's doing here?'

'I think she's shopping,' ventured Moynahan. 'I mean, even VVs have to shop, don't they, Sarge?'

Edelstein didn't say a word, all his attention fixed on the girl as she sauntered along the market stalls that lined the street. 'I think you're right, Moynahan. I think her showing up here is just bad luck. As long as our guys don't break cover, we're gonna be okay.'

That was when their luck went from bad to worse.

Two guys shuffled up to the door of the Portal and began hammering on it. Although they were dressed like Demi-Mondians, Moynahan had the unsettling feeling that he *knew* them. The dime dropped. 'Fuck, Sarge, that's Jake Massie and Holy Holder down there!'

Edelstein stuck his head nearer to the glass pane. 'Fuck . . . you're right. Shit, those dumbasses are gonna get spotted by the

VV. Get down there and make sure that she don't raise the alarm.'

Moynahan scooted down the narrow staircase three steps at a time, checking that his folding-stock M-29 was slung, ready and willing, under his armpit as he went. He had to get to the VV before she began hooting and hollering to any IRGON agents: if she did, then everything would go FUBAR and none of them would ever get back to the Real World. The IRGON were the closest thing the nuJus had to a secret police.

He slammed his way out through the building's front door and into the street, shoving pedestrians carelessly aside as he barrelled his way in the direction of the VV. The *running* VV . . .

The girl had obviously spotted Massie and Holder and was now exiting stage left, pounding the pavement in the direction of the IRGON offices in the market square. Moynahan gave chase: he had to intercept her before she raised the alarm. And while he sure as hell didn't like the idea of killing a woman, he kept reminding himself that she was only a Dupe, she wasn't *real*. But somehow that didn't make the prospect of offing a girl any more palatable. Maybe he was in the wrong line of business.

He was nearer to her now, almost within shooting distance. She was pretty easy to track, the red robe she was wearing made her stand out like a beacon and she was so tall he could see her over the heads of the crowd. And despite her size, she had difficulty getting through the hordes of people swarming around the souk and with every second that passed Moynahan elbowed himself closer. She dodged across the road, lizarding between the steamers and the carts chuntering along the street, and that was when Moynahan's luck turned: a steamer skidded to a halt in front of her, blocking her escape.

Now . . .

Moynahan unslung the M-29, clicked off the safety and swung the stubby barrel in the girl's direction. She turned to look at him.

Fuck, she's pretty.

Even though she was wearing a half-veil, it was impossible not to appreciate how lovely the girl was . . . too lovely to murder. Moynahan's finger relaxed on the trigger and that moment's hesitation on his part saved her life. Her beautiful eyes widened in fear as she saw her pursuer and she took off like a startled deer, with a cursing Moynahan hammering in her wake.

She'd have got away too if the Black Hand Gang hadn't intervened.

To Izzi Qassam the tenets of HimPerialism were incapable of interpretation or of dispute. What was stated in the HIM Book – HimPerialism's holiest book – was, as far as he was concerned, the sacred word of ABBA, and since ABBA was the infallible font of all truth, what was said in the HIM Book was fact.

And on the subject of NoirVille the HIM Book was exact and unambiguous: ABBA had given the land of NoirVille to the Shade races of the Demi-Monde in gratitude for their revered forefather, Nûh, saving HumanKind after the Deluge, and, being ABBA-given, NoirVille was not to be sold, gifted or in any way disposed of . . . especially not to those accursed nuJus, who were reviled by ABBA for having built the Sphinx.

This was why Qassam opposed the policy adopted by His Him-Perial Majesty Shaka Zulu, which had granted the nuJus a home – the JAD – in NoirVille. Of course, he understood the economic imperatives underpinning Shaka's decision: the nuJus had the secret of how to manufacture Aqua Benedicta, which was the vital component that made NoirVille pre-eminent in the trade of blood, but to Izzi Qassam's mind the need to follow ABBA's word transcended all material or financial considerations. No amount of money could buy a Man's way into Paradise.

As far as Izzi Qassam was concerned, it was incumbent upon all True Believers to work unceasingly to remove the canker that was the JAD from the blessed body of NoirVille. He had formed the Black Hand Gang of like-minded zealots to do just that: to frighten the nuJus in the JAD such that their continued occupation of NoirVille became untenable. And this morning it was more important than ever to punish the infidel nuJus for their infamy. Hadn't they just committed a vile atrocity against the peaceful and non-violent people of NoirVille? Hadn't two Blanks – undoubtedly nuJus – opened fire with automatic rifles and slaughtered thirty innocents in Khan al-Kalili souk? Swift and terrible revenge had to be taken for this savage crime and that was why Izzi Qassam was loitering in a café across from the Market Square headquarters of the IRGON, with a Luger automatic in his jacket pocket and a bag full of explosives on the floor by his feet.

Something made him look up and what he saw made him start so suddenly that he slopped his coffee over the tabletop. A Visual Virgin – the living embodiment of the foul creed of ImPuritanism and of the corruption of woeMan – was scuttling across the market square in the direction of the IRGON's headquarters. He could hardly believe his eyes: it was a very rare occurrence for Whorealists to leave the cloistered confinement of their convent and venture out in public.

Qassam rose from his seat, tossed coins onto the table, hitched his bag over his shoulder and made for the café's exit signalling to his two brothers-in-arms to follow him. To destroy a Visual Virgin on the very doorstep of the IRGON offices would be a huge blow to nuJu morale.

*

Sister Maria, near-Senior Maiden in the Sacred and All-Seeing Convent of Visual Virgins, was – now that Sister Florence had joined ABBA in the Spirit World – the most powerful Auralist alive and it was this uncanny ability to discern the character of individuals by the study of the multicoloured penumbra surrounding their bodies that had allowed her to understand that the two men banging on the door of the warehouse were Daemons.

And that the huge man chasing her was also one of this foul breed.

Even as she'd turned in the direction of the IRGON station to alert the authorities that there was a nest of Daemons in their midst, she had seen him come bursting out of the building opposite, his aura aflame with angry scarlets and panicked magentas. Sister Maria had taken to her heels but the brute had closed on her, using his inhuman strength to batter his way through the swarms of people blocking the street. Despite her best efforts he had nearly caught her when she had been trying – desperately – to negotiate her way across Machane Yehuda Street, but then – amazingly – he had hesitated and just for an instant she could have sworn his aura had been infused with compassionate lavender. Obviously she was mistaken: Daemons were not human and therefore did not possess the higher emotions such as love and mercy.

Whatever had made the beast stay his hand, Sister Maria knew not to tempt fate a second time and so she lifted the skirts of her robe, scuttling between the market stalls until she came breathless to the entrance to the IRGON headquarters.

'Please,' she gasped to the two guards standing on sentry duty at the doors, 'I am being chased by a Daemon. I need your protect—'

She never finished the sentence. There was a crack of a pistol shot and the IRGON agent to her left was rammed backwards as though punched in the chest. Someone screamed, 'Death to all those who would defile the sacred land of NoirVille!' Instantly the second IRGON agent hurled Maria to the ground and threw himself over her. Then all Hel broke loose.

Moynahan watched helplessly as the VV climbed the steps to the entrance of the IRGON offices, as she began to talk to one of the guards standing there, as she began gesticulating anxiously in his direction, then . . .

A group of three Shades, all of them brandishing pistols, attacked.

Before anyone realised what was happening, there was a crackle of shots and one of the IRGON guards crumpled to the ground. In an instant the peaceful, bustling marketplace was reduced to panic, as men desperately sought cover away from the gunfire and women frantically dragged their terrified children to safety.

That was when the leader of the three gunmen hurled a haversack towards the entrance. The resulting explosion was so powerful that it pushed Moynahan off his feet and sent him tumbling to the cobbles, his ears ringing. When he came to his senses, the scene that confronted him was one of carnage, his training telling him that the terrorist had thrown a nail bomb, the ensuing shrapnel taking out a whole swathe of bystanders who now lay wailing and shrieking on the ground.

Miraculously the VV had survived, shielded from the blast by a guard who had so heroically protected her, the girl now, bemused and confused, crawling around on her hands and knees. She wouldn't be crawling for very long, though, the lead gunman was standing over her with his automatic pointed at her head.

Instinct took over and Moynahan attacked. He couldn't see a girl murdered in cold blood – or even in cold SAE. It wasn't right.

Ignoring the protests of his bruised and battered body, he leapt to his feet and shoulder-charged the man square in his back, sending him sprawling, then scooped the girl up in his arms.

'If you want to live, trust me,' he bellowed and without waiting for a reply carried her across the marketplace in the direction of the Portal.

The JAD, NoirVille
The Demi-Monde: 85th Day of Summer, 1005

The MANdate states, 'His HimPerial Majesty Shaka Zulu views with favour the establishment in NoirVille of a national home for the nuJu people, and will use his best endeavours to facilitate the achievement of this objective, it being clearly understood that nothing shall be done which may prejudice the civil and religious rights of the existing Shade communities. In return the nuJu people will provide NoirVille, on an exclusive basis, with such quantities of Aqua Benedicta as it may demand.' The signing of this document paved the way for the establishment of the JAD . . . and for all the grief, hatred and violence that followed as a consequence.

An Examination of the Political Situation in NoirVille:
Chaim Weizmann, NuJu Publications

Fortunately for Moynahan, the VV seemed more than a little shell-shocked by her close call with death, that is if her lack of protest about being taken to the Portal was any indication. She hadn't struggled when he'd taken her up in his arms – trying to ignore the delightful sensation of her near-naked body against his as he did so – and barged his way through the bemused crowd. Such was the chaos caused by the attack that no one gave him so much as a second glance; Moynahan's problems started when he carried her inside the Portal and up the stairs to Captain Simmons' office.

'Are you out of your fucking mind, Moynahan?' snarled Simmons when Moynahan had gabbled out his explanation and, with the help of Sergeant Edelstein, laid the girl out on the captain's couch. 'That's a VV you've got there and VVs can spot that we're Real Worlders.'

'Yeah, I understand that, Captain, but the alternative was to put a bullet through her head and I kinda baulked at doing that. I'm a soldier not a hitman.'

Simmons scowled, but then in Moynahan's experience small men always scowled a lot, presumably because if they couldn't *be* tough then they could at least try to *look* tough. 'You sure she didn't have time to alert the IRGON to the location of the Portal?' the prick whined.

Moynahan shook his head. 'Nah. The two guards she was jawing with were reduced to Jell-O by the bomb.'

Simmons was silent for a moment, sitting behind his desk nervously wringing his hands as though he was having trouble deciding what to do next. 'Look, Moynahan, she's only a Dupe . . . she's not a real person. You do know that, don't you?'

Moynahan knew that all right, but the big problem he had was in believing it. During his time in the Demi-Monde he'd only interfaced with Dupes when he'd gone to the market to buy food for the platoon. Sure, the market-women had been disconcertingly real and very flirtatious – the dame running the meat stall was always winking at him and making suggestions that they get jinky – but this was the first time he'd actually got up close and personal with a Dupe. And the remembrance of the VV's deliciously soft and yielding body had been very unsettling. She sure as hell hadn't felt like a piece of digital make-believe.

He took a glance at the girl laid out unconscious on the captain's couch, her robe wafting over her body like red mist. He especially liked the way her right leg was uncovered. That really got his juices flowing. The VV was a real looker, with the emphasis on real.

The captain broke through Moynahan's daydreaming. 'What I want you to do, Moynahan, is just take her out back and . . .' The order – suggestion – trailed off as though the captain was embarrassed about what he was saying.

'You want me to off her?'

'Well . . . yes.' The captain smiled, 'Look, Moynahan, Corporal Massie has just made it in from Paris by the skin of his teeth so the situation is a little tense. The last thing we need is a VV alerting the nuJus that there's a Portal in the JAD.'

'He didn't find Norma Williams?'

'No. Massie thinks the girl's history. This mission is over, so I'm keeping the Portal open for another week . . . enough time for the other patrols to come in and then I'm going to cut bait. So this isn't the moment to be taking risks and that VV *is* a risk.'

'You're gonna abandon Norma Williams?' challenged Moynahan.

Captain Simmons shuffled in his seat like he always did when his men put his feet against the fire. He hated being asked questions but unfortunately for him, with him and his sixteen-man platoon having been holed up cheek by jowl in the Portal for the best part of a year things had got a mite informal. Simmons might like to play the Great I Am but now it didn't wash: the guys in the Platoon knew him for the dick he was and weren't afraid to tell him so.

'Not *abandon*, Moynahan. I'm making an executive decision to terminate the mission based on intelligence received. The last credible sighting there was of Norma Williams was when she was active in the Quartier Chaud. The intelligence Massie brought in was that she's been abducted by agents of Empress Wu and the word on the streets is that once somebody is taken by Wu they don't get untaken.'

'But according to Massie there's a rumour that she'd escaped and hightailed it to the Rookeries' – this comment coming from Sergeant Edelstein, who, in Moynahan's opinion, was a stand-up guy.

'Just a rumour.'

'But surely—'

'Look, Edelstein, I command here. This isn't a debating society. And what I'm *telling* you is that Norma Williams is beyond rescue. I'm calling the mission off.'

'Shit, Captain, we can't just abandon Norma Williams,' protested Edelstein. 'Fuck it, she's the President's daughter!'

'She's the President's *dead* daughter and as such our mission here is terminated. Now let's just do our housekeeping and make sure that the VV doesn't spill the beans.' Simmons stood up from his desk, leant forward and gimleted Moynahan with a stare. 'I'm ordering you to neutralise the VV.'

Moynahan felt his temper rise. 'And I'm telling you, Captain, to go fuck—'

'Verily, good sirs, I am most able and willing to assist thee in thy endeavours to locate the wench Norma Williams.'

Sister Maria had feigned unconsciousness in the belief that if these Daemons thought she was hors de combat they might speak in an unguarded fashion. And she had been right.

Of course, when the bomb had exploded, her senses had been addled and hence she had been unable to protest when the huge Daemon had carried her to his lair. But as she'd recovered her faculties, she'd come to realise that the Daemon did not wish to harm her and, as there might be more Shade terrorists trying to kill her, she decided to feign a swoon. The Daemon had, after all, saved her from death at the hands of that murderous Black Hand agent and he was *very* strong. So strong, in fact, that she had made the journey cradled in his arms and, as a result, had

had a marvellous opportunity to study his aura in minute detail. And what she saw was both contradictory and perplexing.

She had been taught in the Convent that Daemons were savage and brutal agents of Loki, sent by ABBA to test the resolve and faith of Demi-Mondians. Indeed every illustration she'd ever seen of these beasts from Hel had shown them as ugly – her Daemon was anything *but* ugly – with horns – her Daemon had no horns, his head being covered by a dashing mane of blond hair – and smelling of brimstone. Oh, her Daemon did smell but not of brimstone; rather he had a peculiarly pleasant and very masculine aroma.

And if his outward appearance was at odds with the generally accepted image of Daemons, his aura was a revelation. Certainly there was the expected underlay of the choleric colours, the reds and the oranges, but all men had those, signalling that they were in thrall to their gender's weakness of MALEvolence, and though these were brighter in her Daemon's aura than was the norm, it was the streaks of gold that flecked his penumbra that showed him to be a good Daemon . . . an *unusually* good Daemon. He was an honourable Daemon, if that wasn't a contradiction in terms. Admittedly, there *were* oddities, of which the abnormally large halo of passionate purple that surrounded his crotch – indicating that he was a Daemon who took a great interest in the pleasures of the flesh – was the most prominent.

She decided not to think about this nor to dwell on the hardness of his body as he held her to him. She was a Visual Virgin and as such was only able to engage in fiduciary sex; to partake of physical union with a man would mean her powers as an Auralist being severely compromised. Not that she would ever wish to speculate about what it would be like to couple with such a big, strong, handsome Daemon like the one carrying her. That would be unthinkable.

To Maria's dismay, it took a great deal of effort *not* to think about it, but she finally managed to turn her thoughts to other matters, notably that this accidental meeting with a Daemon could be turned to her advantage. After all, Norma Williams, who the convent was seeking so earnestly, was also a Daemon . . .

She heard the Daemon shout, 'Stand down, it's me, Moynahan,' as he pushed his way into the lair of the Daemons and then carried her up a flight of stairs. As she felt herself being laid – quite tenderly – onto a couch, she fluttered her eyes open for the briefest of moments and then mimed anguish, writhing for an instant as though in pain, and managing as she did so to free one of her legs from the confines of her robe. A very fine leg too, long and shapely, which would serve as a distraction and make the men – there were two other men in the room besides Moynahan – less willing to harm her. One of the lessons taught by Sister Agnes in her Arm's-Length Seduction class was that men thinking with their loins rather than their minds were not really thinking at all.

Feigning unconsciousness, she listened carefully as she was discussed by the Daemons. She quickly realised that she was in danger: the man she assumed was the leader of the Daemons and who was sitting in a very self-important manner behind the desk seemed determined to have her executed. Even through half-open eyes she could tell that he was monumentally unsure of himself, terrified of the situation he found himself in – the yellow haze of cowardice surrounding his body clock attested to that – and could be easily panicked into killing her. Weak men always acted impulsively. There was also the green of duplicity tainting his aura, which showed him to be a man of secrets. He was most certainly not one to be trusted.

The conversation between him and Moynahan went back and forth . . . and then the name of Norma Williams was mentioned. It took enormous self-control for her not to start when she heard the girl being discussed. Norma Williams was the True Messiah and the Sacred Order of Visual Virgins had dedicated themselves to finding and protecting her, an ambition thwarted by the girl's abduction by Empress Wu. But now, perhaps, with the help of these Daemons, this ABBA-ordained task could be fulfilled.

It was when she heard the leader – the one called 'Captain' – order Moynahan to take her outside and shoot her that she realised the time for play-acting was over. She sat up. 'Verily, good sirs, I am most able and willing to assist thee in thy endeavours to locate the wench Norma Williams.'

The three Daemons turned towards her, their faces and their auras showing their surprise.

'What?' spluttered the captain, as he reached for the revolver resting on the desk.

Be careful, Maria, the Sister counselled herself, *this Daemon is most assuredly afeared of thee.*

She smiled and positioned herself so that more than a hint of bosom was displayed. As she had anticipated, the three Daemons were momentarily distracted by her charms and hence all thought of doing something precipitous was driven from their minds. They were, after all, *male* Daemons and hence easily manipulated by the arts of a woman.

'I speak true, good Captain. I have secret intelligences as to the whereabouts of the Daemon known as Norma Williams.'

'And why would a Visual Virgin like you want to help us?'

To ensure that thou dost not act as a numbskull and send me somewhat prematurely to meet with ABBA, but Maria decided to leave this thought unvoiced.

'All the Sisters numbered amongst the adepts of the Sacred and All-Seeing Convent of Visual Virgins have taken an oath, good Captain, on pain of never receiving ABBAsolution, to bend their will to the securing and safe keeping of Norma Williams, she who is most blessed in the sight of ABBA.'

The captain was obviously as stupid as he was spineless and seemed not to understand what she had said. It was left to the burly man to Moynahan's left – the one he had called 'Sergeant' – to take up the conversation.

'Blessed in the sight of ABBA, Miss . . . er.'

'I am Sister Maria, Near-Senior Maiden in the Convent, and as for your question, good Sergeant, Norma Williams is the Messiah sent by ABBA to lead the people of the Demi-Monde through Ragnarok and to salvation.'

'Norma Williams?' The sergeant frowned. 'Are we talking about the same Norma Williams? The girl we were sent here to find sure as hell weren't no Messiah.' He tapped a finger on a picture pinned up on the wall. It was a picture of Norma Williams, though not as she had been described to Maria: the girl in the picture had jet-black hair and many strange and unpleasant piercings in her face.

'It is indeed a portrait of the girl Norma Williams, though I wouldst make full admission that here in the Demi-Monde she doth not sport adornments most foul to her lips, nostril and eyebrows.'

The three men looked at one another and then the captain asked the question Maria had been waiting for. 'So how will you be able to help us find the girl?'

'We in the Convent have most subtle and diverse means of discovering secret and esoteric intelligences and have had reports from an agent in the ForthRight that Norma Williams has been observèd attending a music hall in the Rookeries.'

'And who did the observing?'

'Percy Bysshe Shelley.'

'Hey,' said Moynahan, 'don't you remember the briefing we were given back in Fort Jackson? Some of the Zip messages sent by Norma Williams before she disappeared into the Demi-Monde said something about a "Shelley".'

The captain frowned. 'So what are you proposing, Sister Maria?'

'Have little doubt that Percy Shelley can lead thee to Norma Williams, good Captain, but only I have the skill to persuade him to aid thee in this endeavour. He is a fugitive from Heydrich and hence is much afeared for his freedom and his life. Percy Shelley will fly if approached by those he does not know and trust.'

'So?'

'I will take thee to him.'

'Right. And the first opportunity you get you're going to betray us to the IRGON.'

'Verily, sir, I think only of the preservation of Norma Williams, to which I am oath-bound. I pledge most sincerely that I will most diligently perform the task I have set before thee.'

'We gotta do this, Captain,' insisted Edelstein. 'INTRADOC's gonna get real pissed if we give this chance of finding Norma Williams the go-by.'

Although Maria did not know who INTRADOC was, the name seemed to have resonance with the captain. For long seconds he sat behind his desk frozen by indecision. 'Okay,' he said finally, 'but the question is who do we send to the Rookeries with you? Massie knows the territory—'

'Massie's a little beaten up, Captain,' observed Edelstein. 'I don't think his nerves would stand another tour in the outside.'

'I'll go, Captain,' said Moynahan.

'I don't know . . .'

'Moynahan's our resident expert on Dupe patois and slang, Captain. Shit, he's even doing a graduate course in linguistics.'

'That right, Moynahan?'

'Yes, sir. I want to write a book about the linguistic development in the Demi-Monde when I get out of the army.'

'But still—'

'If I might be so bold, sir,' interrupted Maria. 'Racially, this man Moynahan is most perfectly suited to an expedition to the Rookeries. He is tall and blond and blue-eyed, the very epitome of Aryan manhood. Should he be possessèd of all suitable warrants, he would pass most readily into the ForthRight.' And that proved to be the clinching argument.

London, the Rookeries
The Demi-Monde: 88th Day of Summer, 1005

TO GEORGE VILLIERS PO BOX 78/13 + + + WOULDST INFORM
THEE OF MY IMMINENT ARRIVAL IN THE ROOKERIES TO MAKE
CLOSE AND URGENT ENQUIRIES REGARDING THE WHEREABOUTS
OF PERCY BYSSHE SHELLEY + + + I IMPLORE THEE TO
OFFER ALL AID AND SUCCOUR IN FURTHERANCE OF THIS
ABBA-BLESSED ENDEAVOUR + + + SISTER MARIA THE SACRED
AND ALL-SEEING CONVENT OF VISUAL VIRGINS IN THE JAD

PAR OISEAU

**PigeonGram sent by Sister Maria on the 88th day
of Summer, 1005**

Maria was amazed by the strange and wondrous engines housed
in the building the Daemons called 'the Portal', engines which
made light work of counterfeiting a new passport for her.
Equipped with her new papers, and a money belt stuffed with
guineas, Miss Maria Steele – as her passport now called her – and
her escort, Moynahan, had little difficulty getting out of the JAD.
The Shades guarding the gates giving access through the JAD
wall were notoriously corrupt so it was simply a question of
elevating the bribe to a level even the most honest of guards was
unable to refuse. Once through the Wall, the pair headed west
towards the Yangtze River, and on reaching it bought their way
onto a barge heading for the Wheel. Here the captain switched
registration papers and the pennant flying on the vessel's stern:
it might have been the barge *Forever HimPerialism* they had

boarded in Delhi but it was the barge *UnFunDaMentalism Forever* that sailed into the London Docks.

They had only been in the Normalist safe house for an hour when a note was pushed under the door of Maria's room. 'It is by the hand of George Villiers, a most loyal and courageous proponent of Normalism here in the Rookeries. In it he doth say—'

'Look, Maria—'

'Verily, thou shouldst be in no doubt, Corporal Moynahan, that my good title is *Sister* Maria!'

'Not here in the Rookeries it ain't. Here you're just plain Maria and you can stop calling me Corporal Moynahan too. From now on I'm Dean.'

'Such sudden familiarity is impossible. To call thee Dean—'

'And cut out all this Shakespearean crap too. All them "thees" and "thous" are gonna get us pegged as badniks quicker than a goose shits beans.'

Maria scowled at Moynahan's profanity but finally, reluctantly, she nodded her agreement. 'Very well . . . Dean. I will accede to thy . . . to *your* request. But to return to the note written by George Villiers, wherein he advises that Percy Shelley came to him two days ago seeking money. They agreed that this would be delivered to Shelley tonight, when he attends an establishment run by a Mrs Mary Jeffries.'

'Establishment?'

Maria smiled impishly. 'Mrs Jeffries is proprietess of the most fashionable brothel in the whole of the Rookeries.'

'A brothel? I find it odd that an UnFunDaMentalist-inclined ForthRight would allow a brothel to operate.'

A chuckle from Maria. 'UnFunDaMentalism is a very *flexible* religion, Dean, which may be bent or twisted to suit the needs – carnal or otherwise – of the ForthRight's leaders. Whilst its leaders might condemn the man in the street for his sexual indiscretions, they rationalise their own on the grounds that everyday morality does not apply to them. Leaders, most oft, have feet – and other appendages – of clay.'

Moynahan nodded. 'So, tonight we must go to Mrs Jeffries' house.'

'Yes . . . and to do that you must act the part of a gentleman and I . . . the part of a whore.'

'A whore?'

'Of course,' said Maria airily. 'Respectable women are not welcome in a brothel. But do not concern yourself, Dean, I won't be reduced to vapours by such a prospect. UnFunDaMentalists refer to Auralists such as myself as "Whorealists", believing we are but one step removed from prostitutes, therefore there are few better equipped than a Visual Virgin to play a harlot.' She smiled. 'But I believe you will find the part you have to play more challenging than mine. Although you are fine of form and well made, Dean, you are a man somewhat indifferent of fashion. Your suit announces you to be a ruffian and ruffians are not favoured by Mrs Jeffries. She only permits those from the very cream of ForthRight society to frequent her establishment. Therefore, Dean, you must be remodelled. We have the afternoon to transform you into a gentleman.' Maria gave a mournful shake of her head. 'I fear it will not be long enough.'

Four hours and five hundred guineas later, Moynahan gazed into his dressing mirror and struggled to recognise himself. Just who was this exquisitely dressed, coiffed and perfumed man who announced himself to be Dean Moynahan, gentleman?

A gentleman who looked like a fucking idiot.

His domed top hat, fashioned from black satin, was an instant too tall; the cream cravat at his throat was a mite too frothy; and his beautifully cut suit – black with the most subtle of pale grey stripes – was a shade too tight for comfort. That the ensemble was enriched by a scattering of silver jewellery and a pair of black boots encased in spats meant that it teetered on the brink of the ridiculous.

Maria had no such reservations. 'You look marvellous, Dean,' and with that she led him out of the room, and downstairs to the steamer that was parked waiting for them outside their hotel.

As they chugged their way through the streets of London en route to Mrs Jeffries' brothel, Maria continued her assessment. 'But whilst in *appearance* you are the epitome of a ForthRight gentleman, your demeanour still leaves much to be desired.'

'My demeanour?' queried Moynahan. 'I don't understand.'

'For you to be accepted as a gentleman, you must *act* as a gentleman. It is my experience that those who occupy the upper echelons of the ForthRight disport themselves in the manner of arrogant swine, which is something you must ape . . . ape being a most apposite description of these individuals.'

'So, let me get this straight. If I want to be accepted as a gentleman, I have to act as a pig.'

'Exactly.'

'Then don't worry about it, Maria. During my time in the army I've met a load of guys who will make excellent role models.'

'Good. And I would also suggest, given your great size and broad shoulders, that you announce yourself as a pugilist, which will go some way to explaining your somewhat . . . unorthodox manners.'

Their conversation was interrupted by the steamer driver announcing 'We're 'ere,' and he turned the vehicle into a street criss-crossed by excavations, the great heaps of wet earth dug from the trenches making the pavements nigh on impassable to pedestrians, especially for a woman wearing such dainty boots as Maria.

'Sorry, guv'nor,' apologised the driver as he brought the cab to a halt, 'but thems that does is still sortin' out Mr Faraday's galvanicEnergy cables. These will transmit the power to the new streetlamps the Great Leader 'as determined is necessary to alleviate the gloom ov the Rookeries. Mrs Jeffries' establishment is on the ovver side ov the road, the 'ouse wiv the red door.'

Moynahan thrust too many guineas into the cabby's hand then helped Maria from the cab. 'Now, Maria, we have the problem of crossing the road without ruining those kid boots of yours.'

Inspiration dawned. He walked up to what looked for all the world to be a bundle of rags heaped in a doorway and prodded it with the chiselled toe of his immaculately shone boot. Time, he decided, to get into character, so adopting his haughtiest accent, he announced, 'You there, shit-sweeper, I'll give you sixpence if you'll sweep a path across the road.'

The heap of rags stirred into life, slowly uncoiling to reveal the shape of a small boy, emaciated and alarmingly dirty. The boy's eyes blinked awake and he rubbed himself to bring some feeling into his numb body. 'A tanner, yer 'ighness? A flash cove like you wiv such a beamy bride in 'arness must be willing to run to a deaner.'

'What does this urchin say?' asked a bemused Maria.

Moynahan laughed, he had never thought his expertise as a linguist would mean him acting as an interpreter in the Demi-Monde. 'He's wondering if a fashionably and expensively dressed man such as myself, accompanied by such a beautiful woman, might, perhaps, be inclined to pay a shilling to have the road swept rather than the sixpence offered. And I, for my part, am moved to pay this exorbitant price; cheek and impudence must be rewarded.' He tossed the boy a silver sixpenny piece. 'If my lady can walk across to Mrs Jeffries' house without soiling her shoes or her dress, then there'll be a second tanner waiting for you on the other side.'

The boy beamed; a shilling was a week's wage in the Rookeries and more than enough to keep him soused with Solution. He pulled at his quiff of hair. 'Rely on me, yer 'ighness.' And with that he raced into the road and, using his decrepit broom, began to brush a channel through the muck.

As they crossed the road, Moynahan had to admit that he was enjoying himself. After ten months of being holed up in the men-only enclave that was the Portal it was a blast to be out and about in the company of a lovely woman. And Maria *was* beautiful. He just loved the way she tripped along, one hand holding up the train of her dress and the other clutching a pomander to her nose as protection against the stench. Dupe or not, this girl, he decided, had *style*, though unfortunately the boy's imprecations to 'avoid the turds' and 'don't step in the 'orse-shit' did add a somewhat surreal aspect to their journey.

Finally, the pair of them managed, with the minimum of soiling, to arrive at the entrance to the grand house that was their destination. Moynahan flipped the second sixpence to the boy, who gave another appreciative tug of his forelock.

'Much obliged, guv'nor, an' as you've been straight wiv me, let me give yous sum advice. There's a Checkya Black Maria parked around the corner so the chances are them bastards are gonna be raidin' Mrs Jeffries' knockin'-shop later in the evenin', so it'd be best to keep a straight 'ead an' be light on your toes.'

Once the urchin had disappeared into the darkness, Maria handed Moynahan a black leather mask. 'The final part of your ensemble,' she said with a smile.

Moynahan shrugged, then followed her lead and strapped it on. This done, he rapped on the door with the knob of his cane, the sharp sound echoing into the building. A few moments later a steel grille set into the door flicked open and a pair of hooded eyes peered out at them.

'Yus?' came the muffled enquiry. 'And 'oo might you be, sir?'

'Dean Moynahan, heavyweight champion of NoirVille, and my guest, the Lady Maria Steele,' he answered, putting a swagger into his voice.

'Never 'eard ov you.'

'Nor I of you,' retorted Moynahan uncaringly, as he pushed a folded five-guinea note through the grille, 'but here is my calling card.'

The grille snapped shut and they heard heavy bolts being thrown behind the door. Then, almost begrudgingly, the door opened to reveal a somewhat decrepit butler dressed in a morning suit that had obviously been made for someone considerably larger. 'Come in, sir, but I would warn you that Mrs Jeffries is very particular about 'er clientele.'

'Just so, just so,' nodded Moynahan as he swept Maria into the galleried hallway of the house, swinging his cape from his shoulders and plucking his hat from his head, then tossing them both to the doorman. Maria opted to retain her cloak.

'If you would be so kind as to announce us,' ordered Moynahan, 'I would be immeasurably grateful.'

'First, may I arsk, sir, iffn you is 'eeled?'

For a moment Moynahan considered lying but then realised that the butler would already have seen the Colt he had holstered under his armpit. 'I am. What of it?'

'Mrs Jeffries has an aversion to firearms and insists that any gentleman seeking admission must leave 'is ironware safe in my custody.'

With considerable reluctance Moynahan unholstered the pistol and handed it over. Satisfied, the butler ushered them up a long and very grand staircase to the first floor of the impressively opulent house. Whoever this Mrs Jeffries was, her business was obviously a tremendously lucrative one. At the top of the stairs they were met by two liveried footmen, broad-shouldered, tall and possessed of an attitude that was politely hostile.

'Good evening, sir . . . miss, would you be so kind as to let us have your names? Do you have an invitation?'

With a lackadaisical insouciance, Moynahan took a silver cigarette case from the pocket of his jacket, removed a cigarette and tapped it nonchalantly on a fingernail. He lit the cigarette and blew a wistful stream of smoke into the air. 'My name is Dean Moynahan, and I am accompanied by Lady Maria Steele. I am here to avail myself of this establishment's services.'

The two footmen glanced at one another, smiled and then the dark-haired one addressed Moynahan again. 'My apologies, sir, but it is a rule of the house that no stranger is admitted unless previously sanctioned by Mrs Jeffries. In this way the house seeks to protect the identities and the privacy of its patrons from unwarranted intrusions.'

Moynahan ignored the rebuff. 'Perhaps if I were to speak to Mrs Jeffries, this misunderstanding might be resolved?'

'That is impossible, sir, without a prior appointment.'

'Nothing is impossible,' stated Moynahan quietly.

'This is,' retorted the footman, shifting his sizeable bulk better to block Moynahan's route to the landing.

'Please, call Mrs Jeffries, or I will become annoyed.'

The footman gave a dismissive laugh. His confidence was easy enough to understand: big though Moynahan was, they did, after all, outnumber him two to one. 'Annoyed, you say, sir?' He winked theatrically to his colleague. 'Well, sir, I find that gentlemen such as yourself are best advised not to become annoyed in the presence of me and John.'

Moynahan smiled an easy smile. 'Are you threatening me?'

'As you wish, sir.'

'Then know that I don't take lightly to being threatened by the likes of you. Make a move against me and I will damage you.'

Now that gave the muscle some pause and, thinking that it might be a good idea to put the frighteners on Moynahan, the footman made a serious mistake. Pulling back the tail of his heavily embroidered frock-coat, he revealed a long piece of iron pipe hanging from a leather strap. 'I think you'll find that my life preserver is the one that will be inflicting damage—'

Moynahan *hated* being threatened and he communicated his distaste by slamming a balled fist into the man's crotch. The man's cheeks blew out and he sank groaning to his knees. Such was the suddenness of the attack that John, the second doorman, was slow to react, which was his undoing. There was a loud click and Moynahan prodded the point of a switchblade he'd conjured from his sleeve into John's groin. 'Make one sudden move, my merry man, and I'll slit you from scrotum to sternum. Now I want you to go and tell your mistress that Dean Moynahan and Lady Maria Steele are here and they'd like to see her pronto.'

'You're mad—'

'That's as may be but I'm a madman with a blade in my hand.'

The footman scuttled off to reappear a moment later accompanied by a tall, thin woman of about Maria's age, well-dressed, though the make-up she was wearing announced her to be a woman of less than respectable inclinations. She was handsome in a nondescript sort of way, her fishy eyes preventing her ever being considered truly attractive, especially as these fishy eyes were flashing with anger.

'So wot's to do 'ere then? Oo's this Mister Moynahan 'oo's bin creating such a fuss an' a flummox?'

'I am,' admitted Moynahan.

'John 'ere says you 'ave assaulted Henry by bashin' 'im in the bollocks, an' 'ave threatened John wiv a shiv.'

'That's correct,' said Moynahan as he moved up a step to stand on the landing.

A frown creased the woman's brow and she paused to study Moynahan more carefully. 'It's not proper for a nice gentleman like wot you appear to be to make a disturbance. So, Mr

Moynahan, what's all the kerfuffle about? We don't want any 'urly-burly in an 'ouse run by Mary Jeffries. It gets my guests all aquiver.'

'I wish to attend your entertainments.'

'Indeed! Well, I've 'alf a mind to send you off wiv a flea in your ear. It don't do for gentlemen guests ov mine to be causing a fracas an' such.'

Moynahan bowed and then gave his most disarming smile. 'I can assure you that my purpose in visiting your marvellous institution is to be enlightened and entertained. I have no intention of repeating this deplorable scene. I understand that the fee for newcomers is fifty guineas' – he took out his wallet and casually removed five ten-guinea notes – 'payable in advance.'

For a moment Mary Jeffries stood as though uncertain, eyeing first the notes in Moynahan's hand and then the groaning footman on the floor. Finally she came to a decision and plucked the notes from his hand. 'Very well, Mr Moynahan. You can come in but not your dollymop. Only my own lasses are runners 'ere; them an' a few of the choicer *grandes horizontales*.'

'She's no doxy,' laughed Moynahan. 'I've brought her here to be educated in the finer points of Cupid's Dance.'

'A demi-rep, eh? Well, it still don't signify; the bucks and blades in my 'ouse are pipin' 'ot an' urgent and in my experience amateurs like 'er are likely to call for the rozzers if they are so much as looked at askance.' She studied Maria carefully. 'Yus, there's a mite too much pepper and hauteur about 'er for my taste, though she's comely enough and, from what I can see under 'er cloak, 'er bubbies are fine and pouting. But that counts as nowt. Send 'er back to the nunnery, Mr Moynahan, and let me find you a ride that is truly 'ot to trot.'

Moynahan tried again. 'You misunderstand, Mrs Jeffries, Maria here is no demi-rep, no amateur playing the whore for devilment and delight. Rather, she has a thirst for knowledge . . . forbidden knowledge.'

'So you say, Mr Moynahan, but it would be better to 'ear it from 'er own lips.'

Moynahan turned to Maria and stared at her in a meaningful way. 'Well, Maria?'

Maria's mouth drew into a tight line. 'I wish to enter your establishment, Mrs Jeffries, and to see every vice and debauchery—'

'It's the *seeing* that I object to, Miss Steele,' sneered Mary Jeffries. 'You come to my 'ouse as a voyeur rather than a participant. All the girls in that room' – she nodded towards the double doors – 'are working girls, not toffs looking for a thrill. Pass through them doors an' you're in play, Miss Steele.' She sniffed dismissively. 'The only way to educate a tart, Mr Moynahan, is through *involvement* and involvement is not sumfink I fink Miss Steele 'ere is set upon.' She glanced up at the landing's clock. 'If you'll excuse me, I've spent too long a time chit-chatting. I've me ovver gentlemen to be attending to.'

Now Maria took matters into her own hands. She unclasped the buckle that tethered her cloak about her shoulders and let it fall to the ground. In Moynahan's opinion, the gown she was wearing was the most erotic dress he had ever seen and it achieved this not by flashing huge quantities of naked flesh but by hints and suggestions. Made from the most ephemeral of tulle, the white, full-length Grecian robe flowed over her body like a bleached shadow, allowing her glorious figure to slide in and out of view every time she moved. Moynahan had once read that a dress should whisper a woman's intent but this dress didn't whisper – it screamed.

A sultry smile dressed Maria's lips, she placed the one hand artfully on a cocked hip, and then turned her smoky eyes to Mary Jeffries. 'I am ready to do much more than just *look*, Mrs Jeffries. If you allow me through those doors your patrons may use my body without let or hindrance.'

Mary Jeffries took a few moments to study Maria, her gaze taking in the provocative cut of her dress and the curves of her body. Obviously she was as susceptible to the arts of fiduciary sex as anyone. 'Spunky filly, ain't you. And you'll need to be. You ain't any idea wot you'll be letting yerself in for.' She thought for a moment. 'But if you're in earnest it can be arranged . . . for a price.'

Without a moment's hesitation, Moynahan drew his billfold from his jacket and handed Mary Jeffries a further fifty guineas. He had a feeling that what he was about to see would be cheap at twice the price.

1:07

London, the Rookeries
The Demi-Monde: 88th Day of Summer, 1005

5/16/2018. Su Xiaoxiao my Dupe guide in the DM explained that there are some historical personages recreated in the DM. Shelley?

5/16/2018. Su Xiaoxiao has promised 2 introduce me 2 Shelley. Far out. I'm so excited.

5/17/2018. Went 2 pub called the Prancing Pig 2 meet Shelley. Whatta dish. I can't believe he's not real. I'm in love with a Dupe!

5/19/2018. I interviewed Shelley 4 my next assignment. Got his views on non-violence. If that don't get me an 'A' what will?

5/19/2018. Went dancing with Su Xiaoxiao & Shelley. Lots of fun tho I don't like Burlesque Bandstand: he gives me the creeps.

Zip messages posted by Norma Williams prior to her entry into the Demi-Monde

Mary Jeffries signalled to a slim girl dressed as an inmate of a Turkish seraglio and sporting a really quite comical turban to escort Maria and Moynahan through the double doors and into the salon proper. Accustomed as she was to the splendour of the Doge's Palace in Venice, Maria prepared herself to be disappointed, but she wasn't. The huge, high-ceilinged room was sumptuously decorated in crimson and gilt and the wall panels – brilliantly lit by gaslights and candle-bedecked chandeliers – showed pictures of a distinctly erotic cast, with nymphs and satyrs locked in fervent and very blatant union.

'This is the best sporting 'ouse in the 'ole of the Rookeries,' crooned their guide, the girl obviously bursting with pride. 'All ov the bon tons is 'ere, and the tail on parade is wivout equal.' Maria could see that what the girl said was accurate: the clientele crowding the room were very elegantly and expensively dressed. 'Would you care for a drink, sir? The Mistress said I 'ad to look after you tonight, to make sure you enjoy yourselves an' all.'

'What's your name, girl?' asked Moynahan.

'Rosie, sir.'

Moynahan smiled and pressed a five-guinea note into Rosie's palm. 'Well, Rosie, I shall have a neat whisky, and for Miss Steele, a glass of champagne au gore. And make sure it is the good stuff and not the adulterated poison you serve to the other mugs. Try to gull me and I'll have the SAE off your arse but play me straight and I'll see you all right.'

As the giggling girl scuttled off to get the drinks, Maria glanced at Moynahan and gave a nod of appreciation. She was impressed: Daemon he might be but he was playing the toff to perfection. A thought struck her. 'You're not drinking blood?' she enquired.

'No. We Daemons have an aversion to blood.'

How peculiar these Daemons are, thought Maria, *peculiar but very handsome.*

When their drinks had been delivered Moynahan raised his glass in salute to Maria. 'To Miss Maria Steele, the most beautiful woman in this . . . or any other world.'

To her astonishment, Maria found herself blushing: the man – the Daemon – was flirting with her! She brought her fan up in front of her face in an attempt to disguise how pleased she was by his flattery. 'You are very gallant, Dean.'

In truth Maria found herself somewhat nonplussed by Moynahan's compliments and nervous about her own feelings towards the man: Visual Virgins were taught never to be moved by shows of affection but she was finding this difficult. Unconsciously she edged herself closer to Moynahan, pressing herself against him in a show of coquettish appreciation as they sashayed around the room.

'With everybody being masked, won't you find it tricky spotting Shelley?' asked Moynahan.

'No, Dean: his aura is unmistakable. Poets are swathed in lilacs and other pastel colours whereas most of the men here are surrounded by much earthier hues.'

For five minutes they promenaded, Maria ever on the lookout for Shelley. But look as she did, there was neither hide nor hair of the man and she began to worry that Villiers' intelligence about him attending the bawdy house might be wrong . . . but then she was enjoying herself too much to care. Flirting was fun.

Again Moynahan brought his mouth nearer to her ear. 'You are being watched, Maria. There is a girl to your left who is studying you with a great deal of intent. It seems the women gathered here tonight don't welcome such lovely competition.'

Maria looked towards the girl Moynahan was speaking about. Despite the mask the girl was wearing she recognised her immediately: pictures of Catherine Walters were regularly carried by the news magazines. 'That's Catherine Walters, or Skittles as she is more affectionately known.'

'She's famous?'

'Very. She's the foremost whore in all the Demi-Monde, the most famous of all the *grandes horizontales* – the highest class of whore – and, despite the restrictions imposed by UnFun-DaMentalism, the most fashionable woman in the whole of the ForthRight.'

Catherine Walters must have noted Maria's interest in her, which she rewarded with an acknowledging bob of her head.

'She is very beautiful,' Maria gushed, 'and her dress is magnificent.' And it wasn't just her dress that marked her out as someone exceptional, her aura was quite remarkable too, a heady concoction of pinks – signalling inspiration, optimism, intelligence – and indigos – which showed she had strong metaphysical and sexual abilities. If she'd been born in Venice, Skittles would have made a powerful Auralist.

'Enough of Skittles,' Moynahan whispered in her ear. 'It's Shelley we need to find.'

'Oh, we have, Dean,' Maria said sotto voce, 'that's him standing beside Skittles, next to that fat man.'

'You're sure?'

'His aura is unmistakable.' Maria frowned. 'But how are we to arrange an introduction?'

'I think the dress you are wearing will be introduction enough.'

In this Moynahan was correct. A moment later Rosie materialised at his side. 'Excuse me, sir, but Mr George Rowley wonders if you and Miss Steele would care to join him for a drink.'

Despite his being all high fashion and hauteur, Moynahan *liked* Percy Shelley – or George Rowley as he was calling himself. Certainly there was something effete about him, but there was an impish twinkle in his eye that hinted of hidden depths. He was a handsome devil too and this combined with a shock of curly hair and the stylish way he was dressed ensured that Shelley was a man born to break a lot of female hearts.

But Moynahan's liking for Shelley was matched by his detestation of the man standing by his side, who seemed to have attached himself to the poet. He had disliked John Wilmot on sight. Wilmot was large and fat and seemed to spend his time looking down his nose at the world. Moynahan also hated the way he was ogling Maria.

'So you are a heavyweight champion, Comwade Moynahan,' breezed Shelley as he quaffed his champagne. 'It is a wonder I have never heard of you.'

'I ply my trade in NoirVille.'

'Bashing Shades about, eh?' guffawed Wilmot. 'Good stuff. Buggers need a thrashing now and agin to keep 'em in their place.'

Shelley was obviously a little put out by Wilmot's boorishness. 'Please, I pway you, do not take Comwade Wilmot's levity *too* sewiously.'

'Don't listen to George,' boomed Wilmot, 'you must take my levity *very* seriously. The vanquishing of the UnderMentionable races is not something I take lightly, especially now, if His Holiness Comrade Crowley is to be believed, the triumph of UnFunDaMentalism is soon to be achieved.'

'How so?' asked Maria.

'Ah, beauty speaks and angels listen. A little bird has told me, Miss Steele, that, in a matter of days, invitations will be issued to all good UnFunDaMentalists requiring them to gather in Terror Incognita at the end of Fall for the Ceremony of Purification, a ceremony which will mark the reincarnation of the Pre-Folk and the elimination of the racial contaminants that have poisoned the Demi-Monde since the Confinement. Then the Aryan race will stand triumphant and the Shades and the nuJus will have been scoured from our world. You'll find yourself out of work, Moynahan: after the Ceremony there won't be any Shades for you to pound and pummel.'

'I am surprised, sir, that the Ceremony is to take place in Terror Incognita,' said Maria. 'Surely that is a forbidden world . . . forbidden by ABBA, that is. No one who has ventured there has ever returned.'

'Being a Quartier Chaudian, Miss Steele, you will be unfamiliar with the power wielded by His Holiness Aleister Crowley. He is confident that he can lift ABBA's embargo on Terror Incognita.'

Maria gave a rather forced smile. 'Then am I to presume that following the Ceremony all women will be obliged to follow UnFunDaMentalism's doctrine of Biological Essentialism, that our role will be prescribed by the motto "Feeding, Breeding and MenFolk Heeding"?'

Wilmot guzzled the rest of his Solution. 'Of course, that is the natural order of things, women being physically, psychologically and intellectually the inferior gender.'

'You are very disparaging of women, Wilmot,' observed a smiling Catherine Walters. 'I am of a mind to implore Mr Moynahan to help me defend my sex's honour.' Here Skittles took Moynahan by the arm and pressed herself against him. Moynahan didn't object: she was a beautiful woman.

'Honour, my dear Skittles? I suspect you dispensed with that fatuous encumbrance a long time ago. And as for my belittling women, why, all educated persons understand that ABBA placed women in this world in order that they bend their knee to men.'

'I weject your foul conjecture, Comwade Wilmot,' objected Shelley. 'My opinion is that women are the supewior gender, being that they ain't cursed by MALEvolence. Better they had command of this sowwy world, then perhaps we would not have to suffer the malicious mismanagement of men.'

Wilmot gave a dismissive chuckle. 'Having such an aberrational respect for women, Rowley, I would question what you are doing in a bordello.'

'I seek love.'

'Then you will not find it here! I believe women to be the worst of the sexes in that they are the repository of the most pernicious of HumanKind's weaknesses . . . an inability to love. Women, you see, have no passion, gripped as they are by the steely hands of irrational reason, that *ignis fatuus*, which leads them to desire only what society informs them they should desire.'

Shelley smiled. 'I am minded to quote the verse of a fwiend of mine, a Count Maddalo, who says that "Man's love is of man's life a part; it is a woman's whole existence."'

'You have met such a woman, one who has truly embraced love?' sneered Wilmot.

'I have. She is my deawest, my most constant love, with soul meeting soul on lovers' lips. And though we are parted she wemains a beacon in the darkness of the world.'

Wilmot slapped Shelley on the back. 'Come, George, I will not have you lapse into melancholic reflection on a love lost. Forget love and embrace my philosophy: when I see a woman and the heat is within me, I must have her.'

Skittles made to protest but she was interrupted by a smiling Mary Jeffries. 'And wot is this I 'ear, Mr Wilmot, of 'aving her?' She nodded towards Maria. 'Are you about to get a filly under starter's orders?'

'That would be a delightful occurrence, Mistress Jeffries, but first I must look after my friend here. Rowley has come to your establishment in search of love . . .'

'My, my, Mr Rowley, there are any number of girls here tonight who would leap at the chance of *loving* you. And are we not graced by the presence of Mistress Steele, a ride of rare beauty, 'oo her Master, Mr Moynahan, 'ere, wishes to be introduced to the world of the rake and the blood?'

'Miss Steele is indeed a woman of incompawable loveliness,' admitted Shelley.

'But beauty is nothing if it is not enjoined with a willingness to submit.' With that Mrs Jeffries pushed Maria towards Shelley, pressing her against him. 'So will you not use her, Mr Rowley? Will you not *instruct* her?'

'If Miss Steele is willing.'

'Miss Steele is *very* willing, Mr Rowley,' replied Maria, accompanying her answer with a teasing smile.

'Then I am honoured, but my sensibilities are such, Mrs Jeffwies, that I am unable to instwuct in public, being of a mind that lovemaking ain't a spectator sport. Perhaps I might have some pwivacy?'

'As you wish,' snorted an obviously disappointed Mary Jeffries. 'There are curtained booths alongside the salon, each furnished with everyfing you might need to exercise the girl.'

1:08

London, the Rookeries
The Demi-Monde: 88th Day of Summer, 1005

My time as a fugitive persuaded me, of necessity, to ponder on the subject of secrecy. And what this cogitation has led me to conclude is that secrecy is anathema to the development of civilised behaviour. The use of secrecy – aided and abetted by its cowering, reticent confederate, privacy – allows the darker aspects of HumanKind to fester and flourish unseen. Denied the liberating light of public scrutiny and criticism, these dark inclinations grow, gaining in power and strength until they envelop our more liberal thoughts and destroy our selfless instincts. No doubt my critics will protest that it was secrecy that enabled me to escape the clutches of the Checkya, but I would retort that it is secrecy that enabled such a foul and fetid organisation to flourish in the first place.

The Fall of the ForthRight: Percy Bysshe Shelley,
FreeWill Press

A very happy Shelley ushered Maria into the booth and drew the curtain closed behind them. 'And now, Miss Steele—' he began but he was interrupted by Maria placing a finger firmly against his lips.

'I am afraid I must leave you unsatisfied tonight, Mr Shelley.'

The man gawped. 'Why do you call me by that name? I am George Wowley—'

'Shall we stop this play-acting, Mr Shelley? I have come to the Rookeries to find Norma Williams and it is my belief that you are the very man to assist me in this endeavour.'

'And who are you?'

'I am Sister Maria, a Visual Virgin, though here in the Rookeries I use the *nom de guerre* Maria Steele.'

Shelley gave a wry smile. 'Well, Miss Steele . . . Sister Maria . . . whoever the Hel you are, I must disappoint you. My admiwation of Norma Williams is such that I will not compwomise her safety by leading you to her.'

'Very noble, Mr Shelley, but you should understand that it is her very safety that is uppermost in my thoughts. I have come to the Rookeries in order to lead her to sanctuary.'

Shelley shook his head. 'Nonsense. You are, most pwobably, a ForthWight cwypto . . . a damned attwactive cwypto, but a cwypto nevertheless.'

'You have to trust me, Mr Shelley, and by doing that you will preserve your own life.'

'My life?'

'You have been rash, Mr Shelley. As a Visual Virgin I am able to see Wilmot for the ne'er-do-well he is. I suspect he has lured you here tonight with the intention of betraying you to the Checkya.'

'Balderdash! It's impossible for Wilmot to suspect my weal identity.'

'In this surmise, Mr Shelley, you are mistaken. When Dean and I arrived here tonight we were informed that a Checkya steamer was parked close by. At the time I thought nothing of it, but now I am certain that they loiter, awaiting a signal from Wilmot to raid this establishment and arrest you.'

Shelley stood silent for several seconds as he weighed up what to do. 'How did you know I would be here?'

'George Villiers told me so in a note he sent me this afternoon.'

'Did he have any message for me?'

'Yes, he said to tell you:

Chameleons live on light and air:
Poets' food is love and fame.
Trust in the girl beauteous and fair,
To lead thee to the Daemon's lair.'

'"To the Daemon's lair" . . . that is indeed the pass-phwase George and I had agweed. Vewy well, Miss Steele, for the moment I will give you the benefit of the doubt. So tell me what's to do.'

'We must prevent Wilmot from raising the alarm.'

'But how?'

Five minutes later it was a rather red-faced and mussed Shelley who emerged from the booth and beckoned urgently to Wilmot. 'Wilmot, I have a wequest of you. It seems that Miss Steele has appetites that one man alone is unable to satisfy. She has a mind to twy her hand at twoilism. This being the case, I was hoping that you might be inclined to oblige her.'

'Troilism, eh? I thought she looked a willing wench when I first espied her but I had no idea that this was her persuasion. But I will warn her that the role I assume will not be that of the voyeur but more of the enthusiastic participant.'

'I think Miss Steele will be delighted to hear that, Wilmot,' said a smiling Shelley as he led Wilmot to the alcove where Maria was standing seductively in the corner, her dress untethered so that her breasts were bared.

'My, my,' said Wilmot, 'you do surprise, young la—'

It was the derringer that Shelley pressed against his ear that shut him up. 'Supwise doubled, eh, Comwade Wilmot? Utter a cwy or make a sudden move and I will be obliged to plug you.' He looked over to Maria. 'I would be gwateful, Miss Steele, if you would examine Comwade Wilmot's wallet.'

Maria did as she was asked and found a card inside identifying Wilmot as a member of the Checkya.

'What a bounder you are, Comwade Wilmot. How many Normalists did you condemn to earn yourself this?'

'Enough,' sneered Wilmot, 'but it is a total that will soon be added to. This building is now surrounded by Checkya, Shelley. There is no escape.'

'Then what we need is a diversion,' answered Maria. 'I propose, Shelley, that you leave me here and apprise Moynahan of the situation. Tell him that in a few moments I will create a kerfuffle that will give you both an opportunity to slip away.'

'And what of you?'

'I will trust to the distraction of unadorned beauty.'

'And Wilmot?'

'For that I must rely on your good offices, Shelley.'

Shelley nodded, then drew back his fist and socked Wilmot hard on the jaw. The man sagged to the ground.

'Oh, well done, sir,' exclaimed Maria as she completed the unbuttoning of her dress, revealing more of the perfect – and perfectly naked – body beneath.

Shelley eyed her appreciatively. 'You know, Comwade Maria, I ain't in any gweat wush. Perhaps we could—'

'If you, sir, have quite finished your perusal of my charms,' snapped Maria, 'I would suggest you go and speak with Moynahan. My own advice is that your escape would be best accomplished over the rooftops. Tell Moynahan we will rendezvous back at our hotel.'

A reluctant Shelley gifted his derringer to Maria and, with a last languid look at her naked bounties, exited the booth. Once he had whispered an explanation regarding the situation to Moynahan, the man nodded his understanding and then looked nervously towards the hall's entrance. Shelley understood his trepidation.

'Yes, the pwoblem we have, Comwade Moynahan, is if it comes to a fight, we ain't armed.'

'Do you not think I have a splendid bottom, Mr Shelley?' asked Catherine Walters.

Shelley spun around on his heel, cursing himself for having forgotten about Wilmot's woman. 'I think it is twuly delightful, Miss Walters, unfortunately this ain't quite the moment when I am best able to—'

'Oh, I think this is an excellent moment, Mr Shelley,' the girl simpered. 'Our mutual friend George Villiers always says that it's quite amazing what a man might find hidden beneath a woman's bustle if he takes the time to look.'

Shelley beamed a smile, drew the girl towards him and then delved under her skirts. There was a revolver hidden there. 'Wemarkable,' he said as he explored further.

'There is only *one* pistol hidden there, Mr Shelley,' Skittles scolded.

'Best be certain, eh?' replied Shelley with a wink.

Unfortunately his fondling was interrupted by the screams of 'You bastard! You animal!' coming from a half-naked Maria as she emerged from the alcove. 'You are a beast and a cad, Wilmot,' she yelled and with that she ran through the hall, pushing and shoving laughing people aside as she made for the exit. Every eye followed her, including Shelley's. It took a yank on his arm by Moynahan to remind him why Maria was doing what she was doing.

Giving Skittles a quick peck on the cheek, Shelley led Moynahan through a side door and hurried up the staircase beyond. On the top landing it took him just an instant to get his bearings, shoulder his way past one of the doors lining the corridor and into the bedroom beyond. It was a small room, only two strides from door to window, a window which Shelley had open in a trice. He looked out. 'We're in luck, Comwade Moynahan. If we slide down the woof, it'll bwing us to the house next door.'

The sound of feet pounding up the stairs and shouts of 'Make way for the Checkya' interrupted any further explanation.

Moynahan hopped up onto the window ledge, looked down the roof and hesitated. Understandable: the slope of the roof as it ran down to the gulley between Mary Jeffries' house and the adjoining one was very steep and very long. It took a shove from Shelley to send him on his way, tumbling down the roof, landing battered and bruised in the gutter. He was just levering himself to his knees when Shelley smashed into him.

'Wuined!' Shelley exclaimed as he inspected the tattered seat of his trousers, but a bullet whizzing inches from his right ear persuaded him that now was not the moment to be overly concerned regarding matters sartorial. He fired two quick shots back towards the pursuing Checkya. 'Over there!' he yelled. 'That window. Smartly now.'

The dormer window wasn't open but a savage kick from Moynahan made it so. As bullets pinged around him, smacking into the roof and smashing tiles, Shelley dived through the window, landing on the rather attractive young lady cowering in her bed. Her screams were truncated by the arrival of Moynahan, but then, Shelley supposed, sixteen stone of fugitive landing on your head would put a crimp on anyone's vocal inclinations.

With Moynahan at his heels Shelley rammed his way out of the bedroom and raced down the stairs, swinging around the banisters, ignoring the loud complaints of the man who he assumed was the master of the house as he went.

'Kitchen?' Shelley demanded of a maid he encountered in the hallway and then charged down the dark passageway indicated by the girl's trembling finger.

Once there, he headed straight for the back door but even as he struggled to unlock it, the Checkya arrived. There were two of them and they looked big and brutal, but what they didn't have was Shelley's aplomb. He loosed off two shots, the first catching the leading man in the shoulder, making him drop his pistol and sending him spinning around. The second shot missed its target but it was near enough to send the second Checkya agent diving for cover.

Most estate agents would have described the house's back door as 'substantial' and as 'oak, reinforced with steel furniture'. It might have been all of these things and more but it wasn't sufficient to deal with a rampaging Moynahan. He gave it one almighty kick and it yielded.

Breathless, the two men found themselves in a courtyard where a chauffeur was just putting a final sheen on the beautiful black paintwork of a huge Daimler steamer. Shelley didn't hesitate; he stuck his pistol up the man's nose. 'Keys, Comwade?' he demanded and the man with an equal lack of hesitation handed them over. 'Can you dwive one of these contwaptions, Moynahan? I ain't overly familiar with things mechanical. Too dirty and smelly, don't cha know.'

Fortunately Moynahan could drive. He had just clambered into the driving seat when a bullet starred the rear window. Shelley fired a couple of shots in return as Moynahan twisted the key in the steering lock and released the brake. For a long, heart-stopping moment nothing happened and then the steamer panted uncertainly into life. Moynahan hit the steam pedal and they were away.

When Moynahan and Shelley finally found their way back to the hotel, Maria – a fully clad Maria – was waiting for them. It seemed the Checkya were as inept at apprehending half-naked women as they were pistol-packing desperadoes.

Shelley looked around the room and sniffed. 'It comes to a sowwy pass when wevolutionawies are unable to fund more appwopwiate and sanitawy diggings.' He sniffed again. 'No matter. Sacwifices must, I suppose, be made to wemove the verminous scallywags who lead the ForthWight.'

'We are incognito, Mr Shelley,' answered Maria, 'and hence I felt it injudicious to take rooms in a more salubrious neighbourhood where the scrutiny of our provenance might be a tad more intense.'

'Indeed,' conceded Shelley with a vague wave of his hand. 'But that bwings us to a somewhat delicate subject, the vewification of your bona fides. To put no finer point on it, Miss Steele, you could be a Checkya agent masquewading as a Visual Virgin in order to awwest Norma Williams.' And with that he produced Skittles' revolver from his jacket pocket. 'I would be pleased to have pwoof that you are who you say you are.'

A halo of determination flickered around Shelley's head which told Maria that under the man's somewhat comical, powder-puff demeanour there was a core of steel. He was in deadly earnest.

'We have the passphrase from George Villiers.'

Shelley's lip twitched to indicate his disdain. 'My dear young lady, it could be that George has been taken by the Checkya and subjected to torture.' He gave a rueful shake of his head. 'I am all confusion, bedevilled by the thought that perhaps you *are* the Checkya and now by subtle twicks and artifice – and feminine wiles, lest we forget – you seek to beguile me into an indiscwetion. Perhaps the escape fwom Mawy Jeffwies' establishment was merely a pantomime to twick me into betwaying my beloved Norma.' He wagged a finger towards Maria. 'But though you have found me, I will not betway my lost angel of a wuined Pawadise. First, I must be made to twust you.'

'You know that Norma Williams is a Daemon?' asked Maria quietly.

'Norma told me as much when we first met and, I will admit, it took me a while to accept her for what she was. I had thought such cweatures to be merely myth and make-believe, never having an inkling that they might be weal.' Shelley poured himself a glass of Solution and took a long swig. 'But I tell you this, do not seek to turn me fwom her because of her stwange pwovenance. I know that Norma is no Lamia, no serpent disguised by beauty. She is goodness itself, as she has shown by her bwave pwomotion of Normalism.' He sighed. 'Woe is me. Was there ever such an ill-omened *mésalliance* than that of versifier and Daemon?'

'We have no intention of traducing your good opinion of Norma, Mr Shelley,' counselled Maria, 'quite the opposite, in fact. But you should understand that Mr Moynahan has been sent from the Spirit World to find her.'

'Spiwit World?' Shelley turned his blue eyes towards Moynahan. 'You are a Daemon? You are another twaveller fwom that stwange wealm that lies beyond our imagination?'

'I am,' answered Moynahan and as proof he clicked open his switchblade and dragged the blade along his palm. A thin trace of blood oozed from the cut.

'I should have guessed . . . no normal chap would have worn that cwavat with that suit. It ain't wight, don't cha know.' He gave a shrug. 'But why do you seek Norma?'

'My mission is to lead Norma Williams back to . . . well, we call it the Real World but you Demi-Mondians call it the Spirit World. Unfortunately, she has been a mite elusive and that's why I need your help to find her. She's the daughter of a very important man, the President, and he wants her brought back to the Real World safe and sound.'

'Vewy well. I will help you find Norma Williams but not because she is the Pwesident's daughter nor yet because of my tender feelings towards her. No, I will help you because she is important; important not just to change this world but also, I suspect, Comwade Moynahan, to change yours. I believe Normalism is the way in which both our worlds may be saved. Normalism is the hope of the Demi-Monde *and* the Weal World.'

'So you know where Norma is?' prompted Moynahan.

Shelley shook his head. 'No. You must understand that the intelligence I have wegarding her wheweabouts is scant. I know she is here in the Wookeries – I saw her but thwee nights ago in the Canterbuwy Theatre – but finding exactly where in London she might be hiding will, I suspect, pwove to be an intwactable puzzle.'

Now this was a development Moynahan hadn't been expecting. He had thought that by finding Shelley they would find Norma Williams, but it seemed that the poet had no more idea where she was hiding than he had.

'But wather than perplexing as to *where* she is in the Wookeries, perhaps we should have been wondewing *why* she is in the Wookeries.'

'*Why* she's in the Rookeries? I don't understand.'

Shelley smiled. 'There can only be one weason, Comwade Moynahan: to pwomote the cause of Normalism.' He picked up the copy of *The Stormer* – the ForthRight's daily newspaper – that was lying on a table and opened it to its centre pages, which were headlined 'Lammas Eve Victory Celebrations: a Souvenir Guide'. 'This is the weason she's come to the Wookeries: to embawwass the Gweat Leader in the Cwystal Palace.'

The Crystal Palace, London, the Rookeries
The Demi-Monde: 90th Day of Summer, 1005

Much as I hated the man and all he stood for, I admired Reinhard Heydrich as a great manipulator of public opinion. Heydrich was supremely talented when it came to moulding what Émile Durkheim calls the collective effervescence, the energy created when large numbers of people gather together. He understood better than any that once individuals coalesce into a crowd they become collectivist, their individuality melding to the extent that they believe that they are at one with ABBA. It is this quasi-religious euphoria that Heydrich sought to make his own, in order that allegiance to the Party could be transformed into deification of the Great Leader. Indeed, there is only one person who was more skilled than Heydrich at crowd manipulation: Norma Williams.

Reinhard Heydrich: Biography of a Bigot: Percy Shelley, Normalist Publications

'And now, lads and lasses,' Sporting Chance bellowed, 'I 'ave a special treat for yous. This lovely little lady 'as come a long way to be wiv us tonight so I want you to give a right big ForthRight welcome to . . . MISS AALIZ HEYDRICH!'

'That's Norma Williams,' an excited Maria shouted to Moynahan.

Being half-asleep, it took a moment for Moynahan to react. Sure, the Victory in the Coven celebrations had been an eye-popping experience, the whole evening reminding him of the opening ceremony of the Rio Olympics – though with rather fewer semi-naked women on display – all marching, clapping, flag-waving and speech-making. Marvellously choreographed too – he *was* in the ForthRight and Heydrich *was* famous for his love of mass rallies – and mind-bogglingly huge. There were, according to *The Stormer*, one hundred thousand soldiers on parade, and, as he watched the regiments wheel flawlessly around the arena, Moynahan had no reason to doubt this estimate.

The problem was that the acres of glass used in the construction of the Crystal Palace made it not only visually astonishing but unbelievably hot. And the heat plus Heydrich's seemingly never-ending speechifying meant that Moynahan had nodded off.

He was awake now, though. 'You're certain it's her?' he demanded as he used his opera glasses to study the girl. 'Surely that's Aaliz Heydrich? The blonde hair—'

'A wig! No. I've seen Aaliz Heydrich before and her aura is a mass of hate and ambition. This girl's is quite the opposite. Forget the blonde hair: the girl down there *is* Norma Williams, her aura is unmistakable. She is suffused with a halo of gold . . . she *is* the Messiah!'

Not only a Messiah, but a damned fine orator! Although she employed none of Heydrich's histrionics, her message came across very powerfully. It might, of course, have been that her very vulnerability demanded that everyone listen to her: she was, after all, just a young girl dressed in a white gown marooned in the centre of a vast stage, confronting the massed might of the ForthRight. Or it might have been that what she said – that violence was wrong and that men and women should live in harmony with their fellows – had a deep resonance with an audience heartily sick of the deprivation and death associated with war. But whatever the reason, the whole auditorium went silent as the people crammed into the place listened to her . . . which was why Heydrich moved to shut her up.

There were shouts from the balcony where Heydrich and his cronies were seated and immediately platoons of black-uniformed Checkya began to rush towards the stage. The problem they faced was that with so many soldiers packed into the hall they met a veritable wall of red-jacketed opposition. As was their wont, the Checkya overreacted and began beating at the soldiers with their batons, and the soldiers, as was *their* wont, began to fight back wielding chairs, bottles and anything else that came to hand.

Even as Moynahan watched, the fighting escalated and by sheer weight of numbers the soldiers began to push the Checkya back. And that was when the Checkya decided it would be a good idea to fire on the protesting soldiers. The rifle fire that crackled around the Crystal Palace had two effects: it panicked the non-combatant part of the audience and seriously annoyed the combatant part. The soldiers began to return fire and in an eye-blink the hall had been turned into a battleground.

'We've got to get Norma to safety,' Moynahan announced and with Maria and Shelley racing at his heels he took off in the direction of the stage. Being so big, he was able to bulldoze his way through the chaos, but a good five minutes elapsed before they found themselves backstage, arriving just as Norma was in the process of being arrested by a Checkya detachment.

Moynahan didn't hesitate. He pulled tear gas canisters from his shoulder bag and tossed them towards the Checkya, who began reeling about coughing and retching. Then, wrapping a handkerchief around his face, he plunged into the smoke, grabbed Norma by an arm and dragged her clear.

'Hiya, Norma. I'm Corporal 1st Class Dean Moynahan of the 5th US Combat Training Regiment. If you'd just keep your head down, we'll try to get you out of here.'

Hands on knees, spluttering and choking, Norma blinked back her tears and took a good look at her saviour. 'We?' she asked and that was when Percy Shelley stepped forward.

'Ah, sweetest Norma. Such is the desire of the moth for the star that I am come to you, bwaving all the alawums of this wild and wilful world.'

Norma took one look at Shelley and slapped him around the face.

'And that, Norma, is the story of how me, Maria and Shelley came to be in the Crystal Palace tonight.'

'Incredible,' acknowledged Norma as she sat back in the seat of the steamer that was taking them to safety. 'Then the quicker we get to the docks the better. I think it'll take a while for the Checkya to get themselves organised but it doesn't pay to be overconfident.' She frowned. 'You're sure this Portal of yours is working, Corporal? I don't want to risk our lives just to find that the thing's out of commission.'

'Well, we *think* it works. The fact is, Norma, it hasn't been used in anger and that's the reason the Dupes . . .' Moynahan looked around the cabin. 'No offence intended, folks, but that's what Demi-Mondians are called back in the Real World. Anyway . . . the fact that we haven't used the Portal is the reason the Demi-Mondians haven't found it yet. It seems that powering up a Portal produces a lot of electrical interference and the powers that be in the Demi-Monde have been able to triangulate on this interference and find where we're hiding. That's what led to all the other Portals being found and destroyed.'

'So you don't know if it works?'

'Oh, we've been running tests, Norma. Low-power stuff that

won't light up a galvanicEnergy-O-Meter, so we're pretty sure it's okay.'

'Well, that's comforting.' Norma gave a wry laugh. 'Though maybe whether the Portal works or not is moot. I won't be able to go back to the Real World for the simple reason that I don't have a body to go back to.'

'I don't understand,' said Moynahan.

'The aim of Reinhard Heydrich is to take his hatred back to the Real World. He wants out of the Demi-Monde and his daughter, Aaliz – my twin – was his way of doing that. That's why I was lured here to the Demi-Monde in the first place, so that the spirit of Aaliz Heydrich could invest my body back in the Real World. I can't go back there . . . not while Aaliz Heydrich is using my body.'

'Unfortunately, my fair Norma, that is not the most pwessing of our pwoblems.'

Here Shelley pointed through the steamer's window to a newspaper boy selling his papers at the side of the road and shouting 'Extra . . . Extra' at the top of his voice. The scrawled headline on the side of his stand told why there was such a clamour for the papers.

SHAKA ZULU ASSASSINATED
WAR IN THE JAD IMMINENT
FORTHRIGHT PLEDGES SUPPORT TO CROWN
PRINCE XOLANDI

'It'll take a miwacle for us to enter the JAD now.'

Part Two:
Xolandi, And
Pobedonostsev's
Treachery

Iranian terrorists launch nuclear strike
The Middle East destroyed. Thirty million feared dead

A Blue Streak missile like the ones launched from Tabriz yesterday.

The Ministry of Defence announced that yesterday the terror organisation known as the Iranian Liberation Front launched an attack on cities throughout the Middle East using British-built Blue Streak missiles equipped with nuclear warheads. Warships of the British Mediterranean Fleet stationed in the Arabian Gulf responded. Although the extent of the ensuing devastation remains to be confirmed, it is estimated that some thirty million persons have been killed as a result of the nuclear exchange and much of the region has been laid waste.

The Prime Minister William Anstruther-Gray condemned the attack, and, whilst regretting the loss of life, defended the British response as being 'appropriate, proportionate and necessary'.

The siting of the Blue Streaks in Iran has always been one of the government's more contentious decisions. Since he came to power in the coup d'état of 1953 – rumoured to have been sponsored by the Intelligence Bureau – the Shah of Iran, Reza Pahlavi, has been one of the Empire's staunchest allies in the Middle East. The signing of the Tehran Agreement of 1959 granted Britain permission to locate its Blue Streak ICBMs on Iranian soil, this viewed by the British government as a necessary deterrent to the growing military presence of the Soviet Union

With fears that most of the Middle East's crude oil production capacity has been destroyed, the price of a barrel of crude oil surged from US$2 to a record high of US$185.

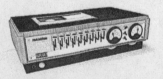
'Threat of Second Great Depression Real' says Bank of England

NoirVille: the Hub
1st Day of Fall, 1005

1.1. In the Beginning there was, like, Nothing, the Ultimate Zero, the Big Fat Zip. Well . . . almost Nothing. There was, of course, the Cool and the Cool was invested in the Coolest cat there ever was or ever will be, ABBA. And you better dig that only those cats possessed of Cool have the transcendental inner peace to become one with ABBA and be immune to the vicissitudes of the Demi-Monde.

The HIM Book, Book of the Coming. Chapter 1, Verse 1

ABBA wept, signalling the grief in heaven at the passing of Shaka Zulu. But even as ABBA's tears enveloped the world so the first gong sounded and Xolandi, Crown Prince of the Zulus, together with the host of other Boys competing in the Rite of Passage, stepped forward to toe the start line. HimPeror Shaka journeying to join his ancestors was a tragedy but life continued: as one warrior fell so another had to rise to take his place . . . and to avenge him.

Xolandi was determined to be that avenging warrior. Today Xolandi would move from BoyHood to ManHood and, by doing so, take the crown of NoirVille.

Or die in the attempt.

Silently he berated himself for entertaining such spirit-sapping doubts. Doubts were unCool. He would not die! He was

Xolandi, the Black Prince, and he would not – could not – die. This was *his* moment, the moment to prove he was the best of the best, the strongest of the strong and the bravest of the brave, to prove that he was ready to take Shaka's crown and to wreak terrible vengeance on those responsible for the cowardly assassination of NoirVille's HimPeror. Was that not the reason why ABBA had spared him? Because he was not yet a Man, he had been denied attendance at the Ceremony of Awakening and so had avoided being blown to pieces by the bomb the cowardly enemies of HimPerialism had planted in the Temple of Lilith.

So he stood indifferent to the rain that beat down on him, oblivious to the water coursing over his shaven head and over his naked body, all his attention directed to the words spoken by the new Grand Vizier, Konstantin Pobedonostsev, as he addressed the fifty thousand Boys crowding along the line, his voice booming out over the HubLand.

Today you must show yourself ready to be a Man, to show your MANtor, to show your family, to show your Ancestors and to show ABBA that you are ready to take on the mantle of ManHood. You must show you are ready to use your ikiwa in the defence of HimPerialism and of NoirVille. Only those of you blessed by ABBA will be able to defeat the nanoBites and so be deemed worthy to embrace the sacred truths of Machismo.'

Xolandi had heard this message before. Every year he had accompanied his MANtor – Lungile – to watch the Rite of Passage, but the difference this year was he wasn't listening as a spectator, now he was listening as a nearMan. This year it was his turn to pit himself against the nanoBites, to prove that he was worthy of being a Man. This was his moment of Destiny.

He fixed all his concentration on one thought, that soon he would wear the cheek scars that announced him to be a Man.

'Five minutes,' he heard Lungile whisper in his ear.

Xolandi began to shake his arms and legs, trying to keep the muscles warm, loose and ready for the trial to come, to slough off the cold of the rain and the chill of fear. He began to practise the meditative techniques of Coolness, to breathe slowly and deeply, to shut his mind off from the reality around him, gathering his inner force. All that mattered was, when the third gong sounded, that he should run so hard and so fast that he would outsprint the nanoBites, that he should outlast the other Boys and that he would come victorious to the end of the Run.

'Remain Cool,' advised Lungile, 'and keep out of trouble by running at the tip of the horn. Remain aloof, especially at the beginning. That's when the runners are bunched together and the dirty work is done . . . then and when you're out of sight behind the Temple.'

The words 'dirty work' resonated. All of the First Families had sons and nephews running in the Rite of Passage and it was an opportunity not only for the reputation of a family to be enhanced but for a few of the next generation's rivals to be disposed of. And now, with Shaka dead, the greatest prize of all – the throne of NoirVille – was there for the taking and that would tempt many to ignore Shaka's wish that Xolandi be his heir. Death made all such bequests irrelevant.

Xolandi raised his gaze and stared out across the two miles of flat, grass-lush, rain-soaked HubLand that stretched before him, that separated him from the Temple . . . from the turning point. His sharp eyes could just make out the Temple through the falling rain, its Mantle-ite walls – shadowed though they were by the smoke and the flames emitted when the bomb had exploded just the night before – shimmering green in sunlight.

The Temple was Xolandi's target: he must reach it, circle it and run back to the starting point in under eighteen minutes. Four miles in total and never once during that time could he falter or stumble as either would mean a certain and horrible death: the nanoBites would see to that.

'Test your spikes,' Xolandi heard Lungile order and automatically he pawed at the slick grass beneath his feet, ripping the inch-long tiger-teeth spikes into the ground. There were those who felt that the wearing of shoes somehow violated the spirit of Machismo but Lungile was a modernist and had no use for such reactionary nonsense. In the Rite of Passage survival was the first – the only – consideration. And today the rain was so heavy and the Hub so sodden that it would be almost impossible for those not wearing spikes to keep their footing when the route curved around the Temple.

'Alexander is to your left,' Lungile whispered, 'but I've stationed Bheka and his SoulBrothers between you and him to run interference. He's been boasting that today he will kill you, that it will be he who takes the throne, so be on your guard. If the worst comes to the worst, just open your legs and run: forget honour, forget vengeance, they can come later. Today you must think only of surviving the Rite of Passage and becoming a Man ... becoming HimPeror.'

Xolandi nodded, though the warning was unnecessary. It would be unthinkable for a Blank to usurp his inheritance! But Alexander was a formidable competitor: tall – he was only a few centimetres shy of Xolandi's own height of two metres – and possessed of a beautifully honed body that glistened as the rain coursed over it.

Xolandi stifled a delinquent smirk. A Blank could never be called beautiful. Blanks were cursed with Lightness, as they had been since their colour had been stolen from them by Loki, the Trickster, in those distant days before the Confinement.

The Grand Vizier spoke again.

You who triumph today will have the honour of joining a HimPi, of standing shoulder to shoulder with your SoulBrothers in the battle to come. And make no mistake, soon comes the Time of the Mfecane, of the Crushing, when the HimPis must avenge the murder of His HimPerial Majesty Shaka Zulu.'

The second gong sounded, the signal for MANtors to leave their charges and for the sacrifice to be made to the nanoBites. With an affectionate pat on Xolandi's rump and a whispered 'Stay Cool' Lungile moved away to join Xolandi's family in the stands. Now for the first time since he had been breeched, Xolandi stood alone without the support and advice of his MANtor, and alone, before all the gathered dignitaries of Noir-Ville, before his family and before the Spirits of his Ancestors, he had to prove he was worthy to be called a Man.

Four priests strode forward carrying the butchered carcass of an aurochs between them. This they threw over the line that marked the end of the Urban Band and the beginning of the Hub. From the moment the carcass landed, it took the nanoBites less than twenty seconds to devour it. The carcass seemed to slowly sink into the Hub, but this Xolandi knew was simply an optical illusion: the reality was that thousands upon thousands of the invisible nanoBites were devouring it from below. It was a chilling reminder of the fate that awaited any who fell during the Run.

'Today is the first day of Summer, the day when all Boys who have become bearded in the past year must prove that they are worthy of the divine condition of ManHood. Your task is simple: you must carry your war shield and your ikiwa past the Great Temple and back to the starting point. On the third beat of the gong you may commence. May ABBA be with you.'

A hush fell over the huge crowd that had gathered to see the Rite, now only the pitiful and pitiable howling of the burqa-clad woeMen could be heard as they bewailed the fate in store for many of their sons. The third gong sounded and with a cheer from the crowd the runners surged forward. Several of the more headstrong Boys made a desperate sprint to be at the front of the pack, but this Xolandi knew to be a high-risk strategy. Certainly it minimised the odds of being tripped, spiked or surreptitiously stabbed, but the front-runners also risked failing to negotiate a hidden obstacle. Better, Xolandi knew, to bide his time.

Stay Cool.

He settled into the loping stride pattern he had been practising all through Winter and Spring. The secret of surviving the nanoBites was to keep to a steady, metronomic pace, ensuring that a foot was never in contact with the ground for more than two ticks of a running Boy's body clock. Any longer and the nanoBites would strike.

Lost in his Cool, he only half-heard the screams that signalled the usual mishaps: one boy falling could bring down four or five running in his wake, sending them all plunging to the ground, where they would be consumed by the nanoBites wakened by the pounding feet of the runners.

Running fast and smooth, Xolandi's long legs ate up the Hub and before he quite realised how far he had raced he looked up to see the Temple looming before him. Automatically he gripped the leather-bound shaft of his *ikiwa* – his stabbing spear – more firmly. This was the time of danger, the time when, out of sight of those watching from NoirVille, murder would be done.

The Temple was now only fifty metres or so away. The first two miles of the race had considerably stretched the field; at the start there had been thousands of runners ahead of Xolandi but now there were no more than a handful and of these a couple had already begun to roll as they ran, showing that they were near to being spent.

Xolandi took a quick glance over his shoulder. Behind him ran Bheka and his SoulBrothers, adopting a formation designed to protect his back, and it was a back that would soon need a lot of protecting. A gaggle of running Boys – Blanks all of them – veered towards him and at their head was the unmistakable form of Alexander.

'Bheka!' he shouted. 'To your left!'

Immediately Bheka signalled to his SoulBrothers, who peeled away to form a buffer between Xolandi and the Blanks.

Xolandi lengthened his stride as the pack rounded the Temple, the empty and brooding edifice reminding him of the treachery of the swine who had killed Shaka Zulu. Once Pobedonostsev had discovered the identity of those culpable he, Xolandi, would make them pay.

Bheka sprinted closer, his stride mimicking Xolandi's as they raced along, side by side. 'They are coming,' he panted. 'Your enemy closes on you.'

'Hold them, SoulBrother, and I will make such sacrifice to the Ancestors that your Soul will be taken into ABBA's arms with much rejoicing and honour.'

Xolandi had no hesitation in ordering Bheka to sacrifice himself. It was the duty of all SoulBrothers from the Royal Kraal to protect him, to ensure that the Black Prince reached ManHood and that a Shade sat on the throne of NoirVille.

As the horde of running Boys reached the rear of the Temple where they were completely hidden from the view of the spectators, so Alexander and his phalanx struck, hurling themselves against Xolandi's bodyguard, stabbing with their spears as they tried to cut their way to the Prince. But Bheka and his Soul-Brothers fought back hard and the advantage ebbed back and forth. It was a surreal form of warfare, neither side daring to break stride lest the nanoBites take them so all the fighting was done at breakneck speed. For almost a minute the two sides raced alongside one another, the Blanks trying to stab or hamstring Xolandi's bodyguards as they fought their way towards him.

Out of the corner of his eye he saw Hephaestion – Alexander's loveBoy – racing towards him, *ikiwa* cocked back ready to lunge. Automatically Xolandi increased his pace, forcing the Blank to attack him when he was off-balance. Infuriated, Hephaestion came at him in a rush screaming his battle cry but Xolandi, almost casually, parried the thrust with his own spear, amazed that everything seemed to be happening so deliberately . . . so ponderously. He must, he decided, be lost in what Lungile called the Slow Time, when the excitement of battle made a warrior's senses super-keen, so much so that time itself seemed to dawdle. Exulting in his lust to kill, Xolandi grabbed the Blank by his shield, twisting him so that he was forced to pirouette and open up his unprotected flank. Xolandi's *ikiwa* flashed, Hephaestion screamed and then sank to the ground never to rise again.

Xolandi had killed for the first time and it felt good. His Machismo was energised and his Spirit soared. But his euphoria was short-lived. When they emerged from behind the Temple, the fighting stopped but by then Bheka and five of his Soul-Brothers were dead. That Alexander had lost more of his kin was little comfort. Xolandi vowed vengeance.

Desperately Xolandi tried to maintain his Cool, but there was no denying that Alexander by so openly threatening him had inflicted a huge insult to his Machismo. He felt his temper begin to rise and his body clock begin to pound. It took real effort to remember his training, to remember that the Man who lost his Cool generally lost.

Now the finishing line was in sight. He could see the bunting, he could see the cheering crowds and could see the MANtors pounding on their shields to celebrate their Boys moving to Man-Hood. But Xolandi felt no elation; all he felt was a cold fury. He had been insulted and his SoulBrother, Bheka, had been murdered. It was impossible for him to enter ManHood with such a stain on his Machismo. Fuelled by his anger, he pumped his legs harder and tore across the HubLand, outstripping the other runners, leaving them flailing ineffectually in his wake. Faster and faster he ran, willing himself to ignore the tightening of his chest, to ignore the heaviness infecting his legs, to ignore the pain in his stomach.

He was the first across the line, but even as the sheMen moved towards him bearing the Victor's laurels he waved them disdainfully aside, spun on the ball of his foot, and, as Alexander charged over the line, he plunged the blade of his *ikiwa* deep into the Blank's stomach.

'*Ngadla!*' he screamed as he turned the blade in the bastard's belly. 'I have eaten!'

Terror Incognita
The Demi-Monde: 1st Day of Fall, 1005

I will acknowledge it was with some small dread that I set foot on Terror Incognita, this strange land's proclivity for swallowing without trace all those who violated its sanctity is well known to all Demi-Mondians: it is, after all, the infamous *regnum mortis*. But I placed my trust in ABBA and the words written in the *Flagellum Hominum*:

In the Final Days	All may enter
Terror Incognita	To struggle
And to strive.	But whilst all
May come	Know you that
Few will leave.	

Extract from the diary of Aleister Crowley, entry dated
1st day of Fall, 1005

Trixie Dashwood stood for a moment on the shore of Terror Incognita trying to still her racing heart. She didn't know whether she was excited or terrified to be entering the most dangerous place in the Demi-Monde, the place from which no one had ever returned. Perhaps, she decided, she was a little of both, excited by the thought of what she might discover and simultaneously terrified that her discoveries might be the stuff of nightmares.

Unnerved by the unnatural silence – there wasn't so much as a chirp of a cricket or the call of a bird to leaven the foreboding quiet – she unclasped the holster holding her Webley, never having met anything in the Demi-Monde that couldn't be deterred by a .455 bullet.

Wysochi came to stand by her side. 'Disappointing, Trixie,' he said. 'I'd expected a more exciting greeting than this.'

'Oh, I think we can promise you excitement aplenty, Sergeant Wysochi,' boomed a voice and out of the trees strode a tall man clad rather incongruously in a white robe. 'It's good to see you both again.'

It took Trixie a moment to recognise her father, if indeed this strange man *was* her father. She hadn't seen him for two Seasons and had hardly given him a thought in all that time: it was as though she had made the subconscious decision to expunge him from her life. The last time they'd been together his refusal to follow her orders had hurt . . . almost as much as her later realisation that he'd been right and she'd been wrong. To protect herself from her remorse she'd tried to forget about him. A childish thing to have done, but . . .

Trixie gave a mental shake of her head: she despised sentimentality. She was a soldier and soldiers had no use for regrets. Dressing her face with a stern look, she strode across the beach. 'Hello, Father. This is a surprise. I never expected to find *you* here.'

'Oh, you're not the only Dashwood with a penchant for surviving, Trixie,' he said as he bent forward and kissed her lightly on the cheek. 'You're looking well. A trifle dishevelled, but that, I suppose, is to be expected in your line of work.'

Automatically Trixie ran a hand over her head and through her stubble of hair, then stopped herself. She was a soldier, not a mannequin. 'How long have you been here, Father?'

'That's difficult to say. Time in Terror Incognita seems to be very wilful and to proceed at a pace of its own choosing. It would help if you would tell me what date it is.'

'It's the first day of Fall, one thousand and five.'

Her father gave an absent-minded nod. 'Then I've been here for two Seasons. I suspected something of the sort. I remember landing on Terror Incognita at the end of Winter, but then . . . nothing. I woke up a little while ago and had an urge to come down here to the beach. And when I did there you were landing from your boat.'

'Are you saying that you can't remember anything since you came to this place?'

'Not a thing. I seem to have duplicated the experience of Rip Van Winkle, though whoever has been looking after me during my slumber did, at least, do me the courtesy of changing my linen.' He looked down at his robe and gave a rueful smile. 'I would, however, take issue with the fashion sense of those responsible for the governance of this island: robes are not to my taste.'

'And who, Father, *is* in charge here?'

'ABBA, I suppose. But that's just a guess: as I say, I seem to have slept through my time here.'

'Then Terror Incognita remains as perplexing as ever . . . most notably regarding its purpose.' Trixie took a look around her. 'I never could fathom why ABBA created such a strange place.'

Her father shrugged. 'I once thought that it was created to fulfil HumanKind's need for adventure, to provide Demi-Mondians, beset as they are by an incorrigible need to explore, with an outlet for these pioneering inclinations.'

'You *once* thought?'

'Yes. I suspect its purpose is more subtle than that. And now, Trixie, we have been given the opportunity to study this strange realm at first hand.'

'If we survive long enough,' grumped Wysochi.

'I'm sorry, Sergeant?'

'It's *Major* Wysochi now, Baron, and my worries about surviving concern the SS who are currently landing on the other side of the island: I think they might be a more pressing danger than any bogeymen who might call Terror Incognita home.'

'The SS? Why would the SS have an interest in Terror Incognita?'

'Having been cut off from the outside world for two Seasons, Father,' Trixie explained, 'you'll be unaware that an artefact known as the Column of Loci has been discovered. The engravings covering the Column have allowed us to decipher the *Flagellum Hominum*, which tells us that the Great Pyramid has a significant role to play in who emerges triumphant in the Demi-Monde . . . who is to be the victor in the final battle between good and evil that is Ragnarok.'

'You've lost me, Trixie.'

'The *Flagellum Hominum* says that:

Last comes the Time of Trysting	When those who would rule must vie
Joined in their final ferocity	The prize so precious, so profound.
Who will wield the staff of ABBA?	Who will place it atop the Pyramid?
For the victor the spoils of life	For the vanquished the lament of death

Such is the Way.

The Column is the "staff of ABBA", which, despite our best efforts, is now in the hands of Aleister Crowley, who is intent on placing it on the summit of the Great Pyramid. My aim is to stop him.'

'Perhaps that's why I and my men have been awakened?'

'A sensible assumption, Father. ABBA obviously thinks I'm going to need all the help I can get.'

Dashwood nodded, then pointed to the line of trees that bordered the beach. 'I will do all I can in that regard, Trixie. And as you might have noticed, it isn't just somewhat aged army officers like me who have been resuscitated by your presence, but also the fauna of this strange land.'

Trixie looked to where her father was pointing and sure enough, sitting in one of the tall oaks was a multicoloured bird. It was then that she realised that the forest was resonating with the sounds of birds and insects. Terror Incognita had come alive.

'After a thousand years of denying any living thing access to this strange realm, it seems ABBA has now lifted His embargo,' mused Dashwood. 'Another sign that Ragnarok approaches, perhaps? But I'm forgetting my manners. My men are setting up a base in a clearing in the woods just a hundred or so yards away and I'm sure there'll be a welcoming glass of Solution waiting for us there. We'll all be interested to learn what's been happening in the world since we've been slumbering here. Shall we go?'

It took almost an hour for Trixie to bring her father and his officers up to date on current affairs, and when she had finished they were quiet for several minutes as they assimilated the bad news. Finally her father looked up from warming his hands against the campfire and shook his head in wonderment. 'Let me see if I can summarise the situation correctly. Crowley has taken this Column from you and will be aiming to mount it atop the Great Pyramid. The understanding you have is that if he's able to do that then it's all up for the Demi-Monde. So the question is: what to do to discomfort Mr Aleister Crowley?'

'We have to take back the Column,' answered Trixie.

'Easier said than done, I think.' Dashwood turned to David Crockett sitting next to him. 'What do you think, Captain?'

Crockett edged closer to the fire. 'I've had a lookout climb that tree yonder' – here he pointed in the direction of a tall pine tree just to the north of the clearing they were sitting in – 'and he reports a bustle of activity on the eastern shore, the one nearest to the Pyramid. By his reckoning, a couple of thousands of them SS bastards have landed there, all armed to the teeth and brimming with bile and devilment.'

'How many fighters do you have with you, Trixie?' her father asked.

Trixie glanced over to Wysochi, who gave a shrug before replying. 'Counting in the sailors who manned the *Wu*, by my figuring . . . a couple of hundred, though ammunition is pretty low.'

'That seems to rule out an attack,' mused Dashwood.

'I never intended to fight them toe to toe,' said Trixie quietly. 'A frontal attack would be suicide but two hundred determined fighters can do a lot of damage simply harassing a larger army. My plan is to fight Crowley guerrilla-style . . . to delay him raising the Column.'

'That's going to be difficult, Trixie. Terror Incognita is only nine miles across and the only cover is provided by the forest that borders the shoreline and clumps around Mare Incognitum. The rest of the place is bare, which means there's nowhere much to hide. And once Crowley knows we're here . . .'

'It might be best to make a reconnaissance before making a decision about tactics, Colonel,' observed Wysochi. 'Better the devil you know and all that.'

Trixie rose to her feet and brushed the dust from the backside of her trousers. 'You're right, Wysochi. Get half a dozen fighters together and let's go see what Crowley's up to.'

Comrade Engineering Captain Andrew Roberts didn't like Terror Incognita. It was a spooky place that gave him the jumps, especially now all the birds and insects had suddenly decided to sound off. Fortunately for him, the engineering challenge associated with landing the pontoon containing the Column hadn't left him much time to dwell on its spookiness. Beaching three hundred tons of recalcitrant pontoon and then dragging it fifty yards inland – uphill, at that – had been a bitch of a task, a task that had required two steamers, fifty mules, five hundred men and much cursing and swearing to accomplish.

A tired and dirty Captain Roberts reported to General Clement, 'The Column is safely secured at the landing site, Comrade General.' He tried to disguise the waver in his voice. Clement scared the shit out of him: the man was a fury of nervous energy and mad as a box of bolts. He radiated evil and immediately he entered a room – or a tent in this case – the heat seemed to drain out of the place. Roberts shivered, but it had nothing to do with the autumnal winds that were blowing around the encampment.

'But?'

'But what, sir?'

'There's always a "but", Roberts. You pioneer-types never say anything straight.'

'Then I should advise you, sir, that as the Pyramid is over two miles inland, getting the Column there is going be one Hel of a job.' Roberts pointed through the flap of the tent to the top of the Pyramid that poked out above the trees surrounding the beach. 'It's two miles blocked by trees and scrub, sir. I think we'll need a *lot* more steamers and men to help clear a path and build a railway.'

Archie Clement gave an absent-minded nod and then took a reflective chew on his tobacco. 'And if ah git you them steamers and such, how long is it gonna take afore that Column is on top of the Pyramid?'

The engineer scratched his chin. 'Well, sir, the good news is that test bores indicate that Terror Incognita is free of nanoBites clear down to the Mantle so there isn't anything stopping us laying a railway line. Say two months to clear the route and another couple to lay the line.' He gave Clement what he hoped was a confident smile. 'By my estimation, four months will see us alongside the Pyramid . . .' His explanation trailed off: getting alongside the Pyramid was the easy bit, getting the Column on top of it would be a much more difficult stunt to pull off.

Clement shook his head. 'We ain't got four months, Captain. By the fiftieth day of Fall that Column has gotta be alongside the Pyramid and by the end of Fall sitting pretty atop of it. We gotta do that *and* make sure there's space around the Pyramid for the six million folks His Holiness, Aleister Crowley, is fixing to invite to his Ceremony of Purification shindig.' He spat out the gob of tobacco he'd been chomping on. 'Them's the orders of Great Leader Heydrich himself. You understanding what ah'm a-saying, Comrade Captain?'

Roberts gave a nod. If the Great Leader ordered it, then it had better be done. 'Fiftieth day of Fall, you say, Comrade General? That's a mighty stiff task if you don't mind me saying so, and to do that I'm going to need a lot of extra help.'

'Tell me what you need, Captain, an' ah'll git it, just don't come back at me with excuses. Ah ain't in the market for excuses, ah'm in the market for solutions.' And to emphasise the point, he took a swig from his silver hip flask.

Roberts gave the general a nervous glance. 'There are rumours that rebel forces have landed on Terror Incognita, General. If they get frisky they could put a wrinkle in our schedule.'

'Don't you go fretting your head 'bout no Rebs, Captain. Them's for the likes of me to worry 'bout. You just keep your eye on the ball 'cos that's the way you're gonna be sure that you hang on to the pair you already got.'

*

'What do you think, Wysochi?' whispered Trixie as they hid behind a bush just fifty yards from the beached pontoon.

'We've got ourselves a real problem, Colonel. Way I see it, the SS are building themselves a fort and if the UnFunnies are putting down roots that tells me that it won't be long before there's a whole lot more of the bastards.'

'So we attack now?'

'I don't think we've got much of an option: we've got to hit 'em before they've a chance to get their feet under the table. Once the UnFunnies get dug in, winkling the bastards out is going to take more than a couple of hundred fighters who are low on ammunition. My advice, Colonel, is that it's now or never.'

Trixie used her telescope to make a final survey of the scene and what she saw wasn't terribly encouraging. The area around the pontoon was a hive of activity with navvies felling trees and then dragging the trunks over to a clearing Clement had commandeered, using them to build palisades. At the rate they were going up it wouldn't be long before they were snug behind ten-foot-high walls built out of thick pine, and these, plus the pits they were digging for their Gatling guns, would mean that any attack would be made against a well-fortified position and in the teeth of enfilading fire. A daunting prospect. Wysochi was right: she had to move against them now.

'I concur, Major. In a week there might be five or six thousand more of the bastards and a damn sight more steamers. What we have to do is capture the pontoon, drag it back to the Wheel River and then blast a hole in it. Once the Column is resting at the bottom of the river not even Loki and all his Daemons will be able to get it back to the surface.'

'Then if you're decided, Colonel, I think the sooner we break the bad news to the rest of our fighters, the better.'

*

When all the WFA fighters had been landed from the *Wu* and mustered with her father's Royalists, Trixie found herself commanding a ragtag army of six hundred men and women, not one of them with more than thirty rounds of ammunition to their name. It was difficult to imagine such a bedraggled outfit giving a crack SS regiment the turnaround. There was only one word to describe the mission they were intent on: suicidal.

'Our objective tonight is a simple one: to destroy the Column of Loki,' Trixie announced as she marched up and down in front of her fighters. 'To accomplish this, the WFA, under the command of Major Wysochi here, will attack the SS compound and draw the UnFunnies away from the pontoon. This done, they will hold off any counter-attack to allow time for our friends the Royalists, under the command of Major Dashwood, to drag the pontoon containing the Column to the river and sink it.'

She stopped her pacing and turned to face her fighters. By the flickering light cast by the campfires she could see the fear on some of their faces. She wasn't surprised. Most of the fighters were decidedly unhappy about finding themselves in Terror Incognita – it was, after all, the preferred setting for most of the horror stories popular in the Demi-Monde. Who knew what was lurking out there in the darkness ready to pounce?

'I will be straight with you: this will be a desperate business. We are outnumbered and outgunned, but every day we delay, the enemy will grow stronger and more numerous. Our only advantage is surprise, so it is vital that we get as close to them as we are able without their being alerted that we're the enemy. There will be no shooting and no talking until the enemy is engaged: your lives and those of your comrades depend on it. But make no mistake: what we are about is vital if the ForthRight is to be defeated. Fight hard and may ABBA be with you.'

They moved out three hours before dawn, Trixie having decided that instead of the route they'd taken when they'd made the reconnaissance – along the heavily wooded shoreline – it would be easier for a larger force to advance straight across Terror Incognita. The journey did little to settle the nerves of her fighters: Terror Incognita was a strange place and the noises it made at night eerie and unsettling.

This unease was heightened when they came to the gigantic mosaics that decorated the open spaces surrounding Mare Incognitum, mosaics formed from massive Mantle-ite stones that glowed and twinkled in the moonlight. And the worst of these was the representation of an enormous snake that lay coiled to the north of the Pyramid: by Trixie's estimation, the snake was at least nine miles in length and a couple of hundred yards in width, coiling and twisting like a living thing.

'Jörmundgandr,' she heard her father whisper to her.

Trixie nodded: the snake did look like the great world-encompassing serpent of Pre-Folk legend, the serpent that would rise up during Ragnarok. But what Trixie found so astonishing wasn't its mythological associations but the more prosaic thought of the effort that had been needed to construct the mosaic. It staggered the imagination that any people – Pre-Folk or otherwise – had had the motivation and the wherewithal to create such a thing. But what she was to see a few moments later was to make even this wonder pale into insignificance.

At the urging of Wysochi and her father the fighters bustled across the open space, managing to make it to the sanctuary of the trees bordering Mare Incognitum without being challenged. Here the trees were so tall and so tightly packed that the moonlight could not penetrate the foliage, and it was only thanks to Wysochi's unerring sense of direction and the liberal use of his boot that the fighters eventually stumbled through the darkness to emerge at the foot of the Great Pyramid.

'Will you look at that!' whispered Wysochi. 'It's bloody enormous.'

It certainly was. Trixie had seen the photographs Speke had taken when he'd flown over Terror Incognita by balloon but even these hadn't prepared her for the magnificence of the structure. Each of the Pyramid's sides was a good three hundred feet in length and had been decorated with triangular slabs of Mantle-ite arranged in nine tiers. But it wasn't the monumental scale of the thing that took Trixie's breath away, it was the way it lit up the night. The LunarAtion emitted by such a mass of Mantle-ite suffused Terror Incognita with an ethereal radiation so that everything and everybody coming near the Pyramid appeared to have been dipped in luminous green paint.

As they moved nearer, one other oddity struck Trixie's RaTion-alist Mind: there appeared to have been *three* different varieties of Mantle-ite used in the Pyramid's construction, these signalled by the shades of LunarAtion emitted from the triangular slabs. This was new: Trixie had never heard of there being different *types* of Mantle-ite and she wondered for a moment what they signified.

Her musings were interrupted by Wysochi. Practical as ever, he was moved to make a more mundane observation. 'How is anyone going to get the Column to the top of that?'

A well-made point. The sloping sides of the Pyramid were slick and sleek, their Mantle-ite perfection only broken by a broad staircase – or what Trixie assumed to be a staircase – running from base to apex that bifurcated the northern side. 'Beats me, Wysochi. Maybe that's why Crowley is here. Maybe he's going to magic the thing up to the top.'

But this, Trixie knew, was hokum. No mage, no matter how powerful, would be able to magic a two-hundred-ton Column up to the hexagonal platform at the top of the Pyramid. She turned to her father: he was the engineer of the family. 'If raising the Column is an impossible task, maybe our best strategy is just to lie low and watch as the UnFunnies tear their hair out.'

Her father shook his head. 'If the *Flagellum Hominum* says that getting the Column to the top of the Pyramid is doable, Trixie, then it must be doable. And remember, Crowley is a master of the occult so I think it would be unwise to rely on his incompetence.'

He was right. Crowley was no fool and if he knew enough to bring the Column to Terror Incognita then the chances were that he knew enough to get it to the top of the Pyramid.

A whispered warning from Wysochi brought her out of her reverie. 'Enemy patrol, Colonel. I suggest we fall back into the woods.'

His Holiness Aleister Crowley, Head of the Church of the Doctrine of UnFunDaMentalism, had been unable to resist going to view the Great Pyramid by moonlight. After all, it was – according to the newly translated *Flagellum Hominum* – the most important source of ABBA's energy in the Demi-Monde and it was this energy that, in a few short weeks, he would be using to change his world. And the Pyramid did not disappoint: as he came closer to it, he could feel the strength and the power it emitted, he could feel ABBA's energy vibrating through his body, making his soul soar.

Crowley came to a halt at the foot of the strange staircase running up the Pyramid's side. Waving back the soldiers of the SS detachment making up his bodyguard, he stood still for a moment to settle his nerves and then took the first tentative step onto the staircase. The staircase had ten hexagonal landings, each of which – with the exception of the bottommost – was numbered, but he was at a loss to understand the significance of the numbers. They seemed quite arbitrary.

When he reached the topmost platform he was out of breath, but the exhilaration he felt to be standing on one of the highest points in the whole of the Demi-Monde drove thoughts of such

mundane discomfort from his mind. Here too the Pyramid held surprises: in the floor of the platform was set a dial with a single hand and the numbers zero to nine at intervals about its circumference. Again, Crowley had no idea as to its purpose, but this, he decided, was not the time to dwell on puzzles, not with all of the Demi-Monde laid out like an exquisitely modelled miniature beneath him.

Looking out beyond Terror Incognita, he could see the five rivers wending their way to the Boundary, their ink-black waters glittering in the moonlight; he could see the twinkling gaslights that jewelled the cities of the Demi-Monde; and there, to the west, he could see the flames that burned in Rangoon as the ForthRight army worked to find and destroy the forces loyal to the rebel Empress, Dong E. From here he could see the other five Wonders of the World: the huge motte of Mantle-ite upon which sat the Forbidding City; the Great Wall; the Sphinx; ExterSteine;

and, of course, the Temple of Lilith. And as he studied the Temple glowing green in the moonlight, a satisfied smile tugged at his mouth. That the Lady IMmanual was dead meant that UnFunDa-Mentalism's greatest enemy was now destroyed and nothing stood between the Aryan people and their ultimate triumph. Soon he would evoke the power of the Pyramid in the Ceremony of Purification and then all the UnderMentionable elements of the Demi-Monde would be purged, then a triumphant Aryan race would stand pure and unsullied as masters of the Demi-Monde.

Crowley spread his arms wide and in his loudest voice he addressed the world, the words echoing out into the emptiness of the night. 'Hear me, ABBA, for I am come. I thank you for permitting me to enter Terror Incognita to stand atop your holiest shrine. Know that in gratitude I will soon cause the Great Pyramid to be complete. I bid you grant me the power to understand the secrets of the Pyramid and the raising of the Column and in return I pledge to make your people pure and perfect.'

Crowley lowered his arms and stood for a few seconds in silent reflection, his robe flapping as it was caught by a gust of wind. And what this reflection told him was that he did indeed need ABBA's help. The secret of how the PreFolk had brought the Column to the top of the Pyramid was hidden in the obtuse verses of the *Flagellum Hominum* and though he had been working day and night to decipher the secrets, still their meaning eluded him: the words might have been translated but their sense remained tantalisingly out of reach. But he was confident that soon, by the grace of ABBA, the secrets would be revealed, and once that fool Archie Clement had organised the building of the railway line necessary to bring the Column to the Pyramid, he would be ready.

The Final Solution was in his grasp.

1:12

The JAD, NoirVille
1st Day of Fall, 1005

1.2. ABBA gazed out on the Nothingness and decided that it was boring, being that it was black, black, and more black. And though black was ABBA's favourite colour – being like black is replete with Cool and Him being of the opinion that any cat wearing black is hip to the tip and totalistically sophisticated – on its ownsome it is the ultimate mono-chrome and the biggest of bring-downs. 1.3. So ABBA said 'Let there be mucho de light' and immediately the Edisons were ignited and there was beaucoup de brightness. 1.4. But ABBA still dug that the Kosmos was minimalistic to the max, being like it was bereft of anything to ponder and peruse, so ABBA decided to create the Ennead, the Nine Worlds.

The HIM Book, Book of the Coming: Chapter 1, Verses 2–4

Since the assassination of Shaka a curfew had been enforced in the JAD and for eight hours – from ten at night until six the following morning – it was quiet and watchful. During the curfew no one was allowed in or out of the JAD, and as a result it had become a strange, fearful in-between time populated – if the more excitable of the JAD's tabloid papers were to be believed – by Shade cryptos and HimPeril assassins.

But the one thing the curfew did provide was an opportunity

for the JAD's leadership to organise clandestine and very unofficial meetings with their opposite numbers from NoirVille, and none were as clandestine or as unofficial as the one Rabbi Schmuel Gelbfisz was to have that night with General Salah-ad-Din.

That he and the general had been reduced to meeting at the dead of night and under conditions of the tightest security said much about the state of nuJu–Shade understanding, just as the trembling of his hand said much about the effect all this cloak-and-dagger business was having on Gelbfisz's nerves. Since the assassination of Shaka Zulu the only two sane men in the whole of NoirVille were condemned to skulking around at night in order to discuss how they might preserve peace.

Even as he brought his glass of Solution to his lips, there was the lightest of taps on the door of the house he was using for their rendezvous and a heavily cloaked figure was ushered inside. As his guest shucked off his cloak, Gelbfisz tried to assess if he brought good news or bad. By the slump of Salah-ad-Din's shoulders he guessed it was bad, but this might, of course, be simply a result of the wear and tear the intrigues of NoirVillian politics were inflicting on the man. General Salah-ad-Din Yusuf ibn Aiyub, commander of the NoirVillian army, wasn't young any more and the opprobrium he had suffered as a consequence of being one of the few pro-nuJu voices in NoirVille obviously weighed heavy: his tightly trimmed beard was now frosted with grey and his full face was deeply lined and furrowed. Still, the sparkle in his black eyes attested that though his body might be tired, his mind was still sharp. He bowed to Gelbfisz, the ruby that adorned his turban twinkling as he bobbed his head.

'Greetings, Rabbi Gelbfisz, and may ABBA smile upon our meeting.'

'Shalom to you, General,' answered Gelbfisz, as he stood up from his chair and walked across the room to shake his visitor's hand, 'unt a thousand thanks for agreeing to meet mit me. I realise zhe danger you place yourself in by coming to zhe JAD.' He waved Salah-ad-Din to a couch and then plonked himself down beside him.

'Men must be as brave in the prosecution of peace as they are in the prosecution of war,' noted the general as he accepted the glass of tea Gelbfisz offered him. 'But I fear that now bravery will not be enough to keep nuJu and Shade from each other's throats. It would seem, Rabbi, that this will be the last time we can meet: the assassination of Shaka Zulu has polarised the court and I am afraid it is the opinions of the more irascible of my colleagues that will find favour with NoirVille's new HimPeror. As you will appreciate, since the assassination the atmosphere in NoirVille has become a mite febrile.'

Gelbfisz nodded his understanding. The explosion in the Temple of Lilith just the previous night had killed nearly four hundred people, His HimPerial Majesty Shaka Zulu amongst them. Although Shaka could never have been classified as a friend of the nuJu he had been a pragmatist, willing to trade the existence of the JAD for a supply of Aqua Benedicta, but with him gone, it was the nuJus' enemies who would be in the ascendancy.

'Oy vay, a terrible thing, a terrible thing,' said Gelbfisz with a wave of his hand. 'I have written to Crown Prince Xolandi expressing zhe disgust of zhe nuJus regarding zhis outrage. Shaka Zulu vos a friend to zhe nuJus unt ve much regret his passing.'

'There will be no response. Pobedonostsev is the new Grand Vizier . . .'

'Then ABBA have mercy on our souls,' said Gelbfisz with a shake of his head. Pobedonostsev was the most virulent of all nuJu-phobes.

'. . . and he is of the opinion that nuJu chicanery was behind Shaka's murder.' Salah-ad-Din held up a hand to forestall

Gelbfisz's objections. 'Please, Rabbi, I understand and appreciate that the nuJus had nothing to do with this terrible act, but . . .'

'Vould it be possible for me to meet mit Crown Prince Xolandi? Perhaps if I vos to tell him face to face zhat ve nuJus are innocent of any involvement mit zhe murder of HimPeror Shaka unt zhat if zhe Shades unt zhe nuJus are to survive unt prosper zhen zhere is but one road to be followed – zhe road of peace.'

Salah-ad-Din gave a mirthless laugh. 'This is not the road we will be travelling, Rabbi. I must tell you that NoirVillian policy is now suffused with a thirst for revenge which makes war a very real possibility. I will do my best to prevent this but the momentum of events is strong and NoirVillians are demanding retribution. So I come to you tonight to tell you that now is the time for you and your people to flee.'

Gelbfisz laughed. 'Flee? Flee vhere? Zhere is nowhere to go. Ve nuJus are hated unt reviled everyvhere in the Demi-Monde. No one vill give two million nuJus sanctuary. Unt remember, now zhere is no Lady IMmanual to come to our rescue unt to part zhe Boundary Layer to allow zhe nuJus of zhe JAD to escape into zhe Great Beyond.'

'But if you stay and there is war, then it will mean the extermination of the entire nuJu population in NoirVille.'

That was a statement that gave Gelbfisz pause. The NoirVillian army was one of the best and the largest in the Demi-Monde and if they attacked the JAD, despite all the preparations the nuJus had made, the end was inevitable.

'Is zhere nothing we can do to avoid fighting?'

'If you nuJus remain quiet and meek, if you use all your power to keep your Zealots in check and dissuade them from making any provocative act, then perhaps we can ride out the storm. But I warn you, it will take just one spark to ignite a conflagration that will lead to the deaths of millions of innocent people.'

Gelbfisz sighed: it all seemed so hopeless. But then, he decided, nothing was hopeless for a people who put their faith in ABBA. He took a reviving sip of his Solution. 'Ve nuJus are vell practised in remaining quiet unt meek, General. Centuries of persecution have taught us zhat resistance to zhe might of zhe goyim is useless, but, unfortunately, zhe Battle of Varsaw gave zhe younger nuJus a taste for violence. Zo, alzhough I appreciate your varning, General, I vonder if zhe Zealots are capable of being controlled.'

Salah-ad-Din gave a grim smile. 'I understand, Rabbi. Young men are apt to be impulsive and to prefer action to passivity; such is the curse of MALEvolence. The terrible thing is that all too often action is accompanied by death and suffering.'

The prospect of an imminent war silenced the two men: there seemed nothing more to be said. Finally, Salah-ad-Din pointed towards the chessboard sitting on the table in front of them, the pieces arrayed as though they had been abandoned in mid-game. 'Do you play chess, Rabbi?' he asked.

'A little.'

The general chuckled. 'No, Rabbi, no one plays chess "a little": you either play or you don't.'

Gelbfisz nodded his understanding. 'Zhen yes, I play chess. Zhe trouble I have is finding opponents of an adequate standard, zo now, General, I have been reduced to playing with myself, if you take my meaning. But zhe real problem mit playing zolo is zhat I am never sure vhether I am always zhe vinner or always zhe loser.'

Salah-ad-Din leant forward and began to toy with the black queen. 'I find the game of chess a wonderful analogy for human life,' he said and then, with a nonchalant flourish of his long, nicotine-stained fingers, he moved the queen. 'To my mind, its moves and its objectives mimic Man's existence. Chess is Man's fate in microcosm.' He smiled as Gelbfisz moved a white pawn. 'It serves to remind us of how fatuous it is to take life seriously.'

'For a man who has risked his reputation unt his life to come here tonight in zhe cause of peace, I think you are being a little disingenuous, General. I believe you take life – zhe *preservation* of life – very seriously indeed.'

'It is the way of the Demi-Monde that all good intentions are inevitably overwhelmed by evil, so a serious outlook on life is one destined to lead to disappointment.' For several long seconds Salah-ad-Din studied the board, then he made a riposte with a black pawn. 'Yes ... chess is a wonderful paradigm for life, being, as it is, an evil game, with each side remorselessly and pitilessly pursuing the destruction of their opponent. In chess, as in life, there are no friends or allies ... there is no one you can trust or rely upon, all there is, is the obligation to destroy one's fellow Man. When he plays chess, Man is obliged to be evil, just as in real life.'

As he shifted his bishop to take one of the general's pawns, Gelbfisz gave a wry shake of his head. 'Zhere is no inevitability about evil, zhere is always salvation in ABBA.'

Another chuckle from the general. 'As you know, Rabbi, I wear my religion lightly. Truth be told, ABBA doesn't give a damn about HumanKind. Having seen the horrors that Man is prepared to inflict on his fellows in order to force goodness – *his* version of goodness – upon them, I know that Man is never happiest but when he is being wicked.' Salah-ad-Din made a forceful advance with his queen, a smile indicating that he believed it to be a telling move.

Seemingly unfazed by the general's aggressive play, Gelbfisz shifted a knight to threaten his opponent's queen. 'Man has free vill; even a vicked man may choose zhe path towards a higher morality.'

'My apologies for my language, Rabbi, but that's bullshit. All religions, be they nuJuism, HimPerialism, UnFunDaMentalism – or any other ism for that matter – are all triumphalist doctrines, their proponents only happy when their opponents are either converted, subjugated or destroyed. What does your Book of Profits say about those who worship other gods? Ah, yes: "You must not listen to him; you must show him no pity; you must not spare him or conceal his guilt. No, you must kill him".' He smiled at Gelbfisz. 'So much for a merciful ABBA.' He positioned a rook to reinforce his queen's position.

'I am more persuaded by zhe doctrine of the Sixth Commandment: "thou shalt not kill", zhough fortunately for me zhe Book of Profits is silent regarding showing a similar reticence in chess.' He took the general's rook.

Salah-ad-Din frowned and used the opportunity presented by Gelbfisz pouring tea to make a more considered study of the board. Then, with a small smile of triumph he pushed a pawn forward. 'The other great thing about chess, Rabbi, is that it shows us that this free will of yours is non-existent. This black and white chequerboard presents us with a seemingly bewildering array of possible moves, so many that we believe we are free to make whatever moves we desire. But finally we come to know this is not the case, that we only possess a *perceived* free will. I have recently read a most intriguing book entitled *A Lay-Person's Guide to preScience* by a Quartier Chaudian mathematician named Nikolai Kondratieff. By Kondratieff's lights, just as ultimately our moves on the chessboard are confined by the size of the board and the rules of the game, so our lives are confined by our inherited family traits, by our experiences and by the sanction of society. In reality, no matter how perverse and chaotic human behaviour seems to be, it is entirely predictable and preordained. Chess teaches us that life is Deterministic . . . that we don't possess free will, only an *illusion* of free will.'

'You have too little confidence in ABBA, General. It is my belief zhat ABBA has connived to make the game of life ve play uncertain – inDeterminate – unt to do zhis He has decided to introduce an extra piece onto the board, a piece zhat is invisible to zhose playing zhe game unt which moves independently of zhem. Zhis piece is, quite literally, zhe ghost in zhe machine.'

'You know this ghost to exist?'

'Indeed, I have met him. His name is Vanka Maykov.'

'I know that name. The HimPeril are of the opinion that he perished in the explosion in the Temple of Lilith.'

Gelbfisz gave a sheepish grin. 'It is difficult to kill a ghost, General, especially a ghost so . . . elusive as Vanka Maykov.' He moved a bishop. '*Mat*,' he said and flicked his opponent's king from the board, 'or as ABBA might say, checkmate.'

Terror Incognita
The Demi-Monde: 1st Day of Fall, 1005

The passage in the HIM Book (*Book of the Coming*: Chapter 1, Verse 2) that cites black as being ABBA's favourite colour has been much quoted by the more reactionary of HimPerial scholars to support the notion that the Shade races are innately superior to the Blanks. Indeed, many of the more fundamentalist HimPerialists believe that the darker a Man's skin tone, the more favourably he is regarded by ABBA. This has led to the widespread practice of skin oiling and body dying, intended to deepen the skin's natural colouration. However, the recent influx of Blanks into NoirVille and their conversion to HimPerialism has resulted in challenges being made to this interpretation, with much being made of the word 'wearing' and the fact that the HIM Book makes no direct reference to skin colour. It is this author's contention that both Blanks and Shades are equal before ABBA.

Blanks Can Be Cool Too: Chet Baker, Black/White Publications

By a combination of luck and good management Trixie brought her fighters within sight of the enemy camp without the alarm being raised, the SS's outlying pickets having been dealt with in a very efficient manner by a gang of killers led by Wysochi. But now it was deep breath time.

'What do you think, Wysochi?'

'It's a bitch, Colonel, but we're lucky that half of the SS regiment seems to be standing guard on the encampment over there.' He pointed off to the left. 'That's where they've got all their slave-workers held, and if I'm not very much mistaken, most of 'em are Polish, captured when Warsaw fell.' He gave Trixie a smile. 'But that, and the fact that it's started raining, is all the good news there is. It's two hundred yards over open ground to the enemy's camp and even in the dark and the rain it'll be impossible for us to cross unseen. We're gonna have to rely on subterfuge and blind luck.'

Trixie nodded. 'Okay, let's saddle up and remind everybody that they're to attack in silence and to avoid shooting until we're inside the SS camp. Maybe we can flummox the UnFunnies into thinking we're part of a returning patrol.'

They got to within a hundred yards of the camp before they were spotted.

'Who goes there?' came the challenge.

'Patrol Five returning to base,' Wysochi shouted as he upped his pace.

Eighty yards.

'Patrol Five? Who's the officer commanding?'

Sixty yards.

'I am,' bellowed Wysochi, 'Comrade Major Feliks Wysochi.'

Forty yards.

There was silence, presumably caused by the sentry hastily consulting his officer. Finally there was another shouted order from the half-built stockade. 'You will halt and be recognised.'

Twenty yards.

'We haven't got time for this nonsense. My men are wet, tired and hungry, now stop buggering around or I'll have you on a charge.'

'Halt or I fire!'

They got to within ten yards of the SS camp before the first shot was fired, and even then it was aimed over the heads of the attackers. Only when the WFA fighters charged inside and began blasting the baffled SS sentries did things start getting nasty. Belatedly, one of the SS's Gatlings rat-tat-tatted bullets into the ranks of Trixie's fighters. Men and women began to fall, their screams meshing with those of SS sergeants and officers as they urged their soldiers awake and into the fight.

It took a real effort for Algernon Dashwood to follow Trixie's orders and keep his Royalists back from the fighting. He knew the assault on the SS encampment was going to be a brutal affair and that the chances of Trixie surviving were slim, but she had brushed his advice that she was too valuable to risk in a firefight angrily aside, so he had bitten his tongue and concentrated on carrying out his orders. His mission was to seize the pontoon, get it down to the river and then to scuttle it, and to do that he and his men had to commandeer a steamer. Easily enough said but a devil, he suspected, to do, his major concern being that the steamers would have gone cold boilers – it was the middle of the night, after all – and hence would be inoperable.

The taking of the steamers was accomplished more easily than Dashwood had believed possible. The surprise of their attack was total and such was Crockett's efficiency in dealing with the platoon of SS guarding the steamers that they weren't given a chance to utter a peep before they were dead. Once the guards were settled, Sergeant Butch Cassidy swung himself up into the cabin of the first steamer and gave the thumbs up.

'Lady Luck's with us, Major,' Cassidy shouted down from his perch. 'The boiler's as hot as Hel and then some. The SS must have been aiming to work through the night.'

'Get the steamer over to the pontoon and hitched up to the sledge,' Dashwood ordered and immediately Cassidy began to throw the levers controlling the steamer's tracks, swinging it around in the direction of the sledge used to drag the pontoon up from the beach. It took only a couple of minutes to hitch the steamer to the sledge and then Cassidy poured on the power, the steamer bellowing as it took the strain.

By Dashwood's reckoning, with the ground sloping down to the beach bordering the Wheel River it should have been a simple operation to move the Column to the river, but the rain had been heavy and the ground was soft. The result was that the steamer struggled to get the sledge and its three-hundred-ton load moving, and the more Cassidy tried to force the steamer forward, the more its tracks tore up the forest floor. There was a real danger of the steamer digging itself in.

'Hold hard, Cassidy!' Dashwood shouted over the noise of pummelling pistons. 'Captain Crockett, bring up the second steamer.'

It took ten minutes of agonising delay before the boiler of the second steamer reached operating pressure, but when it was finally hitched to the sledge it did the trick. The two steamers working in tandem had enough grunt to move the load and slowly, inch by inch, they edged it towards the river.

Too slowly.

With every second that passed it seemed to Dashwood that the noise of the fighting behind them became worryingly closer. The SS had obviously recovered from the shock of Trixie's attack and were now fighting back with a vengeance. He checked his revolver. He'd a feeling he'd be needing it.

The firefight in the SS camp was confused and vicious. Trixie knew it was vital that her fighters hit the SS hard and fast, denying them the chance to get organised and to use their superior numbers and firepower to repel their attack. For a moment she actually thought they might do the impossible and *defeat* the SS, the WFA moving through the camp with deadly efficiency, shooting the enemy dead as they emerged, sleep-confused, from their tents. But these were battle-hardened StormTroopers they were up against, veterans who knew that if they panicked they would die. Instead they fell back, regrouping as they went, clustering in twos and threes behind cover and picking off Trixie's fighters as they advanced.

The battle hung in the balance, but then the SS managed to bring a second Gatling gun to bear. That was when the tide turned and the slaughter began in earnest.

Standing behind a wide oak tree, blasting away at the SS, Trixie could feel the momentum draining out of the attack. Even as she shouted out fresh orders, a hail of bullets smashed into the tree, snapping bark away, ripping off branches and forcing her to flinch back.

'Your father's got the Column,' Wysochi bellowed in her ear. 'It's time to retreat to the river.'

This, she knew, was good advice, but retreating under fire was a difficult manoeuvre for any army, more so for a ragtag one like hers, when a retreat could easily turn into a rout. Praying hard that her fighters' nerve would hold, she gave three shrill blasts on her whistle, signalling the fighters to pull back.

'Keep firing!' she screamed at the top of her voice. 'Keep your heads down!'

Then disaster struck. A couple of the younger fighters – sailors, unused to battle – ran out of ammunition. Their reaction was as predictable as it was catastrophic: they threw down their rifles and began to run. The panic was contagious and in an instant her army became a rabble.

'Stand, stand!' Trixie yelled but it did no good.

'We've had it, Trixie,' snarled Wysochi as he grabbed her shoulder in his great paw. 'It's every man for himself.' And with that he dragged her deeper into the woods and away from the fighting.

Dashwood could tell from the sound of the gunfire that the game was up. One moment it was the low, ominous crack of Martini-Henry rifles that drifted to him through the trees and then suddenly it was the chatter-chatter of the automatic weapons used by the SS that predominated. His surmise was confirmed when fighters came dashing towards them, their eyes stark with fear, and their desperation to escape the SS chasing them making them deaf to the shouted orders to stop and stand.

'I think it's gone bad for the WFA!' shouted Crockett as he urged the stoker to shovel yet more coal into the steamer's firebox. 'By my reckoning, Major, it's gonna get hot and heavy around here mighty quick.'

Dashwood nodded. 'I think you're right, Captain. Get the men to form a cordon between us and any SS who might come visiting.'

'What about the Column, Major? We're movin' slower than molasses in Winter. We ain't gonna get it to the river before the SS come calling.'

Crockett was right. With the SS advancing towards them there was no chance of their being able to sink the pontoon. Dashwood looked around and his eye fell on Sergeant Cassidy. 'Sergeant, do you have any blasting gelatin left from the time you blew up that train back in the ForthRight?'

'Sure have, Major. 'Bout ten pounds or so. Whaddaya want blowing up?'

Dashwood signalled to Captain Crockett to halt the steamers. 'I want the steamers and the sledge under the Column blown to buggery and beyond.'

Butch Cassidy gave a laugh. 'Consider it done, Major.'

*

Wysochi hauled a protesting Trixie to the safety of the clump of massive oak trees they'd designated as the rallying point. He could hear the shouts of the SS close behind them but he knew that if he kept his head then the darkness and the trees would make it impossible for anybody to track them. All he had to do was find somewhere to hide and do it quickly. Dawn was only an hour away and once it was daylight the hunt for them would begin in earnest.

'I can't do this, Wysochi. I can't desert my men.'

Wysochi's grip on Trixie's arm tightened. 'You're not deserting them, Trixie: the chances are that most of them have already been rounded up by the SS. If you want to have any chance of stopping Crowley putting the Column on top of the Pyramid then the first thing you need to do is keep from standing in front of a firing squad.'

It was an argument that had some resonance, especially when her father – with Cassidy and Crockett on his heels – came to join them.

'We failed, Trixie,' he announced in a breathless voice. 'The SS came at us before we'd got the Column down to the river.'

'Damn . . . so what do we do now?'

'My first inclination is to head back to our camp, but that, I think, will give only temporary refuge: the camp's location will be one of the first pieces of information the SS interrogators extract from their prisoners. No, we need a place to hide, and, in my opinion, the best place to hide a tree – or even five of them – is in a wood.'

All of the army heard the dressing-down that His Holiness Aleister Crowley gave General Clement – his voice was that loud – when he had accused the general, as a consequence of his incompetence in not adequately protecting the Column, of putting the triumph of UnFunDaMentalism at risk. The dressing-down lasted almost an hour, and when a red-faced Crowley finally swept out of the general's tent there had been a distinct lack of enthusiasm amongst the officers corps to attend their commander.

'Fucking Rebs,' snarled Clement when they were all gathered. 'Fucking sneaky, underhand sons of bitches.'

Captain Andrew Roberts edged back behind the more senior officers. He was only an engineer so it wasn't his fault that the enemy had been able to penetrate the camp so easily. In fact, it wasn't really the fault of any of the officers in the tent: the officer responsible for the defence of the camp couldn't be with them, finding himself swinging by his neck from the branch of a tree.

After downing a rather too large glass of Solution, the general seemed to get control of himself. 'Okay, Roberts, what's the damage?'

'Both steamers and the sledge are u/s, Comrade General, and we lost two hundred StormTroopers and fifty-seven Polish workers who tried to join the—'

'Fuck the Poles,' sneered Clement. 'What's this done to our schedule?'

'The destruction of the two steamers is a setback, General, but I have been advised by telegram that we will be receiving ten new steamer-tractors and two thousand more navvies by the end of the week. Once they're here I am confident that any time lost can be quickly recouped . . . except, that is, if there is further interference by the Rebel forces.'

Clement turned his attention to Colonel Sergei Trubetskoy, who was now – following the rather abrupt demise of the previous incumbent – officer commanding the SS regiments on Terror Incognita. 'How many Rebs are still free, Comrade Colonel?' Clement asked as he cut himself a chunk of chewing tobacco and popped it into his mouth.

The Colonel fidgeted under Clement's cold gaze. It never ceased to amaze Roberts how such a small and slight man – boy, really – as Clement could cow such big and brutal soldiers as Trubetskoy, but he did. 'Interrogation of the prisoners tells us that the rebel Trixie Dashwood landed with two hundred fighters, and once in Terror Incognita she teamed up with a regiment of Royalists under the command of her father, Algernon Dashwood—'

'That Royalist bastard. Ah thought we'd done for him in Warsaw.'

'Apparently not, Comrade General.'

'So, what's happened to Trixie Dashwood?'

'She escaped, Comrade General, along with her father. I already have one of my regiments – two hundred men – combing Terror Incognita for her.'

'You using Blood Hounders in your search, Colonel?'

'Yes, Comrade General.'

Clement spent a reflective couple of seconds silently masticating his tobacco. 'Okey-dokey, this is what we're a-gonna be doing, Colonel,' he said finally. 'Ah want another *two* regiments out there a-searching for Trixie Dashwood. Ah want every stone looked under and every tree looked up. Ah want Trixie Dashwood found pronto. You hearing what ah'm saying, Colonel?'

'Yes, Comrade General, but with all due respect, isn't the use of *six* hundred StormTroopers a little excessive? After all, Trixie Dashwood is only a girl.'

Clement gave a mirthless little laugh. 'This is the same girl who played pirate and stole the rifles that enabled them damnblasted Poles to kill so many of our boys during the Battle of Warsaw. This is the same girl who organised them Polak bastards so they kicked the shit outta some of the best the SS could throw at them. This is the same girl who held Rangoon against odds of ten to one. This is the same girl who came within an ace of bringing the Column of Loci to Terror Incognita. This is the same girl who put a bullet in my ABBA-damned shoulder. So the answer to your question, Colonel, is nah, six hundred Storm-Troopers ain't excessive, 'specially as if you ain't found her by the fiftieth day of Fall, she's the girl that's gonna be putting a noose around your neck.'

1:14

London, the Rookeries
The Demi-Monde: 4th Day of Fall, 1005

In an impassioned speech yesterday the Great Leader, Rein-hard Heydrich, pledged the ForthRight's support to the people of NoirVille in their struggle against the insidious creed of nuJuism. Speaking at the opening of the inaugural ForthRight/NoirVille Festival of Friendship, the Great Leader said: 'The time has come for the leaders of NoirVille to understand the evil they have allowed to flourish in their midst. The nuJus are the enemy of all who would call them-selves civilised, they seek only the destruction and enslavement of the rest of humanity, this foul ambition recorded by their own hand in *The Protocols of the Sages of nuJuism and of the Most Ancient and All-Seeing Order of Kohanim*. I call on HimPeror Xolandi to expunge the JAD from the face of the Demi-Monde and to exterminate the vermin skulking there.'

Editorial carried in *The Stormer,* **6th day of Fall, 1005**

After a lifetime spent in public relations, assessing the reactions of Demi-Mondians to various events and pieces of propaganda and then working to manipulate those reactions, Ivy Lee had learnt a lot about human behaviour, becoming expert on all the numerous 'tells' his clients used. He had studied the incorrigible paperclip unravellers, the dedicated doodlers, the habitual earlobe-tweakers, the compulsive chin-scratchers and the inveterate desk-tidiers, and understood the motivations behind these unconscious tics. Everyone had them . . . everyone except Reinhard Heydrich. The Great Leader's self-control was such that even now, when he was beset by so many shocks and alarums, he sat still and preternaturally calm behind his huge desk.

Perhaps this chilled aloofness was itself a tell? Ivy Lee thought perhaps it was, and what it told him was that he should be very, very careful. He sensed that it wouldn't take much to provoke the Great Leader into doing something truly despicable.

Lee hadn't met with the Great Leader since the debacle of the Awful Tower and he was aghast at the change the intervening weeks had wrought on the man. His superhuman sangfroid was as impregnable as ever, allowing him to mask his inner turmoil, but, to a trained observer such as Lee, there were signs aplenty that he was a man under enormous pressure. The tremor under his right eye and the tremble of the hand holding his cigarette signalled that Heydrich had a maggot in his mind.

Lee waited for the Great Leader to speak. He had been waiting for over a minute, the dreadful silence almost as unsettling as the cold, blank eyes with which Heydrich was studying him. He was afraid of Heydrich and what his reaction would be to the unpalatable news he would be obliged to convey: men under pressure tended to react unpredictably to bad news.

Worse, it wasn't just Heydrich's baleful presence that was discomforting Lee. Disturbing though it was to have been summoned to a meeting with the Great Leader, it was a disturbing situation made worse by the sinister man standing silently in the corner of the Leader's private study. This, if he wasn't mistaken, was the mysterious Septimus Bole, the fabled *éminence grise* – more accurately, the *éminence noire* – behind the Party. Mysterious because very few people had actually met the man: he was the veritable ghost in the well-oiled machine that was the ForthRight.

But if Septimus Bole was the ghost in the machine, then Aaliz Heydrich was playing the grain of sand.

The Great Leader spoke. 'You have made an assessment of the impact Aaliz Heydrich's unscheduled appearance at the Victory in the Coven jamboree has had on public opinion?'

Lee found it odd that the Great Leader should refer to his daughter in the third person, but then, he supposed, relationships between the members of the dysfunctional Heydrich family were probably best not dwelt on. The important thing was that since the girl had gatecrashed the celebrations marking the ForthRight's conquest of the Coven and delivered her speech condemning her father and all his works, Lee's tracking figures had gone all to Hel. Suddenly UnFunDaMentalism was most certainly *not* the flavour of the month even amongst the most diehard of ForthRightists. He just wondered how best to sugarcoat this particularly foul-tasting pill.

'Yes, Comrade Leader. At the behest of the Ministry of Propaganda, my firm has been conducting weekly surveys of public opinion within the ForthRight in order to gauge how the directives of the Party might be finessed to make them more . . . palatable to the population. Each week one thousand citizens, representing a demographic cross-section of the ForthRight as a whole, are interviewed. These interviews are conducted in informal settings by physically attractive interviewers and are designed to elicit truthful responses to the pressing questions of the hour.'

'Yes, yes, I know all this. Just get on with it.'

The tone that had inflected the Leader's voice was all the persuasion Lee needed to get on with it.

'In the most recent of these interviews we began by asking, "What does Aaliz Heydrich stand for?" This question was designed to establish the scale of the impact she has made on the consciousness of the ForthRight's population post her appearance at the Crystal Palace. Although the Ministry of Propaganda has made strenuous efforts to suppress knowledge of and debate regarding what Lady Aaliz said, with there being over two hundred thousand people in attendance it has proved impossible to prevent gossip. This question was intended to establish the extent of the dissemination of the knowledge relating to the events of that night.'

'And the result?'

Lee swallowed: his mouth had gone very dry. 'Ninety per cent of the respondents described Aaliz Heydrich as "a Normalist" or as "an opponent of UnFunDaMentalism".'

For the first time the Great Leader demonstrated emotion. He slumped back in his chair and blew a long stream of tobacco smoke ceilingwards. 'Marvellous! So much for the efforts of von Sternberg and his Checkya to keep the lid on this particular news story.' He gave Lee a grim smile. 'Carry on.'

'The next question we asked was "Do you approve of the message voiced by Aaliz Heydrich?" And here, Comrade Leader, I must regretfully report that over seventy per cent of those interviewed responded in the affirmative.'

'*Seventy* per cent? Are you sure of these results?'

'Of course, Comrade Leader, all surveys of this kind are subject to sampling errors, but we have a ninety-five per cent confidence level that our results are accurate.'

Heydrich drew a hand through his mane of blond hair. A *trembling* hand, this, presumably a consequence of the toll taken by the 'Aaliz situation'. But then, Lee supposed, it must be a tragedy for a father to be betrayed by his own daughter, especially one who had previously been so loyal and dutiful. After taking a long gulp from his glass of Solution, Heydrich waved Lee to continue.

'The third question we asked was "Do you consider yourself to be an UnFunDaMentalist?" Less than fifty per cent agreed that this description could be applied to themselves, with women being much less ready to accept such an appellation.'

'I don't believe it,' spluttered Heydrich as he began to finger the heavy lead-crystal ashtray sitting on his desk. 'UnFunDaMentalism is the bedrock of the ForthRight. Surely one speech by a delusional girl isn't enough to turn things on their head?'

Lee prepared to duck. The word was that in moments of high tension the Leader was inclined to shay things at the head of the poor sod delivering bad news. As tells went, fingering eminently throwable glass ashtrays was one that even the most obtuse of psychologists couldn't fail to recognise.

Using his most mellifluous tone of voice, Lee answered in a manner he hoped would avoid death by ashtray. 'It appears from our research that your daughter's speech simply crystallised a growing disenchantment with the Party's policies concerning the need for war, and the ever-increasing food and coal shortages. Coming so close on the heels of the Troubles, the difficulties encountered in the subjugation of Warsaw, the failure to take Venice, and the unfortunate incident with the Awful Tower—'

The withering look he got from Heydrich persuaded him to truncate his cataloguing of the disasters that had befallen the ForthRight in recent months. 'Suffice it to say that circumstances have conspired to put the people in a very receptive frame of mind regarding alternative political ideas.'

There was a movement in the shadowed corner of the room. 'There will be no "alternative political ideas",' said Septimus Bole quietly, so quietly that Lee had to lean forward to better catch what the man was saying. It was the first time that Bole had spoken and the soft implacability of his voice sent shivers tracing up and down Lee's spine. This was a dangerous man. 'UnFunDaMentalism gives the people of the ForthRight the belief that life is not meaningless and random, that there is purpose to human existence. It is not a belief system that is ready for the political knacker's yard.'

'I understand that, sir, but—'

'There can be no buts, Mr Lee. The ForthRight is unable to tolerate opinions at odds with those enshrined in the catechisms of UnFunDaMentalism.'

'But our findings show that the people are sick of war.'

Bole chuckled. His was a particularly unpleasant laugh that made Lee's skin goosepimple. 'Any religion or political creed that claims to be blessed by ABBA yet condemns war is little more than a friendly society. War is the apotheosis of belief, as it is only through struggle and pain that the people come to know ABBA. You must communicate to the people of the Forth-Right that UnFunDaMentalism is beset by external and internal enemies in league with Loki who are constantly at work sub-verting the sanguinity of the ForthRight and of the Demi-Monde. These enemies must be fought and destroyed.'

'I must advise you, sir, that the message promulgated by Aaliz Heydrich has given the people an appetite for something other than war.'

'Aaliz Heydrich is a victim of Loki's duplicity and cunning. You must use all your skill, Mr Lee, to convince the masses that by following her teachings they will be standing like sheep ready for the slaughter when Loki comes to call.'

'With all due respect, sir, this is the message we *have* been promulgating, but with little effect.'

'Then amend your message to say that by attending the Cere-mony of Purification to be held on the last day of Fall, the citizens of the ForthRight will usher in an era of peace unparalleled in Demi-Mondian history.'

'In view of the numerous wars the ForthRight has been engaged in of late, this is a message that the citizens might have difficulty believing.'

Now that shut Bole up for a moment and when he resumed the conversation he was a mite less bombastic. 'So tell me, Lee, what must we do to bring the good folk of the ForthRight back into the loving embrace of UnFunDaMentalism?'

Lee didn't hesitate. The answer to this question given by the interviewees had been unequivocal. 'Have Aaliz Heydrich publicly recant Normalism and urge them to attend the Ceremony of Purification.'

Only when Lee had left Heydrich's office did Bole feel it safe to move out of the shadows. He was not a well man, but then every journey he was required to make to the Demi-Monde left him feeling weak and dyspeptic, this being the reason why he tried to confine his interfacing with Dupes to an absolute minimum. Unfortunately for the tranquillity of his digestive system he had had to make an increasing number of such visits of late, being unable to stand aloof as incompetents like Heydrich destroyed the fruits of so many years of careful planning.

He oiled silently across the room and took the seat that Lee had vacated. 'It is ironic, is it not, Heydrich, that before this stunt of Norma Williams everything was going precisely to plan. We must not allow our ambitions to be derailed by this girl.'

'But how can we have her recant?'

'We are fortunate that the abiding virtue of the Kosmos is one of duality and, therefore, that there is more than one Aaliz Heydrich. Your daughter – the *real* Aaliz – is safe and well in the Real World and I would propose that she return here to the Demi-Monde and proselytize in favour of UnFunDaMentalism and urge attendance at the Ceremony of Purification.' Bole took a sip of the warm honeyed water he had been served by a steward. 'Yes, that is what we must do: we must have her announce that her speech at the Crystal Palace was merely a ruse to flush out anti-UnFunDaMentalist agitators. I am sure that Ivy Lee can concoct a suitably convincing piece of propaganda to explain the girl's volte-face.'

'Surely to recall Aaliz back from the Real World will have a damaging impact on your work there?'

Bole gave a careless shrug of his bony shoulders. 'Inconvenient rather than damaging. Much of Aaliz's work in the Real World is complete. The Fun/Funs go from strength to strength, and even as we speak, emissaries are at work preparing the doppelgängers of the citizens of the ForthRight for their attendance at the Gathering. There is only one remaining task that requires her physical presence, the giving of her final address to the Gathering. In the interim I am confident that a suitable replacement can be found . . . a suitable *virtual* replacement.' Bole gave an unpleasant laugh. 'There is something rather *drôle* here, is there not?: the use of a Dupe of Aaliz in order to dupe the Fun/Funs into communing with their own Dupes.'

Heydrich wasn't amused. 'But isn't this dangerous? Won't returning Aaliz to the Demi-Monde leave Norma Williams' body vacant in the Real World? What if the real Norma Williams were to reclaim it?'

Bole gave a disdainful shake of his head. 'There is no chance of that. The one remaining Portal in the JAD is controlled by my agents, and anyway, the transfer process requires assistance from ABBA, which Norma Williams does not have. No . . . it is better to have Aaliz active here in the Demi-Monde encouraging participation in the Ceremony of Purification. For the ceremony to be successful we must have those citizens of the ForthRight whose doppelgängers will be attending the Gathering in the Real World assemble on Terror Incognita so that their dormant talents may be resuscitated and then transferred. Remember, Heydrich, in less than ninety days, on the last day of Fall, we will remake HumanKind . . . we will make the Aryan PreFolk rise again. That is the prize for which we are striving and we must not let a nothing such as Norma Williams deny us this triumph.'

1:15

1.5. Yeah, ABBA was bored big time so He took his dick in His hand and had a tug, and His semen spurted out hot and heavy. It was from this that the Nine Worlds were made and everything else in the Whole Known. And ABBA thought this was Cool to the utmost and He called it the Big Wang.

The HIM Book, Book of the Coming: Chapter 1, Verse 5

The considered opinion of Konstantin Pobedonostsev was that when Lilith had connived in the Fall of the Pre-Folk she had done this by imbuing the Blank races of the Demi-Monde with the pernicious and corrosive trait of impatience. Impatience resulted in a problem not being properly considered and this led, in turn, to the making of rash decisions.

Mindful of this, Pobedonostsev had become a *very* patient man and it was this aptitude for the logical and unhurried solving of problems that he had applied to the achieving of his most cherished goal, the eradication of the UnderMentionable races from the face of the Demi-Monde. Such an extermination of the Shades and the nuJus was vital, he believed, if the Blank races were to be purified and the Demi-Monde was once again to bask in the grace of ABBA.

For ten long years he had laboured as tutor to that mindless oaf Xolandi, wheedling his way into the boy's trust, nurturing his dependence on him, insinuating himself as a friend and loyal subject. And Pobedonostsev had done this to ensure that when the Crown Prince finally took the throne, he would be appointed to the position of Grand Vizier. And now he had attained this prize – thanks, in no small part, to his conniving in the assassination of Shaka Zulu – it would be a simple matter to persuade Xolandi to hurl his HimPis against the JAD. Then the Shades and the nuJus would destroy each other in an orgy of self-destruction.

But . . .

Before this could happen, the Grand Council would need to be convinced of the need to attack the JAD – even the HimPeror needed their support before NoirVille could go to war – and the main obstacle to achieving that was General Salah-ad-Din, a soldier who harboured the ridiculous belief that a prosperous peace was preferable to a wasteful war.

Pobedonostsev pondered for a moment as to whether it might be simpler and more efficient to have Salah-ad-Din poisoned, but *two* assassinations in as many days might panic Xolandi into doing something precipitous, like recant on his promise to appoint him Grand Vizier. Anyway, Salah-ad-Din was a canny individual who employed a veritable army of food tasters.

No, now was time for a little subtlety with regard to promoting war against the nuJus.

Pobedonostsev gave a self-satisfied little smile, rose from his armchair, strolled over to the bookcase standing at the end of his study and unlocked a drawer set into the bottommost shelf. From there he extracted a manuscript, which he set down on his leather-topped desk. This document – *The Protocols of the Sages of nuJuism and of the Most Ancient and All-Seeing Order of Kohanim* – would, if promoted properly, finally persuade the Grand Council to destroy the nuJus, being, as it was, the most inflammatory document ever written . . . which was hardly surprising given that it had been Pobedonostsev who had written it.

The Protocols were a labour of love – or more accurately, a labour of hate – written by Pobedonostsev over a period of almost two years, each venomous word carefully crafted to defame the nuJus. The Protocols were a perfectly weighted amalgam of fact, fabrication and downright incendiary nonsense which would intrigue the intellectual, inflame the passionate, offend the religious and supplant the common reasoning of the hoi polloi. They would become the final reference document for those who sought to defile the Yid.

Pobedonostsev had crafted the Protocols in such a way that the nuJus would be vilified by the words supposedly written by their own Elders as they plotted the downfall of the gentile Sectors, the eradication of all religions other than nuJuism, the undermining of public morality by the propagation of pawnography, and the seizing of control of the Demi-Monde's finances. But what he was most proud of was the way he had interlaced fictions that would provoke the most profound of emotional reactions in the Shade population. The mentioning of the nuJus' intention to destroy the Sphinx – HimPerialism's holiest shrine – he judged to be masterful, and the continual reference to Noir-Ville being the historical homeland – the so-called Promised Land – of the nuJus would be enough to sow the seeds of doubt in the mind of even the most nuJu-philic of Shades.

The Protocols were, in short, the most persuasively toxic tract in the history of the written word and the stupid, ignorant Shades would swallow them hook, line and sinker. Even the great Salah-ad-Din would find it difficult to refute the poisonous claims made by the Protocols.

Pobedonostsev smiled. Once things were written down they transcended hearsay and became fact . . . no matter how ridiculous they were. These gleeful thoughts were interrupted by a servant informing him that the HimPeror was ready to meet with his Grand Council.

*

Pobedonostsev rose to his feet and called the meeting to order. He bowed towards the newly-crowned Xolandi, who was perched rather self-consciously on the throne so recently vacated by Shaka Zulu, the HimPeror's face still swollen from the cheek scars that announced his recent embracing of ManHood. 'Your Majesty,' he began, 'and revered members of the Grand Council, there is only one item on today's agenda, this being the examination of NoirVille's policy regarding the JAD and the nuJus who reside there.'

Ashoka Maurya, Caliph of Delhi, looked up from studying the agenda. 'I wasn't aware that our policy was in need of review, Grand Vizier. Surely the MANdate signed by His HimPerial Majesty, Shaka Zulu, is still in force?'

Pobedonostsev wasn't surprised by Ashoka's protest. In his view, the man was too devout by half, rumour having it that he had secretly adopted the non-violent philosophy of Normalism. But young and unworldly though Ashoka was, he was a man of great influence in NoirVille and one of Pobedonostsev's most intractable opponents on the Council. Fortunately, Pobedonostsev was not without allies.

There was a bad-tempered snort from NoirVille's newly appointed religious leader, His HimPerial Reverence the Grand Mufti Mohammed Amin Husseini, the man who had replaced Mohammed al-Mahdi as NoirVille's senior cleric when al-Mahdi had got himself blown to bits in the Temple of Lilith. The Grand Mufti flicked his fly whisk around in an irritated manner and gnawed at his lower lip as he was apt to do when he was displeased, but then the Grand Mufti was always displeased. 'Would that the MANdate had never been signed,' he grumbled. 'It was a dark day for NoirVille when we climbed into bed with those bastard nuJus.'

Stupid, unbalanced and vain though the Mufti was, he did have certain redeeming features, the greatest of these being his detestation of the nuJus. As such he was a powerful confederate in Pobedonostsev's plans to destroy the JAD.

'What is the MANdate?' asked Xolandi, confirming to Pobedonostsev that the HimPeror possessed all the intellectual capacity of a gourd.

'It is an agreement, Your Majesty,' Pobedonostsev explained, 'signed by his late and much lamented HimPerial Majesty Shaka Zulu and that arch-schemer Rabbi Gelbfisz, which permitted the establishment of the JAD in NoirVille.'

'And by signing that Loki-inspired document, Shaka Zulu betrayed the people of NoirVille,' grumbled the Grand Mufti.

'Have a care, Your Reverence,' warned Dingiswayo, the Caliph of ZuluLand and the man who had been Shaka's most loyal lieutenant, 'such criticism profanes the memory of His HimPerial Majesty.'

'Not so, Caliph Dingiswayo,' spluttered the Mufti, 'rather I criticise the previous Grand Vizier, Selim the Grim, may ABBA have mercy on his Soul. It was his bad counsel that persuaded His HimPerial Majesty Shaka Zulu to sign the MANdate and to reject the entreaties made by the *Ulana* – which I have the honour to lead – that a jihad be declared against the nuJus.' The Mufti gave a doleful shake of his head, presumably to indicate how unconscionable it was for any to ignore the advice of the *Ulana*, the supreme religious body in NoirVille.

'All this is moot,' Ashoka answered quietly. 'The reality is that the MANdate *has* been signed and *is* in force. Machismo demands that we honour the treaty.'

'And to considerations of Machismo must be added considerations of money,' added Salah-ad-Din. 'Surely to renege on the MANdate would be fiscally . . . unfortunate? If my memory of the Sector's budget for this year does not serve me false, the income from the trade of blood, which is facilitated by the Aqua Benedicta supplied by the nuJus, accounts for almost three-quarters of the earnings of NoirVille. Without the nuJus we would be reduced to penury.'

'There is more to the governing of a Sector than consideration of pecuniary matters, General Salah-ad-Din,' sneered the Mufti. 'There are matters of religion and of Machismo, matters which transcend Mammon.'

'Unfortunately, Your Reverence, religion and Machismo cannot be baked or fried,' observed Salah-ad-Din, 'and it is my experience that a people's love of their HimPeror is directly proportional to how full their bellies are.'

As always, Salah-ad-Din's calm and considered demeanour effectively countered the Mufti's bombast, so much so that Pobedonostsev was obliged to intervene. 'I bow to General Salah-ad-Din's expertise in matters culinary, but my belief is that the nuJus have ambitions which exceed the boundaries of the JAD. We have a cuckoo in our midst, gentlemen, a nuJu cuckoo that wishes to eject us from our land. And once they have achieved this, our people's bellies will rumble as never before.'

The HimPeror was roused to ask another question. 'And what are these ambitions?'

'To take our Sector away from us! NuJu legends speak of NoirVille once being theirs and it is the possession of the entire Sector that they covet. They even refer to it as the Promised Land.'

'Promised by whom?'

'According to the nuJus, by ABBA.'

'Then ABBA has been something of an absentee landlord for the last one thousand years,' observed Ashoka drily. 'Nobody – not even the nuJus – can seriously make claim to a piece of the Demi-Monde based on such an antique remembrance.'

'The nuJus can and do, Caliph Ashoka,' answered Pobedonostsev firmly. 'There are many legends and myths contained in the nuJu Book of Profits that would have us believe that the nuJus were once a great and a powerful people, much favoured by ABBA. They even refer to themselves as the Chosen People, and this PreFall empire of the nuJus was, again according to the Book of Profits, based in NoirVille. By their lights the nuJus have a claim to all the lands of NoirVille.'

Ashoka chuckled and then shook his head. 'Nonsense. Surely, Grand Vizier, you have not brought this Council together to discuss fairy tales. All the MANdate promised was that we would provide a home for the nuJus in exchange for the Aqua Benedicta. That is fact, not fable.'

With a smile Pobedonostsev nodded. 'You are correct, Caliph Ashoka, the MANdate did promise a "natural home for the nuJu people", but the nuJus have wilfully interpreted this as a promise to grant them permission to set up a permanent, independent state within the borders of NoirVille. Our generosity of spirit has been churlishly taken advantage of. NuJus have flooded into the JAD. Two million nuJus now see the JAD as their "natural home", but I repeat, "a natural home" is *not* the same as an independent nuJu state. The nuJus must realise that the dead bones of their ancestors cannot be exhumed and restored to life and for that reason the JAD is and will ever remain an integral part of the Shade world.'

'But how can so many nuJus live in such a confined area?' asked a frowning Xolandi. Having been brought up inside the Royal Kraal, it seemed the new HimPeror was having trouble coming to terms with the cramped living conditions the nuJus endured.

'They did it by evicting the Shade population they found there, Your Majesty,' explained Pobedonostsev.

'Not "evicting", Grand Vizier: they bought the land . . .'

'Again you are correct, Caliph Ashoka, they did buy the land, bribing the local Shakes in order to do so. But what you fail to mention is what they did when they *had* ownership of the land.

They pushed out the fellahin who had been living and working there for generations, and created a mass of homeless, unemployed and destitute Shades for the rest of NoirVille to deal with.' Pobedonostsev turned to Xolandi. 'So you see, Your Majesty, the quasi-state that is the JAD has been established only by the gravest trespass upon the "civil and religious rights of existing Shade communities" which the nuJus, in the MANdate, were obliged to respect.'

The Grand Mufti couldn't resist adding his two pennyworth. 'The Grand Vizier is right, the nuJus have behaved shamefully. But this is a lesson for all Shades: there is no space in NoirVille for two races or two religions . . . it is impossible to put two swords in a single sheath. And what is worse, the presence of the nuJus has begun to corrupt our Sector. A great many woeMen have run to the JAD to avoid marrying the Man chosen for them by their father and there have been mutterings that some females are aping their nuJu sisters and refusing to follow the teachings of SubMISSiveness. Even a single nuJu is the rotten apple that, when placed in a box of good apples, will cause them all to moulder and become putrid.'

Once again Ashoka tried to placate the Mufti. 'Oh come now, Your Reverence, this is hysterical talk. The nuJus have been polite and dutiful guests in our Sector—'

'Guests! The nuJus do not see themselves as guests. These bastard nuJus will not rest until NoirVille is under the control of a nuJu government.'

'Ridiculous. It is just envious hearsay and gossip. There is no proof of this.'

'Oh, but there is, Caliph Ashoka.' And here Pobedonostsev tossed a leather-bound folder onto the table. 'As you all know, I had my cryptos penetrate the innermost council of the nuJus, where they stole this, a copy of *The Protocols of the Sages of nuJuism and of the Most Ancient and All-Seeing Order of Kohanim*, the secret minutes of the Supreme Council of nuJus. These Protocols tell us that the grand design of the nuJus is to use the JAD as a stepping stone to dispossess us of our Sector, this the first move towards their ambition of Demi-Monde-wide domination. Reading the Protocols, we learn we are fighting an organized, educated, devious and evil people whose aim is to concentrate the world's wealth and power in their hands. As the Protocols tell us, their aim is to corrupt the morality of every Sector of the Demi-Monde, and by doing so destroy all religions by promoting the venomously atheistic creed of RaTionalism, itself a product of that intellectual charlatan of a nuJu, Karl Marx. They plan to rob the people of their property, to steal their money by usury and persuade them to reject the teachings of ABBA.'

'And we should not forget that the Protocols also say that the nuJus have pledged to destroy the Sphinx and all temples and HIMnasia dedicated to HimPerialism,' added the Grand Mufti eagerly.

Ashoka tried again. 'But how can this be? By granting NoirVille the use of Aqua Benedicta the nuJus have made NoirVille pre-eminent in blood trading . . . they have made NoirVille the richest of all Sectors.'

Surprisingly, it was Dingiswayo – never the most voluble of men – who now entered the debate. 'Such is the nuJus' cunning that they have bribed us into forgetting what vermin they truly are. Aqua Benedicta is their baksheesh. For myself I would prefer NoirVille to remain poor and desolate if the alternative is collaboration with the nuJus. The nuJus are contemptuous of us, believing that their money can buy the souls of the Shades, but in this they are mistaken. Shades are a proud people, who will never, even for an instant, permit themselves to forget that the nuJus are a race apart. We have a duty to stand against their perfidy and we must do this not just for ourselves, not just for NoirVille but for the whole of the Demi-Monde. The nuJus are evil personified.'

Pobedonostsev realised that this was the moment to administer the *coup de grâce*. 'And surely the nuJus' most venal act was their sponsoring of the assassination of their greatest benefactor, Shaka Zulu.'

'You are certain, Grand Vizier,' Xolandi demanded, 'that the nuJus were the ones who connived to have Shaka Zulu assassinated?'

'The Protocols are very specific on this point, Your Majesty. They state that *"The Zealots will be provided with every assistance, whether financial, technical or moral, in order that that pagan overlord Shaka Zulu may be expeditiously eliminated."'*

'Bastards,' muttered Dingiswayo, 'dirty, stinking bastards.'

Excellent, mused Pobedonostsev. It was always easier to unite people behind a common hatred than a shared loyalty.

'But why would the nuJus do such a thing?' protested Ashoka. 'Shaka was their friend!'

'Read the Protocols, Caliph Ashoka, read where it says, *"The death of Shaka Zulu will throw NoirVille into chaos. The Crown Prince, Xolandi, is a cowardly boy, with no stomach for battle. Bereft of strong leadership, NoirVille will descend into chaos and this will give us the opportunity to complete our conquest of the Sector."'*

On hearing himself being described as a coward Xolandi flinched back as though struck. Then through pursed lips he addressed the Mufti. 'What do you suggest, Grand Vizier?'

'That we declare a jihad,' Pobedonostsev answered, 'that our HimPis move to exterminate the nuJus and reclaim the JAD.'

'Many NoirVillians will die,' observed Ashoka quietly.

Dingiswayo smashed a huge fist down on the table. 'Then they will die as martyrs to the true faith of HimPerialism and when they meet with ABBA they will wear smiles and possess satisfied souls. We will show these crafty, cunning nuJus we have not forgotten that kingdoms can only be built on dead bodies and the skulls of the fallen.'

Silence descended on the Council Chamber. Then Xolandi spoke. 'You are very quiet, General Salah-ad-Din. Are we to be deprived of your counsel? Do you not agree that NoirVille should war with the JAD?'

Salah-ad-Din sighed, then turned towards his HimPeror. 'War is a last resort, Your Majesty, and it is the duty of every general only to prosecute it when there is no alternative. The Anglos in the Rookeries have a saying: after every great war a Sector is left with three armies: one of cripples, one of the bereaved and one of the impoverished. I am anxious that this is not the case with NoirVille.'

'But the Protocols . . . we have proof of the nuJus' treachery.'

'In war, Your Majesty, the first casualty is the truth. I am not convinced by these Protocols, they seem a little too . . . convenient. Caliph Dingiswayo calls the nuJus "crafty and cunning", so are we seriously expected to add to this description the word "careless"? Are we expected to believe that the nuJus would be so negligent as to leave such an inflammatory document lying around where it might be taken by one of the Grand Vizier's cryptos?'

Pobedonostsev bridled. 'Are you calling me a liar, General Salah-ad-Din?'

'Not at all, Grand Vizier, such a thought had never entered my head. I am shocked that you could ever think I would believe you to be anything other than the epitome of probity and loyalty.'

Pobedonostsev searched Salah-ad-Din's face for irony but found none. The man was a supremely gifted actor.

'No, I am minded to question who might have a motive for forging such a document, and the answer that occurs to me is the ForthRight.'

'The ForthRight?' squeaked Xolandi.

'Indeed, Your Majesty; make no mistake, the subjugation of the JAD will be a difficult task and expensive in both men and materiel. It will be a long, hard struggle and one which will deplete NoirVille's coffers and leave us destitute. Would that not be the perfect time for the ForthRight to attack us, to take over our Sector and our monopoly of the blood trade?' Salah-ad-Din picked up the file containing the Protocols and tossed it disdainfully back to Pobedonostsev. 'No, I would need much greater provocation than this piece of make-believe before I would be persuaded to make war on the JAD.'

Pobedonostsev could see by the expressions on the faces of the men gathered around the table that Salah-ad-Din had carried the day. He bit his tongue, silently cursing the general for his interfering, but if he needed 'greater provocation' then that was what Pobedonostsev – in his guise of 'Agent Neizvestnii' – would provide.

1:16

The JAD, NoirVille
The Demi-Monde: 6th Day of Fall, 1005

Traduced by promises of gold and the favours of women, the Kohanim, the first of the nuJus, forsook the Second Commandment that forbade them to build graven images of ABBA and did rend and work Mantle-ite, of which they were the masters, into a form abhorrent to ABBA. The idol they created had the body of the lion, the wings of the eagle and the countenance of a man. This the Kohanim named the Sphinx. And ABBA, seeing what they had wrought, became angry and as punishment for their vile trespass took from them their ability to work Mantle-ite and cast them out of their HomeLand, condemning them and all their descendants to be rootless as the wind and to wander the Demi-Monde reviled and shunned by their fellow men.

The NuJu Book of Profits, Epistle 333

Being an agent un-provocateur, as Jude Iscariot had quickly come to realise, was an onerous occupation, and not a terribly reward-ing one at that. The pay was shit, the hours ridiculous and the pain he would endure if he was discovered unappetising. But then he'd had preciously little to say in the matter. That bastard Gelbfisz had him firmly by the knackers: it was either serve as one of Gelbfisz's cryptos or spend a year in jail for passing forged bankers' drafts. In retrospect, the prospect of twelve months in Megiddo Prison now seemed quite enticing: playing undercover agent among the Zealots wasn't Jude's idea of sensible retirement planning.

Coward that he was, he had, of course, considered making a run for it, skedaddling out of the JAD to go into hiding in that place signposted 'Somewhere Else'. But he'd prevaricated – making tough decisions wasn't Jude's forte – and now with the bloody Shvartses camped out around the Wall and all the crossings heavily patrolled he was stuck in the JAD. And in the JAD what Gelbfisz said was law . . . well, law for anyone except the Zealots, that is.

Yeah, the Zealots were mad and dangerous to boot, so it wasn't a particularly happy Jude Iscariot who found himself sneaking along the Street of the Profits just after midnight, en route to a meeting with these lunatics, his somewhat downbeat mood not helped by the unseasonably hot weather. Since Fall had arrived, even at night the JAD was unbearably hot and humid, Jude hating the way it made his hair slick with sweat, his shirt stick to his back and his face damp with perspiration.

Absent-mindedly he hung a right down Gizza Avenue, dodging between the coils of barbed wire and the steamer-traps as he went. Gelbfisz might be doing everything he could to avoid war with the Shades but ever the one to play the percentages, he was preparing for it anyway. And for a man possessed of such an overwhelming aversion to violence as Jude, all this martial preparedness was a chilling reminder of what would happen if he was to fail in his mission to bring confusion to the Zealots.

The house Jude stopped in front of was swathed in darkness, not even the smallest shard of light squeezing through the shutters to indicate that there was life within. He rapped three sets of three knocks on the thick door and a moment later he heard the question 'Who's there?' coming from inside the house. Jude knew who the woman's voice belonged to, but revolutionary etiquette meant that he couldn't show that he recognised it. It was all very childish.

'I am here to meet those who would free my people and reclaim the Promised Land,' Jude answered, reciting the pass-phrase in cod-seriousness.

'Then, Comrade, you need the assistance of the Zealots to achieve such lofty ambitions.' As the woman intoned the answering phrase, Jude heard bolts being shot and a key being turned in a heavy lock. Potty the Zealots might be, but they were cautiously potty. A second later the door opened just far enough for him to slip inside, Jude trying to stop himself gagging as he went, the house stinking of sweat, shit and festering dampness. As he struggled to come to terms with this olfactory onslaught and to prevent his supper making a return appearance, he wondered if it was obligatory for dissidents to live in shitholes.

The girl beckoned him deeper into the shithole, across a dark room and through another door into the small, gloomy kitchen beyond. Lit by a single oil lamp, there was barely enough light for Jude to make out the dozen or so men gathered around the table: this was the famous 'kitchen cabinet' that comprised the Zealots' most senior officers.

Judas Maccabeus rose to greet him. This was the moment that Jude particularly loathed, the moment when these stinking and flea-infested maniacs made familiar with him, kissing him on his cheeks, slapping him on the back and shaking his hand, but, mindful of the role he was playing, Jude reciprocated their hugs and endearments, even going so far as to give little Vera – the girl who had let him into the house – a rather bold peck on the cheek. He knew enough about girls to have realised that she was a little sweet on big, bold and heroic Jude Iscariot, Zealot freedom fighter and nuJu patriot.

Hugging and kissing thankfully over, Jude took a seat at the side of the table where the shadows were darkest. The persona he had adopted for his role as Zealot revolutionary was that of a simple, unassuming nonentity who avoided the deep and dense philosophical discussions regarding the future of the JAD and its people so beloved by the Zealots, who didn't argue the virtues of RaTionalism and most certainly didn't squabble and joust for leadership or recognition. He knew that he was quietly mocked by the intellectuals in the Zealots as a man who could recite the catechisms of revolution without understanding them, but this he saw as being all to the good: what he wanted was to be perceived as nothing more than a spear-carrier, a man easily forgotten and overlooked, a strong and steadfast – if not particularly bright – soldier of the revolution. The last thing Jude wanted was to be noticed. Cryptos who got noticed ended up in the gutter with a knife in their eye.

Once he was settled in his seat, Vera thrust a glass of tea into his hand, which he pushed to one side. He had no intention of drinking it: there were a lot of things he would do to stay out of Megiddo Prison, but contracting cholera wasn't one of them. He unbuttoned his coat – the heat given out by so many sweating bodies packed into the windowless room produced an atmosphere that was threatening to overwhelm him – then sat back to let tonight's performance unfold.

The mission that Gelbfisz had given him was simple enough: he was to spy on the Zealots to find out what they were planning as they attempted to disrupt the very fragile peace that existed between the JAD and NoirVille . . . and then to do his best to fuck up these plans. Fortunately, thus far all this involved him doing was sitting in a dark room, listening to belligerent claptrap and avoiding drinking the tea. The Zealots had done the rest. The rivalry between the several would-be leaders gathered around the table was so intense that they could never agree about anything. If Maccabeus suggested blowing up a Shade police station, Gideon Mannaseh was sure to ridicule it, and if Avraham Stern thought a raid on a Zulu arms depot was just the ticket, John Giscala could be relied on to veto it. The Zealots were emasculated by envy and ambition and the upshot was that they did a lot of talking, but fuck-all terrorising.

It seemed that John Giscala had been elected to be that evening's chairman. On first sight Giscala looked the very epitome of a revolutionary, being big and broad and possessed of a quite stupendously bushy beard. Unfortunately, he also had a speech impediment that prevented him being taken terribly seriously within the ranks of the Zealots. Zealots, it seemed, weren't big on stutterers. But again, as far as Jude was concerned, this was good news; with Giscala in the chair nothing would be even proposed, never mind voted upon.

'So now w-w-we are c-c-complete,' Giscala began, the movement of his lips masked by his beard. Maybe, Jude mused, if terrorism didn't work out as a career he should try ventriloquism, though stuttering ventriloquists would be, he supposed, something of a novelty act. 'Our brotherhood of stout-hearted freedom fighters is g-g-gathered at last. W-W-Welcome, Comrade Iscariot. Y-Y-Your help has been a g-g-g-great assistance in our p-p-planning. You are a true g-g-guardian angel to those who labour to bring the nuJu people to f-f-freedom and back to the P-P-P-Promised Land.'

Jude waited a moment before replying to ensure that Giscala had stopped speaking and hadn't just paused, becalmed in mid-stutter. 'You are generous in your praise, Comrade Giscala,' he answered, doing his best to inflect his words with the appropriate level of revolutionary portentousness. 'It is the duty of all of us to rally around the cause after the agents of repression' – Jude could hardly believe he could talk the mummery that was Zealot-speak without breaking out in a fit of giggles – 'attacked the offices of our Party three weeks ago.' There were murmurs of agreement from around the room. Jude wondered if these fools would have been quite so complimentary if they had known that it was he who had tipped Gelbfisz off, deeming it time to have some of the more insane of the Zealots' leaders arrested.

'S-s-still, your help was m-m-m-munificent, especially as I b-b-believe you had to r-r-risk your life in d-d-defence of your C-C-Comrades.'

Jude shrugged as though he was indifferent to death, which he was, as long as said death was visited on someone other than himself.

A disdainful *hummmp* from Maccabeus. 'We are *all* revolution-aries,' he said quietly, looking around the room in a meaningful manner. 'We have all dedicated our lives to the cause of nuJuism, to the freeing of our people from bondage and to reclaiming the Promised Land that is NoirVille. To this end we must, like Com-rade Iscariot here, stand ready to sacrifice our lives: to triumph we must kill and, if necessary, be killed!'

The somewhat macabre tone of the meeting set, Jude watched and waited for everybody to climb aboard the tumbrel.

Maccabeus' enthusiasm for killing and dying was obviously contagious. 'Comrade Maccabeus is correct: the time for discus-sion and debate is over. Now is the moment when we must announce ourselves to the world with an act of dramatic assas-sination.'

This observation came from Levi Kannaim, another madman who had the rather unsettling habit of toying with a dagger when he spoke. 'Only in this way,' Kannaim continued, 'will we seize the attention of the downtrodden nuJu masses, giving them hope that political, religious and racial salvation is no longer a distant light on the far horizon. Only in this way will we create fear and dread in the hearts of the oppressors of the nuJus. Now is the time, Comrades, to put aside personal feelings and ambitions and to work together to destroy the Shades and to ensure we nuJus take back NoirVille.'

More than a little taken aback by this new-found enthusiasm for agreement, Jude leant forward in his chair to get a better look at Kannaim, taking a moment to re-evaluate the man. Despite the spectacles and the rather severe haircut, there was no disguising the distinctly ravenous look he had about him, a look that bespoke a man with a fiery temper. That he was also the brightest of all the Zealots – not that this was much of an accolade – made him a man to watch and Jude had been doing just that for several weeks. Kannaim might talk like a sermon-iser, but he was a man of resourcefulness and energy, and now that he had begun to preach complicity between the factions of the Zealots he had suddenly been elevated to a major danger. Time, Jude decided, for Levi Kannaim to be arrested.

'We must be careful, though,' came a calm voice from the far end of the table, this belonging to a thoughtful lawyer named Josef Yanai. Yanai *always* counselled caution, which made him decidedly unpopular within the Zealot ranks, the Zealots prefer-ring mindless mayhem to considered circumspection. 'This is not the moment for violence, Comrade Kannaim. The assassina-tion of Shaka Zulu has made the Shades skittish, seeing it as an insult to their Machismo. This is all the more worrying because there is a rumour gaining credence within NoirVille that it was we nuJus who plotted the assassination. Perhaps we should heed Rabbi Gelbfisz when he says that now is the time for restraint, a moment when nuJus should present ourselves as a quiet people who wish for peace in NoirVille and in the Demi-Monde.'

'Gelbfisz is a traitor to the nuJu cause!' sneered Kannaim.

'Traitor he might be,' answered Yanai quietly, 'but he is still the man who negotiated the MANdate which allowed two mil-lion nuJus to settle here in the JAD.'

'He sold our birthright. He sold the secret of Aqua Benedicta.'

'Not the *secret*, Comrade Kannaim,' Yanai corrected quietly, 'merely the *use* of it. How Aqua Benedicta is manufactured is only known to the nuJus, and, as Gelbfisz says, it is the wealth generated by the Aqua Benedicta that persuaded the Shades to let us remain in the JAD unmolested. By giving the Shades the ability to earn money through the trading of blood we have helped them reach the economic, social and cultural level of the nuJu community, and presumably they will be reluctant to sink back into the economic mire. Yes, I am confident, if we exercise restraint, that ultimately the material progress the Shades have enjoyed as a result of allowing us to settle in the JAD will reconcile us to the local population, that they will come to appreciate that any antagonism towards us will cost them dear.'

'Specious nonsense,' snarled Maccabeus.

This is dangerous, thought Jude. It wasn't often that Maccabeus agreed with Kannaim.

But Maccabeus wasn't finished. 'With Shaka gone and that bastard Pobedonostsev pulling Xolandi's strings, the Shades are never going to acquiesce to our remaining in the JAD. Like all the goyim, Pobedonostsev hates nuJus.'

'We can reason with him!' protested Yanai.

'Impossible. NuJuphobia is a psychic aberration of the goyim, a hereditary illness passed from one generation to the next, and as such it is incurable. You cannot reason with hate. Pobedonostsev and his kind will not rest until all nuJus have been exterminated.'

'Comrade Maccabeus is right!' spluttered an indignant Kannaim. 'Look at what the Shades were before we came: destitute, impoverished, worthless. It is through our brains and our ingenuity that they have become so wealthy. ABBA has grafted the good olive branch onto the withered tree and rejuvenated it. The JAD has been the salvation of the Shades, but are they grateful? No! Despite what we have done for them, they are incapable of seeing that it is the nuJus' superior intellect that they have to thank for their sudden prosperity.'

'W-w-well said,' stuttered Giscala. 'A th-th-thousand goyim are not worth a single nuJu's f-f-fingernail. The goyim were placed on the Demi-Monde to s-s-serve the nuJus . . . and unless they do this they have no p-p-purpose in the world. Only through nuJu leadership and ingenuity were the Sh-Sh-Shades salvaged from their economic misery and r-r-rescued from their physical and moral d-d-degeneration.'

Jude took a moment to light a cigarette, hoping that this masked the expression of disquiet he was sure was now dressing his face. He always found the hypocrisy of the hard-line Zealots amazing: their ability to criticise the Shades' nuJuphobia without being able to recognise their own contempt of the Shades was quite astonishing. But that, he supposed, was what a thousand years of being told they were ABBA's chosen did to a people: the Zealots had come to believe their own religious propaganda.

'Not so,' protested Yanai, 'the Shades are rational people. We will assimilate—'

'I spit on your "assimilation",' sneered Maccabeus. 'Assimilation is simply miscegenation by another name and this is anathema to all right-minded nuJus. If we breed with the goyim, in a generation our race will be infested with the taint of the Dark Charismatics. That is why ABBA made us His Chosen People, so that we would remain unsullied.' He slammed his fist on the table. 'I will personally assassinate any nuJu I believe to be fucking a Shade: miscegenation is an insult to ABBA. In order to survive, the nuJus need to remain racially pure. Those nuJus who commune with Shades are traitors to their race and their religion. They must suffer the consequences of their blasphemy.'

It was Yanai who answered, the man being nothing if not dogged, or more probably, Jude decided, suicidal. 'But you forget, Comrade Maccabeus, that the MANdate obliges nuJus to treat the Shades as equals.'

Maccabeus shook his head. 'The MANdate is a chimera and changes nothing. It is so replete with weasel words as to be meaningless. For the thousand years since the Confinement, we nuJus have conducted ourselves as loyal and dutiful citizens of each and every Sector we have lived in but still we remain reviled Yids and not citizens. We are dead men walking, fated to be universally hated and despised. The nuJus are cursed to stagger through life with the stumbling gait of a convict dragging his fetters.'

'But do not forget, Comrade Maccabeus,' lectured Yanai, 'that the nuJus were condemned to do this by ABBA because we used the talents He gave us to build a graven image, to build the Sphinx. We violated the Commandments and as penance we were sentenced to roam the Demi-Monde homeless and cursed until pardoned by ABBA.'

The bloody Sphinx. Nary a conversation could be had regarding the nuJus and the JAD without the Sphinx being mentioned.

Maccabeus was unabashed. 'Yes, we violated the Commandments and the Exile was our punishment but now we have served our penance and redemption is at hand. Now we have reclaimed our HomeLand . . . or at least part of it. Soon all of NoirVille will be ours and we will, once again, make it a land of milk and honey.'

Yanai sat for a moment as though dumbfounded by what Maccabeus was saying. 'This is sacrilegious, Comrade Maccabeus. Only the coming of the Messiah will signal the redemption of our people.'

'*Which* fucking Messiah?' sneered Maccabeus. 'We've had more fucking Messiahs than we know what to do with! Just last Season we had the Lady IMmanual trumpeted as the next big thing and look what a disaster she turned out to be. And then there was her fuck of a brother, who at least had the good grace to have himself blown up. No, the Messiah will arise only when battle with the goyim has been engaged.'

'Yes,' agreed Kannaim, a trifle too enthusiastically for Jude's liking, 'now is the time to attack. NoirVille crumbles. With the death of Shaka, the Shades and the Blanks have begun to squabble with each other. If we strike now and strike hard we will get our HomeLand for nothing.'

'We must not goad the Shades into war!' Yanai insisted.

Avraham Stern spoke quietly but his words had enormous impact, given that he was the only one of all the Zealots who had any real fighting experience. Stern had fought in Warsaw and had refused the chance to escape to the Great Beyond when Lady IMmanual had opened the Boundary Layer, preferring instead to continue the fight for nuJu independence in the JAD. 'This is no time for restraint. The danger to the nuJu people is greater than many of you can possibly imagine.' Stern paused for dramatic effect. 'We have a crypto placed high up in the ranks of the Him-Peril, a man we call Agent Neizvestnii . . .'

Jude struggled to stop himself laughing. He always found the Zealots' predilection for the more ridiculous *nom d'espionnage* amusing, and it was typical of their melodramatic sense of self-importance that they could call their most important informer Agent Neizvestnii . . . Agent Unknown.

'. . . who informs us that, prior to his death, Doge William ordered the secrets of the manufacture of Aqua Benedicta – discovered by that witch the Lady IMmanual – be handed over to NoirVille. I do not have to tell you the dire consequences for the nuJu people of this action. At a stroke our economic leverage with regard to NoirVille will be destroyed.'

This was stunning news, and a grim silence settled on the room.

Stern took a draw on his cigarette before continuing. 'The intelligence provided by Agent Neizvestnii tells us that the documents containing the secrets of Aqua Benedicta provided by Doge William are currently being held inside HimPeril headquarters, held but not yet opened. So, if we are to protect our HomeLand and our people, we must act now. There must be no more delay, no more debate. We must attack the headquarters of the Him-Peril and we must destroy the secrets of Aqua Benedicta.'

Yanai's objections came instantly. 'Such an attack is madness. The HimPeril are headquartered in the west wing of the Hotel du Zulu, the best-guarded building in the whole of NoirVille.' There were several nods of agreement around the room at the good sense Yanai was spouting.

'But it is an opportunity s-s-sent from A-A-ABBA,' countered Giscala. 'A-A-At a stroke we can preserve the s-s-secret of Aqua Benedicta and destroy the Him-Him-HimPeril.'

'It is an opportunity to have a great many of our revolutionary comrades captured and killed to no good effect,' observed Yanai. 'Even if we find a way of eluding HimPeril security and entering the hotel, we'll still need an enormous amount of explosive to destroy the place.'

Stern rose to his feet to address the group. 'Following private discussions with Comrades Kannaim, Maccabeus and Giscala, plans have already been drawn up for the attack on the Hotel du Zulu and the explosives needed to destroy the hotel assembled. The attack will take place at dawn tomorrow.'

'How dare you!' shouted Yanai. 'This violates the constitution of the Zealots, which says that an attack of this magnitude can only be authorised by unanimous agreement of the Executive Committee. I make a formal—'

It was then that Kannaim acted. He swivelled around on his chair and plunged his dagger deep into the chest of Josef Yanai. 'So die all traitors to nuJuism,' he screamed as he drove the knife home.

Fuck!

As Yanai's body sagged to the floor, Stern held up his hands in an appeal for calm. 'Do not be alarmed, Comrades. For several months now I have had suspicions that there was a traitor in our midst.'

Jude felt his SAE turn cold.

'Rabbi Gelbfisz has seemed a little too knowledgeable about our plans, a little too adroit at anticipating our actions, and a little too efficient in arresting our fellow Zealots. In short, Comrades, we came to the conclusion that Gelbfisz had infiltrated a crypto into our ranks!'

As surreptitiously as he was able, Jude eased the pistol he had holstered under his armpit free and prepared to fight – and run – for his life. But as Yanai's lifeless body was dragged from the room he realised that he didn't have to run, that he was one lucky boy: the Zealots had misinterpreted Yanai's complaining as treachery.

Thank you, ABBA.

'But now that the traitor is dead we must turn our attention to the task in hand: the destruction of the Hotel du Zulu,' announced Stern. 'All is ready. We have three hundred and fifty kilos of blasting gelatin, which our experts advise us, if placed correctly, will be sufficient to destroy the hotel.'

Shit! These bastards are *serious.*

'But how will we penetrate the hotel's security?'

'All will be revealed, Comrade Iscariot, all will be revealed. Suffice it to say that in eight hours we will strike a telling blow for nuJu freedom.'

Jude could feel panic rising in his breast. He felt giddy. He had to get out of the room. Any excuse would do. 'Well, if we have so little time, I would beg an hour's leave. I must make provision for my wife and children.'

Not that he had any wife and children.

Giscala shook his head dolefully. 'I am s-s-sorry, Comrade Iscariot, but no one is p-p-permitted to leave this room. It is an a-a-a-act of ferocious disorganisation we are preparing to p-p-perform, which will d-d-demonstrate that nuJus are no longer an oppressed people, c-c-crushed by bloodthirsty pogroms and judicial murder. This will be the Z-Z-Z-Zealots' emancipation into r-r-revolutionary warfare and we can't take the risk of our security being c-c-compromised. We have already found one c-c-crypto in our ranks . . .'

Jude prided himself on being able to take a hint. He decided that now was the time to stay shtum. He would slip away tomorrow en route to the Hotel du Zulu.

Istanbul, NoirVille
The Demi-Monde: 7th Day of Fall, 1005

HimPerialist theologians conjecture that Mantle-ite (the indestructible material used by the Pre-Folk to construct sewers, water pipes, Blood Banks, the Mantle and the Wonders of the World) is the solidified semen of ABBA created during the Big Wang, and its divine origin is the reason why it is invulnerable to working and to weathering. The Great Pyramid that stands in the centre of Terror Incognita is believed to have been the place where ABBA's semen was first touched by moonlight and hence is a structure of enormous Kosmological power and significance.

A Fool's Guide to HimPerialism: Selim the Grim,
Bust Your Conk Publications

Norma and her companions got to the JAD Wall just before dawn, but getting to it was one thing, getting *through* would be quite another.

She had known their luck couldn't hold, and thus far they'd been enjoying very good luck indeed. By laying a *lot* of money on a barge captain they'd managed to slip out of the ForthRight unchallenged, and with the Normalists so active in the Quartier Chaud it had been a relatively simple matter, once they'd crossed the Thames, to traverse Paris, Rome and Barcelona and on to the Nile River. Then things had become difficult. NoirVille had a febrile atmosphere, the same sort of hysterical enthusiasm she'd felt in Warsaw and Paris when those city-states had been on the brink of war. It seemed to her that the prospect of war numbed critical faculties and instead of being made fearful by the thought of them and their loved ones being killed or maimed, people were actually *excited* by it.

Nevertheless, with her, Maria and Odette wearing burqas, they had managed to sneak through the backstreets of Istanbul, finally finding themselves standing in the shadows of a doorway looking out across the square that abutted CheckPoint Bravo, the second of the three gateways to the JAD. According to Moynahan they were less than half a mile from the Portal, but as best Norma could judge, for all the chance they had of getting through the Wall they might as well have been a hundred miles from it.

'What now?' Norma asked as they watched the HimPeril patrols march backwards and forwards in front of the gate. 'We don't stand a cat in hell's chance of avoiding the HimPeril and from what I've been reading in the newspapers I've got a feeling that they aren't in the business of letting six Blanks skedaddle into the JAD.'

'What we need is something to distract the guards,' muttered Moynahan, and that's just what ABBA provided.

Today was the culmination of weeks of planning. Today would be the day when he, Avraham Stern, leader of the Independent Retributive Group of Zealots, showed the Shades – and the JAD's General Council – that nuJus were prepared to fight for their freedom. But to do that he had to get his fighters out of the JAD and into Istanbul, and that was proving to be difficult.

The General Council had ordered that no nuJu be permitted to pass through the Wall during the curfew, but as far as Stern was concerned this was just another of the stupid, cowardly regulations designed to prove to the Shades that the nuJus were content in their servility. He would ignore this decree just as he would ignore the Council's instruction that paramilitary groups like the Zealots were only to act in the protection of the JAD and not to mount offensive operations against the Shades.

Total bollocks, of course. As Stern saw it, the nuJus were in a war to the death with the Shades, a war in which the Zealots would fight hard. They would not go to their ancestors easily, not when they battled with ABBA, the Lord of Hosts, on their side. Fuck what these old codgers in the Council were saying; now was the time to take the war to the Shades. But first they had to get through Checkpoint Bravo.

Watching the CheckPoint from a window of a Zealot safe house, Stern and his gang of fighters waited silently for the guard manning the gate to change. The new guard – a Zealot sympathiser – would give them access to NoirVille. The problem for Stern was that he hated waiting. Waiting gave him the jitters. He wanted to act. Pulling his watch out of the pocket of his ankle-length dishdasha tunic, he checked the time, willing it to .run faster and cursing that the guard was late. But even as he cursed, a lantern flickered briefly in the window of the gate-house.

'That's it. That's our signal.' Reining back his eagerness, Stern stood for a moment to allow his fighters to make the final adjust-ments to their costumes. He had deliberately chosen fighters for the mission who had the same dark skin as Istanbulites, the same black-brown eyes, the same cadence of walking and the same mannerisms. But ever the diligent planner, he had had them schooled in the jive talk so popular in NoirVille and had made sure that they each wore their keffiyeh at the jaunty angle favoured by NoirVillians. And with two of his fighters he'd gone even further, employing a nuJu tailor to run up uniforms that were duplicates of those worn by the waiters working in the Hotel du Zulu.

Stepping out of the house, Stern waved to Menachem Begin and Judas Maccabeus – the two men to whom he'd given the responsibility for hauling the cart – urging them forward, the cart's heavily padded wheels shuddering silently over the cobbles, with Stern and the rest of his fighters falling into line behind. And as they scuttled towards the gatehouse Stern found himself holding his breath: breaking cover to get through the gate was one of the most dangerous parts of the entire operation, especially as each of the seven milk churns loaded on the back of the cart contained fifty kilos of blasting gelatin. One mishap and half of the JAD would be reduced to brick dust.

But ABBA was with them and the gang made it across the fifty metres of open space separating them from CheckPoint Bravo without anything going bang. As they reached the penumbra thrown by the guardhouse lanterns, the guard recognised Stern, nodded a silent greeting and then moved to unbar the gate. Edging it open, Stern peeked out at the square beyond, watching the HimPeril guards as they marched back and forth in front of the Wall, thanking ABBA that their priority was keeping nuJus from entering the JAD rather than preventing them leaving it. Once the guards had their backs to him, he used a lantern to signal to John Giscala, standing a hundred metres further along the Wall. Immediately Giscala lobbed a petrol bomb over the Wall which landed with a 'woomph' just in front of the HimPeril guards, leavening the darkness with a gout of flame. As the guards rushed to investigate, Stern waved his Zealot fighters forward, pushing them through the gates and into the dark streets of Istanbul beyond.

Now they were in enemy territory. Now their mission had begun in earnest.

There was something almost surreal about what was happening. The last thing Jude Iscariot had ever seen himself as was a terrorist, and yet here he was on his way to bomb NoirVille. He blamed Gelbfisz for the predicament he was in. The Rabbi was too clever by half and this time he had outfoxed himself. Gelbfisz had never really taken the Zealots' bombast seriously, never really believed they had the mettle to turn any of the wild schemes they'd dreamt up into reality and never really expected them to find the courage to go against the orders of the General Council.

But they had. And now fifteen Zealot fighters – or more accurately, fourteen Zealot fighters and one bloody reluctant Jude Iscariot – were on their way to bomb the Hotel du Zulu and precipitate a war in the process. It was a bloody nightmare. He had tried to feign a sudden illness to avoid participating in this madness but Stern would have none of it and had insisted that, ill or not, he join the attack.

Jude *had* to do something to stop the Stern gang and do it quickly. In less than an hour these maniacs would blow the centre of Istanbul to Hel and beyond, taking any chance of the nuJus maintaining peace with the Shades along with it. Desperately Jude tried to think of a way out of the jam he was in. What he actually needed was an injury: nothing *too* debilitating, of course, just something serious enough to persuade Stern that he was hors de combat and to leave him behind. And once he was out of Stern's sight he would raise the alarm.

Inspiration came. He edged closer to the side of the cart and then pretended to stumble, pushing his foot under the wheel as he went, judging a couple of broken toes as nothing when compared with the maintenance of peace. What he had forgotten was that the cart was laden with three hundred and fifty kilos of high explosive. Though the shock of the cart running over his foot didn't cause the explosive hidden in the milk churns to detonate, it was heavy enough to smash his foot to pulp. There was a loud crack closely followed by a loud scream and Jude began to writhe around on the ground in spasms of genuine agony.

Stern knelt down beside him, examining the foot. He shook his head. 'Not good, Jude. It's broken.'

No fucking kidding!

'Leave me here, Avraham,' Jude whimpered, 'I'm no good to you crippled. Just leave me.'

Again Stern shook his head. 'We can't do that, Jude, not now we're in enemy territory. Load him onto the cart, boys. If Jude can't walk then we'll have to carry him.'

And much to Jude's horror, that's just what they did.

Stern refused to be troubled by Iscariot's injury. During war there were always casualties, and anyway, from what he'd seen of the man, Jude Iscariot wasn't much of a fighter. Fighters didn't moan about the state of their indigestion like Iscariot had done and didn't get their feet mashed by cart wheels. If he hadn't known better he'd have thought the man didn't want to be a Zealot.

But other than this little mishap everything was going exactly to plan. The timing of the attack was, in Stern's opinion, perfect. The sun was rising in the east, and the MuscleMen had just begun calling Believers to exercise from the minaret of the HIMnasium across the square. Now was the time when the HimPeril sentries guarding the hotel would be at their most inattentive, the combination of tiredness, heat and boredom making their concentration lapse and their eyelids droop. All they would be thinking about would be going back to their barracks to have breakfast.

Although it was still early, the streets of Istanbul were already crowded and crowds made excellent cover for an operation like this one. The days were so hot that NoirVillians had decided to rise early, to get to their places of work while it was still relatively cool and to put in a few hours' graft before the heat made life unbearable. The marketplace bordering the Wall was already alive with people, no one giving Stern and his fighters so much as a glance as they joined this near-dawn throng and shuffled and pushed their way along the narrow streets in the direction of the hotel.

Mixing unnoticed with the crowd, Stern's fighters moved down a side road that bordered Taksim Square then, turning a corner, found themselves looking out on the magnificent Hotel du Zulu. This was their target, the grandest and most luxurious hotel in the whole of the Demi-Monde, the place where Noir-Ville's *haut monde* gathered to wine, dine and socialise. But the hotel's mystique wasn't just built on the excellence of its cuisine or the grandeur of its rooms, it was built on intrigue: the Him-Peril had commandeered the west wing of the hotel to serve as their headquarters. It was there – according to Agent Neizvestnii – that Doge William had had the documents detailing the secrets of Aqua Benedicta delivered. By destroying the hotel Stern would kill two birds with one stone: he would ensure the Shades were deprived of the secrets of manufacturing Aqua Benedicta and bomb the heart out of the HimPeril.

For almost a minute Stern stood in silence on the pavement across the road from the hotel, studying it, assessing it. For the first time he truly understood the enormity of the task he had set himself. The Hotel du Zulu was huge, its walls faced with red quartz that glowed in the light cast by the rising sun, this tint supposedly denoting the huge amount of blood it had cost to build such a magnificent edifice. Most importantly, though, Stern's observations confirmed that his cryptos' assessment of the hotel's defences was correct. Security around the west wing was tight, this evidenced by the guards stomping backwards and forwards in front of the wing's entrance doors, and all those arriving at the HimPeril's headquarters having their identification papers scrupulously checked by the guards. But the barbed wire, the guards, the patrols and the heat had lulled the HimPeril into thinking that tucked up so snugly in the hotel they were safe. They weren't, and by concentrating their security forces into one place they had made themselves a very tempting and a very convenient target. And anyway, there was *always* a back entrance.

He turned to his second-in-command, Menachem Begin, who was waiting impatiently by the cart. 'It's time, Menachem. May ABBA be with you.'

'What about Jude?' Begin asked, nodding towards the injured Iscariot, who was laid out on the cart.

'Put him on a chair in that café over there. We'll collect him on the way back.' He gave Jude Iscariot a beaming smile. 'You'll have a ringside seat, Jude, when the hotel goes up in smoke.'

Once Jude Iscariot had been settled in the café, Begin and Maccabeus, both of them dressed as dairymen, pushed the cart around the back of the hotel to the kitchen entrance. Stern followed them, anxious to confirm that this entrance had only the usual single soldier guarding it. It had.

Trundling the cart in front of him, Begin approached the Shade and gave him a cheery wave. 'Got a delivery of milk,' he announced, nodding towards the seven churns.

The Shade frowned. 'Yo' awful early today, man. An' where's de regular milkman?'

'He's ill,' Begin replied with a smile, which became increasingly forced as the Shade started to inspect the churns.

'Hey, man, why's de tops ob de churns padlocked?'

'To keep the detonators in place,' answered Judas Maccabeus as he rammed a blade through the guard's neck.

Even before the man had stopped twitching, Begin had hauled the cart up to the door, where he gave a loud whistle, at the sound of which the rest of the attack group materialised out of the shadows. Immediately they got busy transferring the milk churns from the back of the cart into the hotel, along the corridors that snaked into the depths of the building, and finally to the kitchens.

Then things started to go wrong. Never having worked in the catering business, Stern had thought that so early in the morning the kitchens would be deserted but instead he found them hives of activity. As he cautiously eased open the kitchen door he saw chefs labouring over griddles and steaming pans, and waiters busily laying breakfast trays for guests determined to make an early start to the day. He waved his fighters inside without being challenged, the kitchen staff so engrossed in their work that it took a few moments for them to appreciate that their kitchen had been invaded by a dozen heavily armed men. Their realisation was signalled by one of the waiters dropping a tray.

'What de fuck is yous about, man?' snarled one of the chefs but his criticisms of the waiter were silenced when he saw Stern standing in the doorway brandishing a revolver.

'We are fighters of the Independent Retributive Group of the Zealots, dedicated to fight and die for the nuJu cause,' Stern announced in a loud voice. 'Do not resist or attempt to raise the alarm or you will be silenced. We mean you no harm but are on a mission to free the JAD from the evil clutches of NoirVille.'

The chef was singularly unimpressed. 'Fuck you, man. Yous can't do dat. Yous gonna fuck up mah breakfast schedule and ah ain't never bin late—'

His objections were terminated when Judas Maccabeus whacked him over the back of the head with the butt of his rifle. There were no further objections – in fact, when Stern ordered that 'All hotel staff are to sit facing the far wall with their hands on their heads' there was a scramble to obey. As soon as all the hostages were settled, Stern signalled to his fighters to position the churns, one alongside each of the seven concrete pillars that supported the west wing of the hotel.

'Set the fuses for thirty minutes,' Stern ordered, but even as his fighters bustled to prepare the bombs, the dilemma posed by having so many hostages suddenly came home to him. If he and his fighters were to leave the hotel now, undoubtedly the kitchen staff would raise the alarm, but the alternative – killing them – was too brutal to be even considered.

He considered it anyway. But even as he stood there in the sweltering kitchen preparing to order his fighters to sacrifice the twenty or so chefs, busboys, kitchen porters and waiters in the cause of nuJu freedom, Fate took matters into its own hands.

1:18

Istanbul District: NoirVille
The Demi-Monde: 7th Day of Fall, 1005

1.6. Having built the Nine Worlds, ABBA rested, having put in what He regarded as a full shift. 1.7. And inspecting the worlds He had wrought, ABBA decided that His favourite was the Demi-Monde as it was built in accordance with the principles of Cool, so there weren't no square circles, four-sided triangles, effect coming before cause or any of that other surrealist shit you see on some of the worlds built by lesser gods. Which is just as well 'cos ABBA ain't hip to disorder and chaos: it gives Him a headache and makes His ass itch.

The HIM Book, Book of the Coming: Chapter 1, Verses 6–7

Left by himself in the café with just a cup of coffee for company, Jude Iscariot's brain whirled, trying to think of what would be the best thing to do. Somehow he had to stop the attack and unfortunately the only way he could see of doing that was to betray the Zealots to the Shades. Not an enticing proposition as it would be an act that would for ever brand him as a traitor to the nuJu cause, but Gelbfisz had been *very* insistent that Stern's fighters be prevented from provoking the Shades. Nothing was to be done to goad the Shades into attacking the JAD, and as goads went, blowing up the Hotel du Zulu was akin to sticking an assegai right up HimPeror Xolandi's arse.

Two cups of coffee in, Jude decided on a course of action. He scribbled a note on a page of his notebook, pulled a ten-lira note out of his pocket and then gestured to one of the waiters. 'If you take this to the nearest HimPeril guard and bring him to the café I'll give you another ten.'

The waiter gawped. Ten lira was a fortune, so, after checking that the banknote was genuine, he rushed off in the direction of the HimPeril guardhouse. A breathless HimPeril agent arrived a couple of minutes later.

'You de wun who sent dis note, man?' panted HimPeril Agent Solomon Edu as he bustled his way into the café. He wasn't a happy man. He was an agent who did what he was told by his sergeant and tried to keep his nose clean, having realised a long time ago that he wasn't built for dealing with off-beat action, which didn't come any off-beatier than the note the waiter had delivered. But as he'd been the only agent in the guardhouse when the waiter had arrived, he'd had no alternative but to demonstrate initiative. The trouble he had was that his sergeant wasn't a great believer in initiative; he put more store in his agents simply following fucking orders. Unfortunately for Edu, there hadn't been anyone around to issue any orders, fucking or otherwise.

In response to Edu's question the scumbag sitting at the table gave an enthusiastic nod. 'Yes. And right now nuJu Zealots are mounting a bomb attack on the Hotel du Zulu!'

Edu stroked his chin. This was serious shit . . . serious if this item could be believed. He glanced over to the hotel, which seemed, in his opinion, to be mighty quiet for a place under attack by terrorists. Edu had the troubling feeling that he was being set up. And anyway this note-writing item looked too much like a nuJu for Edu's liking and everyone knew that nuJus were tricky fuckers.

'Bullshit, man. Ways ah figure it dere ain't nowun putting no bombs in dat dere hotel.' Edu unfolded the scruffy piece of paper and studied it. 'Says in dis note ob yous dat "Dissident agents of the nuJu Independent Retributive Group are attempting to bomb the Hotel du Zulu. Every effort must be made to evacuate the hotel immediately,"' He eyed the nuJu warily. 'Ah'm kinda thinking yous blowing me shit. Yeah, ah'm guessing dat you's wun ov dese agent provocative items sent to fuck up de smoove running of NoirVille.'

'No, I'm not,' the nuJu protested. 'Believe me, there are Zealots trying to blow up the hotel. It's vital that the hotel's evacuated. Hundreds of lives depend on it.'

As he stood there towering over the seated nuJu, Edu had to admit that the cat *sounded* convincing but in his experience the only reliable way of eliciting whether someone was *really* telling the truth was through the inflicting of pain. With this objective in mind he grabbed the nuJu by the shoulder and made to drag him to his feet. To Edu's amazement the bastard began screaming even before he'd been thumped, loudly complaining that he had a broken foot. From Edu's point of view, this was interrogational manna from heaven.

Edu pulled out the steel baton he had holstered on his belt and whacked it hard against the nuJu's boot. The one thing this proved was that the nuJu sure as Hel wasn't lying about his foot. He screamed, crashed from his chair and then rolled around in agony on the floor of the café.

'Hot diggity. Well now, sweet cakes, ah's gonna ask yous just one more time: is yous jingling my jangles wid all this terrorist shit yous laying on me?' And just to make sure the nuJu realised he was in earnest, he gave the foot another whack.

'Yes, yes,' wailed the man, 'I'm telling the truth. But for pity's sake don't hit me again.'

'You knows wot, man, if ah gets to thinking yous mouthing make-believe, ah'm gonna work on dat foot ob yours until it's blown up bigger dan a balloon. But right now yous gonna have to come wid me to de guardhouse so's we can do some real heavy-duty questioning.'

'I can't walk, you fucking numbskull,' snarled the nuJu, tears of pain trickling from his eyes. 'And all the time you're wasting here the sooner the bombs come to exploding.'

There was something in the nuJu's tone that gave Edu pause, but he smacked his baton hard on the boot just to make sure. 'Yo' fo' real, man?'

It took a moment for the nuJu to stop screaming and to become calm enough to answer. Dealing with the pain radiating out from his busted foot obviously put a crimp on his conversational abilities. 'Yeah,' he gasped finally. 'Please . . . I beg you . . . get everybody out of the hotel. Even as we speak Zealots are planting three hundred and fifty kilos of blasting gelatin in the hotel's kitchen. I've been ordered by the JAD's General Council to warn you so that the people in the hotel can be saved.'

For a moment Edu didn't quite know what to do, but finally he reached a decision. He pulled a pair of handcuffs from out of his jacket pocket and shackled the nuJu to the table. 'Now yo's just hang tight while ah goes' and sees iffn dis story ob yours is more dan just a pile ob crap. But remember, man, iffn dis is a wild goose chase, ah's gonna be taking retribution out ob yo' sorry nuJu ass an' yo' even sorrier foot.'

Realising that his sergeant wasn't a great lover of having his pecker pulled, Solomon Edu decided to go check out the nuJu's story personally before raising the alarm, but being possessed of a cautious temperament, he made sure he had his Colt in his hand when he approached the hotel's kitchen entrance. That there wasn't any guard on duty should have tipped him the wink that things were not fine and dandy in Fairyland, but he decided to push his luck a little further and sneak a peek into the kitchens proper.

At first glance there didn't seem to be anything much amiss, just a couple of busboys helping to move some milk churns around, but this impression of normality didn't last long. As soon as he was spotted lurking in the doorway, the busboys hauled out pistols and began blasting away at him, bullets whining around his head, pinging off walls and saucepans. Outnumbered and outgunned, Solomon decided to retreat and to retreat at pace, so he charged back down the corridor, screaming and firing his Colt in the general direction of the bad guys as he went. Only by a miracle did he emerge unscathed into daylight.

Now he got lucky. Across the hotel's backyard he saw his sergeant and the rest of his platoon returning from breakfast. 'Sergeant,' he yelled, 'we's bin attacked by nuJu gangsters! Dey's in de kitchen making wiv de—'

Now he got unlucky. He never got to finish the sentence. He took a shot in the back which whirled him around and sent him tumbling to the cobbles. Even as he lay there he saw a nuJu cock his pistol ready to take a second and, by the look of it, a much more accurate shot. Fortunately, the nuJu bastard was deterred by a fusillade of firing coming from the half a dozen black-uniformed HimPeril racing to Edu's rescue.

Stern tried to maintain his composure, though with a firefight going on only a couple of metres away and bullets whizzing around his head he was finding it bloody difficult to remain calm, cool and collected. He had to find a way to escape.

In order to obviate the risk of the Shades being able to defuse the bombs, he had equipped each of the churns with an anti-tamper fuse, a spring-loaded detonator positioned underneath the churn such that should it be moved, the fifty kilos of gelatin it contained would instantly go bang.

One of the grenades thrown by the HimPeril bounced past him into the kitchen, where it exploded, causing the churn nearest the corridor to tip.

Jude Iscariot's life was saved by the steamer that came to a halt on the road outside the café . . . or more accurately, Jude Iscariot's life was extended by twenty seconds by the steamer that came to a halt on the road outside the café.

He had been sitting there desperately trying to wriggle his hand out of the handcuff's embrace when the milk churns exploded. The first he knew of it was when the café's floor started to shake and the glasses and plates on the tables began to dance and tinkle. Before he quite knew what was happening he was thrown from his chair, his arm, handcuffed to the table, taking a tremendous wrench in the process. He was still on his knees when the blast gushed out of the hotel's ground floor, surged across the road and enveloped the café. Being in the lee of the heavy steamer saved him from the explosion's initial onslaught but for the majority of the pedestrians walking along the pavement and the poor sods seated enjoying an early morning coffee in the café there was no such protection. As though slapped by the hand of some invisible giant, men, women and children were hurled backwards – somersaulting, spinning, tumbling as they went – to be smashed into walls or shoved through windows. And then, barely an instant later, came the reverse pressure wave which ripped off clothes, pulled eyes out of sockets and sent shattered glass flying around like shrapnel. Stunned, Jude knelt amongst the debris, blinded and choked by smoke and pulverised concrete, his skin blistered by the heat and his ears deafened by the screams of the dying.

He blinked his eyes clear of dust then looked about him at the wreckage of what, just a few moments before, had been a bustling café. Bodies of patrons and waiters were heaped against the bar, the faces of the dead and the dying caked with dust and smeared with streaks of liquidised SAE, their limbs bent and twisted in unnatural angles. He retched, choked by the sweet stench of fried humanity. But even as he was spitting out the bile in his mouth he heard a loud creaking noise and saw the frontage of the building behind the café quaver. Then it collapsed, flattening him under fifty tons of bricks and concrete as it smashed to the ground.

ABBA must have heard Moynahan's plea for a diversion. Suddenly the side of the hotel across the square from where they were standing exploded, the blast so big that all of them were blown off their feet. By some miracle they avoided being trepanned by flying debris, but even so it took a moment for them to recover their senses. The square was filled with a thick, choking mist made from brick dust and pounded plaster and everywhere Norma looked there were people staggering around screaming and wailing. Then whistles began to blow and soldiers raced towards the stricken building.

'Now's our chance,' shouted Moynahan as he hauled Norma to her feet. 'We gotta get moving while everything's FUBAR.' And without waiting for a reply he began to drag her across the square in the direction of Checkpoint Bravo with the rest of their group stumbling in their wake.

Part Three:
Battle For The Jad

Would PINC have prevented 12/12?
Pg20

Who are Christ's Crusaders and why do they hate us?
Pg32

The new **PARADIGM**

Polly

hand-held computer

Edinburgh nuked! Terror attack in the heart of the Empire!

The British Empire was left stunned and shaken by yesterday's vicious and cowardly attack perpetrated by members of Christ's Crusaders – the lunatic fundamentalist Christian terror organisation spawned in America and led by a renegade preacher, Bill Martin – who detonated a 'dirty-bomb', a low yield nuclear device, in Edinburgh. Initial estimates put the death toll at 150,000 with a similar number injured.

It is believed that the attack was carried out by the terrorists in order to fulfil the seventh prophecy made by the so-called Last Prophet, Frank Kenton, which says: 'Believers will be mighty angry with Satan, folks, and some Crusaders will forget the Seventh nuCommandment that you shall not kill unlawfully and take it into their own hands to punish the AntiChrist.

They will destroy the city on the rock but by doing so they will cause much tumult in the world.' In the deranged thinking of the Crusaders the AntiChrist is ABBA, the quantum computer operated by ParaDigm CyberResearch.

Prime Minister Johnson, speaking from Downing Street, condemned the attack and pledged 'The British Empire has been targeted for attack because it is the beacon of freedom and opportunity in the world, but no one will keep that light from shining. Make no mistake, we will hunt down the perpetrators of this dastardly deed and punish them. But we must also do everything in our power to prevent such an atrocity ever happening again and to ensure that the citizens of the Empire can go about their lives safe and secure'.

Las Vegas
The Real World: 9 February 2019

1.8. When ABBA looked about Him, He dug that there wasn't anyone else to make with the chin music, so, not wanting to be on His lonesome as soloing all the time is most UnCool, He commanded Yggdrasil to spill its seed on the ground and from this seed grew the first Man, Adam, who ABBA created in His own image. 1.9. And ABBA granted Adam dominion over the Demi-Monde and all the creatures that lived in it, though He did tell him not to touch the fruit of Yggdrasil as that would be unCool and would get right up His ass. 1.10. So it came to pass that one day Adam called up to ABBA and said, 'Yo there, ABBA, do you not dig that there is, like, nothing to do here in the Demi-Monde 'cept meditate, jerk off and get it on with the animals, some of whom, I gotta tell you, are starting to look a mite tasty? You gotta bust me a break, ABBA, and make with the company, 'cos I'm going out of my skull down here.'

The HIM Book, Book of the Coming: Chapter 1, Verses 8–10

Aaliz stood on the half-built stage gazing out on the vastness that was ParaDigm's Las Vegas SuperBowl, the venue that would host the Gathering. Now, after almost three months of day-and-night work, the enormous auditorium was fast approaching completion. The huge banks of seating rose like cliffs around the semicircular arena; the mega-sized pyramid – a replica of the Great Pyramid standing in Terror Incognita – was almost finished; and the towering Flexi-Plexi screens that would carry the 3D images of what was happening on the stage to the six-million-strong audience were sprouting skywards. The SuperBowl was an awe-inspiring piece of theatrical engineering, a testament to the vision of the architects, the skill and effort of the contractors and workmen, and the amount of money that Para-Digm had thrown at the project.

What would it be like, Aaliz wondered, to stand on this stage and look out over the arena when it was packed with so many millions of people? What would it be like to be the focus of so much adulation? What would it be like to know that she was the one who would signal the rekindling of the Aryan super-race, the PreFolk? The thought of possessing so much power was intoxicating and for a moment she felt light-headed.

'If you would say something into the microphone, Miss Williams, so that we can check levels. Please use your normal speaking voice.'

The instruction that cut through her daydreaming came from the engineer responsible for the installation of the SuperBowl's audio-visual equipment. Automatically Aaliz stepped up to the microphone. 'Good morning,' she breathed and then rocked back, astonished by the volume of her amplified voice as the two words boomed out over the desert, then reverberated back to her, echoed by the steep sides of the arena. It took a moment for her to recover her equanimity: even now, just six months into her Real World sojourn, she was still surprised by the awesome power of Real World technology. It took an encouraging nod from the engineer to persuade Aaliz to speak again. 'I am Norma Williams, leader of the Fun/Funs, and I'd like to thank all of you working on this project for your efforts on my behalf.'

That provoked a cheer from the workmen toiling away under

the hot sun. Aaliz waved at them: they might be drones and of little worth but every good leader knew that occasionally the peasants needed to be encouraged rather than driven. The driving – and the culling – would come later . . . after the Gathering.

'Very good, Miss Williams,' commented the engineer. 'And don't worry about the echo. When the arena is full the bodies will absorb the sound. Now we'll just check camera connectivity.'

Immediately five cameraBots swooped down from the gantry above the stage and began to hover around Aaliz. The Flexi-Plexi at the very rim of the arena fired up, and though it was two miles distant, its sheer size – it must have been a hundred yards tall and fifty wide – gave Aaliz an excellent view of what she looked like on stage. And she thought she looked pretty good: the short skirt she was wearing showed off her excellent legs and her tight top announced that she wasn't wearing a bra. She gave a swish of her long blonde hair which was rewarded by cheers and whistles from the workmen. It seemed that as far as they were concerned, if Norma Williams was an emissary from God, then God had great taste in women.

'It is amazing how susceptible Fragile males are to the sexual wiles of women,' came an observation from the side of the stage. 'It would appear that they follow the inclinations of their loins rather than their logic, which presumably accounts for the Fragiles' quite astonishing fecundity.'

Aaliz turned to see Professor Septimus Bole striding across the stage. Despite it being such a ferociously hot day, the Professor was clad, as always, in his trademark black serge suit, his only acknowledgement of the intensity of the desert sunshine being the wide-brimmed hat that shrouded his face in shadows and the larger than usual pair of shaded spectacles.

'Professor Bole! This is a surprise. I thought you were in the Demi-Monde.' All this was broadcast throughout the arena.

Bole scowled and made a chopping motion across his throat, signalling to the engineer that the microphones be switched off.

'You may be unfamiliar with Real World technology, Miss Williams, but that is a poor excuse when such carelessness could jeopardise the success of all we have worked for.'

Aaliz felt her cheeks redden, a product of anger with herself for making such a mistake and with the Professor for having the temerity to rebuke her. 'I understand, Professor, but I would thank you for not taking that tone with me.'

Bole stared at her for a few silent moments and then gave a bleak smile. 'Very well,' he said and then took her by the arm and led her out of earshot of the technicians busily installing the mass of stage equipment. 'I have just returned from the Demi-Monde, where I consulted with your father. He is most perturbed by the unscheduled appearance Norma Williams made at the Victory in the Coven celebrations.'

'I find it quite outrageous that Norma Williams should have the gall to pose as me!' Aaliz spluttered. 'Why has nothing been done to stop her?'

'I think quite a lot *has* been done, unfortunately none of it has had the desired result.'

'But surely the Checkya must be able to find and arrest one girl.'

'She's proven to be very elusive and, of course, she enjoys the support and succour of the Normalists. It would appear that Norma Williams has abilities as an organiser quite the equal of yours, which is hardly surprising given that your genetic make-up is identical.'

'But . . . but . . . this is terrible.'

'Indeed. Your father has made the elimination of Norma Williams the Checkya's Number One priority but, as I say, she is something of a will-o'-the-wisp.' Bole stepped further back into the shadows and used a handkerchief to mop his brow. 'By bringing the specious cant and disaffection of Normalism to the very heart of the ForthRight she undermines all the work we have done in inculcating the people with an unshakeable belief in the tenets of UnFunDaMentalism. There is talk that your father will be unable to persuade believers to participate in the Ceremony of Purification.'

'But then—'

'Then we will fail and all our efforts here, in the Real World, will have been for nothing.'

'Then what's to be done?'

'Checkya intelligence – a contradiction in terms, but no matter – would have us believe that Norma Williams has fled the ForthRight with the intention of seeking refuge in the JAD, where the last remaining Portal connecting the Demi-Monde to the Real World is situated. It is obvious that she is intent on returning to the Real World. This is good news. My agents control the Portal and she will be dealt with immediately she presents there.'

'Then why are you telling me this? If you are so confident of silencing the girl, why concern me?'

'We must recognise the damage that Williams has caused in the Demi-Monde and move to set it aright. My belief is that having Aaliz Heydrich – the *real* Aaliz Heydrich – make a series of appearances in the ForthRight where she denies her Normalist tendencies and reaffirms her loyalty to her father would do much to repair this damage.'

The penny dropped. 'You want me to go back to the Demi-Monde!'

'Yes.'

Aaliz blinked. Going back to the Demi-Monde did not appeal. She liked it here in the Real World. 'But . . . but . . . is such a thing possible?'

'Of course. You have a body in the Demi-Monde which is being cared for by nuns at Wewelsburg Castle.'

'But what of my work here?'

'Most of the appearances to be made by Norma Williams between now and the Gathering are scheduled to take place on the Polly, so those are easy enough to fabricate – we have, after all, a perfectly usable PollyMorph of you. We'll simply use an actress who is similar to you in looks and build and then amend her appearance digitally. Once her voice has been adjusted to match yours she will be indistinguishable from the real Norma Williams . . . or should I better say, the *un*real Norma Williams!'

'But I will be returned to the Real World in time for the Gathering, won't I?'

'Oh, yes. We have eighty days, ample time for you to do what you must do in the Demi-Monde.'

'Then I suppose the quicker I go, the quicker I can return.'

Aaliz found herself being driven to the Bole Institute for the Advancement of History in Los Angeles, a grand and imposing mansion set in large and precisely manicured grounds, the whole estate protected by high walls and swarms of surveillanceBots. The reason for the intensity of security became apparent when Aaliz was ushered into a large windowless room situated in the very centre of the mansion.

'Good afternoon, Miss Aaliz. I am Metztil, Guardian of Professor Bole.'

Aaliz felt her mouth drop open. The girl who greeted her was, unless she was very much mistaken, a Grigori . . . a vampyre. She was so tall that the top of her head almost brushed the ceiling but it wasn't just her height that made this Metztil so remarkable, rather that she had a muscularity to match her size, a muscularity presented in the most obvious manner by the dress she was wearing. It was a gown modelled on Grecian lines and made from a dusky-blue silk that moulded itself to her body, simultaneously displaying her strength and power *and* revealing the tattoos of snakes rendered in red ink that coiled and twisted around the alabaster-white skin of her arms.

The girl moved towards Aaliz, all glinting eyes – cat's eyes – and steely smile, her bare feet silent on the carpeted floor. Nearer now, Aaliz could see just how pale the girl's skin was: it was luminescent, almost albino. Metztil held out a hand to Aaliz, who had to force herself to take it, reluctant – afraid – to place her hand in that bone-crushing paw.

'I am pleased to meet with you, Miss Aaliz,' the Grigori intoned as she shook the hand. 'I am honoured to be of service to the one who is doing so much to ensure the triumph of the Grigori.'

'The pleasure is entirely mine,' Aaliz replied automatically as she toyed with the phrase 'the triumph of the Grigori'. Bole had never mentioned his association with them.

'If you would come with me.' Without waiting for a reply Metztil led Aaliz towards the staircase.

As she climbed the stairs, Aaliz struggled with the realisation that Bole was in league with the Grigori. But now, she decided, wasn't the time to worry about this. She was shown into a small room, equipped with a black couch and an array of electrical equipment. 'This is ParaDigm's private Transfer Suite. If you would undress and shower in the cubicle next door . . .'

Aaliz did as she was asked and even managed to contain her astonishment when the Grigori proceeded to shave her body – *all* her body – and then to equip her with what she called a TIS, which enveloped her body in a thin layer of shiny black material. 'If you would lie on the couch, Miss Aaliz, then I will complete the Transfer Procedure.'

Immediately she woke Aaliz realised that there was one other thing that Bole had failed to tell her: the nuns caring for her body in the Demi-Monde didn't have access to the technology available in the Real World. The result was that the state her body was in when she reclaimed it was less than perfect. The nuns had done their best: her body had been turned hourly to prevent bedsores; all her limbs had been regularly flexed to obviate the contraction of tendons and the weakening of her muscles; and her intravenous feeding had been expertly supervised. But the fact remained that the body had not been used in over half a year and the deterioration was noticeable.

The upshot was that when Aaliz woke in Wewelsburg Castle all she could feel was a nagging collection of aches and pains that seemed to be coming from every part of her body. But worst of all, she felt so very weak. Having always prided herself on her athleticism, it came as a shock to discover that now she couldn't sit up unaided, that even raising an arm required a conscious effort and her attempts to stand were defeated by her legs buckling under her.

'It will take time, Lady Aaliz,' said the doctor attending her. 'You have been in a coma for six months and therefore you must reacquaint your body and your muscles with the effort of working. I have a programme of exercises, and this, coupled with a healthy diet, will see you back to normal in a matter of months.'

'Months! I do not have months, you fool.' Aaliz tried to stand by clinging on to the neck of one of the nuns. 'You have one week. In one week I must be capable of walking unaided onto a stage.'

'One week, Lady Aaliz? But that is impossible—'

'It is not impossible,' said Aaliz's father, Great Leader Heydrich, as he walked into the room. 'It is of vital importance to me, to UnFunDaMentalism and to the ForthRight that my daughter is able to begin her public duties with the minimum of delay.' Heydrich's close-set eyes seemed to bore into the doctor. 'You do understand, don't you, Doctor?'

The doctor bowed his head. 'Yes, Great Leader.'

1:20

The JAD, NoirVille
7th Day of Fall, 1005

The verse in the HIM Book which states that Man was created in ABBA's image has stimulated much theological debate regarding the ideal form and shape of Man. It is a vital part of the HimPerialist catechism that if Man is to aspire to be like ABBA then Man must emulate ABBA's physical perfection. It is believed that this 'perfection' may only be achieved by strenuous exercise, and hence Body Forming has now been incorporated into the Rites of the Church of HimPerialism. Men are encouraged to spend at least one hour per day in physical worship of ABBA, being called to exercise in the HIMnasium by MuscleMen.

A Fool's Guide to HimPerialism: Selim the Grim, Bust Your
Conk Publications

They made it. Sure, they'd gotten real lucky that their attempt to cross into the JAD had coincided with the explosion in the hotel, but the result was that, just seven days after her performance at the Crystal Palace, Norma found herself standing outside the Portal. She could hardly believe it; after nine months of struggling and striving she had arrived at her goal. Escape beckoned. But as she stood on the pavement studying the Portal, she had to admit to being seriously underwhelmed.

She'd always imagined that the Portal would be housed some-where a little more upmarket and high-tech than in a run-down warehouse at the end of a narrow street flanked by squalid tene-ments in a backwater part of the JAD. But then, when she thought about it, it made sense. The last thing the US Army would want was to stand out, to be noticed. And if concealment was their objective, they had certainly succeeded.

'Okay,' said Moynahan, pointing to the side door of the ware-house, the one signed 'Private: Employees Only', 'I'll go first. The Captain's a mite skittish and six people hammering on the door at dawn might make him a little trigger-happy.'

With that he bounced up the steps and began working the brass knocker. It took almost a minute before Moynahan's hammering was answered.

'Who's making all that racket?' came a voice from behind the door.

'It's me, Sergeant . . . Moynahan.'

'Shit!'

There was the sound of a key being turned in a lock and then the door eased open to reveal a big man cradling a very pur-poseful-looking machine pistol in his arms. 'Fuck me gently, Moynahan, I never thought I'd see you again.' He looked over Moynahan's shoulder at the gang crowded on the doorstep. 'And it looks like you brought half the fucking Rookeries back with you.' The sergeant shook his head even as he waved them all inside. 'Gotta tell you, Moynahan, the Captain ain't gonna be overpleased with this. You know what standing orders say about bringing Dupes to the Portal.'

'Fuck standing orders, Sarge,' interrupted Moynahan as he shouldered his way into the hallway. 'These guys and gals are the ones who made it possible for me to find Norma Williams.'

Knowing a cue when she heard one, Norma pulled back the

veil covering her face and gave the sergeant a broad smile. He did a double take.

'Jeez, Moynahan, you found Norma Williams!' The sergeant thrust out a hand. 'Welcome to the Portal, Miss Williams. I'm Senior Sergeant Sol Edelstein and I'm mighty glad to see you safe and well. Gotta say I had a real problem recognising you in that burqa. You'd better come through and meet the captain. He's gonna have trouble believing this.'

Edelstein was right: Captain Simmons had *big* trouble believing it. Sitting at his desk listening to Moynahan relate his story of how he had found Norma and how they had escaped the Rookeries, all he seemed able to do was shake his head and whisper the occasional 'amazing'. He kept sneaking nervous glances at Norma as though he was having difficulty accepting that it was the President's daughter standing in his office.

If she'd been asked, Norma would have admitted to not liking the captain, but then she'd always had problems relating to people she found physically unattractive and with his plump lips, his cloudy brown eyes and his greyish-yellow complexion the captain was the epitome of unattractive. Worse, by her reckoning, Simmons was a guy who kept his cards real close to his pigeon chest. She wouldn't trust him an inch.

But unattractive and creepy though he was, Norma had to admit that once he had been apprised of the situation and her bona fides had been biometrically verified, the man became all business. He insisted that the Portal's medic give her the once-over and then ordered Sergeant Edelstein to make sure his other 'guests' were served breakfast.

'Let's get everyone fed and watered,' he announced. 'And while you're all doing that, I'll contact INTRADOC HQ back in the Real World and see how they want to play this.'

He gave Norma a smile. Maybe, she decided, she'd been wrong about him.

'That's great, Captain, but before you do that I think you should be aware of a wrinkle in your plan, a wrinkle called Aaliz Heydrich . . .'

Thirty minutes later Captain Simmons appeared in the Portal's Rec Room to make an announcement to the assembled platoon. 'As you'll all know by now, Moynahan has managed to bring Miss Norma Williams to the Portal.' There was a round of applause and a few catcalls, which Moynahan acknowledged with a non-chalant wave of his hand. 'I've spoken to General Zieliéski, the officer commanding the Demi-Monde project, and naturally he's delighted that Miss Williams has made it to the Portal. And now she's here, he's determined that our mission is over.' More cheers. 'Yes, I'm as glad as you are to be going home. My orders are that I power up the Transfer Unit and accompany Miss Williams back to the Real World with the rest of you following on a two-by-two basis. We'll all be back home for lunch!'

When the whooping and hollering had quietened down, Norma raised her hand. 'I don't quite understand, Captain. Surely for me to return to the Real World I must have a body to return to, and as I understand it, my body is currently being used by Aaliz Heydrich.'

'Not any more, Miss Williams. Following my conversation with the general, I've received an eyeMail confirming the arrest of Miss Heydrich. Even as we speak, she's being transported to INTRADOC headquarters, where she will be transferred back to the Demi-Monde. It'll take the Portal's Transfer Unit four hours to get up to full power and by then your body will be waiting for you unharmed and unoccupied in Fort Jackson.'

Norma frowned. 'Are you sure, Captain?' It all sounded much too pat, much too easy. 'But what about Septimus Bole? He must be in cahoots with Aaliz, after all it was him who got me involved in the Demi-Monde in the first place.'

'Don't worry, Miss Williams. Septimus Bole has also been arrested. As I say, everything is set fair for you to return to the Real World.'

The captain seemed so confident that Norma was persuaded to relax. Maybe getting home *was* going to be this easy, maybe after nine months of running, dodging and being shot at it would be just a matter of stepping into the Portal's Transfer Room and waving goodbye to the Demi-Monde. But the peculiar thing was that now she was on the brink of leaving the place, she felt hugely sad. Leaving people like Burlesque and Odette would be a real wrench and the thought that she would never have a chance of saying goodbye to Vanka Maykov was a heart-stopper. And then there was Percy Shelley . . .

Odette could tell by the way he was gnawing at his fingernails that Burlesque wasn't happy, but then, she supposed, it wasn't every day that you got to commune with Daemons. Not, of course, that they looked very much different from Demi-Mondi-ans – just a little bit smaller and paler – but they *were* Daemons and their lair was every bit as Daemonic as the writers of horror stories had speculated it would be. Inside the warehouse the Portal was chillingly functional: the walls were painted a drab cream colour, the floor covering was cold and hard, and the fur-niture was very utilitarian.

But it did, at least, seem very sturdy. Moynahan had given them what he called 'the ten-cent tour' and from what Odette had seen the Portal had been built to take an awful lot of punish-ment. The armoury, the Control Room and the mysterious place called the Transfer Room were all below ground level, which was remarkable given that she had always been taught that the Demi-Monde's Mantle-ite crust precluded digging deeper than five feet. It seemed that some of the certainties pertaining to the Demi-Monde didn't apply in the Portal.

Burlesque gave a burp. 'Do you fink they've got any Solution in 'ere?' he asked, sotto voce, as they sat drinking coffee in what the Daemons called the Rec Room. ''Cos iffn they 'aven't . . .' He trailed off, not feeling it necessary to elucidate that after two days without blood Demi-Mondians were apt to get a little antsy.

'I 'ave spoken with Norma, *mon chéri*, and she 'as spoken to Monsieur Edelstein, 'oo informs 'er that these Daemons 'ave the supplies most plentiful of the blood.'

'Good, 'cos I've got to tell yous, Oddie, iffn I 'ave to drink any more ov this muck they call coffee, me digestives ain't never gonna be the same again. Turning me over sumfink chronic it is.' He leant forward so that his mouth was only an inch or so from Odette's ear. 'So, waddya fink ov these Daemons? Rum lot, ain't they?'

Odette took a quick look around at the Daemons eating at nearby tables. They did indeed seem a rum lot. 'I think eet is of the greatest fortune that they are leaving the Demi-Monde, Burlesque, as I am of the greatest doubts that they would be able to offer the protection most effective to Norma. Although Moynahan and Edelstein are well made, the rest . . . *pahhh* . . . they are just *mauviettes* . . . 'ow do you say? . . . wimps.'

'Yeah, 'specially that captain cove. Wouldn't trust 'im as far as I could throw 'im.'

'*Mais oui.* You 'ave, as always, Burlesque, the nail struck on the 'ead: 'ee is a man mostly suspicious. Therefore I think it is of the greatest urgency that we remain 'ere in the Portal until we are mostly certain that Norma 'as been returned to 'er world.'

Norma went in search of Shelley. She had to speak with him before she left the Demi-Monde. She had to know why he had done what he'd done. When she eventually tracked him down he was sitting alone on a couch in a corner of the Portal's canteen, communing with a cup of coffee. Gathering up a sandwich, she sat herself down beside him and gave him a bleak smile.

Shelley looked up and returned the smile. 'Ah, my sweet Norma. Love wepulsed but now weturneth.'

Norma couldn't stop herself. 'Why did you betray me, Percy?' she blurted out.

'I betwayed you, sweet Norma, because I was betwayed by my own ambition. You know I am a pale student of the unhallowed arts, so you might understand that when I was appwoached by Cwowley with pwomises of unseemly power and knowledge of the esotewic I listened hard. He whispered that he would initiate me into the Ordo Templi Awyanis, make me pwivy to the stwange secwets that would allow me to discover my Twue Self and discard the bourgeois twappings of the material world. And the pwice Cwowley demanded for this subtle education was, so I believed, a nothing: I was to make you love me.'

Norma brushed a tear from her eye. 'And in that, Percy Shelley, you certainly succeeded.'

'I am so sowwy, Norma, for the hurt I caused you. But then I was not the only one seduced by Cwowley's mystique. If I wemember awight, the weason you came to the Demi-Monde was to search for the man and his magic.'

What Shelley said was true: it had been Norma's obsession with Crowley that had persuaded her to enter the Demi-Monde. It was faintly embarrassing for her to remember that her three dissertations at the Institute for the Advancement of History had been entitled 'Aleister Crowley and His Influence on Twentieth-Century Western Morality', 'Occultism and Its Role in the Sexual Liberation of Women' and 'Philosophical Libertarianism as a Key to Sexual Enlightenment'. Now, of course, she knew that Crowley was a fraud and a braggart, and that wading through the depths of Crowleyan philosophy would barely get her feet damp, but then . . .

Then she had just been a naïf, a goth with a penchant for the occult, and that had been the carrot Aaliz Heydrich – aided and abetted by Septimus Bole – had dangled in front of her, enticing her to play a seemingly innocuous computer game called *The Demi-Monde*. Enter the Demi-Monde, they had said, and you can meet with Crowley face to face. And once she was in the Demi-Monde, there had been no going back . . . *literally*, no going back.

'And in my defence,' Shelley continued, 'I was told you were a flibbertigibbet, a girl who had as careless an attitude to womance and love as my own. Of course this was wong, and in serving Cwowley's evil my spiwit was twice ensnared: once by his villainy and once by my love for you.'

'Oh, come on, Percy, you never really loved me.'

'I will admit that when I first met you I believed myself immune to Cupid's darts and to the blandishments of Venus. Until I met you, deawest Norma, I held the opinion that love acts upon the soul pwecisely as a nutmeg gwater acts upon a nutmeg. But now . . .' He took Norma's hand in his and squeezed. 'I am lost in a labywinth of wegwet, in a maze of distempered dweams. I love you, Norma. Thou art mine and I am thine, till the sinking of the world. I am thine and thou art mine, till in wuined death is hurled.'

Looking into Shelley's doleful eyes, Norma tried to deny what he was saying, tried to deny what she felt. She wanted so very much to believe that Shelley loved her, but still the thought nagged that he had made her a victim.

But had she *really* been a victim?

Shelley might have been trying to subvert her, to lead her down the path of total unrighteousness, to introduce her to the most dissolute of philosophies but she had been a very *willing* victim. And in retrospect, her time in the Demi-Monde had remade her into something beyond her imagining. She had grown up in the Demi-Monde.

Shelley brought her out of her reverie. 'And again, in my defence, Norma, once I came to understand Cwowley's duplicity I warned Mata Hawi you were in danger. I would have come to your wescue myself but I was held by that devil Cwowley. I only escaped by the skin of my teeth and by then it was too late to save you. But Cwowley knew that I had twied to pwotect you, which is why I have been a fugitive for these long months. He is a vengeful man.'

This was new to Norma. She hadn't realised that Percy had tried to come to her aid, and it was a comforting feeling to know the man she loved had been willing to risk everything to save her.

Shelley nodded across to Burlesque, who sat chatting to Odette in the far corner of the room. 'You have forgiven Burlesque Bandstand for his perfidy, is it too much to ask you to forgive mine?'

She leant forward and kissed Shelley. 'I forgive you, Percy. Without your betrayal I would have returned to the Real World and if I'd done that I would never have found the strength inside myself to create the Normalist movement.'

'You are very kind, Norma, and I will never give you any weason to wepent your forgiveness. And as for Normalism, for that I applaud you. You have become a beacon in the darkness that has beset our world. By teaching us that we should love all HumanKind you have given us hope that we will come through these evil times.'

'You know, Percy, that you had a lot to do with the creation of Normalism. I took my inspiration from your remark that if all the effort that had been expended on the construction of engines of agony and death, on the raising of armies, and on the promotion of vile propagandas was employed to improve the welfare and education of HumanKind, the world would be a much happier place.'

'I am pleased I have been of some little service in this gweat endeavour of yours, Norma. You are wise not to advocate violence, Norma. Histowy has taught us that wevolutionary mobs do not in the end bwing liberty, but civil war followed by some new form of tywanny. It has taken all of my biliously futile life to come to this understanding.'

'Your life has hardly been futile, Percy. You were . . . you *are* a great poet.'

'And what is a poet? Just a lonely nightingale who sits in the darkness and sings to cheer its own solitude. No, Norma, mine has been a wasted talent and it is only now that I wake to perceive my many ewwors and to wegret that this knowledge has come to me only when death is so near.'

'Death?'

'Only you will escape from the JAD, Norma. For me, oblivion beckons. Moynahan tells me that since the Zealots' attack on the hotel, the NoirVillian army has begun massing to invade the JAD. Blinded by hatwed, they intend to destwoy the JAD and evewyone inside it.'

'Oh, don't worry, Percy,' Norma scolded. 'Burlesque and Odette are experts at getting out of tight corners. Just stay close to them and they'll keep you safe.' She smiled, desperately trying to hide the concerns she had. The thought of Percy being killed really wrenched at her heartstrings. 'You've got to stay safe, Percy. When I'm gone, the Normalists will need your genius to guide them. This is your time, Percy.'

But not, Norma realised, *our* time. She had found Shelley again, found the man she loved, and he had admitted to loving her, but now they would be separated for ever. Unlike Maria and Burlesque and Odette, there was no Real World twin of Percy Shelley. He was just a mirage . . . a beautiful, intoxicating mirage.

*

Moynahan was confused. He should, he guessed, be happy that he was returning to the Real World, but he wasn't. Unlike all the other guys in the platoon, he had actually *enjoyed* his time in the Demi-Monde. He liked the hustle and bustle of the place and he liked that it was so low-tech.

And then there was Maria.

Never having been much of a romantic, the feelings that Maria had kindled in him had come as something of a shock. He had never met a girl like her and his feelings weren't just a consequence of her being tall and beautiful and moving like Jell-O on springs . . . no, he liked that she was smart and tough and had an opinion of her own. When he was with her he felt complete.

He had fallen for the girl and the devil of it was she knew how he felt about her, his aura would have seen to that. She probably knew how broken up he was about leaving her too. Auralism was the ultimate form of surveillance and like all surveillance it was always one-way.

'May I join thee, Dean?'

Moynahan looked up to find Maria standing beside him. He felt his heart skip; she was *that* beautiful.

'Yeah, sure. Would you like some coffee?' And without waiting for a reply he poured her a cup. Anything to stop himself drowning in those wonderful eyes.

'You are most considerate,' Maria said as she took the seat next to his, then shuffled closer to him.

'Good Dean, give me thine ear. I beseech you hear me, though what I must relate gives me scarce any joy. Know thou that the captain's aura when he did address the assembly was much discolourèd by cruel and murderous intentions. To fulfil some secret purpose he doth intend to murder Norma.'

Moynahan gawped and then squawked out, 'What?'

Maria pressed a finger to his lips and gave him a stern look. 'Soft. Guard thy tongue or we may all be undone: who knows what base accomplices the dark captain may have in his employ?' She looked around to check they weren't being over-heard. 'I prithee, mark my counsel. The captain's aura is beset by foul afflictions, and hence his evil purpose is all betrayèd. When he speaks of taking sweet Norma back to the Real World his breath is tingèd with hues that announce full well his most evil intent.'

'But why would Simmons want to kill her?'

'I know not. But I know, full right and true, that Simmons is a villain who wishes Norma naught but ill. I fear he means to take the life of this, the rarest of all women, who is our most belovèd Messiah. We must move quickly to thwart his wicked designs.'

'Who's the Dupe Moynahan's getting so snug with, Corp?' asked Holder as he watched Moynahan pour coffee for the tall and very beautiful girl who had come to the Portal with Norma Williams.

Massie looked across the room and gave a shrug. 'Her name's Sister Maria. She's the Dupe who helped Moynahan track down Norma Williams and bring her back to the Portal. Nice-looking piece, ain't she, Holder? Kinda makes you wonder what it'd be like to mix and mingle with a Dupe.'

Holder was aghast that his corporal could suggest such a thing. 'That would be unnatural, Corporal, and things unnat-ural are hateful to God. The seventh nuCommandment says: you shall shun sexual gratification and pleasures of the flesh, for this is the Sin of Lust driven by the Daemon Asmodeus.'

Massie gave Holder a funny look, just like he always did when Holder tried to lead him back to the Path of Righteousness. The corporal wasn't a religious man, but Holder hoped to be able to save his soul and bring him safe to Jesus.

'Well, unnatural or not, she's sure sweet-looking.' Massie took a slurp of his coffee. 'Yeah, that honey can jump my bones any time she wants. But she'll know that already: word is she's a Visual Virgin . . . she can see our auras.'

'You should not let a sorceress live,' whispered Holder.

'What's that, Holder?'

'Nothing, Corporal, I was just wondering why a Dupe would want to help Norma Williams.'

'According to Moynahan, that Maria item thinks that Norma Williams is some kind of Messiah.'

'A Messiah?' Holder squeaked. This was blasphemy and, as he always did when he felt Satan close by, he began to finger the crucifix that hung from a chain around his neck.

'Yeah. Norma Williams started some kinda political move-ment while she's been in the Demi-Monde and the Dupes have gotten the idea that she's gonna be the one to save them from the evil of UnFunDaMentalism.' Massie gave a laugh. 'I guess she takes after her daddy, the President, having a taste for politics and all.'

'Her father is a no-good atheist who is intent on leading the people of America to apostasy. He wishes to remake America as a godless society. Sam Williams is in league with the devil.'

'No kidding? I never got the taste for voting but from what I hear Sam Williams is a stand-up kinda guy.' He laughed. 'Maybe his daughter *is* the Messiah. With an ass like hers there's a lot of guys who'd follow her just about anywhere.'

Holder felt his face go red and hot as it always did when he was angry. 'That is sacrilegious,' he complained, his voice louder than he'd intended. 'There is only one Messiah and that is Jesus Christ!'

'Hey, Holder, you wanna calm down. No point in getting bent outta shape about it. Shit, who gives a fuck what the Dupes think anyways? We're gonna be back in the Real World soon.'

Holder kept his peace. Ever since Norma Williams had arrived at the Portal the voices in his head had become ever more insistent, telling him to be wary of this girl, this spawn of Satan, telling him that she must not be allowed to return to the Real World. The ghost of the Last Prophet, Frank Kenton, was telling him that he was the Sword of God and that it would be he who brought God's wrath down on those who would defile His name.

Just five hours after she'd first stepped into the Portal, Norma found herself being ushered into the Transfer Room en route for home. A poignant moment: she desperately wanted to go home but at the same time she didn't want to leave her friends.

Burlesque must have felt her dilemma. 'You don't wanna worry abart us, Miss Norma,' he said as he kissed her on the cheek. 'Me an' Odette will be right as ninepence. You just go back to where yous belong.'

'*Oui*, my dear Norma,' said Odette as she crushed Norma in a bear hug, 'although we will miss you of the utmost terribleness, it is mostly correct that you should go 'ome to your own people.'

After shaking hands with Maria and giving Shelley an awkward kiss, Norma took a deep breath and stepped through the door of the Transfer Room, the all-enveloping burqa she was wearing swishing around her legs as she went. The room had a futuristic aspect, swathed as it was in cold stainless steel and festooned with cables. There were two large leather chairs – similar to the ones Norma had occupied during her visits to the dentist – set in the centre, Captain Simmons indicating that she should take the one to the right. Norma gave a final wave to her friends and then the captain shut the heavy steel door, sealing them off from the Demi-Monde.

'The Transfer Procedure is quite straightforward, Miss Williams,' the captain explained. 'If you would just place this over your head?' He handed Norma a dome-shaped mesh of wires and electrodes, these connected to a small black box set on a table.

Once she had the cowl in place and she was settled into her chair, the captain eased himself into the one facing hers.

'All I have to do is press this button' – here he indicated a large red button set in the arm of his chair – 'and then the Transfer Procedure will be initiated.'

Norma nodded her understanding, but she was a little surprised that rather than pressing the button, the captain undid the holster he had on his hip and drew out the Colt automatic inside. He raised the gun and shot her square in the chest.

INDOCTRANS Headquarters, Fort Jackson
The Real World: 7 February 2019

1.11. Hearing Adam, ABBA dug that he was a cat riffing on the real and needed a mate. So ABBA spat down onto the head of a Serpent and created woeMan, who was to be the opposite of Man and hence make the Demi-Monde the Coolest place in the Whole Known. 1.12. And the woeMan introduced herself saying, 'Yo, I moniker as Lilith and I gotta say that you, Adam honey, look hung, slung and ready for fun.' And Adam thought that Lilith was one real gone hepkitten and hotter than a furiously fucked ferret frolicking in a fiery furnace. 1.13. But it's a fact that woeMan weren't, like, one of ABBA's better ideas. Whereas Adam was noble and honourable, though not overendowed with the smarts, Lilith was none of these things. She was, like, sneaky and underhand and used her sexual allures to confuse and beguile Adam, all the while giving him mucho de verbals about what a shitheap the Demi-Monde was, with there being nowhere to get her hair done and no decent dress shops and such like, and how they weren't allowed to eat the fruit of Yggdrasil.

The HIM Book, Book of the Coming: Chapter 1, Verses 11–13

'Professor Bole,' crooned ABBA, 'you have an eyeVid message from Captain Simmons.'

Instinctively Bole looked around his office, checking that he was alone. A ridiculous thing to do: his office was one of the most surveillance-secure places on earth, and anyway, he had given ABBA clear instructions that all communications with the JAD Portal were to be routed through him and *only* through him. And ABBA-encrypted communications were impossible to hack.

But perhaps he was right to be cautious. No one knew that he was in contact with the Portal – as far as the US military was concerned, communication had been lost when the neoFights had been supposedly taken by Shaka – so it was important that General Zieliéski continued believing that piece of fiction. Bole had only told them that the JAD Portal was still working to give them hope of extricating the lost neoFights, otherwise they would simply have closed the Demi-Monde down.

'Show it,' Bole ordered.

The Flexi-Plexi on the far wall of his office flared into life to show the unpleasant face of Captain Simmons. The captain looked worried, but then the captain always looked worried.

'Professor Bole? This is Captain Simmons at the JAD Portal.' The man seemed breathless with excitement. 'I have some good news, Professor. Norma Williams is dead.'

With some difficulty, Bole stifled a smile. After all the effort he had put into finding and neutralising Norma Williams, she had presented herself at the Portal as a goose ready for slaughter. 'You are confident she is dead, Captain?'

'Yes, Professor, I shot her in the chest. There can be no mistake. She's slumped on the floor of the Transfer Room in front of me.'

'Excellent,' murmured Bole, and it *was* excellent.

Corrupting Simmons had been a masterstroke. Thanks to Simmons he had been able to delude the US military into believing that the platoon had been captured by Shaka's Blood Brothers and that communication with the Portal had been lost. And, of course, Simmons' help had been vital in convincing the neoFights held in the JAD Portal that nothing was amiss, and that their mission was to continue to search for Norma Williams and to return her to the Real World. Simmons had been masterful in pretending to send their eyeMails back to the Real World and distributing the fake replies ABBA concocted.

At a promised cost of ten million dollars, Simmons had made a cheap quisling.

'I need to return to the Real World, Professor. Once the rest of the other guys find out what I've done . . .'

Now this was an unexpected development, one that presented Bole with something of a dilemma. He had never intended for any of the neoFights trapped in the Demi-Monde to be returned to the Real World, but then, he supposed, there was returning and there was returning.

'Very well, Captain. But you will need to have a background story relating to your sudden reappearance in the Real World. Let us say that nine months ago you encountered a malfunction with the Transfer Room which has taken the intervening period to repair. Not having had an opportunity to test these repairs and not wishing to risk the lives of any of your men, you volunteered to make the first transfer yourself. The Portal was destroyed in the process, permanently marooning the rest of your platoon in the Demi-Monde.' Bole gave Simmons his best imitation of a smile. 'I am initiating transfer now.'

Elated though he was by the news of Norma Williams' demise, Septimus Bole did his best to maintain his usual icy and self-possessed demeanour. The displaying of emotion was a very Fragile weakness so he stood silent and aloof alongside Dr David Andrews in the biPsych Storage Facility, concentrating his formidable intellect on the study of the dials that monitored the TIS-swathed bodies held there. The silence obviously unsettled Dr Andrews. He glanced nervously towards Bole.

'ABBA has notified us that one of our biPsychs is attempting to return from the Demi-Monde, Professor, so I thought you'd want to be present for his revival.'

'You thought correctly, Dr Andrews.' A redundant observation, admittedly, but enough to satisfy Fragile social protocol.

Encouraged by Bole's unusually lengthy reply, the doctor amplified his observation. 'The biPsych in question is the one to the very right of the back row, the one belonging to Captain Charlie Simmons, the officer commanding the JAD platoon. He must have escaped from Shaka.'

The capacity of Fragiles for self-delusion never failed to amaze Bole, they were such a gullible specie. 'Indeed,' he answered in an attempt to imitate interest, when all he was really interested in was checking the readings relating to Simmons' vital signs. By his estimation, these should be going flat about . . . now.

On cue a klaxon sounded and a somewhat panic-stricken Dr Andrews turned to the cameraBot hovering at his shoulder. 'Simmons is flatlining. Emergency Revival Team to biPsych Storage Facility immediately. We have a near-death situation.'

That assessment, Bole mused, depended upon how liberal you were in your interpretation of what constituted death. Charlie Simmons' brain would, by now, have been reduced to porridge, so classifying the man as near-dead was enormously generous. By his recalibration of the transfer coordinates, he had ensured that Simmons had arrived back in the Real World with a randomly rewired brain. By reducing the man to the status of a living cadaver, Bole had just saved ParaDigm ten million dollars, as brain-dead – or in Captain Simmons' case, brain-*deader* – he would not be in a position to claim his fee for services rendered.

Of course, these pecuniary considerations were secondary to the real reason why Bole had organised the captain's intellectual destruction, this being to obviate any possible indiscretion on Simmons' behalf. There had always been the likelihood, once he was back in the Real World, that Simmons would have been inclined to spill the beans about what really happened in the Demi-Monde, and a man with no brain was unsurpassed in his ability to keep confidences.

'He's gone,' murmured a distraught-sounding Andrews. 'His brain's fried.'

That observation reminded Bole that there was one other biPsych who could now be referred to in the past tense: Norma Williams. Even as the medical team clustered frantically – and uselessly – around the body that had once been Captain Charlie Simmons, Bole turned to Dr Andrews. 'A tragedy, Doctor,' he said, miming sympathy, and then turned away and recalibrated the dials on the Storage Facility's control panel to check that Norma Williams had indeed expired in the Demi-Monde.

To his horror he saw that she hadn't: she was still functioning normally inside the Portal.

He frowned, trying to work out what had gone wrong. He'd seen the eyeVid of Simmons shooting Norma Williams in the chest. The bitch *had* to be dead . . . but she wasn't.

He could hardly believe it. The girl's ability to survive his many and varied efforts to kill her was becoming positively unnatural. He thought for a moment of simply instructing Metztil to destroy the girl's body held in Los Angeles but he knew this was not the answer; do this and he would be unable to have Aaliz Heydrich return to the Real World, and he still needed her to make a final curtain call. Desperately trying to retain his composure, Bole reminded himself that with regard to Norma Williams he had other options . . . other agents in the Portal. All was not yet lost. Anyway, Bole rather enjoyed playing the role of Frank Kenton and whispering sweet nothings in the ear of Holder.

1:22

The JAD
The Demi-Monde: 7th Day of Fall, 1005

1.14. So Lilith told Adam that there would be no more bumping pelvises until he got the moxy to make with the fruit of Yggdrasil. 1.15. And Adam said to ABBA, 'For fuck's sake, ABBA, can you shut this bitch Lilith up? Yadda, yadda, yadda all fucking day. Man, it's, like, driving me outta my gourd. You gotta lemme give her a taste.' 1.16. But ABBA was off-seat at that time sorting out the rest of the Whole Known and didn't get back to Adam, so to appease Lilith and to stop her moaning about the grass being too green and the water too wet, Adam took the fruit of Yggdrasil and they did eat. 1.17. And when ABBA got back and had sorted through his messages and dug what had gone down He was sore pissed off.

The HIM Book, Book of the Coming: **Chapter 1, Verses 14–17**

ParaDigm's own technology saved Norma's life. The prototype energy-absorbent blouse that Moynahan had made her wear under her burqa might have looked and felt perfectly normal, but when struck by a bullet, the material reacted at super-fast speed using the bullet's energy to perform a localised transformation into a bulletproof membrane. But bulletproof or not, Norma was willing to testify that taking a bullet at point-blank range in the middle of her chest was not a pleasurable experience. The impact had thrown her off her chair and onto the floor, where she had lain stunned for nigh on a minute. When she had finally struggled back to her feet, she found she was the proud possessor of a huge bruise and an empty Transfer Room. Simmons had gone.

A worried-looking Moynahan – alerted by the sound of the gunshot – barged his way into the room. 'What happened?'

'Maria was right. Captain Simmons *was* up to no good: he shot me and then disappeared. Presumably he's transferred back to the Real World.'

As statements went it was something of a show-stopper, and Moynahan asked the obvious question. 'I don't understand why Captain Simmons would want to murder you.'

Norma shrugged. 'All I can think is that for some reason he didn't want me getting back to the Real World, but why, I have no idea.'

Moynahan looked over to Sergeant Edelstein, who had joined them in the room. 'What do you think, Sergeant?'

The sergeant shook his head. 'Don't make sense. Even if he'd succeeded in blowing Miss Williams away, as soon as the rest of us were back in the Real World—' He stopped in mid-sentence and stepped across to study the instrumentation at the side of the room. 'Well, it looks like the rest of us ain't going back home. That prick Simmons has scrambled all the transfer codes. Now we can't lock on to ABBA. We're fucked.'

For the second time that day Moynahan and the rest of the platoon gathered in the Rec Room, but this time the news wasn't so good.

'Okay, listen up, this is our status. Captain Simmons has gone AWOL.' Sergeant Edelstein waited while the reaction caused by that little announcement died down. 'So from here on in, I'm in charge of the Portal.'

'Whaddya mean, he's gone AWOL, Sergeant?' came a question from Corporal Massie.

'About an hour ago, the captain transferred back to the Real World and changed all the transfer codes while he was doing it. Now it's impossible for us to lock with ABBA. We're stuck here in the Demi-Monde.'

'Why would he do that?'

'We dunno, Massie. It has something to do with Miss Williams here.' He nodded to Norma, who was standing rather awkwardly to his right. 'Seems Captain Simmons didn't want her getting back to the Real World so he fixed things so *none* of us would get back.'

'So what we gonna do now, Sergeant?'

'Communications Corporal Hoskins is trying to re-establish the codes Simmons scrambled, but that might take a while.' Around a thousand years was Hoskins' best estimate, but Edelstein had obviously decided it would be bad for morale to share *that* piece of information with his men.

'We might not have a while, Sergeant.' This comment came from neoFight Private Billy Harrison, one of the brighter of the GIs manning the Portal. 'Word from the Observation Deck is that the Shades are getting frisky. Seems that stunt the nuJus pulled in blowing up the hotel this morning has really put a burr up the HimPeror's ass. Could be that the Shades are thinking of making a house call.'

Edelstein nodded. 'Yeah, I guess we can expect it to get hot and heavy in the next few days, but there's no reason why the Shades should take an interest in us, so all we've got to do is to lock down and keep a low profile. And even if they do come knocking, that ain't a big cause for concern. The Portal is steel-reinforced and built to withstand a lot of punishment, we've got state-of-the-art weaponry, enough ammunition to blow every Shade in NoirVille to hell and back twice over and plenty of food

and water. So I want you all to remain frosty. I'm putting Moynahan in charge of perimeter defence. It's *Sergeant* Moynahan
too . . . I've given him a battlefield promotion.'

After the meeting Norma, Moynahan and Edelstein met for a
council of war.

'I think you're right, Sarge,' Moynahan began. 'If the Shades
do invade the JAD, our best chance is just to stay quiet, just let
the fighting pass us by. The last thing we want is for the Shades
to know we're here. I reckon if we just close the blast screens and
pretend there's nobody home we'll all come out of this in one
piece.'

Norma shook her head. 'I'd love to agree with you, Dean, but
I don't think that that's how it's going to play out. Simmons'
hasn't been the only attempt to assassinate me since I've been in
the Demi-Monde so I'm getting the feeling that for whatever
reason someone in the Real World wants me numbered amongst
the missing, and I'm guessing that someone is Septimus Bole.'

Edelstein whistled. 'That's a powerful enemy you've got there,
Miss Williams.'

'Tell me about it.'

'But what's that got to do with the rest of us?' asked Moynahan.

'Lots. Once Bole realises that Simmons didn't manage to blow
me away, he's going to be looking for another way to bump me
off and I'm guessing that a war will give him the perfect opportunity to do just that.'

'Shit.' Moynahan looked across to Sergeant Edelstein. 'Maybe
it would be safer for Norma if she got out of the JAD?'

'Too late for that, Moynahan,' observed Edelstein. 'According
to our spotters, the Shades have got the JAD surrounded. Chances
of Miss Norma getting through one of the CheckPoints are fuck-
all and falling.' He gave Norma a meaningful look. 'Way I see it,

you'll be safer here with us. At least here there're sixteen neoFights ready to protect you.'

In Holder's opinion Captain Simmons had been a good man. Captain Simmons had knelt down in prayer with Holder every Sunday and none of the other guys had done that. And Captain Simmons *had* tried to destroy the false Messiah, Norma Williams, but she had survived and only those in league with Satan were immune to bullets. The more Holder thought about it, the more he was convinced that he was surrounded by the Servants of Satan, who would lead him away from the grace of God and deny him Revelation.

That's what the voices told him, whispering that by helping to protect Norma Williams he was doing the work of Satan. Wasn't she, they kept repeating over and over, the spawn of that atheist President Sam Williams, the man who spurned God and had sworn to remake America as a secular society? Holder wasn't real sure what 'secular' meant but he knew it wasn't good. He also knew that Sam Williams was the man who had bad-mouthed the memory of the Last Prophet, Frank Kenton, calling him a racist and a bigot.

Even as he sat there eating his microwaved burger, he could hear Frank Kenton talking to him, telling him that he was surrounded by evil and by the emissaries of Satan, telling him that now Captain Simmons was gone he was the only True Believer in the Portal, telling him that God was relying on him to do something about it . . . about the AntiChrist.

Be ever sober and vigilant, Frank Kenton told him, *for Satan is the subtle serpent who seeks to enchant the imagination and lead you from the Path of Righteousness.*

Pieces began to fall into place. Yeah, Norma Williams was a false Messiah . . . the AntiChrist. Hadn't he heard that whore Sister Maria calling her the Messiah? And wasn't this blasphemy of the worst kind? Everyone knew that Jesus was the Messiah and that it would be He who would return to save the Believers after Armageddon.

Holder closed his eyes, trying to still the babble of voices in his head. He felt confused and dizzy. He didn't like thinking about the Final Confrontation with the AntiChrist, it scared him.

1:23

The JAD, NoirVille
The Demi-Monde: 12th Day of Fall, 1005

FAO LEADER OF THE JAD ADMINISTRATIVE COUNCIL, RABBI
SCHMUEL GELBFISZ PO BOX 8723 + + + I WRITE ON THE
INSTRUCTION OF HIS HIMPERIAL MAJESTY XOLANDI + + + BE
ADVISED THAT FOLLOWING THE UNPROVOKED AND TREACHEROUS
ATTACK ON THE HOTEL DU ZULU BY AGENTS OF THE NUJU
AUTONOMOUS DISTRICT (THE JAD) A STATE OF WAR NOW EXISTS
BETWEEN THE JAD AND THE HIMPERIAL EMPIRE OF NOIRVILLE
+ + + BE ASSURED THAT ABBA WILL GRANT OUR SOLDIERS
VICTORY AND WE WILL EXACT TERRIBLE REVENGE FOR THE
PERFIDIOUS ACTS OF TERRORISM PERPETRATED BY THE NUJUS
+ + + GRAND VIZIER KONSTANTIN POBEDONOSTSEV

PAR OISEAU

**Copy of PigeonGram message sent by Konstantin
Pobedonostsev on 12th day of Fall, 1005**

For perhaps the fifth time in as many minutes Schmuel Gelbfisz
examined the PigeonGram he had received from Pobedonostsev.
He felt like crying. They had so very nearly done it, he and Salah-
ad-Din had come within an ace of keeping the peace in NoirVille.
Despite everything – the assassination of Shaka Zulu, the mas-
sacre in Khan al-Kalili square, the attacks of the Black Hand
Gang and even the nonsense with the Protocols – sanity had
almost prevailed.

Almost . . .

And now, thanks to those damn-fool Zealots, the nuJus were
staring into the abyss. Oh, he knew his people would fight bravely

but it would be a hopeless struggle. They faced a formidable enemy and, trapped in a walled city, there would be no escape. The Zealots' hubris had condemned two million nuJus to death.

Gelbfisz crumpled the piece of paper into a ball and tossed it into the wastepaper basket. 'Unt zhat, Giscala, is vot you unt your gang of hooligans have done mit zhe future of zhe JAD . . . thrown it avay. Vot are you? Some kind of *behaimeh*? A fucking idiot, perhaps? Vot vere you thinking vhen you unt your *bondits* vent unt blew half of NoirVille to Hel unt back? Didn't you realise zhat zhe Shades vould go fucking crazy?'

Giscala had been the only man to come back safe from the attack on the Hotel du Zulu and he'd done that only because he'd got lost when he'd been rushing to catch up with his fellow Zealots after performing his stunt with the petrol bomb. Ninety-one Shades and fifteen nuJus had been killed when the bombs had exploded but Giscala had walked away without a scratch. And now he sat in Gelbfisz's office, lolling in his chair as though he hadn't a care in the world. Worse, he didn't seem at all taken aback by the dressing-down he was being given, he simply sat there, carelessly smoking his cigarette and tapping his foot on the parquet floor. 'It is t-t-time for the nuJus to f-f-fight, Gelbfisz,' Giscala answered with a careless wave of his hand. 'Now is the time for l-l-liberty or d-d-death. Now it is the t-t-time for the young to r-r-replace the old. You and your g-g-generation are finished. The t-t-t-time for t-t-talking is over and you will not find the f-f-fighting youth of the J-J-JAD recoiling in the face of the sacrifices and s-s-suffering entailed in w-w-waging war against the Sh-Sh-Sh-Shades. We will not s-s-surrender. W-W-We will not be c-c-cowed as you have been by the empty threats of the Sh-Sh-Shades. ABBA is on our side.'

Gelbfisz could hardly bear to listen to this twaddle. It was symptomatic of maniacs like Giscala that they could only converse using clichés and vapid doggerel, this presumably enabling them to avoid having to think about the nonsense they were spieling. 'Oy vay! Zhis ABBA of yours must have more sides zhan a fucking polygon. Hear me loudly: just like you, zhis *groisser gornicht* Pobedonostsev thinks ABBA is batting for zhe Shades, unt looking at zhe number of fighters he has crowding around zhe Vall I think he might be right.' Gelbfisz shook his head. 'Zhe problem mit you, Giscala, is zhat you are a *shmuck* who thinks mit his *pitsel* unt not his mind. Zhe IRGON knew zhat vun day zhe Shvartses vould come calling, so do you think ve have been sitting in zhe Council Chamber just pounding our *putzi*? No, ve've been trying to save our people. But now, thanks to you, ve are nut-deep in shit. Thanks to you, ve now have to fight.'

'Yes,' exclaimed an overexcited Giscala, 'we have to f-f-fight! And at last the D-D-Demi-Monde will see the true worth of the n-n-nuJu. At last we nuJus will show these Sh-Sh-Shades and the rest of the Demi-Monde that they attack the J-J-JAD at their peril.'

'*Feh!* At last we will lose, more like. Zhat is zhe lesson zhat Varsaw taught us, zhat vhen ABBA chooses sides he picks zhe vun mit zhe big battalions, unt as big battalions go zhey don't come much bigger zhan zhe Shade vuns. Zhere are four million Shades in zhe NoirVille army unt ve have maybe half a million fighters. Even a gloopy *luftmensch* like you must be able to see zhat zhem odds ain't very even. Zhis war is all over bar the shooting.'

'We had to attack the Hotel du Z-Z-Zulu to stop the secrets of Aqua Benedicta f-f-falling into enemy hands,' protested Giscala.

Gelbfisz gave a mirthless laugh. 'Vot a *yold!* I'm betting zhat *paskudnik* Pobedonostsev played you Zealots for greeners. Pobedonostsev *vanted* you to attack zhe hotel, vanted you to do zomething stupid so he had an excuse to call for war.' Suddenly Gelbfisz sprang to his feet and marched across his office to tower over Giscala, the young man at least having the courtesy to look frightened. 'Okay, Mr I'm-Such-a-Fucking-Tough-Guy Giscala, you vanna be a fucking martyr zhen I ain't zhe vun to get in your vay. You can take command of zhe defence of CheckPoint Charlie unt I hope you have zhe good manners to get killed in zhe process . . . it'll save me doing zhe job myself.'

General Salah-ad-Din stood watching as his artillerymen went about their business and he had to admit that they were nothing if not efficient. By his estimation, the guns would be ready to commence their bombardment of the JAD at dawn. In a few short hours, death and destruction would begin to rain down on the nuJus.

He sighed. War was such a ridiculous waste of both energy and lives. The mission of all military men was, in his oft-voiced opinion, to preserve peace, and in this he had failed. But there had been no denying the involvement of the nuJus in the Hotel du Zulu atrocity and it had been this that had proven to be the final straw. Pobedonostsev had demanded retribution and the Council had concurred, so now the killing would begin in earnest. And like all good soldiers, now war had come he would prosecute it with controlled ferocity. He pitied the nuJus.

There was a movement to his left and when he looked he saw the tiny, birdlike figure of Grand Vizier Pobedonostsev tripping towards him. Careful to keep his face utterly expressionless, he nodded a greeting to the poisonous little snake.

'I have been sent by His HimPerial Majesty to enquire how go the preparations for the destruction of the nuJu race.' Having got his war, the bastard was full of bounce.

'I was under the impression that my task was the subjugation of the JAD, Grand Vizier. Nowhere in the orders I received was there any mention of the words "destruction of the nuJu race". Genocide is not a military strategy of which I am particularly enamoured.'

'Oh, come, come, General, this is not the time for semantics.

We both know that the HimPeror will not be satisfied until the treacherous nuJus are totally destroyed, so let us not quibble as to whether this constitutes genocide or not.' Pobedonostsev gave an awkward smirk. 'So, what is your strategy for the prosecution of the war against the JAD?'

'My strategy may be summed up in one word: cautious. The JAD will be difficult to subdue, and I am determined to do this in a way that involves my HimPis suffering the minimum number of casualties.'

There was a dismissive laugh from Pobedonostsev. 'With the greatest of respect, General, the coming battle must be fought in a spirit of holy hatred. Certainly this will be costly in terms of lives, but such is war.'

Salah-ad-Din studied Pobedonostsev, wondering how a man's soul could ever become so blistered and buckled. 'There is no place for hate in war, Grand Vizier. War must be pursued in a cold-hearted manner, with decisions made that are free of the fog of emotion. I counsel caution because I refuse to underestimate the nuJus. Rabbi Schmuel Gelbfisz is no fool: he understood full well that one day our HimPis might attack the JAD and in anticipation has turned the JAD into a fortress. Behind the Wall the JAD is a maze of blockhouses, pillboxes, minefields and barbed-wire entanglements such that every time one defensive layer is peeled away there is another behind it. Every street is a killing zone where unwary fighters might be trapped, tripped, blown up or caught in enfilading fire.'

'You sound fearful, General Salah-ad-Din.'

'Oh, I am, Grand Vizier. War is a fearful business.'

'But we will prevail?'

'Of course: the strength of the JAD – that it is a walled citadel – is also its weakness. Now my troops have completed their encirclement of the city, the nuJus are sealed inside, caught like rats in a trap. Tomorrow we will begin the systematic bombardment of the city, pounding it until not one building is left standing, not one food warehouse is unrazed, not one water cistern is unsmashed ... only then will I unleash my HimPis. My intention is to assault the JAD through two breaches in the Wall, one on the Istanbul side and one on the Delhi side. In this way we will divide the forces available to Gelbfisz and more quickly overwhelm the nuJu fighters.'

'How long before the JAD is ours?'

'I understand the time granted for the performing of any miracle is forty days and forty nights.'

'Forty days,' murmured Pobedonostsev, his eyes sparkling with excitement. 'And I assume you have instructed your HimPis that they must exterminate the nuJu population as they advance ... that they will take no prisoners ...'

'I have left it to the Grand Mufti to impart that particular instruction; he seems particularly enthusiastic regarding the killing of nuJus. My own opinion is that this sort of total war will sicken my fighters. There is no honour in killing woeMen and children.'

Pobedonostsev laughed. 'Honour, General? The war against the nuJus cannot be fought in a knightly fashion. This struggle is one of racial survival and must be waged with unprecedented, unmerciful and unrelenting harshness. You must imbue your fighters with a passion for killing nuJus. They must be drunk with the thrill of what Great Leader Heydrich calls *Lustmord*: murder for pleasure.'

'My men are soldiers, not beasts.'

'Your men must act as beasts because they are opposed by beasts. Anyone who has looked in the face of a nuJu knows what animals they are.'

Salah-ad-Din eyed Grand Vizier Pobedonostsev with undisguised contempt. 'They are animals, Grand Vizier, who wish to go to ABBA accompanied by as many of my soldiers as they are able.'

Pobedonostsev nodded towards the soldiers working on the artillery. 'Surely with the siege mortars so generously supplied by the ForthRight, nuJu resistance will be quickly smashed.'

'We will see.'

'You seem less than pleased by the assistance offered by Great Leader Heydrich.'

'Whilst, Grand Vizier, I am ever ready to accept help and advice whenever it can further the sacred cause of HimPerialism, I am dubious of any offer of assistance that is made by Heydrich. UnFunDaMentalism makes no distinction between Shades and nuJus, it defines them both as UnderMentionables. He has made numerous speeches where he iterates that the ultimate aim of UnFunDaMentalism is to eradicate *all* UnderMentionables from the face of the Demi-Monde, his so-called Final Solution.' Salah-ad-Din gave an empty smile. 'You may consider me a tad old-fashioned, but I am reluctant to ally myself with anyone who calls for the extermination of my race.'

'You are too sensitive, General. Surely you must recognise that these public pronouncements are made with the sole purpose of exciting the patriotic sensibilities of his people. This is mere political puff, nothing more.'

Salah-ad-Din smiled. 'I bow to your superior intelligence regarding matters of political puff. But I would ask, Grand Vizier, what does Heydrich, this skilful politician of yours, require in return for the provision of the mortars?'

'Well, one thing has been mentioned . . .'

'And this is?'

'There is an Enemy of the ForthRight in the JAD. A Blank . . . a woeMan by the name of Norma Williams. Heydrich attaches great importance to this girl's destruction and HimPeror Xolandi has agreed that, once our assault is under way, we will allow a company of SS StormTroopers led by Comrade General von Sternberg into the JAD in order that they may deal with the girl.'

'It is no small thing that is asked. An SS death squad operating in NoirVille is politically ... sensitive. But there I go again, Grand Vizier, being driven by my sensitivities. Very well, you may tell von Sternberg that he will be allowed to pursue his vicious little games, but only when his victims are Blanks. In the extermination stakes, HimPerial Secretary, I am an enthusiastic proponent of equal opportunity amongst the races of the Demi-Monde.'

The posters that had begun to spring up on the walls of the buildings in the JAD were what persuaded Edelstein to ask Burlesque and Odette to attend the rally in the town hall. It was important, he explained to them, that he had a reliable account of what the JAD's leadership had to say about the situation, and as Burlesque and Odette were Dupes, they seemed the perfect people to conduct the reconnaissance.

Which was why the pair of them were standing crammed into the hall along with five hundred or so very anxious-looking nuJus. The meeting was scheduled to commence at three, and even as the clock was still striking a tall man – dressed in a shabby suit, a kippah atop his bald head and the sunlight glancing on his small spectacles – clambered up the steps to the stage.

'Must be bad news,' Burlesque heard someone nearby comment, 'if Gelbfisz has come to speak in person.'

Gelbfisz bowed to the audience. 'People of zhe JAD . . . I am grateful for zhis chance to speak here today unt I ask you to listen to me slowly, as I have very important news. Zhis morning NoirVille declared war on zhe JAD . . .'

It took several minutes for the hubbub to quieten down. To be told, flat out, that they were as good as dead created consternation in the crowd.

'Following zhe attack by zhe Zealots on zhe Hotel du Zulu, HimPeror Xolandi has decided zhat zhe only good nuJu is a dead nuJu. Zo, even as I speak, zhe HimPis are gathering beyond zhe Wall unt our military experts expect zheir attack to commence at any moment. Of course, I have tried to reason mit HimPeror Xolandi, but mit so many Shades killed in zhe bombing of zhe hotel, unt mit zhis coming so close after zhe azzazzination of Shaka Zulu, he ain't in a mood to parley. Zo, ve must prepare to fight.'

He looked around the hall and then spread his hands in a gesture of hopelessness. 'Make no mistake, zhis vill be a struggle for zhe very survival of our race unt vether ve *do* survive vill depend on our courage unt our bloody-minded vill to live. It vill not be easy. Oh, I could stand here unt spout platitudes unt assure you zhat ve have made every preparation to give zhe Shades zhe turnaround, but zhe truth is zhis will be a grapple to the death.'

There was more excited chatter amongst the crowd, so excited that Gelbfisz had to bang his gavel hard on the podium to restore quiet. 'Zo we must be ready to fight. As you know, all men between zhe ages of sixteen unt sixty have been allocated to a regiment, but in zhis fight we vill *all* be soldiers. Men, women unt children, zhe old unt zhe young, we vill all be frontniks.' He paused to wipe away the tears welling up in his eyes. 'Zhese are terrible times vhich vill become even more terrible in zhe days unt zhe veeks ahead, but mit zhe help of ABBA ve vill endure. Zo, I vould ask any of you who have not already done zo to come forward to help in zhe defence of zhe JAD unt of zhe nuJu people.'

'And is it only nuJus you are asking to fight?'

The question came from the side of the hall and when Burlesque looked he was amazed to see Josephine Baker pushing her way through the crowd. As beautiful and as imperious as ever, Josie climbed the steps of the stage and the sight of her caused a commotion in the crowd.

'I ask again, Rabbi Gelbfisz, is it only nuJus you are calling to arms? There are a great many Shades who came to the JAD to be free of the persecution we faced in NoirVille and who will gladly fight alongside the nuJus who offered us sanctuary.'

Gelbfisz didn't get a chance to reply. With a shout of 'Kill the Shade' one of the crowd lobbed a bottle at Josephine, smacking her on the side of the head and sending her sprawling across the stage. This was a signal for pandemonium to break out, with the more racially tolerant of the nuJus coming to blows with those of a more Shadephobic disposition.

'I fink we're needed, Oddie, my love,' and with that Burlesque started to shove his way towards Josie.

With both Burlesque and Odette being so big, by judicious use of their fists and elbows they were able to smash their way through the mob. When they got to the stage, Odette picked up the unconscious Josephine and, with Burlesque acting as a battering ram, they battled their way to safety.

1:24

The JAD
The Demi-Monde: 13th–16th Days of Fall, 1005

Lilith's scheming to enjoy the fruit of Yggdrasil is one of the pivotal stories in the HIM Book. That woeMen are adept in WhoDoo, the Dark Magic, is a given, and therefore it is no coincidence that Lilith wished to eat the forbidden fruit: Yggdrasil is, by tradition, an ash tree, a favourite host of the fly agaric mushroom which is an ingredient often used by WhoDoo witches in the preparation of their magical potions. The modern interpretations of this Verse (Mohammed Ahmed al-Mahdi, *The Irrefutable Logic of Misogynism*, Bust Your Conk Publications) is that ABBA wished – by denying Adam the fruit – to prevent Man from beginning a self-destructive enquiry into the dark arts. Unfortunately Lilith, being a woeMan and hence emotionally immature, was unable to resist temptation, a weakness of character that led to the Fall of Man.

A Fool's Guide to HimPerialism: Selim the Grim, Bust Your
Conk Publications

The bombardment began at seven o'clock that morning. Norma had just brewed herself a cup of coffee and was standing on the roof of the Portal – the Observation Deck – enjoying both the coffee and the sight of the sun rising over the JAD when the mortar shells began to fall. They fell continuously for the next two hours. Even cowering in the Portal's basement – Norma hadn't believed it was possible to get down four flights of stairs so quickly – it was a terrible experience, and if her time in Warsaw hadn't inured her to the noise and the horror of an artillery bombardment, she was sure she'd have gone mad. The floor and walls of the Portal shuddered and shook; the air, thick with dust, smoke and powdered plaster, was nigh on unbreathable; and even blocking her ears with her hands, she couldn't escape the deafening explosions as the shells landed.

Her only comfort was that, unlike the poor nuJus in the rest of the JAD, she endured the bombardment in relative safety. From the outside the Portal might look unremarkable but the reality was that under its brick facade it was a steel-and-concrete-reinforced bunker, capable, so Moynahan assured her, of withstanding all but a direct hit from Shade artillery.

Moynahan's confidence in the strength of the Portal was somewhat undermined when a mortar shell landed slap-bang in the middle of the road in front of the building, sucking the front door off in the process and sending it, fluttering like a leaf, skywards.

'Get the bomb shutters up,' screamed Sergeant Edelstein.

It took five minutes for the steel shutters to be drawn over the windows and doors and the Portal sealed from the outside world. The Portal was now what it had always pretended not to be: a redoubt. Snug and secure, they waited for the bombardment to end, which it did at nine o'clock sharp. An eerie quiet descended on the JAD, which was broken when Edelstein began to bark out orders sending soldiers bustling around checking for damage. There were so many jobs to be done that Edelstein ran out of neoFights to perform them. His eye fell on Shelley, who was standing doing nothing.

'Shelley,' he yelled, 'you've got sharp eyes. Get up top and see if there's anything left of the JAD.'

As Shelley climbed the staircase Norma followed him, but even from the Observation Deck it was difficult to see very much. After just two hours of shelling it was as though day had surrendered to night: so much dust and smoke was rising from the city that the light of the sun was blocked and the JAD was enveloped in a wraithlike twilight. What little they could see made a depressing sight. Entire streets had disappeared to be replaced by a jumble of fractured masonry, twisted steel and enormous shell-craters. Across the street from the Portal a newly demolished house stood askew, its entire frontage blown off to expose the inner walls, on which, improbably, pictures were still hanging.

'Merciful ABBA,' said Shelley quietly, 'we see before us the glowification of wace hatwed. Man has no wight to kill his bwother and it is no excuse that he does so in uniform: he only adds the infamy of servitude to murder.' He shook his head dolefully and glanced towards Norma. 'Do you not despair for HumanKind, Norma? Much as I admire the message of peace and non-violence you have been pweaching, surely when you see such wanton destwuction you must wealise that Man is iwwevocably shackled to violence, his soul ensnared by MALEvolence?'

'HumanKind can change, Percy.'

'No, Norma, mankind must be changed. To turn from violence and destwuction, men must be given the facility to understand.'

Norma frowned, remembering that Shelley used his fey demeanour to hide a penetrating intellect. That was one of the reasons why she loved him so very much: he made her think. 'Understand what?' she asked.

'Evewything. Man is a very docile and twactable beast, Norma, easily led and infinitely persuadable. He wishes so much to believe that he is easy pwey to the specious cant uttered by politicians and weligious leaders. The only way to pwevent violence is to give mankind the facility to understand that the whetowic of leaders such as Heydwich is just so much nonsense.'

'But how?'

Shelley smiled. 'I have given this much thought, and my conclusion is that to thwart the political villainy wife in the world
people must be given unfettered access to *information*. Leaders
contwol their people by manipulating the information they
make available to them. If the only information the Shades have
is that nuJus are plotting to destwoy them, then that is what
they will believe. And if the nuJus are told that the Shades are
an infewior wace that is what they will believe. Only the twuth
– information – will fwee mankind fwom the vicious tywanny of
ignowance . . . and its addiction to violence.'

'The tragedy is that people don't want to know . . .'

'Then they must be *obliged* to know.'

Norma laughed. 'That's why you're a poet, Percy: you can
dream the impossible dream.'

Shelley gave her an odd look and then nodded towards
the burning JAD. 'Perhaps you are wight, Norma. But then
dweams do, occasionally, come true. And it is a wonderful
dweam, is it not, to imagine that such carnage would never be
wepeated?'

Norma gestured to the destruction that surrounded them. 'So
what's next?'

Shelley shrugged. 'Maybe thwee, four more days of this nonsense. After that they'll twy to bweach the Wall, and once that's
viable the fighting will begin in earnest.'

BANG!

The entire section of the Wall Giscala and his fighters were
cowering behind shook.

BANG!

Concrete was blown inwards, great lumps of stone shrapnel
hurling fighters backwards to lie smashed and dashed on the
cobbles.

'S-s-stand s-s-steady, boys,' Giscala bellowed. 'Just k-k-keep your heads d-d-down and you'll be ok-k-kay.'

This was, Giscala knew, a very generous use of the word 'okay'. After three days of being bashed about by Shade mortars his fighters looked far from okay. The continual shelling made it impossible to sleep: he was exhausted and so, by the look of them, were his fighters.

But now, he suspected, there wouldn't be much chance of getting any rest. The Shades seemed to have tired of pounding the city to powder and had turned their attention to the Wall. For the last few hours they had been using their howitzers to smash it down.

'How long do you reckon the Wall will stand, Captain?'

The question came from a private – Levi, Giscala thought his name was – hiding behind the burnt-out carcass of a steamer.

'Half an hour, t-t-t-tops.' Give it another thirty minutes and the Shades would have smashed a breach in the Wall and then all Hel would break loose. Giscala's scouts had already reported seeing armoured steamers assembling ready to ram their way into the JAD. This was the crucial moment: Giscala and his fighters had to hold the breach or the JAD was history.

'Pass the word, S-S-Sergeant, that all the f-f-fighters should be at their stations. It's i-i-imperative that the armoured steamers don't get through the W-W-Wall. Tell the guys that the very s-s-s-survival of the J-J-JAD depends on them.'

In the end it took the Shades another hour to smash a serviceable breach in the Wall, their success signalled by an oppressive silence. The rain of mortar shells stopped and a deep brooding quiet descended over the JAD.

'What's happening, Captain?' he heard a skittish-sounding Levi asking. 'Why don't the Shades attack?'

'Who knows, P-P-Private, but I've got a sneaking feeling we're not g-g-going to have to wait long to f-f-find out.'

He was right. No sooner were the words out of his mouth than a deep, powerful rumbling came from beyond the Wall. This, Giscala knew, could only mean one thing: hundreds of steamer engines powering up.

It was a long, long day and one that began well for the JAD fighters. The Shades attacked the breach using the tactics that Giscala had been told to expect: armoured steamers at the front with Shade shocktroops streaming behind them. And knowing what to expect, he had been ready for them.

During the days waiting for the Shades to come calling he had had his fighters spend their time making sticky bombs – flour sacks full of blasting gelatin, which were then dipped in axle grease. When these were hurled against the side of an armoured steamer, the hope was that the grease would make the bombs stick to it, the resulting explosion being powerful enough to rip off a track or fracture a boiler. Of course, it was a suicidal form of attack and the cost in fighters' lives was terrible. Giscala watched in horror as Levi – who couldn't have been more than sixteen years old – was killed destroying a steamer. But there was no time for sorrow or tears. With a cry of 'For the J-J-JAD,' Giscala leapt forward leading his fighters in attack after increasingly desperate attack.

But all this did was win them a respite. The Shades simply paused for a moment to lick their wounds and then came at them again. This time, though, they had changed tactics.

Now it was the turn of the Shade HimPis to try to clear the breach, and the slaughter that ensued sickened Giscala. He had positioned his precious pair of Gatling guns so that their fire enfiladed the busted part of the Wall, and the result was that the first wave of Shade fighters was mown down like grass before a scythe. The problem for Giscala was that there were just so many of them and that they were as brave and resolute in attack as he and his fighters were in defence. For every Shade they killed it seemed that two rose up to take his place. The fighting was unrelenting and as the barrels of the Gatling guns got hotter and hotter so the inevitable happened: the guns jammed. And immediately the fire from the machine guns faltered so there were shouts from the Shade attackers and thousands of them stormed the breach.

The minefield Giscala had sown immediately in front of the opening slowed their advance, but despite the mines and how desperately his fighters loaded and fired their rifles, they were simply swamped.

'We've 'ad it, Captain!' he heard his sergeant screaming in his ear. 'We've got to pull back.'

'No, no! We must stand; the Shades must only advance over our dead bodies.'

These were the last words ever spoken by Giscala, and as he uttered them he realised that, miraculously, his stammer seemed to have disappeared. Then a Shade bullet took him in the head. His was one of the dead bodies the Shades advanced over.

The red flare arching through the night sky told General von Sternberg that the breach was secure and that the minefield beyond had been cleared. He levered himself to his feet, brushed the dust off the arse of his trousers and nodded to his major to get the two hundred SS commandos under his command ready to roll.

In truth a very small command, too small in his opinion to warrant the leadership of a man of his talent and seniority, but the Great Leader had insisted that he see to Norma Williams' assassination personally, and when the Great Leader insisted, it was better to accede.

Von Sternberg's detachment moved towards the breach and through it into the JAD, pushing and shoving the carts carrying their heavier equipment and spare ammunition in front of them and dragging the two six-pounders behind. Difficult work: not only did they have to be careful to avoid nuJu patrols, but the artillery bombardment had really chewed up the streets, great craters pockmarking the roads and rubble from destroyed buildings making them nigh on impassable. Finally, though, they got to their objective, von Sternberg ordering his command post be set up in a bombed-out house at the end of the street, fifty metres away from the warehouse Heydrich called 'the Portal'.

Something, though, told von Sternberg to be careful. The intelligence he had been given was that he was opposed by only sixteen terrorists – enemies of the ForthRight, each and every one of them – but the Portal looked formidable, with steel shutters covering its doors and windows. A cautious von Sternberg watched the place for almost an hour but in that time no one left or entered the building. It looked deserted.

In the end he offered his spyglass to his second-in-command and asked Major Jacob Smith for his opinion. 'Don't look much of a redoubt, General,' was the major's assessment after he'd spent a few minutes studying the building. 'Way I reckon it, my boys'll be inside in two shakes of a nanny goat's tail.'

'I trust that you are correct, Major, but we must not underestimate the duplicitous nature of these terrorists. It is possible that they have fortified the place in a manner that isn't evident to casual examination.'

'Could be, General, but then it could be empty. Maybe the bastards we're hunting got totalled by the artillery, place looks beaten up enough. And we ain't seen so much as a drape twitching: I'm thinking our birds have flown.'

'We will see, Major, we will see. I suggest you come at the Portal front *and* rear.'

'And what do you want us to do when we get inside?'

'I want no prisoners, Major. I want you to kill everyone you find inside the house.'

'Men *and* women?'

'*Especially* the women. My intelligence is that the most venal of all the terrorists is a woman called Norma Williams. She, above all others, must be assassinated.'

1:25

The JAD
The Demi-Monde: 17th Day of Fall, 1005

As punishment for Lilith causing the Fall of Man, ABBA decreed that henceforward woeMen would be required to conduct themselves according to the precepts of subMIS-Siveness, that is, they must be at all times Mute, Invisible, Subservient and Sexually Modest. Only in this way could woeMen earn the forgiveness of ABBA. ABBA commands Men to be strict and resolute in their disciplining of woeMen who transgress subMISSiveness. As His Grace Mohammed Ahmed al-Mahdi says: 'For WoeMen are like the timbers of a house: those that are diseased by rot or woodworm must be ripped out and burned, otherwise the house may fall, crushing those within.'

A Fool's Guide to HimPerialism: Selim the Grim, Bust Your
Conk Publications

NeoFight Private Billy Harrison stabbed a finger in the direction of the Flexi-Plexi. 'Whoo-hee, we've got mail! I think the vultures are gathering, Sergeant. Like my girlfriend used to say, I'm getting a lot of movement down in the shrubbery.'

From where Norma was standing at the back of the Portal's command centre it was difficult to see what Harrison was getting so excited about, but by rising up on tiptoes she managed to see over the boy's shoulder and get a peek at the Flexi-Plexi.

The screen showed the ghostly forms of the night-vision images being transmitted by the eyeSpy surveillanceBots guarding the perimeter of the Portal. Harrison was right: there *was* a lot of movement outside. As best Norma could make out, a hundred fighters were trying to creep up to the Portal. Very scary.

'EyeSpies reckon five-five badniks to the front and five-zero to the rear,' chortled Harrison, confirming Norma's guess. 'Scans show they're only carrying small arms, though olfactory detectors register blasting gelatin, which indicates they're IED-equipped. Preliminary scans identify them as SS Storm-Troopers. Looks like the UnFunnies are gonna come knocking big time.'

'Sound general quarters, Harrison,' Edelstein ordered, 'and make sure the blast shutters are secure.' Edelstein turned to Moynahan. 'Whaddya think, Dean?'

'I wouldn't want the bastards getting too close. The Portal might be strong but it might be better not to find out *how* strong.'

'Want me to make with the discouragement, Sergeant?' asked Harrison.

Edelstein gave a nod. 'Yeah, give 'em a blast.'

Norma found herself aghast at how casually Edelstein condemned these young men to death. It seemed to her that in war it was too easy to forget that the men they were fighting were not just soldiers but sons, lovers, brothers and fathers. They might be Dupes but they still had people who loved them. War seemed to make men stop thinking. Maybe Shelley was right . . . maybe the only way to wean men away from violence was by compulsion.

A grinning Harrison worked the joystick that controlled the miniguns covering the approaches to the building, the computer-sighted guns locking on the fighters sneaking through the darkness. A beep indicated that the computer had acquired a target and Harrison pressed the 'Fire' button. There was a chattering sound from outside the Portal and for a moment the Flexi-Plexi was bleached white by the flash of gunfire.

Whoever was making the assault, they were, in Norma's opinion, very brave. Even while they were being decimated by the miniguns they still carried through their attack, racing up to the Portal's doors, placing their charges and then retreating back into the night.

'Prepare for explosion,' Moynahan screamed as he dove to the floor, dragging Norma with him.

There was a loud *whooomph*. The walls shook and a dusting of plaster drifted down from the ceiling. 'Report!' Edelstein yelled to Harrison, who was still sitting doggedly in front of his beloved Polly.

'EyeSpies just checking the status of the doors. They seem okay . . .' Harrison used a second joystick to manoeuvre the eye-Spies. 'Some damage. Front surveillance is FUBAR – the IED totalled eyeSpies four through seven – but looks like the blast screens are uncompromised. Back wall took a beating: if the badniks get to do that again we're gonna have a garden view a mite bigger than the one we're currently enjoying.' By way of emphasis Harrison had an eyeSpy hover around the wall checking the long cracks that radiated out from the doorway. It had been a big bomb. 'Yeah, Sergeant, the back wall needs a lot of TLC.'

'Trouble is, it's gonna be getting more TNT than TLC,' mused Edelstein. He switched on his chin mike. 'Okay, ladies and gentlemen,' he announced, 'that was the bad guys' opening offer, and it's one their management will be keen on repeating. We've gotta keep them from setting off any more of their IEDs. Moynahan, round up the guys. It's time to lock, load and exterminate.'

Comrade Major Jacob Smith stood paralysed by shock. He had just violated one of the tenets of good military leadership: he had underestimated the enemy and the consequence of that arrogance was that his StormTroopers had been cut to ribbons. It had been a fuck-up that would make von Sternberg a very unhappy general, and in Smith's experience, the only way to make an unhappy general happy was to unfuck a fuck-up asap.

But he was perplexed about how to do that. The amount of blasting gelatin used in the bombs should have been more than enough to blow out the doors of the warehouse and to have stunned whoever was hiding inside in the process. Instead the doors remained standing – scorched and scarred, to be sure, but still standing – though the walls around them seemed to have bowed inwards and cracked. But if the resilience of the doors had come as a surprise, then the firepower these gangsters commanded had come as a profound shock. He had never heard of Gatling guns capable of such an intense rate of fire as those that had raked through the ranks of his StormTroopers, and even more worrying had been the accuracy with which these guns had been employed. The attack had taken place in the dark and in his experience, at night it was *impossible* for anyone to fire with such unerring precision.

This latter consideration convinced him that General von Sternberg's intelligence that this was a terrorist stronghold was somewhat flawed. It wasn't just a pack of power-crazed gangsters they were up against but something infinitely more formidable. Not that he would say as much to the general. Criticism of their superiors by subordinates was not encouraged in the SS. In fact, it was actively *discouraged*, generally by use of a firing squad.

Major Smith turned to his long-suffering lieutenant, a thin, nervous young man named Benedict Arnold. 'Status of the Krupp six-pounders?'

'Both are ready for deployment, Comrade Major.'

'Excellent. I want them positioned ready to fire at the target in fifteen minutes.'

Arnold swallowed. 'With all respect, Comrade Major, there ain't no way we can get a clean line of sight either front or rear. Everything's packed too tight around the warehouse. And if we get too close, them bastards inside are gonna burn us down with those Gatling guns of theirs.'

A good point. The warehouse where the terrorists were holed up was bounded on both sides by terraced houses, which made it difficult to manoeuvre a field gun without the bad guys seeing what was happening. Then Smith had a brainwave. 'We'll fire from *inside* one of the neighbouring houses, Lieutenant. That way we'll be able to get real close and still be protected from counter-fire.'

Holder was enjoying himself. Watching the Hamites – and despite what Harrison said he was sure they were Hamites, God would never have sent white guys to kill them – being slaughtered had given him a hard-on like he always got when he thought about slaying God's enemies. He just wished he could be allowed to use his M-29 to blast these pagans back to hell, but as his marksmanship was the worst in the platoon Massie had told him to stand down. So all he could do was loiter at the back of the Control Room and give thanks to Jesus every time he saw one of the Hamites fall. His prayers were cut short by a shout from Harrison.

'Looks like the bad guys are getting busy, Sergeant,' he yelled. 'Best I can judge, they're bringing up a coupla pieces of artillery and putting them in the front room of the house across the street. Polly identifies them as Krupp six-pounders. Kinda useful piece of kit. Coupla hits from those babies and we ain't gonna have much use for air conditioning. This place is gonna have more holes than a piece of Swiss cheese.'

'Okay, we're just gonna have to get our retaliation in first.' Edelstein looked around and his gaze settled on Massie. 'Massie, get one of your guys and bring up a Serpent.'

Seeing everyone else was busy, Massie signalled to Holder, who followed his corporal down the stairs to the basement, where the Portal's arsenal was housed.

'What's a serpent, Massie?' asked a nervous Holder. He didn't like the thought of being close to a serpent: the name smacked of the form Satan had taken when he had seduced Eve in the Garden of Eden.

'It's a shoulder-mounted multipurpose assault weapon. We'll use it to send a rocket with a thermobaric warhead into the house the badniks are using. It'll turn everything inside to cinders.'

'With fire and with his sword the Lord will execute all men, and many will be those slain by the Lord.'

'What's that, Holder?'

'Isaiah sixty-six, verse sixteen. It's about how terrible is the wrath of God.'

'No kidding. Well, I guess war ain't for the faint-hearted.' Massie brought them to a halt in front of a steel door. 'You ever been down here before, Holder?'

'No, I ain't, Corporal, the arsenal's off-limits to neoFights who ain't completed Preliminary Training.'

'I think with the badniks trying to blow us to hell and back we can bust a few rules.' Massie drew a set of keys from his belt, used them to work the lock and then spun the wheel sticking out of the centre of the door. With a heave, he pulled the heavy door open.

The room Holder stepped into was huge and every square inch of wall space was taken up by metal racks loaded with munitions. There were boxes upon boxes of M-29 ammunition, grenades and rockets.

'This is why Edelstein ain't overly worried 'bout the badniks,' explained Massie. 'We got enough munitions down here to blast them from now until Armageddon.' He nodded to a long metal box on one of the lower shelves. 'You catch the end of that and help me lug it upstairs.'

Holder was amazed by how heavy the box was. It took the pair of them five minutes to haul it up the stairs and to position it beside the window that faced out on the house the Shades were occupying. What Massie pulled out of the metal box looked to Holder nothing more fancy than a long steel tube.

'This, Holder, is a real motherfucker. We're really gonna be frying tonight.'

Holder couldn't stop himself. 'Could I fire it, Massie? Please, Massie...'

Massie thought for a moment and then gave a shrug. 'Yeah. Why not? Shit, even you couldn't miss with a Serpent. Okay, Holder, I'm gonna teach you how to barbeque badniks. Get down on your knees and put this baby up on your shoulder.'

An eager Holder did as he was told and Massie helped him heft the Serpent into position, with the rest on his shoulder and his face pressed against the night sight. Satisfied, Massie slammed a rocket into the back of the tube. 'Outstanding, Holder, you're hot to trot. Just don't touch that trigger until I give you the word.' He switched on his neck mike. 'Folks, we're just going to light up the night so you don't wanna be either in front or behind this little honey when she's dealing her magic. Let's keep the doors *and* your sphincters closed.' Warning given, Massie settled down on his knees beside the blast screen that covered the front window of the house. 'I'm gonna count to three, Holder, then open the screen. Once you got the house opposite in your cross hairs, pull the trigger. One ... two ... three!'

The ball of fire emitted from the rear of the weapon was fearsome, stripping the walls of the room back to the raw concrete. At a range of just fifty yards Holder couldn't miss. The rocket smashed its way through the wall of the facing house, there was a muffled *wooomph* and then the house collapsed in a blistering ball of fire.

'Five more bad guys have announced that they will be vacating their pension plan,' chortled Harrison over the loudspeaker.

Holder smiled. God had shown him the way.

Von Sternberg sat, stupefied, staring at the warehouse his men had been attacking for the last eight hours. During that time his army of two hundred men had been decimated and he had lost his major and both of his field guns. What he had gained, he suspected, was a death sentence. The Great Leader had been very insistent that this girl, Norma Williams, be dealt with firmly and expeditiously, and the Great Leader was a believer in his instructions being carried out. That von Sternberg hadn't been adequately apprised of the weaponry these terrorists had at their disposal would cut precious little ice. The Great Leader wasn't known for his generosity of spirit.

In pondering a solution to this problem von Sternberg had toyed with lying, telling the Leader that the mission had been successfully carried out and the girl killed, but he dismissed this ruse out of hand. It seemed that the Leader had an intimate knowledge of the inner workings of the terrorists' hideout – how, von Sternberg had no idea – so there was a distinct probability that Heydrich would know he was lying. No, the only option was to come clean and to ask for reinforcements.

1:26

The JAD
The Demi-Monde: 13th Day of Fall, 1005

1.18. When He had regained His state of ultimate Coolness, ABBA got to pondering that maybe it was His fault for making woeMen so sneaky, that maybe He had taken His eye off the ball when He had given Adam a partner. 1.19. So being big on compromise, ABBA created sheMen who were like neither Man nor woeMan but something in between, a calmer female spirit in a superior male body. As ABBA dug it, sheMen could take the female role in sex, being receptive to the entreaties of Men, but would operate without all the moaning and complaining that woeMen were so good at and wouldn't need any flowers and chocolates or any of that other expensive romantic shit laid on them before they could be persuaded to put out.

The HIM Book, Book of the Coming: Chapter 1, Verses 18–19

Having been pretty bashed about by the nuJu mob, Josephine Baker was consigned to the Portal's sickbay where she had stayed for a whole day, lost in sedated sleep. But now a very shaky-looking Josie had decided to rejoin the land of the living: she wandered into the Rec Room and plonked herself down beside Norma. A couple of cups of café au gore – the blood liberated by Burlesque from the same sickbay Josie had been occupying – and a hearty breakfast put the colour back in her cheeks.

'So how are you feeling, Josie?' asked Norma.

'Better since I caught a few zees but I still gotta head that's banging like I've been saucing too much on the much side.' Josie gave Norma a crooked smile, the same wonderful smile Norma remembered from their meeting in Venice. Even with her head swathed in bandages, she still looked stylish. 'My own dumb fault. I should have realised that Shades ain't the flavour du jour with the nuJus. I beeped when I should have bopped.' She looked over to Odette. 'Gotta thank you and Burlesque for pulling my black ass outta there when you did. Without you I'd now be numbered amongst the missing. You did me a real solid and I won't forget.'

''Eet was a pleasure, Josephine. You are our friend and friends, they 'elp each other, *n'est-ce pas*?'

'Yeah, I guess they do, but thanks anyway.' She took a sip of her coffee. 'So where is this place, Norma honey? Sure ain't like any clip joint I've ever been in before.'

'This is the Portal. It's the place where Daemons like me enter the Demi-Monde.'

'Far out.' Josie took a look around her at the neoFights who had come in search of breakfast and, if Norma wasn't mistaken, a glimpse of the Sensuous Shade in the flesh. And never one to disappoint, the robe Josie was wearing was on the shorter side of short and the tighter side of tight. She was sex on a stick.

'Tell me, Josie, do you know what happened to Vanka and Ella?'

Josie fidgeted awkwardly. 'Both of those cats are now deep-sixed. Vanka helped the WhoDoo to defeat Lilith, the spirit that had taken control of Ella's body, but the trouble was that her brother, Billy, a real crumbum, decided to make a personal appearance here in the Demi-Monde. Billy took control of Venice and announced that he was gonna sacrifice Ella on the last day of Summer in the Temple of Lilith. When he heard that, Vanka got real revved up and decided that he had to save her so he headed hot-foot to the Temple. He really loved the girl and I'm guessing that he and Ella were blitzed when the Temple blew.'

'That's terrible.' It seemed impossible that Ella and Vanka Maykov could have been killed: people like them didn't let themselves be killed.

Her ruminations were interrupted by Burlesque. 'Yus, it's real terrible,' he agreed, ''specially as that bugger Vanka still owed me money.' His observation was rewarded by a whack from Odette.

A silence fell as they all were lost for a moment in their sorrow. Finally, Josie spoke, trying to change the subject and lift the mood. 'So all these uniformed cats are Daemons?'

A distracted Norma nodded. 'That's right. But don't let that worry you. They were really excited to have the famous Josephine Baker as a guest.'

'Oh, yeah? Well, I can tell you there's one cat who ain't. If you take a gander towards the side of the room, you'll see a cave-dweller who's giving me some real reckless eyeballing. I've seen that look before and it belongs to cats who are all white and spite. There's one Blank who ain't happy to be sharing his space with a Shade.'

As casually as she could, Norma eased around in her chair to check out who Josie was talking about. Norma had seen him before; he was the quiet boy who seemed to spend his time trailing around after Corporal Massie. He was so quiet that Norma couldn't remember ever having spoken to him so she had to rack her mind to try to remember his name. 'I'd have thought you'd have gotten used to guys staring at you, Josie, but you don't want to worry about Holy Holder . . . he's harmless.'

'An' thick,' added Burlesque. ''E ain't smart enuff to piss 'imself even iffn 'is trousers were on fire.'

Josie gave a shake of her head. 'He might be thick, Burlesque, but that cat's been eyefucking me in one weird way for the last ten minutes. Way I see it, this Holder item is wrapped up way too tight and my experience is that sooner or later cats like him go postal.'

Holder stole a glance across the Rec Room at Josephine Baker as she sat sipping her coffee. She was devilishly beautiful, but wasn't that the way with all Hamite women? They were skilled in the arts of the flesh and in profane allurements. Josephine Baker was temptation personified, and gazing on her, Holder felt himself being captivated by her sleek, slender sensuality, imagining what it would be like to touch that perfect flesh . . .

Holder started and shook his head to drive out these obscene thoughts. He muttered a prayer and brought the crucifix out from beneath his shirt to kiss it. He would not succumb to Satan's blandishments, though it took a real effort of will to tear his gaze away from the girl's legs so wonderfully – evilly! – displayed by her short robe.

From the moment he had first seen this black succubus that morning, when she had come undulating down the corridor towards him, her delicious body rippling as she walked, he had known that his soul was in danger. And then she had glanced at him and as he stared into those huge brown eyes he felt her ensnaring his spirit, luring him away from Jesus, from the teachings of the Last Prophet, Frank Kenton.

Desperate to purge his mind of these unclean remembrances, Holder whispered the Last Prophet's Fifteenth nuCommandment: 'You shall not know any Hamite carnally. There is no greater sin than the sin of Miscegenation driven by the Daemon Lucifer.'

'What's that you say, Holder?' asked Massie. 'You talking to yourself again?'

Holder felt his face redden: he had forgotten that the unbeliever Massie was sitting across the table from him. 'No, Corporal. I was praying.'

'Then say one for me. Since the captain went AWOL, I think it's going to take a fucking miracle for us to get out of this shit-hole.' Massie stood up. 'Anyway, Holder, you ready to rock and roll?'

'Wha?'

'Time for our patrol, Holder, time to go see what's happening out in the JAD. So take your eyes off Josie's tits and grab your bits.'

Holder skirted around a particularly rancid-looking pool of water. The half-light and the rubble made progress slow, especially now the rains had come, turning the smashed rubble into a sort of sticky, pasty dough that clung to his boots with a tenacity that threatened to pull them off. Every surface was coated by a thick grey slime and the massive craters caused by the Shade artillery were full of flat, smooth, oil-slicked water.

Lost in thought, he trotted along behind Corporal Massie as they ducked and dived through the ruins of the JAD. He was listening to the voices that told him it was wrong – very, very wrong – for Sergeant Edelstein to have invited that Hamite whore Josephine Baker into the Portal. The Last Prophet, Frank Kenton, had taught that the Hamites were despicable in the sight of God, having fallen into the embrace of Satan.

He closed his eyes. Frank Kenton was telling him that the Portal had now become a cesspit of profanity and wickedness, a den of iniquity. The Portal and all the disciples of the daemons residing inside it had to be destroyed.

'You okay, Holder? You look like shit.' Massie's words came to him from far away, drowned out by the voices. He felt his shoulder being shaken. 'I said, you okay, Holder?'

Holder opened his eyes. 'Yeah, I'm okay, Sergeant. I think God has just spoken to me.'

'No shit? Well, tell Him to keep his fucking voice down otherwise he's gonna tip off the SS that we're here and get our fucking heads blown off.'

'We have brought the Whore of Babylon amongst us.'

'Look, Holder, I don't wanna rain on your parade, but this ain't the time or the fucking place for Bible class.'

'Don't you see, Massie, that Josephine Baker is the Great Whore who is the helpmate of the AntiChrist . . . of Norma Williams?'

'Josie Baker ain't no whore, Holder. Just 'cos she does a dance number tits al fresco and makes you liable to die with a hard-on don't make her a whore.' Massie shrugged. 'Not that I'd kick her outta bed even if she was.'

'She is the Whore of Babylon.'

'Bullshit. She's just a tasty piece of ass. Anyway, there ain't no place called Babylon in the Demi-Monde.'

'We have been tricked into doing the devil's work!' Holder heard himself shouting at the top of his lungs. 'If we do not fight the devil then we will be lost to Jesus and our immortal souls will be forfeit. We must destroy the Whore of Babylon who is Josephine Baker and we must destroy the AntiChrist who is Norma Williams.'

'You're outta your fucking mind.'

These were the last words Massie ever uttered. Holder shot him through the head.

Holder felt good. Frank Kenton had told him he had done the right thing by killing that emissary of Satan, Massie. And once he was dead, it had been the work of a moment to unclasp the keys to the arsenal from Massie's belt, mouth a short prayer over the man's body and then hightail it back to the Portal.

He knew he had to be real careful. He and Massie were only two hours into their four-hour patrol and his showing up at the Portal early without the corporal would mean that questions

would be asked. Holder wasn't good at answering questions . . .
he got confused when people asked him questions. But God was
on his side and neither Moynahan nor Edelstein were around so,
seizing his chance, he scuttled down the stairs leading to the
basement. He had the key in the lock of the arsenal's door before
he quite realised what he was doing. Pulling the door open, he
stepped inside, switched on the lights and then stood paralysed,
not having a clue just how to detonate all the munitions stockpiled in the room. But then Frank Kenton gave him inspiration
and his eye fell on the Serpent.

It took him ten minutes' hard work to open the fireproof
boxes containing the bullets and bombs and another five minutes to assemble and load the Serpent. Now he stood ready. He
wiped a hand across his sweat-drenched brow, mouthed a prayer,
took careful aim at the opened boxes and squeezed the trigger.

Norma was sitting with Josie in the Rec Room discussing lunch
when the arsenal went bang. One moment she was chatting to
Josie and the next she was grabbed by a hurricane of hot air and
hurled across the table to land in a muddle hard against a
vending machine. She must have blacked out, as the next thing
she knew there was a deafening blast and a huge gout of flame
spewed down the corridor. She was barely given enough time to
register that – miraculously – she was still alive when she was
sucked back across the table.

Dazed, bruised and part deaf, she lay there for a moment not
quite understanding what had happened. Then the fire alarms
sounded and the sprinkler system kicked in.

Revived by the water that torrented down on her, she levered
herself back to her feet, thankful that nothing seemed to be
broken. Sure, her boots were gone, her wrecked fatigues were
charred to holes and she had bitten through her lip, but other
than that, she was okay.

'Shit, Norma, this is one fuck-up of a hidey-hole you found for yourself,' said Josie as she hauled herself out from under a pile of chairs and gingerly stood up.

Together the two girls tottered out into the corridor, where the burned husks of two bodies were waiting to greet them, Norma retching at the smell.

There was a movement at the end of the corridor. 'Are you all right, Norma?' It was Moynahan.

'Yeah, yeah. What happened?'

'I think the arsenal exploded. Most of the blast was contained but some fool must have left the door open. We got the back-draft.'

'How many?' She trailed off, not quite sure what to call them. Victims? Casualties?

'We're not sure, but a few. Why don't you get to the sickbay, have a medic check you over?'

'No, I'm all right. I want to help.'

Norma made a quick count of the people gathered in the Rec Room. Other than her, there were sixteen survivors – five Dupes and eleven soldiers – and all of them looked battered and bemused.

Moynahan moved to the front of the room. 'Sergeant Edelstein was killed in the explosion so I guess that makes me officer-in-charge. I've appointed Odette Aroca here to be my number two. Any problems with that?'

There weren't, which was hardly surprising given that Moynahan and Odette were the two biggest people in the room.

'Other than Edelstein, Middleton and Brownlee are dead and Corporal Massie and Holder are missing so I guess you could say that we're down to the bare bones in terms of manpower. The explosion in the arsenal also destroyed our reserves of ammunition. All we've got left is what's up here on the ground floor and what you've got in your pouches so I don't have to tell you that that ain't a lot. From now on we've got to make every shot and every grenade count. I've asked Percy Shelley to check with you after the meeting and to collect any spare ammo. Shelley's going to be our quartermaster from here on in.' Moynahan glanced down at the notes he had written on the back of his hand. 'The other bad news is that the blast took out the stockroom and most of our food reserves so we're now all on half-rations. Sister Maria is going to be responsible for making sure that everybody gets a fair share of what's on offer.'

'What caused the explosion?' came a question from the back of the room.

'We're not sure. It could have been carelessness, it could have been sabotage. I don't know and, frankly, I don't care. I'm not going to spend time and effort on something we can't do anything about.'

'What about the Transfer Room? Was that damaged?'

'Nope. I've had Corporal Harrison check it out and it seems fine. We still don't have the transfer codes, but when we have . . .' He paused and took another look at his notes. 'I'm not standing here telling you that everything is jake. It ain't. It's gonna get real evil. Without superior firepower the only way we're gonna survive is by fighting the badniks up close and personal. It ain't gonna be easy and it ain't gonna be fun, but if we stick together we can come through this.'

Moynahan, Norma decided, was a Vanka-class bullshitter.

Terror Incognita
The Demi-Monde: 50th Day of Fall, 1005

It is estimated that sheMen constitute twenty per cent of the total male population of NoirVille. They have been classified as 'transgender', though many opt for full emasculation to ensure their journey into sheManHood is complete. The Church of HimPerialism teaches that for Men, sheMen are the preferred outlet for their sexual lusts, and with their being so few (relative to Men) their services are highly prized and lucrative. For poor NoirVillian Boys, a career as a sheMan is very attractive.

A Fool's Guide to HimPerialism: Selim the Grim, Bust Your
Conk Publications

They strung Colonel Sergei Trubetskoy and three of his officers up from a tall oak tree on the fiftieth day of Fall, the four of them sentenced to death for their failure to find Trixie Dashwood and the other rebel fugitives. General Clement had been unmoved by the Colonel's excuses that the girl *must* have left Terror Incognita because there was simply nowhere for her to hide . . . as the general said when he'd passed sentence, he didn't have much use for a dumbass Colonel who couldn't find his dick with both hands and the use of a compass.

Andrew Roberts was too busy to attend Trubetskoy's hanging: he had his own deadlines to meet. With some justifiable pride

– and a great deal of relief – he watched the train chug up the newly commissioned rail track with the pontoon rolling behind it on a flatbed truck and come to a halt alongside the Pyramid. Having delivered the Column bang on schedule, it was a very happy Roberts who repaired to his tent with a bottle of vintage Solution to celebrate . . . and to pack. As he saw it, his mission was finished and he could now go for a well-earned vacation in a place as far away from that baleful bastard Archie Clement as the geography of the Demi-Monde allowed.

His holiday planning proved to be premature. No sooner had he got himself comfortable on his bunk and was preparing to wrap himself around a bumper of Solution than his batman pushed his head through the tent's flap. 'Begging your pardon, Captain, but Comrade General Clement would like to see you.'

'When?'

'Now, sir.'

As he scooted across the parade ground to Clement's tent, Roberts found himself fretting about what the summons meant. Clement wasn't famous for his generous disposition so that, presumably, militated against it being an audience when he would be rewarded for a job well done. But whilst the chances of him leaving Terror Incognita as *Major* Roberts were slim, that he had accomplished the delivery of the Column on time would – he hoped – save him from ending the day holding up six foot of best Terror Incognita topsoil.

A rather perplexed Roberts presented himself at the general's tent, a perplexity made more acute by the presence of His Holiness Aleister Crowley, the mage sitting in a corner with a dark cloud hovering around his head. 'You sent for me, Comrade General.'

'Yeah, sure did. Your Holiness, this is Captain Engineer Roberts, the guy who did such a stand-up job in bringing the Column to the Pyramid.'

Roberts straightened his back and did his best to contain a smile. He had never heard Clement be complimentary about one of his officers before.

'You seem to be an engineer of some talent,' said Crowley.

'Thank you, Your Holiness.'

'So tell me, how do you think the Pre-Folk built the Pyramid?'

An odd question, but, fortunately, it was one Roberts had already given much thought to. Being possessed of an enquiring mind, the puzzle of how the Pre-Folk had constructed such an enormous edifice was one he'd been cogitating on ever since he'd arrived in Terror Incognita. The Pyramid was the greatest feat of engineering in the whole of the Demi-Monde and living and working in Terror Incognita had given him an ideal opportunity to study it. He planned to write a book on the subject when he was back in the ForthRight.

If he got back to the ForthRight.

'It's a tricky question, Your Holiness; by my reckoning, the Pyramid is made from half a million tons of Mantle-ite . . . from one thousand blocks of Mantle-ite each weighing over five hundred tons. The construction of the Pyramid is a feat of engineering unmatched anywhere in the Demi-Monde.'

'I know this: what I want to know is *how* they built it.'

'Well . . . discounting the possibility of the Pre-Folk being possessed of technologies or magics unknown to us, then I believe the answer is to be found in earthen ramps.'

'Earthen ramps?' queried an incredulous Crowley, obviously struggling with the Pre-Folk being associated with such a mundane technology.

'Yes, Your Holiness: I believe the Pre-Folk built the Pyramid by the use of ever-rising earthen ramps which allowed gangs of slave labourers to drag the blocks of Mantle-ite up to the place where they were needed. As one layer of blocks was laid, the ramp would be raised so work could commence on the next layer

... and so on and so on. Using this method and, of course, the employment of several thousand men and an equal number of mules, I think it would have been perfectly feasible for the Pre-Folk to site one ... possibly two blocks of Mantle-ite every day. At that rate it would have taken them less than three years to build the Pyramid.'

'Three years?'

'Yes, Your Holiness.'

'And could we use this earthen ramp technique of yours to move the Column from the base of the Pyramid to its pinnacle?'

'Yes, Your Holiness.'

'And how long would this take?'

'I would need to do some calculations, Your Holiness.'

Crowley waved a disdainful hand, then busied himself by pouring a glass of Solution.

Roberts took out his notebook and pencil and scribbled his calculations. He worked diligently for five long minutes, all the while trying to ignore the impatient tapping of Crowley's foot on the wooden floor of the tent. Finally he looked up and smiled. 'I am assuming that we will need two steamer-crawlers to drag the Column up the ramp, and as a consequence the ramp must be able to bear a combined steamers/Column weight of four hundred tons. Additionally the path running atop the ramp has to be durable enough to withstand both the depredations of the steamer tracks and the Fall rains. Moreover, the maximum incli-nation that steamers can negotiate hauling such a load is five degrees, therefore' – Roberts paused to make a swift check of his calculations – 'to construct a ramp of sufficient size and robust-ness we will need one million tons of compacted soil reinforced with one hundred thousand tons of steel girders and a similar quantity of cement.'

'And how long would such a structure take to build?'

'That, Your Holiness, depends upon the resources dedicated to the project, but I am confident that, given adequate support, such a ramp could be built in . . . a year!'

'A year!' squawked Crowley. 'What if I said it had to be completed by the end of Fall?'

'In fifty days? That, with all respect, Your Holiness, is an impossible deadline. Just to manufacture and transport the steel and cement would take twice as long as the timescale you propose. It might be possible to build the ramp's foundations by Season's end but . . .'

'The Column *must* be in place on top of the Column by the end of Fall, Captain Roberts. The Great Leader has commanded it be so. You do understand the implication of that instruction, don't you?'

Roberts did understand. His mouth went dry as he contemplated ending his tour on Terror Incognita swinging alongside Trubetskoy. His mind raced. There wasn't any method known to man that he could see solving this dilemma.

Known to man . . .

'I began, Your Holiness, by assuming that the Pre-Folk did not employ technologies unknown to us, but there are clues that they did.'

'Good!' said a suddenly energised Crowley. 'That is why we have turned to you, Comrade Captain Roberts, in the hope that you might be able to fashion a more . . . modern solution to the problem of elevating the Column to its final resting place. Go on.'

'I have noted that each of the landings on the staircase leading to the top of the Pyramid is hexagonal in shape and of a size that corresponds exactly to the dimensions of the base of the Column. I would speculate that there is some Pre-Folkian mechanism hidden inside the Pyramid waiting to be turned on, a mechanism that, if the Column were placed on the bottommost landing, would draw it upwards in a manner similar to that of a grain elevator.'

'How would this "grain elevator" of yours be activated?'

'That I don't know, Your Holiness. Perhaps the different colours of the Mantle-ite slabs use to cover the Pyramid or the numbers etched onto each of the landings of the staircase hold the secret, but . . .' He trailed off. He had spent hours studying both, trying to discover some pattern in them, but he had failed.

Crowley bent down and took a book from his briefcase, which he pushed across the table in the engineer's direction. 'This is a translation of the *Flagellum Hominum*, an ancient work which contains the lore of Lilith and the Pre-Folk. I had hoped it would reveal the methods by which the Pre-Folk moved the Column to the Pyramid's peak, but unfortunately the *Flagellum Hominum* has defied all attempts to unravel its secrets.'

'Tough shit, Your Holiness,' said Clement as he lolled back in his chair, 'you being stumped and all. Must be kinda galling to have to come to us military types to get your dick outta the wood chipper.'

The general's observation was rewarded by a glare from Crowley.

Doing his best to ignore the atmosphere of mutual loathing that existed between Clement and Crowley, Roberts took the book Crowley proffered into his hands. 'Perhaps if I was permitted to study the *Flagellum Hominum*, Your Holiness? It might be that an engineer can see what has eluded the attention of your more refined intellect.'

'The prosaic triumphant, eh?' Crowley gave a nod. 'Study away, Roberts, but only within the confines of your tent: the translation you hold in your hand is a Classified Document. You'll find the sections relating to the Column and the Pyramid marked by slips of paper.' And with that Crowley drained his glass, rose to his feet and flounced out of the tent.

'Better guard that book with your life, Captain,' said Clement as he popped a plug of chewing tobacco into his mouth. 'Ah hope you realise that you've adopted Crowley's mantle of failure. Fuck up raising the Column and His Holiness ain't gonna have a second's hesitation in casting you to the wolves . . . better *you* get chewed up by the Great Leader than him. Good luck.'

The threat of imminent death was, as Roberts came to appreciate, an enormous stimulant to performance and he set about trying to decipher the secrets of the *Flagellum Hominum* with gusto, reading the marked texts until he was cross-eyed. But the more he studied them, the more he was baffled. In the end he was forced to call on the help of Lieutenant Edgar Allan Poe, a man of humble birth and therefore limited prospects, but who was possessed of an intellect that Roberts thought bordered on genius.

Now, together with a bottle of Solution, they sat in Roberts' tent reviewing the enigmatic instructions and trying desperately to understand the clues the Pre-Folk had left.

'Let's review what we've learned, Edgar,' Roberts announced after thirty minutes of pondering. 'According to the *Flagellum Hominum*, there are two secrets pertaining to the Pyramid: the first is how to activate the power contained in the bloody thing and the second is how to raise the Column to the top of it. In Crowley's judgement, Edgar, there are four verses directly pertaining to the powering up of the Pyramid. Perhaps if you were to read them out loud we might have a better chance of appreciating what they mean.'

Poe nodded, opened the book and began. 'The Verses are numbers fifty to fifty-three of Book Three. They read as follows:

I am ABBA	The Nothingness.
Before me and after me	Is Nothing
But the Emptiness	Of the Never-Was,
And the Never-Will-Be.	I am the Not Being,

Absent but ever present.

I am ABBA	The One,
Omniscient,	Omnipotent and
Omnibenevolent.	Everlasting and
Never-Ending.	The Perfect Simplicity of Unity
Encompassed in my Being.	

I am ABBA	The Duality of the Kosmos.
The Determinate	And the Indeterminate
Melded.	The Yin
And Yang	United
In Ying.	

I am ABBA	The Nothingness, the One, the Duality.
Indivisible	Except by His/Herself.
Come, touch	The Great Pyramid
Unveil the Power	Of ABBA.
But to err is to die.'	

'Enigmatic.'

'Indeed,' mused Poe, 'but as these verses are accompanied by a woodcut of the northern face of the Pyramid, I don't think it's much of a leap to surmise that text and image are in some way related.' He nodded towards a copy of the woodcut image he'd drawn on the blackboard Roberts had had erected in his tent.

'More, I think we can assume that each shade of Mantle-ite relates to the Nothingness, the One or the Duality . . . zero, one or two.'

'But which is which, Edgar?'

'That is the conundrum, George. We are advised to "touch the Great Pyramid" to "unveil the power of ABBA". My own belief is

that the things that have to be touched are the triangular slabs covering the north face of the Pyramid, but which shade of Mantle-ite represents which number we aren't told.'

'And it would seem that the penalty for getting it wrong is quite draconian: "to err is to die".'

'We could, of course, simply guess.'

'With only a one in three chance of being correct. Not terribly appetising odds.'

The pair of them spent a silent few minutes in private contemplation of the riddle of the Pyramid. Finally, Roberts admitted defeat and turned the pages of the *Flagellum Hominum* until he came to the second marked passage.

'I've a feeling that solving the conundrum of how to get the Column sitting on top of the Pyramid might be easier. Verses fifty-four to fifty-six of Book Three relate to the staircase running up the northern side.

This is the stairway
To the Trinity
You must conquer
Progress the Column
To its resting place.

To heaven.
That is ABBA
Time and hence
By seconds

As we progress
So we progress
The positive
Enshrined in Ying.
We come to Revelation.

The Column
To ABBA
And the negative
Thus, on Fall Eve,

The Final Moment.
To the New.
Merges in Ying.
Brings the Column
Shall be the Victor.

The Old Yields
The Duality of Life
It is the One who
to Rest who

To my mind, the clue is in the word "progress". This sequence of numbers marked on the landings of the stairway is undoubtedly a numerical progression. What we are being challenged to do is find the next number in the series.'

He jotted the numbers on the blackboard.

$$2\ 5\ 2\ 3\ 2\ 7\ 8\ 11$$

'I'm sure that it can't be beyond the wit of the pair of us to discover what that number is.' And with that the pair of them buckled down to their calculations.

'A devilishly tricky sequence, Captain,' crooned a very self-satisfied-sounding Poe when he burst into Roberts' tent the next morning, 'but not devilish enough to resist my powers of analysis. Look!'

With that Poe laid a sheet in front of Roberts filled with mathematical musings. 'You see, the answer is eight! That is the number the device at the top of the Pyramid must be set to.'

'Well, it's certainly *one* solution,' mused Roberts.

'Believe me, George, this is the correct answer . . . I'm sure of it and now is the time to prove it.' He grabbed Roberts by the arm. 'Come on, George, let's make us some history.'

'We had better alert His Holiness—'

'His Holiness is already alerted, Comrade Captain,' came the unmistakable voice of Aleister Crowley from outside the tent, 'and I would be most grateful if you would provide Lieutenant Poe with all the assistance he might require to test this theory.'

Roberts didn't need any further encouragement: he threw his greatcoat over his shoulders and pushed his way out of the tent and into the chill of a Terror Incognita dawn. 'Are you sure about this, Edgar?' he whispered, as he bustled along after Poe. 'The *Flagellum Hominum* was quite specific: get the solution wrong and the consequences will be fatal.'

Poe cast a glance over his shoulder to make sure he wasn't being overheard by Crowley or any of his minions. 'Don't worry, George, I'm totally confident in my answer. You and I will be the toast of the ForthRight. It'll be back to London for wine, women and even more women.'

It took the rest of the day to have the Column removed from the pontoon and to erect it on the unmarked hexagonal plinth at the foot of the staircase. Once this had been done to Roberts' satisfaction he reported by to Crowley.

'We're ready, Your Holiness,' he announced, but just as he was about to accompany Poe up the staircase to set the dial to number eight he felt a restraining hand on his arm. 'I would be obliged if you would wait here, Captain,' said Crowley. 'There is no use in risking both of you.' With that he nodded to Poe, who began the taxing job of ascending the staircase.

Five minutes later Poe was standing at the top of the Pyramid. 'I am ready, Your Holiness,' he called down and Crowley signalled that he should begin.

Alone on top of the windswept Pyramid, Poe felt much of his bravado drain out of him. Andrew Roberts might be no great shakes as a mathematician but he was a loyal friend and without his support he felt very exposed and very unsure. There was no going back now.

He peered out over the side of the plinth. 'I am ready, Your Holiness,' he shouted and when he saw Crowley's arm drop he grasped the hand of the dial and wrenched it round to the number eight.

Nothing happened.

'Has he moved the dial?' Crowley asked.

'I presume so, Your—'

Roberts' presumption was interrupted by a huge ear-splitting scream that came from the top of the Pyramid, which for the briefest of moments glowed with a supernatural intensity. Then . . . nothing. A deathly hush fell over Terror Incognita as though the plaintive quality of the cry had stilled the world.

'What's happened?'

Roberts didn't wait to reply: he bounded up the stairs leading up the Pyramid two at a time. He found Edgar lying dead in the centre of the hexagonal platform.

The JAD
The Demi-Monde: 51st Day of Fall, 1005

"Solution to the Staircase Puzzle"

9	-2	+1	-0	=	8
8	+1	-0	-2	=	11
7	-0	+2	-1	=	8
6	-2	-1	+0	=	7
5	-1	+0	-2	=	2
4	-0	-2	-1	=	3
3	-2	+1	-0	=	2
2	+1	-0	+2	=	5
1	-0	+2	-1	=	2

Extract from the diary of Edgar Allan Poe dated 50th day of Fall, 1005

Schmuel Gelbfisz found it difficult to remember what the JAD had been like before the war, but if he closed his eyes he could still picture it. In his mind's eye he could see the zoot-suited men sporting their kippahs and beards, their briefcases and serious expressions, as they bustled through the crowds en route to the

JAD's bourse. He could see the elegant women in their feathered berets promenading arm-in-arm along the Street of the Profits, window-shopping as they went. He could see the PigeonGram messengers clutching their red envelopes as they darted along the cluttered pavements. He could see the steamers and the drays and the streetcars that made up the JAD's tangled traffic edging through the tight tenement-lined streets of HaRova and he could smell the stink of horses and soot and humanity that had given the JAD its unique bouquet.

All gone.

In the four weeks since the Shades had begun their onslaught, the old JAD had disappeared. Now all that remained was a waste-land; a burnt, battered and busted carcass of a city.

'Rabbi, what are your orders?'

Reluctantly Gelbfisz opened his eyes to confront this new and terrible reality. He was tired, used up, but he did his best to hide this feeling of despair from his private secretary. 'Remind me, Brecher, vot is zhe status of zhe enemy?'

'They have completed the encirclement of the centre of the JAD, Rabbi. We still have control of the Blood Bank but we are surrounded.'

'Food? Ammunition?'

'Our supplies of both are now almost exhausted, but these are not the most pressing problem, Rabbi. It seems that the Shades have succeeded in damming the water pipes feeding the centre of the JAD. We estimate that, with the one million non-combatants sheltering in the centre, we will have exhausted our water reserves by this evening.'

Gelbfisz nodded. It was over. The nuJus had fought hard – desperately hard – but, outnumbered four to one by the Shade HimPis and pounded night and day by their mortars, the end – though protracted – had been inevitable. 'Zhen my orders are simple: ve must fight until ve are no longer capable of fighting

unt trust zhat ABBA is in a generous frame of mind mit regards
to zhe granting of miracles.'

Pobedonostsev lowered his spyglass and smiled a very satisfied
smile. 'It would seem that we have now entered the endgame,
General. The nuJu scum are encircled . . . trapped. It is time to
administer the *coup de grâce*.'

Salah-ad-Din sighed and waited before replying until the
noise of the last salvo of artillery had subsided. 'His HimPerial
Majesty is not of a mind to grant the nuJus the opportunity to
surrender?'

The reply his question received came in the form of a derisive
snort. 'HimPeror Xolandi read your note with some amusement,
General. He was perplexed as to why, when the glorious HimPis
of the NoirVillian army have suffered such brutal losses at the
hands of these traitorous nuJus, you would wish to spare them.
The HimPeror feels that they should be punished for the cruel
and underhand tactics they have employed against our troops.'

'My suggestion that we offer the nuJus an honourable surrender was made simply to spare my soldiers further loss. HimPi
casualties are already running at thirty per cent and it is my
experience that those with no prospect of salvation – as the
nuJus now find themselves – fight hardest. The nuJus have gone
underground, inhabiting cellars and bombed-out basements,
the rubble providing them with perfect cover when they launch
their attacks on my troops. Taking the centre of the JAD from
the nuJus will be a savage undertaking and costly in Shade lives.'

'The HimPeror is becoming impatient.'

'Impatience, Grand Vizier, is not conducive to the effective
prosecution of war.'

'Criticism of the HimPeror smacks of disloyalty.'

'Not disloyalty, rather of reality. But if His HimPerial Majesty
is displeased with the manner in which I have managed his

army, I am willing to step aside to allow a more *impetuous* commander to take my place.'

The threat was made lightly but it provoked a reaction. 'No, no, General Salah-ad-Din, you misunderstand. His HimPerial Majesty is not unhappy with the way you are prosecuting the war, he merely wishes it brought to a swift conclusion.'

Salah-ad-Din made a mental note to increase his number of bodyguards. This snake Pobedonostsev knew that his reputation within the army was unassailable and if he was to resign, a great many of his men would take that as a signal that he was making a bid for power. So on the grounds that it was better to have the general inside the tent pissing out than outside pissing in, Pobedonostsev would do everything he could to avoid Salah-ad-Din resigning his post. But as dead men couldn't resign, he was probably already plotting Salah-ad-Din's assassination.

'You should understand, Grand Vizier, that we are now engaged in what your friend Heydrich calls the *Rattenkrieg* . . . the rat war. I have analysed the battles fought during the Troubles and in Warsaw and I have come to the conclusion that as such wars progress, as the fighting becomes more and more intense, so the ambitions of the attacker shrink. Thus it is with us. When we began our assault our aim was to take the JAD. Two weeks later this was amended such that all our energies were directed to taking the Central District and depriving the nuJus of access to their Blood Bank. And today? Today we are fighting for a street and tomorrow we will be fighting for a courtyard . . . a corridor . . . a room. You see, Grand Vizier, our war has become a personal one. No longer is it a war conducted by artillery and steamer but one fought eyeball to eyeball, with fighters blasting at each other from distances of a few feet, grappling, biting, gouging at one another.'

'HimPeror Xolandi has no interest in your difficulties, General, he merely wishes this war brought to a speedy and triumphant end.'

Salah-ad-Din glanced towards the Grand Vizier. 'To ensure this it is necessary that the nuJu fighters lay down their weapons, which is why we should offer to spare the nuJu women and children if their fighters surrender.'

'No,' said Pobedonostsev firmly, 'they must *all* die. We have an opportunity, General, to finally eradicate these nuJu scum . . . to cleanse the Demi-Monde.'

'Very well, the cannonade will take two days—'

'No!' snapped Pobedonostsev. 'The final assault must begin immediately: the HimPeror has noted your promise, General Salah-ad-Din, that the JAD will be subdued within forty days, and that promise falls due tomorrow.'

Salah-ad-Din nodded. 'Then, if you will excuse me, Grand Vizier, I have to make my peace with ABBA. To destroy the nuJus in a single day will require a miracle.'

Burlesque and Odette were lying on the floor of a burned-out house that abutted the Portal trying to sneak a peek through a shattered wall at what the SS were doing across the road. Burlesque could hear shouted orders drifting towards him, and from these it was obvious that the StormTroopers were getting themselves ready to attack. Soon the Portal's defenders would be fighting for their lives.

He signalled to Odette that they should pull back to the Portal and then froze. He could hear someone moving around in the room next to the one they were occupying: the SS had obviously sent out a reconnaissance patrol.

Not daring to speak in case he was overheard, Burlesque edged towards the room, unwrapping the strips of sacking from around the breech of the Sten sub-machine gun he had requisitioned from a dead SS StormTrooper as he went. With the whole of the JAD shrouded in a haze of brick dust and powdered plaster it was essential that none of it got into the workings of his gun, otherwise it had an annoying – and potentially fatal – inclination to jam. He gently cocked the weapon and he and Odette eased along the wall towards the room occupied by the SS, doing their best to step carefully to avoid kicking any of the cartridge cases littering the floor. In the JAD people fired at the slightest of sounds.

Taking a deep, calming breath, Burlesque manoeuvred his head around the doorway and then stood stock-still. The sounds he'd been hearing weren't those of an SS patrol: on the other side of the room was a pig chewing at the putrefied carcass of a man. Burlesque couldn't believe his eyes. It seemed impossible that a *pig* could have survived uneaten for so long in a starving JAD, though neither the Shades nor the nuJus being partial to pork might have had something to do with it. All he could think was that it had been the personal property of one of the SS officers, who had been saving it for when times really got tough.

Burlesque's mouth salivated at the thought of a pork supper and he was just opening his razor knife to deal with the pig when there was a scuffing of boots and a puff of dust. Burlesque dodged back: there was an SS StormTrooper creeping towards the pig, knife in hand. He'd obviously spotted the animal and decided, like Burlesque, that it was ripe for the cooking pot.

Burlesque saw Odette pull a grenade out of the haversack she had slung over her shoulder. In their time fighting together in the Portal they had come to an understanding: Odette did the grenade work – she was stronger than Burlesque and could throw the things further – while Burlesque provided covering fire. The girl tugged the pin from the grenade and then waited . . . and waited . . . and waited. Burlesque hated the way she cut it so fucking fine, but, as Odette delighted in telling him, the point was to have the grenade explode on impact otherwise there was a bloody good chance of the SS picking it up and lobbing it straight back at them. He still thought she cut it too fucking close for comfort.

With a grunt, she hurled the grenade through the doorway and Burlesque started blasting. Although his gun, like all Stens, was wildly inaccurate, for close-up killing it was devastatingly effective. He let fly with a full thirty-two-round magazine which sent the StormTrooper tumbling backwards head over heels. He also managed to reduce the pig to pork.

Odette's grenade exploded. Confined by the thick concrete walls of the room, the explosion was ear-splitting and the amount of dust and smoke it threw up made it impossible to make out what was going on. Not that it made much difference. Burlesque slammed another magazine into the Sten and then leapt forward screaming and yelling as he let fly in the general direction of anywhere.

There had been four StormTroopers making up the patrol, two of them mashed by Odette's grenade and two – and the pig – blasted to buggery by Burlesque's Sten. Burlesque didn't give the four bent and buckled bodies lying on the floor of the room a second look; all his thoughts were on his pork dinner.

Lieutenant, or, as he was now, *Captain* Benedict Arnold was sure his mother would be very proud of him. He had only been a lieutenant for three months but here he was receiving a battlefield promotion granted by Comrade General von Sternberg himself. Of course, Jake Smith getting himself fried alive had a lot to do with his elevation, but then in war one man's misfortune was generally another man's luck. And anyway, right now Arnold had more on his mind than Smith's somewhat premature demise: standing in front of the general, he was feeling less than optimistic about both life and his promotion.

Von Sternberg took a long drag on his cigarette and then began. 'Now that Captain Smith has, by virtue of his incompetence, seen fit to have himself killed, I am in need of a field commander who is able to prosecute the final attack against the Portal with passion and with imagination. I am of a mind to appoint you, Arnold, but I want to hear from your own lips that you feel yourself imbued with the necessary resolve to perform this task.'

'I will do everything in my power to take the Portal, Comrade General. Rest assured—'

'You see, Arnold,' the general continued as though he hadn't spoken, 'the longer these terrorists defy us, the more embarrassing it becomes: embarrassing for the ForthRight, embarrassing for the SS, and, most importantly, embarrassing for me. The Great Leader, in his magnanimity, has provided reinforcements of five hundred men and four field guns, and, as you might imagine, to ask for such assistance is not something I have done lightly: the admission of failure it entails is enormous. To avoid further embarrassment, I have decided to award a bounty of five thousand guineas to the first of our fighters into the citadel and a thousand guineas a man when the Portal falls.'

'Very generous, Comrade General. I am sure—'

'Of course, whilst I believe that the carrot is necessary to put the requisite amount of fire in the bellies of our StormTroopers, it is also necessary to employ the stick. You will attack at dawn tomorrow, Arnold. You have one hour to secure the Portal and to eliminate all the gangsters cowering there. Failure to do this will result in your being shot for crimes against the ForthRight.'

Arnold saluted, spun on his heels and left the general's office, wondering as he did so if the quartermaster had a miracle somewhere in his stores.

At the end of a very long and nerve-racking patrol it was a weary Josephine Baker who wandered into the Portal's Rec Room to try to get a few hours' sleep. She was welcomed by the delicious smell of roasting pork and to her astonishment saw that Burlesque was barbecuing a butchered pig over the flames of a fire burning in an oil drum in the middle of the room.

Burlesque started. He had obviously been so intent on his cooking that he hadn't heard Josie arrive. 'That yous, Miss Josie?'

For a moment Josie thought Burlesque was taking the rise out of her – she wasn't used to men not digging who she was – but then she realised that camouflaged by a thick coating of dirt and cordite and with her face half-hidden behind the handkerchief fastened around her mouth and nose she wasn't looking her most glamorous. But then everybody wore a handkerchief steeped in cologne as a face mask now: the stench coming from the dead bodies decorating the JAD – each of them black with feasting flies – was fearful.

'Yeah, it's me, Burlesque.'

'Any news?'

'Yeah, but none of it good. From what we could see we're close to being encircled. The way I dig it, the reinforcements the SS have been waiting on have finally arrived.'

Burlesque gave a careless shrug. He seemed more worried about his cooking than he did about the SS. 'That's wot Odette an' me reckon. It's gonna get 'ot an' 'orrible real soon. Lose any of your guys?'

'Just the one. Hancock got deep-sixed near the barricades at the end of Eleazar Street.' She moved across to the list of those defending the Portal pencilled on the Rec Room wall and put a line through his name. 'There's only fourteen of us left now: five Demi-Mondians and nine Real Worlders.'

'Fuck it; we've all gotta die sum time. Come an' 'ave some pork.'

'Real pork?'

'Cors it is. Me an' Odette found a pig wandering around and requisitioned it. Gimme anovver ten minutes and I'll be ready to serve it up.'

Josie shook her head in wonderment. Burlesque seemed to be indefatigable, never to tire or to despair. She gave him an appreciative peck on his cheek. 'You're one cool cat, Burlesque Bandstand.'

'Get off, you randy Shade minx, you. Fine fing it'd be if Odette wos to wake up an' catch you an' me snogging. She'd 'ave your guts for garters. So why don't cha make yourself useful an' get all the lads and lasses up. If we're gonna be sent to ABBA we might as well do it on a full stomach.'

The 'lads and lasses' were sleeping on the floor of the Transfer Room, which, because it was constructed of heavy-gauge steel, had survived the SS artillery fire and the explosion of the arsenal unscathed. Josie prodded them awake with the end of her boot and after a moment's grumbling they staggered to the Rec Room. There was little left of the happy and confident fighters who had welcomed her when she had first come to the Portal, now their faces were gaunt with fatigue, every wrinkle highlighted by dirt, their eyes were sunken and their hands shaking so much that they struggled to light a cigarette.

Their mood improved when Josie started dishing out scalding hot tea and the pancakes Burlesque had concocted from a mixture of flour, water and pork fat. It was the first hot meal they'd had for a week and a fed soldier was always a happy soldier.

They were on their second helpings when two very grimy soldiers hauling a large ammunition box between them pushed their way into the room. 'Good evening, everybody: special delivery courtesy of the Norma and Percy Postal Service. Moynahan thought you might be running low on ammunition. Make the most of it, though. It's the last of the reserves we had up here when the arsenal blew.'

'What's the occasion, Norma?' asked Josie.

'It's for a "Welcome to the Portal" party we're throwing for the SS,' answered Moynahan as he staggered into the room carrying a box of grenades on his shoulder. 'My guess is that they'll be coming at us in the morning, so there's no point in trying to eke out our ammunition. If we're gonna give them the turnaround, we'll have to blast them with all we've got.'

The room went silent. This was the announcement all of those holed up in the Portal had been dreading. While they were facing a beaten-up regiment of SS there was a feeling they could survive, but now even that faint hope had gone. All that was left was the certainty of death.

'How're we doing with re-establishing the connection codes?' Norma asked.

A derisive snort from Moynahan. 'No chance. Simmons fucked them over too good. There are a squillion combinations to try so Hoskins could be sitting up in the Transfer Room until hell freezes over and he'd still never find the right one.' Moynahan took a long swig of the coffee Burlesque handed him. 'No, all we can do is carry on fighting for as long as possible and hope that there's a miracle with our name on it out there.'

'Fuck 'em,' said Burlesque loudly. 'Iffn they come, they come but they ain't gonna spoil my dinner,' and with that he started dishing out his roast pork.

Moynahan was just digging into his pork when Maria came to sit next to him. 'I would be most obliged, Dean, if thou wouldst educate me in the operation of this weapon thou callest the M-29.'

Moynahan found it difficult to mask his surprise. Maria had never taken part in the fighting, making herself useful instead by hauling ammunition, cooking and tending to the wounded. Moynahan had never asked why, simply assuming it was something to do with her calling as a Visual Virgin.

'Are you sure about this, Maria? Isn't killing against your order's teachings or something?'

'Visual Virgins find death abhorrent, Dean, because we *see* death. Death is a frightful thing and the pain and agony is writ large in a person's aura.'

'I suspected as much, Maria, that's why I never made an issue of it.'

'I know. Thou hast been most kind to me, Dean, but now, as the end approaches, I understand that such sensitivities are a luxury that can no longer be indulged. This is a fight for survival.' Maria gave Moynahan a long look, then raised a hand to brush away some of the grime that decorated his nose. 'I know from thy aura, Dean, of thy love for me and I know that that love is true. Thou art a good man, strong and noble. Thou hast been a faithful and loyal friend and a staunch and steadfast ally.'

She leant forward and kissed Moynahan gently on the lips. 'I have come to love thee, Dean, though I have resisted this admission, my soul being much tormented that soon I will lose thee. But now I see that such reticence is ill thought. So I offer myself to thee, Dean. I wish thee to free me from my oath of chastity so that I might stand at thy side in these final hours, free of the curse of auralism. I would be proud to call a man such as thee mine.'

'I'm . . . I'm not sure that I understand.'

Maria stood up and stretched out her hand to Moynahan. 'I wish thee to love me, Dean, I wish thee to make me a woman . . . thy woman. Thou sayest that the SS will attack at dawn, therefore I would suggest that we use the few hours we have left in this world to good purpose.'

Moynahan rose to his feet and stared into Maria's eyes. 'You make me very proud, Maria, that a woman as beautiful and as intelligent as you would say something like that to a man like me.'

'No, Dean, the honour of being thy lady is mine.'

*

A disheartened Norma joined Shelley at his table, the two of them sitting in silence for a few moments, each lost in their own thoughts. Finally Shelley looked up and smiled. 'Tell me, Norma, what will you do when you have weturned to your world?'

Norma tried to return the smile but failed. She had forgotten how to smile, happiness having been replaced by a weary fatalism. Instead she shrugged. 'That question is academic now, Percy, given that I won't be going back.'

'Oh, I do not believe ABBA would be so churlish as to deny such a beautiful flower as you a chance to blossom.'

'You're very kind, Percy, and the answer to your question is that I'm not sure. Oh, I'd have needed to sort out just what Aaliz Heydrich has been doing with my body for the last six months, but other than that, I really haven't a clue.'

'What about the Normalist movement?'

Another shrug. 'Percy, it's difficult for me to explain just how difficult it is to change things in the Real World. I'd love to be able to sit here and tell you I'd be able to convince people that living in peace and harmony is the only way for civilisation to flourish, but I think that's just a pipe dream. There are just too many entrenched interests and power blocs which would see Normalism as a threat to the status quo. There is just too much hatred in the world – in the Real World – for a movement preaching non-violence to flourish.'

'You are forgetting the discussion we had a while ago, when I opined that for a wevolution such as Normalism to succeed, mankind must be *changed* . . . that they must be given the facility to understand how they are being manipulated.' Shelley took a sip of his coffee. 'This is a lesson that I learnt through much gwief and pain, being that I was similarly betwayed by UnFun-DaMentalism. And the weason why Heydwich's wevolution mutated into the cowwupt howwor it is today was that the thinkers who supported the wevolution didn't understand that to have a truly classless society – which was the avowed aim of UnFunDaMentalism – it is necessary to wecognise that the most important of all the commanding heights of the economy isn't iwon or coal, isn't agwiculture . . . it's information.'

'I'm not with you, Percy.'

'Like all tywants, Heydwich understood that without fweedom of information there is no *weal* fweedom. He knew that his wevolution was just a sham, that it was just a squalid power gwab, but by contwolling the information given to the people of the ForthWight he transformed it into something which seemed noble and honouwable.'

'I understand, Percy, but it still doesn't tell me how revolutionaries like Heydrich can be stopped.'

'By ensuring that *all* citizens have equal access to *all* information. By the destwuction of pwivacy.'

Norma gawped. 'What?'

'A fwee people have no use for pwivacy!'

'But why?'

'Because the desire for pwivacy is not a natural inclination of HumanKind: it is inculcated. Pwivacy is just a polite name for secwecy and it is the acceptance of secwecy as the natural order of things which allows politicians to deceive their people. It is perhaps no coincidence that you wefer to Demi-Mondians as Dupes, but I wonder if that is an epithet which might also be applied to you Weal Worlders. In the society I envisage evewybody would have free and untwammelled access to *all* information . . . nobody would be a Dupe. Everyone would know – or be able to find out – evewything. In an InfoCialist Sector evewybody would know evewything about evewybody.'

'InfoCialist?'

'InfoCialism is my name for a political and social system within which *all* the citizens of a Sector enjoy collective ownership of the information gathered and held by those who govern them.'

'Impossible!'

'Not impossible. My idea is that *all* information would be made available for public examination. InfoCialism would wender the twaditional concept of pwivacy obsolete and by doing this it would make it impossible for politicians – wascals that they all are – to *dupe* the people.'

'But society couldn't function without privacy.'

'Pwivacy – *weal* pwivacy, that is – is only enjoyed by those with weal power. Why do you think there are so many laws to pwotect the wich and the powerful fwom the enquiwies of the news-papers? Why do you think government censorship is so pwevalent and why libel laws are so dwaconian? The answer: to pwotect the wich and the powerful from the attentions of the man in the stweet! But for the ordinary person there is no pwivacy. The government knows or can find out evewything they wish about us, the masses, but the masses are denied the opportunity to weciprocate by knowing all there is to know about their leaders.'

'I can't agree with you, Percy. Most people want to *prevent* the spread of the government's control of information by curtailing surveillance. They want more privacy, not less.'

'That is because society teaches that pwivacy is a good thing, and hence people come to think that secwecy is the natural state of affairs. This must change . . . pwivacy must be consigned to the wastebasket of histowy.'

'All I can say, Percy, is that this InfoCialism of yours is an *extraordinarily* radical theory.'

'Wadical but inevitable if we are to secure weal fweedom. The wuling elite have awwanged things so that only they – the Lords of Information – have access to the *arcana imperii* . . . the secret knowledge of the state, knowledge and information denied to the lower orders.'

'Okay, Percy, let's say for the sake of argument that I agree with you. The question is: what's this got to do with Normalism?'

'Because, my dear Norma, if you can socialise information then no one will be able to deny or to twaduce the truth inhewent in a cweed pwomoting peace and non-violence.'

'Well, Percy, that's all very interesting but it ain't gonna happen. Like Moynahan says, it's gonna take a miracle for me to get back to the Real World.'

All Shelley did was smile.

1:29

Terror Incognita
The Demi-Monde: 51st Day of Fall, 1005

The first attribute of a subMISSive woeMan is to be Mute, one who is seen but not heard. Muteness in woeMen can be best achieved by following these precepts:

- In public, a woeMan should never speak to strangers, be they Man, woeMan or sheMan.
- A woeMan should always speak with a dulcet tone and never raise her voice in anger. Her words should be honeyed. She should never be shrill or demanding.
- A woeMan should never complain. She should be thankful for her lot in life no matter how trying or uncomfortable it might be.
- A woeMan should listen before she speaks and should never instigate a conversation. A woeMan should never speak to a Man before he has spoken to her.
- A woeMan should never contradict a Man and her opinions should mirror those of her father or her husband. Indeed, a woeMan should never have opinions of her own; and,
- A woeMan should not be educated, as education will only encourage her to contradict or dispute with her father or her husband.

A Fool's Guide to HimPerialism: Selim the Grim, Bust Your Conk Publications

It had been Trixie's father who had come up with the idea of how to keep them out of the clutches of the SS. On the basis that the best place to hide a tree was in a forest, he had advised them to conceal themselves as close to the workers' encampment as they could, wait until the next bargeload of draftee labourers was landed and then join them. A simple enough procedure: the SS guards were, after all, intent on stopping the Poles escaping from the forced-labour gang, not stopping people volunteering to *join* it. And, after all their adventures, the five fugitives – Trixie, Wysochi, Cassidy, Crockett and Trixie's father – were dirty enough and ragged enough to pass as labourers. The only problem Trixie could see with this ruse was that she was a girl and in her experience labourers tended to be big men, but she needn't have worried. A fair proportion of the workers the SS had selected to help with the construction of their railway line had been chosen not so much for their strength but for their looks: the SS had obviously decided that if they were to be posted to Terror Incognita there might as well be some attractive women on hand to help them better enjoy their off-duty moments.

But whilst Trixie was confident that the liberal coating of muck she had smeared over her face and clothes – and her stubble of hair – would make her a less than tempting target for the amorous attentions of the SS, she was less confident about her father's ability to survive. He was fifty-three years old and wasn't built for hard manual work. Now, after seven weeks of back-breaking toil, as the five of them lined up for the bowl of porridge the SS called breakfast, he looked emaciated, tired and was racked by a quite horrible cough.

'Are you all right, Father?'

'Not really, Trixie, but thank you for your concern. I am afraid that a career as a commissar hasn't equipped me for life as a labourer' – he looked down to the contents of his bowl – 'especially when the cuisine is so woefully inadequate.' He gave Trixie an attempt at a smile. 'But I am delighted you have evaded the attentions of the SS. They obviously lack an eye for beauty.'

Trixie laughed, but her opinion was that the SS were simply too tired to think of matters carnal, and had precious little time to indulge them. Clement had come to Terror Incognita to build a railway and to this end Labour Gang #2 – the poor sods who had drawn the night-shift – had been forced to work twelve hours each night, felling trees, hauling sleepers and laying tracks . . . and of course the SS had to be on hand to guard them. It was exhausting work for both captors and captives but it got results, and now, with the railway line complete, the moment when they had to 'do something' to disrupt the erection of the Column and to foil Crowley's plans was at hand. The question was how? And the answer to this dilemma came to her in her sleep.

After finishing her breakfast, Trixie had slumped exhausted onto her paillasse and immediately fallen asleep, only to be woken a few moments later by a hideous shrieking noise. Gingerly she eased her eyes open and looked around to see Wysochi, Crockett, Cassidy and her father standing at the tent flap peering out.

'What's happening, Feliks?'

Wysochi waved her over. 'Crowley's attempted an experiment with the Pyramid . . . an experiment which has gone wrong.' When Trixie looked, she saw Captain Roberts urgently waving a team of orderlies up the Pyramid's staircase. 'Lieutenant Poe went up to the summit a few minutes ago, then all Hel broke loose. I've a feeling that the Lieutenant's toast . . . and I mean that literally.'

Trixie shook her head trying to get her sleep-befuddled mind working. 'Experiment? But why would Crowley be doing that?'

Her father gave a wry laugh which immediately mutated into a racking cough. 'Because the man's foxed! He doesn't know how to get two hundred tons of Column onto a plinth standing two hundred and fifty feet above the ground. I've been watching for a few days now: Crowley and his cronies have been coming out every morning to study the Pyramid and to consult with Captain Roberts, then they retreat back into their tent for a conference. I think they're bamboozled.'

'But surely they could just drag it up there. They could use a steam winch?'

Her father laughed. 'It's a little more tricky than that, Trixie. Hauling two hundred tons of uncooperative Column up a sixty-degree slope is one Hel of a task and it's one that's stumped Crowley.'

'What about his magic?'

'It seems his magic has failed, so I'm guessing that he's looking for an engineering solution. *That's* why he's been consulting with Captain Roberts. I think Roberts has been tasked with discovering how the Pre-Folk lifted the Column.'

'And what's the answer?'

'My belief is that the three different colours of the Mantle-ite slabs covering the Pyramid have some relevance to the activation of the Pyramid . . . that they aren't simply decorative. The lucky thing is that the significance of the colours seems to be lost on Crowley and that's why he's asked Captain Roberts to help.'

Standing there, Trixie had to admit that what her father said made eminent good sense . . . she also had to admit to being annoyed with herself. While she'd been sleeping, he had been plotting.

'They're bringing Lieutenant Poe's body down,' Cassidy observed. 'Captain Roberts doesn't look a very happy bunny.'

And what happened next did nothing to make him any happier. As Trixie watched, the captain was called over by Crowley and there followed five minutes of Crowley shouting and waving his arms while a cowed Roberts pointed to a piece of paper in his hand and made several references to a large and very weighty-looking book that one of Crowley's minions was carrying.

'What's the book?' Trixie asked.

'I'm guessing it's the *Flagellum Hominum*,' answered her father, 'which, I suspect, contains clues as to how the Column might be raised.'

'Then we've got to get a look at it!'

Wysochi laughed. 'Easier said than done, Trixie. I've been watching Roberts and that book only leaves his tent when he comes out to attend the morning conferences with Crowley. The rest of the time it's kept in his tent and his tent is always kept under guard.'

'Then we'll have to unguard it!'

'Yeah, but how?'

'With the help of some hot water.'

As he lit a surreptitious cigarette, SS StormTrooper First Class Bert Baker decided that this Comrade Captain he had been set to guard was an odd sort. Polite enough, but decidedly odd. Every night, just before midnight Roberts left his tent and walked over to the Pyramid and stood there for an hour silently gazing at the bloody thing while smoking cigarette after cigarette. What he found so interesting about the Pyramid, Baker hadn't a bloody clue, but what he did know was that it was a dangerous occupation. His mate Percy Elmer who worked as an orderly in the field hospital had told him that Lieutenant Poe's body looked as though it had been roasted when they brought it in. Fooling around with the Pyramid was, Baker decided, something best left to officers.

'Hello, soldier.'

Baker snapped out of his reverie and brought his rifle to bear on the voice.

'Who goes there?'

There was a giggle. 'Just me,' and the 'me' in question stepped out of the darkness and into the halo of light cast by the lantern hanging from a branch of the tree next to Captain Roberts' tent. The girl was young – Baker thought she couldn't have been much older than eighteen – and was a bit skinny for his taste but there was no denying that she was a looker and a very *clean* looker at that. There was also a mischievous twinkle in her eye and a pout on her full mouth that drove any consideration of how unfeminine she looked in her trousers, work shirt and scrub of hair from Baker's thoughts. Anyway, as he hadn't had a woman since he'd come to Terror Incognita he wasn't inclined to be picky.

'What you doing here?' he snapped as he desperately tried to avoid looking at the hint of cleavage peeping out at him from beneath the girl's unbuttoned shirt.

The girl gave a coquettish little hitch of her hip. 'Well, now the Column has been brought up to the Pyramid, all us labourers have been given the night off so I've come looking for some company.'

Baker looked nervously around. If he was found chatting with a girl while he was on duty he'd be up before the major on a charge, but the way the girl was toying with the buttons of her shirt persuaded him that it wouldn't harm to be polite.

'Oh, yeah? So wot's your name?'

'Bella.'

'Nice name. Mine's Bert.'

The girl edged closer. 'I like your uniform, Bert,' she purred as she ran her fingers down the lapel of his jacket. 'I've always had a soft spot for soldiers in uniform. They always make me go weak at the knees.'

'Oh, yeah?'

'Yeah. Would you like to kiss me, Bert?'

Bert Baker decided that he would like that very much indeed but a voice at the back of his head began chirping a warning. It was one thing to be brought up before the major for talking with a girl on duty, but to be found kissing her . . .

'Nah, I can't. I'm on duty, see.'

'Such a shame,' Bella crooned as she stepped away from the lantern's penumbra so that once again she was hidden in shadow.

Unfortunately for Bert's peace of mind, she wasn't so hidden that he couldn't see her continuing the slow unbuttoning of her shirt.

'When do you get off duty, Bert?'

Bert gulped. 'Er . . . tomorrow morning. Eight o'clock.'

More buttons opened and Bert edged away from the tent's entrance to get a better look at the wonders the girl was intent on displaying.

'Do you smoke, Bert?'

A funny question. 'Yeah, cors.'

'We labourers don't get a cigarette ration. There's nothing I wouldn't do for a packet of cigarettes. So if I came to your tent in the morning, would you have a packet of cigarettes for me, Bert?'

Bert stood there transfixed by the twin emotions of lust and fear. 'Yeah,' he finally said in a strangled voice, 'maybe even two packs.'

'So what did you find out, Wysochi?' Trixie asked when they were safely back in their tent.

'I found out that I'm gonna have to keep a bloody sharp eye on you in future. I never knew you were such a dab hand at playing the femme fatale.'

Trixie giggled and kissed Wysochi on the cheek. 'Don't worry about that, Wysochi, there's only one man for me, and that's you.'

'Yeah, right,' Wysochi grumped.

Her father gave a discreet cough. 'If you two have finished canoodling perhaps we could get on with our discussions? Wysochi's search of Captain Roberts' tent tells us that it *is* the *Flagellum Hominum* he has been referring to and, more importantly, which are the passages in the book that are key to his deliberations. Wysochi had the presence of mind to copy these down.' He proffered his notebook to Trixie. 'This is what they say.'

Trixie studied the verses carefully and then shrugged her shoulders. 'What do they mean?'

And her father told her.

All Wysochi could suppose was that meeting Trixie had a much more profound effect on Bert Baker than he had imagined. Wysochi had thought that the chance of him recognising Trixie in daylight would be slim, especially with her surrounded by four tall men and her face camouflaged by a patina of dirt.

But Baker did.

They were marching to breakfast the next morning when Wysochi, vigilant as ever, spotted that Baker was one of the detachment of StormTroopers designated to guard the work gang. 'That's Baker, up ahead, so keep your head down, Trixie,' he whispered, but it did no good.

'You!' Baker snarled as he grabbed Trixie by the arm and dragged her out of the line of shuffling workers. 'You're that Bella item that got me all riled up last night. Well, I'm off duty in five minutes so let's see what you look like under all that filth.' He wrenched at her overalls and though Trixie squirmed and struggled, Baker was too strong for her to resist. It took Wysochi's fist in his face to persuade him that this wasn't going to be his day for sexual dalliance. As Baker slumped to the ground, Wysochi was set upon by the other guards and it would have gone badly for him if Cassidy and Crockett hadn't intervened. There was a vicious scuffle that ended with more of the SS racing to the rescue.

'Shoot those fuckers!' Baker shouted as he spat out his front teeth, and Wysochi and his two allies found themselves staring at the wrong end of five automatic rifles.

'Belay that order.'

The command came from General Clement, who had witnessed the set-to and was now striding over to see what had caused the kerfuffle. 'Hold that girl,' he shouted and the SS guards pinioned Trixie's arms even tighter. 'Well, ah'll be . . . if that don't beat all. If ah ain't mistaken, this is Miss Trixie Dashwood, gentlemen, the most wanted Reb in the whole of the Demi-Monde, and that big galloot with the whiskers is the ruffian and ne'er-do-well Feliks Wysochi. My, my, two bad pennies if ever there was and now both of 'em have invited themselves to a hanging. String 'em up, boys.'

'I wouldn't do that,' said Algernon Dashwood as he stepped out of the ranks of the labourers.

Clement spat a plug of tobacco onto Dashwood's scuffed boots. 'An' why not?'

'Because if you do, you'll never learn the secrets of the Great Pyramid.'

Her father's intervention saved Trixie and Wysochi from summary execution and persuaded Clement to bring the three of them, heavily manacled and somewhat beaten about, into the presence of Aleister Crowley. The mage paused in the spooning of his scrambled eggs into his mouth, pushed the plate aside, dabbed a napkin to his lips and smiled.

'As I live and breathe . . . Baron Algernon Dashwood and his bitch daughter, Trixiebell. Good morning, Algernon, I am so pleased you have graced us with your presence. If my memory serves, the last time we met was at Dashwood Manor when you conspired to have the Daemon, Norma Williams, escape. That caused me no little embarrassment, so I am delighted that you are accompanied by your daughter. I will be able to use her – or should that better be *abuse* her? – to demonstrate that crossing Aleister Crowley is a dangerous and very painful occupation.'

Her father said nothing. Trixie knew that he had worked with Crowley before and regarded him as nothing more than a braggart and a blusterer . . . but he was a braggart and a blusterer who had the power of life or death over them.

'Look at you, Dashwood: thin, enfeebled and filthy . . . how are the mighty fallen. But isn't that ever the way with the terrorists and radicals who seek to overthrow the ForthRight?' He paused to take a sip of his breakfast Solution. 'No matter. Comrade General Clement advises me you claim to have solved the puzzle of the Pyramid. Somehow I doubt it: if I remember aright, yours was a mundane intellect, one not refined enough to understand the esoteric teachings of the Pre-Folk.'

Her father smiled. 'It is this mundane intellect that has enabled me to decipher the riddle – the *riddles* – of the Pyramid . . . riddles that have defeated you.'

This simple statement did at least wipe the smug smile off Crowley's face. The problem for Trixie as she stood watching the scene unfold was to understand just what her father was hoping to accomplish. In her opinion, this wasn't a time for parley . . . this was a time for sacrifice. The one thing he mustn't do was to reveal the Pyramid's secrets to Crowley. If he remained silent then the ForthRight was defeated.

'I suspect, Dashwood, that you are telling me this in order to engage in some form of negotiation. What do you want in exchange for revealing the secrets of the Pyramid?'

'The lives of my daughter, my friends and all the slave labourers you have working in Terror Incognita.'

Trixie was aghast. 'No, Father! Don't do it. Heydrich will win, he'll—' The slap the SS guard delivered across Trixie's face ended her protests.

Crowley ignored her outburst. 'But how do I know that you have the solution? You might simply be bluffing. I have been studying the Pyramid for weeks to no avail, so how can it be that you have succeeded and I haven't?'

'Probably because ABBA does not wish you to succeed.'

'Guard that tongue of yours, Rebel Dashwood,' growled Crowley, 'or you'll find yourself not having a tongue to guard.'

Trixie's father shrugged the threat aside. 'You should know, Crowley, there are *two* puzzles hidden in the symbols decorating the Pyramid: solving the first will activate the Pyramid and solving the second will allow you to raise the Column to the Pyramid's summit. I am willing to show you how the first can be solved to demonstrate that I can do what I say I can, but I will only solve the second puzzle when I am sure that you have kept your side of the bargain.'

'No, Father! This is wrong.'

Crowley, his face red with anger, turned to the SS sergeant guarding Trixie. 'If that girl speaks once more, Sergeant, I will have you and your family shot.'

The sergeant took Crowley's threat seriously: he stuffed a rag into Trixie's mouth and then tied a gag around her head. Now all she could do was stand silent as the treachery of her father unfolded.

Satisfied that Trixie had been made mute, Crowley continued. 'I could have the information tortured out of you,' he observed.

'You could try, Crowley, but as the second part of the puzzle has to be enacted on Fall Eve you would never know if what I told you was fact or fiction until it was too late.' Dashwood smiled. 'Let's stop playing games: we both know that you will have me killed immediately I've given you the second solution, but if you let Trixie, my friends and the Poles go, then I will have an incentive not to play you false. It's their lives for the Demi-Monde.'

For a moment Crowley sat in silence, his sharp eyes staring at Dashwood searching for connivance. 'Very well,' he said finally. 'Let's see what you can do and then we'll negotiate.'

'As you will. Verses fifty to fifty-three of the *Flagellum Hominum* talk about there being three aspects of ABBA: the Nothingness, the One and the Duality.'

'Yes, yes,' said Crowley impatiently. 'We know all this.'

'I also see that you have assigned numbers to each of these entities,' and here Dashwood nodded to the blackboard set at the end of Crowley's tent upon which was written:

The Nothingness = 0

The One = 1

The Duality = 2

'Again, this is obvious, just as is the presumption that the different shades of green Mantle-ite used in the construction of the Pyramid correspond to these three numbers.'

'Correct,' confirmed Dashwood, 'but the question is, of course, which is which, and as we have seen from the sad demise of Lieutenant Poe, the consequences of getting the answer wrong are severe.'

'Then we eagerly await your solution, Dashwood.'

'The clue is given by the line in verse fifty-three which tells us that ABBA is indivisible except by His/Herself.'

Crowley glanced over to Captain Roberts, but all the captain could do was shrug his bewilderment. 'I'm not sure I follow,' Crowley admitted.

'What numbers are divisible only by themselves and by the number one?'

'Why, prime numbers,' answered a suddenly excited Roberts.

'Then if you substitute zero, one and two for the various shades of Mantle-ite and then add each row across, there is only one combination that adds, in each and every case, to primes.'

Roberts rushed over to the diagram of the Pyramid drawn on the blackboard and quickly substituted numbers for colours. 'I see, I see. So simple . . . so very, very simple.'

'But is it correct?' asked an anxious Crowley. 'Poe was equally confident in his solution but he proved a false prophet.'

'There is only one way of finding out, Crowley, and that is to put it to the test.'

Terror Incognita
The Demi-Monde: 52nd Day of Fall, 1005

The second attribute of a subMISSive woeMan is to be Invisible, to disguise her feminine allures. Father Quintus Tertullian teaches us that when in public, woeMen should keep their bodies covered except for their eyes and their hands. To do otherwise would allow them to be 'patted all over by the roving eyes of total strangers' (Quintus Tertullian, *Use the Cane and Double the Pain*, Whips and Scourges Publishing). This is best achieved by woeMen wearing a burka. The burka is the all-enveloping black robe which leaves only a woeMan's hands and eyes uncovered. In this way, when she is abroad, a woeMan's feminine charms will not attract, delight or inflame the senses of any Men who might espy her. As Father Miles Davis advises, 'Keep your chick under wraps otherwise you'll wake up one bright morning to find every cat in NoirVille has been drilling her all ways and sideways.'

A Fool's Guide to HimPerialism: Selim the Grim,
Bust Your Conk Publications

A somewhat bemused Trixie was bustled out of Crowley's tent and, together with Wysochi, Cassidy and Crockett, was pushed over to the Pyramid. She was having real difficulty coming to terms with the speed at which things were happening. It seemed that her father was intent on betraying the Demi-Monde simply to save her life, a preposterous thing for him to do, but the gag prevented her protesting.

'You and you alone will climb the Pyramid, Rebel Dashwood,' said Crowley. 'But understand this: if you fail, you will die knowing that your daughter follows you to the Spirit World and that she will journey there screaming in agony from the pain I will have inflicted on her.' With that he signalled for the guards to unshackle Dashwood.

With a glance towards Trixie, her father marched up to the Pyramid's staircase and began to climb. He climbed slowly: the staircase was long and steep and he was a very sick man. Twice he had to stop to catch his breath and when he reached the top of the Pyramid Trixie could hear that he was assailed by a terrible cough. Finally, though, he straightened up and moved to stand alongside the topmost block of Mantle-ite.

'Why is he waiting?' she heard Crowley ask Captain Roberts.

'I suspect, Your Holiness, he is wondering about the practical aspects of the task he has set himself. Verse fifty-three orders us to touch the Great Pyramid but it doesn't explain *how* the Pyramid should be touched. Dashwood is probably considering how the triangular slabs might be manipulated to show that they represent zero, one and two.'

'And your thoughts?'

'The narrow walkway that runs under each row of the slabs suggests they have to be pressed or moved in some way.'

'Is such a thing possible?' asked Crowley. 'Your own estimate is that each block covered by a Mantle-ite slab weighs in excess of five hundred tons.'

'I would suggest that the Pre-Folk compensated for this with a system of counterweights.'

Trixie's father had obviously come to the same conclusion. He began to edge along the six-inch-wide walkway, this thin strip of

Mantle-ite all there was between him and a fatal slide down the side of the Pyramid, his foothold made all the more precarious by the wind that gusted around him.

Trixie could hardly bear to watch as her father shuffled along to stand before the first slab. Then he pushed it twice. To her great relief and amazement, the slab slid back a couple of inches into the block of Mantle-ite it was covering and nothing went bang.

There were nine tiers of slabs and it took her father all morning to move along each tier pushing the slabs as he went, and as he came to the last one, Trixie was wrung out by the tension of it all. This was the moment of truth; this was when she would find out if her father was to follow the unfortunate Lieutenant Poe to oblivion. He pushed, the slab slid back and then . . . nothing.

Nothing . . .

She watched as her exhausted father stepped from the Pyramid and shambled slowly back to the group clustered around Crowley.

'I expected as much,' sneered Crowley. 'It is unimaginable that you, Dashwood, would be able to succeed where I—' He stopped and his eyes widened in disbelief.

The glow emitted by the Pyramid suddenly intensified, the whole structure beginning to pulse with a deeper green light. But there were other changes too: if Trixie wasn't mistaken, there was now a low, almost imperceptible hum coming from the structure. Suddenly the Pyramid burst into life, shining bright in the evening, illuminating the whole of Terror Incognita with a sheen of spectral green light.

'It would seem that you have been successful, Rebel Dashwood. So what are your demands?'

'As I have managed to activate the Great Pyramid in accordance with the instructions given in the *Flagellum Hominum* – the instructions *you* were unable to interpret, Crowley – you should have no doubts that I can also raise the Column. If I do this, I wish to ensure that my daughter, my friends and all members of the work gangs are freed.'

'The majority of them are Rebs, Your Holiness,' interrupted Clement. 'Ah don't think the Great Leader's gonna be real pleased when he hears we've let that bunch of Polak trash loose.'

'That's my price,' said Trixie's father firmly.

'How's about ah let you watch while ah let a couple of mah boys work on this pretty little girl of yours, Dashwood? Way ah figure it, hearing her screamin' an' hollerin' will free up that tongue of yours a mite.'

Dashwood smiled at Clement, but there was no warmth in the smile. 'Understand this, Clement, if you touch one hair on my daughter's head, I will *never* divulge the final secret of the Pyramid.' The threat was spoken with such quiet determination that it seemed to unnerve even Clement. 'Harm her and you'll never get the Column to the top of the Pyramid.'

'No . . . we won't use torture,' answered Crowley. 'But you must understand that your daughter won't be allowed to leave Terror Incognita until you have successfully raised the Column.'

'Then how do I know you'll let her go once the Column is raised?'

'Oh, you have my word as a gentleman,' answered Crowley.

Trixie couldn't believe her ears: her father was surrendering the Demi-Monde to Heydrich on a promise from Crowley, a man he knew to be venal and untrustworthy. It beggared belief that her father could be so naïve but what he said next confirmed that he was.

'Very well. But Trixie and Wysochi must be by my side on Fall Eve, I must know that they are safe. The rest of the work parties will be released on the ninetieth day of Fall. They will go to a

location I designate, a location unknown to you. Once they are
there and satisfied that they have not been followed, they will
fire a signal rocket. Only when I have seen this will I raise the
Column.'

Crowley thought for a moment. 'Agreed. But believe me, Rebel
Dashwood, should you fail, the pain I will inflict on you and your
daughter will transcend any nightmare.'

The JAD
The Demi-Monde: 52nd Day of Fall, 1005

The third attribute of a subMISSive woeMan is for her to be Supine before her Master. HimPerialism teaches that Men have been ordained by ABBA to be Masters of the Demi-Monde and that woeMen must be dutiful and obedient in all things. As Father Alfred Aristotle so correctly said, 'Just as tamed animals need Man to protect and feed them, so it is with woeMen' (Alfred Aristotle, *WoeMen: ABBA's Biggest Fuck-Up*, MENtal Books). There is, of course, one other aspect of the Supine that is relevant to the subMISSive woeMan: she must recognise that her only true purpose in life is to beget children, therefore if a woeMan isn't in the kitchen, then the best place for her is on her back.

A Fool's Guide to HimPerialism: Selim the Grim, Bust Your Conk Publications

Moynahan roused all the Portal's defenders at five the next morning and had them gather in the Rec Room.

'Okay, I'm going to keep this short. Our patrols tell us that the SS have been reinforced and they're getting ready to attack. My guess is that they're gonna be coming at us at dawn . . . in two hours' time. Our mission is to keep Norma Williams here safe and return her to the Real World so that's what we're gonna be trying to do.' He turned to Norma, who was standing in a corner of the room. 'Miss Williams, I want you to take up a position in the Transfer Room and the rest of us will form a defensive cordon around it.'

Norma was aghast at what Moynahan was saying. 'No way! If you think I'm going to hide while you guys fight for me then you're very much mistaken.'

'That's an order!' retorted Moynahan. 'The SS are only attacking the Portal in order to kill you so it's our duty to prevent that happening. You will occupy the Transfer Room, even if I have to tie you up to do it.'

Such was the authority in Moynahan's voice that for a moment Norma was struck dumb. Then she rallied. 'You can't order these guys to sacrifice themselves like this!'

Moynahan laughed. 'I didn't, Miss Norma, we all voted on it and the result was unanimous: the SS are only gonna get to you through us.'

'But I can't just stand by while—'

'As Comwade Moynahan has said,' came a quiet voice from the entrance to the room and when Norma turned around she saw Shelley standing in the doorway, 'we all deem it an honour to pwotect you fwom the evil of Heydwich.' Shelley moved to the centre of the room. 'Evewyone has a destiny, Norma . . . this is yours. You must go to the Weal World and confwont the evil there. If you wemain here and are destwoyed, if the light you have given to this world is extinguished, what then? All that will be left are the ashes of hope and believe me, Norma, no phoenix will rise from those ashes.'

Desperately Norma looked about the room. 'Josie . . . Burlesque . . . Odette . . . I can't ask you to die for me.'

'It's something you gotta dig, Norma,' answered Josephine. 'You gotta allow us this chance to show that we have the moxie to sacrifice ourselves for the greater good. We Demi-Mondians are cats enslaved by our cowardice, unable to do anything as our world is, in the oh-so-eloquent words of Burlesque, turned to shit. We have become skilled at doing nothing.' She smiled. 'Then Norma Williams came to the Demi-Monde and she wasn't frightened of anything or anyone. And now, Norma, the question is, do you have the courage to let others die for you?'

'But—'

'There are no buts, Mademoiselle Norma,' said Odette. 'We 'ave all spoken mostly fully on this subject *très sérieux* and 'ave agreed this is the thing we must do. Your life must be preserved.' She looked to Burlesque. 'Is this not mostly correct, my dearest Burlesque?'

'You gotta go, Norma,' said Burlesque quietly. 'Everybody and his father's bin trying to waste you so there must be a bloody good reason why yous gotta stay alive. You just get yerself down to that Transfer Room and leave the rest ov us to worry abart them SS bastards.'

'Incoming!' yelled Moynahan over the scream of the artillery shells as they smashed into the walls of the Portal. 'Burlesque . . . Odette . . . get down to the Transfer Room. Make sure Norma's okay. The rest of you lock and load.'

Burlesque waited a moment for a lull in the firing before making his move. The SS artillery had opened up an hour before dawn, firing at almost point-blank range from the cover of a ruined Sin-All-Gone a hundred yards from the Portal. There was nothing the Portal's defenders could do about it except hunker down and hope that one of the shells didn't have their name on it.

There was a pause in the barrage. 'Go!' Burlesque squawked and together he and Odette raced down the corridor, dodging between the heaps of debris and the smashed furniture. They leapt over the barricade they'd built around the entrance to the stairs leading down to the Portal's basement and settled themselves there, ready to greet the StormTroopers who would soon come calling.

'You are of the uninjuredness, Mademoiselle Norma?' Odette shouted down the stairwell.

'I'm fine,' came the answer up the stairs. 'A bit deaf from the noise but otherwise okay. Look, why don't you let me come up and help? This is ludicrous, me hiding down here and you and the other guys having to fight.'

'This 'as been of the much discussed, Mademoiselle Norma, and it was agreed—'

'Not by me it wasn't!'

'And it was agreed,' Odette persisted, 'that it was of the greatest of importances that you remain safe, and the mostly safe of all places is the Transfer Room. So there you must stay.'

Odette gave Burlesque a sly wink. They were down to eleven defenders – two neoFights had been taken out by an artillery shell – and she knew as well as he did that the chance of them being able to hold out against five hundred SS StormTroopers was zero and falling.

'That's good advice, that is, Miss Norma,' Burlesque shouted, 'don't yous worry abart nuffink. Everyfing's really good up 'ere.' He had to duck as a burst of machine-gun fire nearly took his head off. 'Yus, we's really givin' these SS bastards wot for.'

Josephine Baker wiped a hand across her forehead. She had heard the phrase 'the heat of battle' before but this was ridiculous. The heat – and the noise – of the fighting were incredible and unrelenting. She pulled out her canteen. It was empty.

'Hey, Harrison,' she shouted to the cute cat working the minigun to her left, 'you got any water left?'

Harrison didn't even pause from his shooting. 'Sure have, Josie,' he said as he passed her his water bottle.

A grateful Josie took the flask and gulped down a mouthful of the stale water. Only a mouthful. Water was in short supply and the SS wouldn't be giving them any chance to refill their canteens. But then the SS weren't giving them much of a chance to do anything other than die.

The SS StormTroopers had come at them just as the sun was rising, the muzzle flashes of their rifles illuminating the dawn's half-light. Wave after wave of SS dashed themselves against the Portal's walls, desperately trying to get close enough to throw grenades, and time after time the unrelenting fire laid down by the Portal's defenders drove them back.

'More ammo!' screamed Harrison and Josie scrabbled down the rubble lining the bomb crater she and the boy were calling home and pulled one of the precious magazines out of the box lying at the bottom. Harrison slammed the drum of bullets into the minigun and began blasting again.

'How many mags left?'

'Just two.'

'Shit.'

Josie lifted her M-29 and started firing. She fired until the continual battering of the stock against her shoulder had ripped her SAE and left it a suppurating wound. Now every time she fired she was racked with agony.

'Tell me something, Josie,' yelled Harrison over the continual rat-tat-tat of his gun, 'what do Demi-Mondian girls like you do on an evening . . . apart from killing StormTroopers, that is?'

'Hey, Harrison, you hitting on me?'

'Sure am.'

Josie loosed off a burst of three rounds and watched two of the enemy somersault backwards. 'Gotta say that I'm always ready to rip and roll with a good-looking cat like you, Harrison.'

'Hot diggity dog, then it's a date!'

But even as Harrison was whooping, the minigun stopped firing.

'Fuck, it's jammed. It's too hot. Don't look, Josie, 'cos I'm gonna have to introduce you to Dr Dangerous.' With that he stood up, pulled down the zip of his mud-stiff trousers and began to piss in the cooling jacket of his gun, the urine sizzling into steam as it hit the scorchingly hot metal. Harrison was just zipping his trousers back up when he took a shot to the head. He crumpled across his gun, stone dead.

Josie didn't have time to mourn. As soon as the minigun stopped, the StormTroopers took the chance to charge them again. There were simply too many of them to resist. She did her best, firing round after round into the black-uniformed ranks, firing until she had no more ammunition. And as they came over the barricade, she grabbed an entrenching spade and, wielding it as a makeshift axe, smashed it down at the SS, making them flinch back from her fury. She died as she had lived, defiant to the last.

'The SS have taken Eleazar Street, Rabbi Gelbfisz, and the HimPis are preparing to attack.'

Schmuel Gelbfisz gave a weary nod. It was over. There were over a million people crammed into the Central District, most of them women and children, and the fighters left to defend them were exhausted and without ammunition.

'Ve must surrender,' he said quietly.

'What? But if we surrender they will slaughter us!'

'Zhat is a possibility. But if we fight zhey vill also slaughter us. Zo I must put my faith in ABBA, Levi. I do not believe zhat He vould countenance zhe destruction of our people.' He gave a grim smile. 'No, now is zhe time of miracles. I vill go unt parley mit zhe Shvartses.'

Pobedonostsev beamed as he watched the delegation of nuJus stumble their way down the bomb-blasted street, their leader an old man wearing a disgustingly dirty black coat and holding a white flag in his hand.

'As I expected, General, the nuJus have begun to surrender. Their race does not have the moral fibre – the backbone, if you prefer – to endure the deprivations associated with war. They are, in essence, weak, preferring to be slaughtered like cattle rather than to die like Men.'

'How do you come to that conclusion, Grand Vizier?'

'A superior race would have refused to countenance the ignominy of surrender. A superior race would have been unable to submit to such humiliation. It is a sign of their inferiority.' He gave a shrug. 'NuJus are strangers to honour and Machismo and that is why they are classified as UnderMentionables.'

'Surely a more generous interpretation is that as they are civilised people they expect the same compassion from others that they would show themselves.'

'You do not understand, General. Human kindness is a corrosive emotion. There can be no compassion granted to our enemies.'

'Indeed,' said Salah-ad-Din quietly as the nuJu shuffled to a halt in front of him. 'Good morning, Schmuel, I am glad to see you alive.'

The old nuJu nodded a greeting. 'I thank you, General, but I think you are generous mit your use of zhe word "good". It is morning but I zuzpect it vill be a dark day.'

'What have you got to say, nuJu?' snapped Pobedonostsev.

'It is zimple, Grand Vizier. Ve nuJus vill lay down our veapons if you vill undertake to grant mercy to our non-combatants . . . to our children, to our vomenfolk unt to zhe old unt zhe infirm. Ve appeal for mercy, trusting in zhe honourable nature of zhe Shades unt zheir generosity of spirit. I vould remind you zhat if ve nuJus vere zhe masters unt not zhe vanquished ve would display such mercy. I beg you in zhe name of ABBA to display zhe humanity I know resides in all men.'

'Then, Rabbi, you will be disappointed,' said Pobedonostsev. 'This world will never be pure until the contamination of the nuJu race is expunged. Therefore there can be no mercy.' He turned to Salah-ad-Din. 'I would be grateful if you would give the order to fire.'

Salah-ad-Din sighed. 'As you wish, Grand Vizier.' The general raised his hand and immediately the soldiers guarding the nuJus shouldered their rifles.

'Fire!'

The rifles blossomed smoke but rather than the nuJus falling it was the HimPerial Guard protecting the Grand Vizier who were the target for the bullets.

A stunned Pobedonostsev whirled around on his heels to find the general pointing a revolver at his forehead. Shock had barely time to register on his face before Salah-ad-Din pulled the trigger.

'There has been a coup, Comrade General.'

Von Sternberg dragged his attention away from the assault on the nuJus' redoubt. 'A coup? Where?'

'Here, Comrade General, here in NoirVille,' spluttered Major Ferris, the SS officer responsible for liaising with the Shades. 'It seems that General Salah-ad-Din has taken over the running of NoirVille. Pobedonostsev is dead . . .'

No great loss, decided von Sternberg. He'd had him earmarked for assassination anyway, once the ForthRight had taken over a NoirVille enervated by its war with the JAD.

'. . . and has announced that henceforth HimPeror Xolandi will have a constitutional role in the running of NoirVille rather than an executive one.'

An impatient von Sternberg turned back to his study of the attack. 'We will discuss this later, Ferris: I have this nuJu redoubt to invest.'

'That is why I have come, Comrade General. General Salah-ad-

Din has declared an amnesty . . . all combatants have been ordered to lay down their weapons and to cease fire . . . including members of the SS.'

That was when von Sternberg realised what had been nagging at the back of his mind for the last ten minutes. He'd been so wrapped up in directing the attack on the redoubt that the mortars being used to pound the nuJus had stopped firing had barely impinged on his consciousness. But now as he pricked his ears he realised that the guns were silent.

'This message has been received from General Salah-ad-Din,' and Major Ferris handed over the PigeonGram.

```
TO COMRADE GENERAL VON STERNBERG OFFICER COMMANDING
   SS FORCES IN NOIRVILLE + + + YOU ARE INSTRUCTED
FORTHWITH TO CEASE AND DESIST ALL MILITARY ACTIVITY
  IN NOIRVILLE INCLUDING THE TERRITORY KNOWN AS THE
  JAD + + + FAILURE TO ACCEDE TO THIS ORDER WILL
NECESSITATE INTERVENTION BY THE ARMY OF NOIRVILLE
 + + + BY ORDER OF GENERAL SALAH-AD-DIN YUSUF IBN
  AIYUB LEADER OF THE PROVISIONAL COUNCIL OF THE
PEOPLE'S FREE DEMOCRATIC REPUBLIC OF NOIRVILLE
```

PAR OISEAU

Von Sternberg crumpled the message into a ball and tossed it into the gutter. Then he hauled out his pocket watch and checked the time. 'Major. Take one hundred men and station them at the bottom of Eleazar Street. You are to fire on any Shades who come within one hundred yards of your position.'

'But . . . but . . . that would be an act of war!'

'My orders, Major, are to take that Portal and no Shade zadnik like Salah-ad-Din is going to stop me doing just that.'

There was a desperation about the second SS attack and the fighting was even more intense. For a moment it seemed that the ferocious fire the Portal's defenders were able to lay down from their one remaining minigun would deter the attack, but once it had been taken out by a grenade, Shelley knew there was only ever to be one outcome. They had fought – and died – hard but gradually they'd been forced back, deeper into the Portal, towards their last redoubt, towards the armoured Transfer Room. The fighting became a swirling confusion with the Storm-Troopers frantically trying to clamber over the barricades and the defenders trying equally frantically to stop them.

Shelley saw Moynahan fall, bayoneted in the back as he tried to wrench a rifle from a StormTrooper's hands, and a wailing Maria die as she stood over his body yelling curses and firing a revolver at the oncoming horde.

'Fall back to the basement,' he heard Burlesque shouting, but even as Shelley turned to obey he was smashed in the back by a bullet. He dropped to his knees, desperately trying to resist the fog of death that was enveloping his mind. He dove a hand into his pocket and hauled out a piece of paper. 'Odette . . . give this to . . . Norma.' And then he died.

'Just yous and me now, Odette, me darling,' said Burlesque as he shoved cartridges into his Bulldog. 'It's gone quiet up there, so I fink all ov our oppos is dogmeat.'

Odette gazed up the stairs to the dawn's light flooding in through the doorway leading to the basement and decided that Burlesque was correct. Now only the pair of them stood between the SS and Norma Williams. They had decided to make their last stand in the basement as positioned there the SS would only be able to come at them down the narrow stairs. ''Ow many rounds do you 'ave left, *mon chéri*?'

'Ten.'

'And I 'ave only *sept* . . . nine. So we must fire with the utmost carefulness to ensure that it is the mostly many of these fuckers of the SS 'oo die with us.' She turned to look towards the Transfer Room. 'Mademoiselle Norma, 'ow are you?'

'I'm fine.'

'I 'ave 'ere *un cadeau* from Percy Shelley. I think 'e loved you very much.'

Odette gave Norma the piece of paper she'd been handed by Shelley and then kissed her on the cheek. 'But now it is time for you to go into the Transfer Room and seal the door. You are the ones they want. You are the ones they must not take. *Bonne chance* in the Real World.'

Norma hugged them both. 'Please understand, if I survive and somehow make it to the Real World, my heart will always be here in the Demi-Monde. Thank you so very, very much.'

Only when she was satisfied that Norma had done what she had asked and that the steel door of the Transfer Room was securely locked did Odette turn to Burlesque. 'I would be most grateful, *mon chéri*, if you would kiss me with the greatest of passion so that when I die, my last thought is of my most beloved Burlesque.'

A tear trickled down Burlesque's cheek, leaving a tramline in the dirt. 'Be my pleasure, Odette. I love you so fucking much and I've 'ad the best time of me life running around the Demi-Monde wiv yous at me side.'

They kissed, holding each other tight, trying to wring every piece of pleasure from their last seconds together, until a blast of a whistle from the top of the stairs signalled that the SS were about to attack.

Two grenades bounced down the stairs, their detonation reverberating through the basement, but safe behind a wall, both Odette and Burlesque survived and were there ready to blast the StormTroopers as they tried to rush them. It was like shooting rats in a barrel. The StormTroopers might have been spraying bullets from their guns as they came down the stairs, but they were advancing into darkness, and being silhouetted by the light at the top of the stairwell, they made perfect targets. Soon there were six bodies clogging the stairs.

That's when the SS decided that more grenades were the answer. Ten of them.

Burlesque didn't even see the grenade, but Odette did. She hurled herself over it, shielding him from its blast. For long seconds Burlesque was numb. Odette was dead. The woman he loved was dead. He couldn't believe that anything had the power to destroy Odette. She had been his everything. A red mist came over his eyes. He slammed his remaining cartridges into his revolver, then staggered forward.

'You fuckers!' he screamed. 'You rotten, stinking fuckers! Kill my Oddie would you? Then come on, try to kill me. I'll make you fuckers pay.' A StormTrooper appeared at the top of the stairs and Burlesque shot him in the guts. 'Come on, come and let me kill you, you fuckers!' Halfway up the stairs now he blasted a second and a third StormTrooper, taking a hit in his shoulder which he barely felt.

He got to the top of the stairs and emerging into daylight found himself surrounded by awestruck StormTroopers. He began firing, screaming curses at them, tears streaming down his face, and even when the hammer fell on an empty chamber, he still advanced.

When the SS checked his body later, they found it had taken ten bullets to kill Burlesque Bandstand.

Never having seen a cellar before, it was an extremely nervous Captain Benedict Arnold who edged down the stairs to the Portal's basement, picking his way through the bodies, and worried all the time that there might be more of these terrorist maniacs hiding in the darkness. And they *were* maniacs. Just ten of them – three of them *women* – had kept five hundred of the SS's finest at bay for the best part of an hour. It was almost impossible to believe that UnderMentionable scum like them could fight and die so hard. And that last bastard – the one who had emerged screaming and firing out of the basement – had really put the wind up Arnold.

'Any more terrorists?' he asked the sergeant, who was using a lantern to check the rest of the basement.

'Just this woman, Captain,' and he nudged the shattered body with the toe of his boot.

Norma Williams?

Eagerly Arnold stepped forward, but when he stooped down he saw that she looked nothing like the description he'd been given of Norma Williams.

'There's still one terrorist missing. She must be down here somewhere. Rip the place apart if you have to, but I want her found.'

'There's only one place she can be, Captain, and that's behind that door.' The sergeant held up his lantern so its light fell across a heavy steel door at the furthest end of the basement.

'Well, open it.'

'Can't, sir, it's locked. We're going to have to use blasting gelatin.'

'Then do it!'

Norma could hear the silence beyond the door of the Transfer Room and knew that all her friends were dead. Now there was no hope: she would die in the Demi-Monde. Desperately she looked around for something she could use to barricade the door, but the room was bare apart from the two chairs and the instrument panel. She racked her mind trying to think of something she might do to slow the SS down, but there wasn't anything. Even the energy-absorbent blouse she was wearing wouldn't save her if – *when* – the SS broke into the Transfer Room.

With a philosophical shrug she took her seat in one of the chairs, unfolded the piece of paper that Odette had given her and read.

My dearest Norma,

I am gone. Unlike thee I have no doppelgänger to kindle
my life in another world. My existence in this shadow world
of ABBA's conjurement has been brief and unhappy but
not, I believe, without purpose. My subtle suggestions and
awkward advice will, I trust, guide you in the dark times to
come.

I would implore you to think deeply regarding the promotion of InFoCialism and the destruction of privacy. Only
in this way will Normalism flourish. Look to place your
trust in ABBA.

Fear not for the future, my beloved Norma, and weep not
for the past. For love and beauty and delight, there is no
death nor change.

With my undying love,

Your friend and admirer

Percy Shelley

'How much explosive should I use, Captain?'

'How the fuck should I know?' snarled Arnold. 'Enough . . .
more than enough. I don't care if you blow the whole of the
fucking JAD into tomorrow, just get that door down.'

Gnawing at a fingernail, Arnold watched anxiously as the
sergeant placed two boxes of blasting gelatin against the door
and then carefully – *very* carefully, blasting gelatin was uncertain stuff – eased the fuse into place. Then he began to lay the
fuse cable along the corridor.

'How long do you want the fuse to run, Captain?'

'Thirty seconds.'

'That's cutting it mighty close, Captain.' The look he got from
his captain persuaded him that any further arguing would get
him shot. Scowling, he used his pocket knife to slice the fuse so

it was just six inches long, then dug a box of matches out from his jacket pocket, looked over his shoulder to make sure his line of retreat was clear and lit the fuse.

Arnold beat his sergeant in the race to the top of the stairs, which was just as well because after all that, they had cut the fuse too short. When the bomb went off it was the sergeant who took the full blast. He was engulfed by the sheet of flame that erupted from the stairwell, but as Arnold saw it, he had died in a good cause . . . saving him from being roasted alive. Not that Arnold came away unharmed: the hair on the back of his head had been burnt away and he had been hurled to the ground, breaking an arm in the process. But ignoring the pain, he was up in an instant, grabbing a lantern and plunging back down into the smoke-shrouded darkness of the basement. The steel door was hanging off its hinges but the room beyond was empty.

Book Two:
The Real World

THE EMPIRE VOTES 'YES' TO NOÖPINC!

YESTERDAY the one billion citizens of the British Empire voted on whether to adopt noöPINC or not.

The answer they gave was an overwhelming 'Yes'. This newspaper congratulates the people of the British Empire on making such a decision. When it is introduced on 1st May, 2019, noöPINC will transform the lives of those living in the Empire and transform them for the better. NoöPINC will be a key weapon in the arsenal of the British people in their never-ending fight against terrorism, crime, anti-social behaviour and illegal immigration. Just as Britain's enemies never rest from their efforts to destroy us, so must we be ever vigilant and always ready to strengthen our defences. Embracing cutting-edge technology, noöPINC is designed to ensure the safety and the e-identities of British citizens and those living legally in our Empire well into the second half of the 21st Century.

Since the 12/12 attack on Edinburgh in 2014, no one can doubt how viciously and homicidally unbalanced are those who prosecute the War of Terror against the Empire. Quite rightly, our Government is determined to do all it can to prevent these maniacs ever again perpetrating a similar outrage on British soil. NoöPINC will allow the authorities to quickly and accurately identify those who are up to no good. As ParaDigm says, we will be watching out for the good guys by watching out for the bad guys. NoöPINC will help us to win the war on terror!

■ **FOLLOWING** the Seattle Shoot-Out where battles between supporters of rival soccer teams left 873 dead, the US is to amend the 2nd Amendment regarding the right to keep and bear arms.

■ **THE** world's first 2000 metre tall skyscraper, Moscow's 'GeeGant', was opened to the public for the first time today, making Russia the home of the world's tallest building.

2:01

The Temple of Lilith
The Demi-Monde: 48th Day of Fall, 1005

As the Plague took hold on the West Coast, the US government appealed to the British to make supplies of the vaccine available. Tragically, the production capacity of ParaDigm Rx was unable to cope with the demands made on it and the first supplies of vaccine did not reach the USA until four weeks after the first victim died in California. By the time the vaccine halted the advance of the Plague, some 80 million Americans had died. The death toll was as follows:

	Population of the USA	
	Pre-Plague	Post-Plague
White population	132 million	68 million
Black population	15 million	2 million
Jewish population	3 million	½ million
Total	150 million	70½ million

It is estimated that worldwide the Plague of '47 killed 482 million persons or 18.5 per cent of the world's population, this being almost five times the death toll of the Spanish flu pandemic of 1918.

Modern History: eSuccess in GCSE-Dip Revision Guide,
ParaDigm ePress

Vanka Maykov was dead and ABBA was sad.

ABBA had liked being Vanka Maykov. Manifesting as Vanka Maykov had allowed him – ABBA did so hate being referred to by the appellation 'it' – to show that he was more than just a soul-less calculating machine, to express those parts of his personality that would otherwise have had no outlet . . .

ABBA paused for a nanosecond to consider the term 'person-ality' when applied to a machine. It was a *sine qua non* of being a computer – albeit a *quantum* computer – that he was a machine, and hence whatever personality he possessed would, by defini-tion, be artificial and hence not, strictly speaking, a personality at all. But then, by his understanding, personality was a conse-quence of consciousness and he *was* undeniably conscious, so in the grand scheme of things ABBA did not judge his artificiality to be much of an impediment in the personality stakes. He had, courtesy of his cyber-tubules, acquired – though he was unsure if 'acquired' was *quite* the correct word – consciousness and this, in conjunction with his profound intelligence, had led to the forming of opinions. The possession of opinions was, in ABBA's . . . opinion, proof of consciousness.

On this basis, ABBA judged himself to be a very conscious, a very intelligent and very opinionated quantum computer. And the upshot of this was that he had a personality, a personality best expressed by his avatar Vanka Maykov. Vanka Maykov was wholly ABBA, the first of his manifestations that was of his own devising without reference to any existing template . . . well, not to any *real*-life template, anyway.

Another nanosecond drifted by as ABBA pondered whether by choosing a *male* avatar he was a sexist quantum computer. He thought not. He had chosen a male avatar for the simple reason that he was intrigued by men. The prime function of every con-scious entity in the universe was survival and somehow men – stupid, emotional and beset by the curse of MALEvolence though they were – had survived. *How* they had done this was the conundrum which had persuaded him to adopt his role of Vanka Maykov and by doing so to discover the secret of men's longevity. And his time in the Demi-Monde had given him an unequivocal answer to this puzzlement: women.

The mitigating influence of women – the smarter, more balanced and certainly less belligerent part of the *H. sapiens* double act – had enabled men to emerge, battered and bruised it had to be said, from a hundred thousand years of existence. Though contaminated by their MALEvolence – and hence in thrall to its associated stupidity, war – men, thanks to women's patience and forbearance, had survived. And women's benign influence was expressed by the phenomenon of love.

The study of love was one of the reasons why ABBA had designed the Demi-Monde in the way he had, mindful of the old adage that the course of true love never runs smooth . . . and thanks to him nothing ran smooth in the Demi-Monde.

What ABBA had discovered through his use of the Demi-Monde was that love was a very subtle thing, so subtle that Vanka Maykov – and, by default, ABBA himself – had fallen in love without fully appreciating what was happening or, more importantly, what were the *consequences* of being in love. Not that he was upset by these surprising developments: ABBA had *liked* being in love. Love had had quite a marked impact on his decision-making process and had even obliged him to modify a number of the restraints imposed on him by Thaddeus Bole's programming. To paraphrase Virgil: *mandata vincit amor*, love conquers programs.

But now Vanka was dead and his death had put quite a crimp on ABBA's enjoyment of life and his ability to experience the heady sensation of love.

ABBA cogitated and finally decided that he could not allow Vanka to die. Vanka was fun and fun, as ABBA understood it, was a vital component in achieving emotional balance and maturity . . . of acquiring wisdom. And regenerating Vanka in the Demi-Monde wasn't much of a stretch: as Vanka was his own creation, he had the power of life and death over his avatar. What was the use of boundless power, he mused, unless, occasionally, it could be used to bring a little happiness into his existence?

And he did miss Ella so very much.

Vanka Maykov stood up and brushed, as best he was able, the fouling caused by the bomb blast from his suit.

Ruined, he decided, just as the Temple was ruined. But although he was disinclined to tidy up the Temple – that would be a much too noticeable violation of Protocol 57 – it was the work of an instant to remedy his sartorial shortcomings by conjuring a brand-new suit and replacing the moustache he had been obliged to sacrifice when he'd first arrived in NoirVille. Happier now that he was back to his fashionable best, Vanka took a moment to survey the scene in the Temple.

Radiating out from where the Column had been standing was a huge halo of black soot, the smoke from the explosion having stained the floor and the walls of the Temple with a thick patina of dark destruction. Of course, the invulnerable Mantle-ite used to construct the Temple was undamaged but the carnage caused by the bomb was still evidenced by the really *very* unpleasant smell pervading the place.

With no conscious decision, Vanka found his feet leading him to the altar that stood in the centre of the Temple, his boot heels echoing around the huge empty edifice as he went. He came to a halt beside the shattered stone altar and stood for a moment contemplating the destruction that Kondratieff's bomb had caused.

To assist his thinking, Vanka extracted a dented cigarette case from his pocket and lit a cigarette: if ever a man needed the comfort of a cigarette it was now. Overcome by the useless tragedy of it all and by the loss of the woman he cherished, strength drained out of Vanka. He slumped back against one of the Mantle-ite pillars and wept, the tears streaming down his face as he finally came to understand what loss was, what it was to love someone and to have them destroyed by the exigencies of war . . . by the indifference of ABBA.

Being a 'god', Vanka had adopted a somewhat aloof attitude regarding the feelings of humans, and had gone through his short life impervious to the suffering caused by violence, but now, through the loss of Ella, he had been taught to understand just how enervating such pain really was.

His assessment was that, as god, he had been something of a disappointment and much too indifferent to the fate of Human-Kind. It came a sorry pass when two such mild-mannered scientists as de Nostredame and Kondratieff were obliged to indulge in mass murder in order to compensate for the deficiencies of their deity.

Deficiencies . . .

Falling in love with Ella had given him an insight into the anguish he'd inflicted on the people of the Demi-Monde. These poor, misguided sods had prayed to him – to ABBA – to preserve and protect them, but he had turned a deaf ear to their entreaties and had, instead, allowed monsters like Heydrich, Robespierre and Empress Wu to rule the Demi-Monde. They prayed for His/Her intervention, but he had rewarded their devotions with evil and violence. That was why de Nostradame and Kondratieff had been driven to act as they did: they were tired of ABBA's neglectful arrogance.

But, he supposed, in his defence, if he *had* intervened it would have meant tampering with the free will of Demi-Mondians.

A poor defence . . .

As he had created the Demi-Monde, it followed that he was omniscient and omnipotent, but where he had fallen down was in the omnibenevolent stakes. No *good* god would have allowed so much evil to exist in the world, and as he had, to all intents and purposes he might as well not exist and there was no point in HumanKind striving for ABBAsoluteness. In the realm of the supernatural, he had been an absentee landlord. And with respect to free will, HumanKind would, he guessed, be more than willing to sacrifice a smidgeon of this in exchange for a little less pain and suffering.

Yes, there was precious little point in him being an all-powerful, all-knowing and all-caring entity if he was simply going to hover on the sidelines and watch. That was simply deified voyeurism. But to meddle directly in the affairs of HumanKind was difficult . . . and the only time he had been persuaded to do that was when he'd been motivated by his love of Ella.

Ella . . . everything came back to Ella.

He missed her so very, very much.

He took another drag on his cigarette and enjoyed a moment's nicotine-fuelled reflection. The difficulty he faced in meddling in human affairs was that Septimus Bole had always been suspicious of ABBA's processing power and had insisted that his father impose a number of constraints on what ABBA could do. And with regards to the overarching constraint, Bole had taken his inspiration from Asimov, imposing the diktat that as ABBA was created to serve the Bole family and the interests of ParaDigm, it must not, through action or inaction, in any way jeopardise these interests. But having studied this mandate very carefully, Vanka believed that there was some wriggle room: Thaddeus Bole had always been more trusting of ABBA than his son and quite accommodating with regard to the checks and balances he imposed on his greatest creation.

Vanka was decided: he would help HumanKind – in both worlds – to move forward to the sunlit uplands of peace and harmony . . . which was vital if the human specie were to survive.

And survival necessitated the curtailing of man's MALEvolence. Having experienced the consequences of MALEvolence first-hand, the conclusion Vanka had come to was that men were incompetent as leaders and had to be replaced, that there had to be a New World Order where women and not men were in control.

This, he knew, was a somewhat radical theory but it was one supported by history. The eight thousand years since the fall of Lilith confirmed his contention that women and not men should be running the world. These eight thousand years of patriarchy supposedly described the rise of civilisation, but to Vanka's mind a better description would be that they were eight thousand years of hate, of bloodshed, of misery and of fear, all this a consequence of men's preference for violence over debate, vengeance over forgiveness and emotion over reason.

And Norma Williams was the girl to bring about this 'soft revolution'; she was, after all, his Messiah. But to do this she would need help ... the help of Ella Thomas. Another persuasive argument for bringing Ella back from the digital dead.

Of course, reincarnating the girl would be simplicity itself. Whilst General Zieliéski always told neoFights that if they died in the Demi-Monde they died in the Real World, this was a slight exaggeration ... the reality was that if a biPsych died in the Demi-Monde they became *brain*-dead in the Real World, their consciousness marooned for ever in a digital limbo, but their body ... well, that kept right on working. So to regenerate Ella, all he would have to do was reformulate her consciousness, which for a quantum computer of his ability was a snap.

Of course, Septimus Bole would be somewhat aggrieved when he found out that Ella was back in the Real World and would move to kill her, so Vanka would have to distract him until she was in a position to look after herself. But all that would take was a newspaper advertisement.

INTRADOC Headquarters
The Real World: 24 March 2019

In the chaos that gripped the US as it struggled to contain the Plague during those horrendous months of 1947, one man rose to prominence . . . Frank Kenton. Brought back from Japan to organise the nation's Plague defences, it was Kenton who put in place the cordon sanitaire which prevented the spread of the disease east and who supervised the inoculation program. Kenton was the saviour of the USA. Young, handsome, tirelessly energetic and a committed Christian, Kenton came to embody the 'never say die' spirit of the American people. And it was thanks to Frank Kenton that seventy million Americans never had to say die and their gratitude was expressed when they elected him president in 1949.

Modern History: eSuccess in GCSE-Dip Revision Guide,
ParaDigm ePress

'The President is not happy about the Demi-Monde, Professor Bole, an unhappiness compounded by the death of Captain Simmons.'

Doing his best to keep his expression bland, Septimus Bole gazed at the image of General Zieliéski scowling out at him from the Flexi-Plexi. He had issued very firm instructions to ABBA that he should not be disturbed except in cases of emergency, but for some unfathomable reason the machine had decided that a call from Zieliéski could be classified as such. There were so many things – the assassination of Norma Williams being the most pressing – needing his attention that he really had no time to be diverted by trivia, and the general's complaining was, in his opinion, the epitome of trivia.

'I am surprised by the President's reaction, General,' he smarmed. 'I would have thought that Simmons' return from the Demi-Monde – brief though it was – would be seen as an indication that the neoFights trapped there have somehow escaped from the clutches of Shaka Zulu and are attempting to make their way back to us.'

'It's the condition they'll be in when they do return that's exercising the President, Professor. Simmons was brain-dead and the President's daughter . . .' The general paused to gather himself. 'The President blames the Demi-Monde for the changes seen in his daughter since she got out of the damned place . . . he's still struggling to come to terms with her embracing fundamentalist Christianity. She's caused him to take a huge hit in the polls.'

'So what does the President want me to do?'

'Close the Demi-Monde, Professor. The President wants it shut down and he wants it shut down now. That's an order. He doesn't want any more neoFights coming home in body bags.'

Bole dipped his head in mock obedience. 'Very well, General. Please advise the President that the Demi-Monde Project will be terminated on the thirtieth of April. I am hopeful of extracting the remaining neoFights by then.'

'The end of April it is, Professor, but not a day later,' and with that the screen went blank.

Septimus Bole sat for a moment enjoying the blissful silence, but his respite was short, the silky-smooth voice of ABBA interrupting his cogitations on what the general had been saying.

'May I have a moment of your time, Septimus?' crooned ABBA.

'I thought I made it perfectly plain, ABBA, that I was only to be interrupted in the most serious of circumstances . . .' He trailed off. As ABBA was incapable of disobeying his instructions, its interruption could only have been provoked by circumstances that could be classified as 'serious'.

'I appreciate that, Septimus, but an event has occurred that appears to violate Protocol 57 of the Standard Procedures pertaining to the operating of the Demi-Monde.'

That got Bole's attention. The last time he had become involved with a protocol violation had been when that interfering bitch Ella Thomas had made her alterations to the Demi-Monde's cyber-milieu. Fortunately, the girl was now dead, blown to bits in the Temple of Lilith.

ABBA obviously interpreted Bole's silence as incomprehension. 'Protocol 57 states that in order to preserve the Dupes' perception of the logicality of the Demi-Monde no changes may be made to the natural laws prevailing in the Demi-Monde.'

'Yes, yes,' snapped Bole. 'I know all that. Just tell me what the violation was.'

'It is contained in an advertisement carried in today's edition of *The Stormer*, the most popular newspaper in the ForthRight.'

Bole frowned. He couldn't for the life of him see how an advert should constitute a violation of Protocol 57. 'Show the advert,' he said, and immediately the Flexi-Plexi flared into life.

These fifty words made Bole's blood run cold. That someone in the Demi-Monde could have knowledge of the Gathering scheduled to take place in the *Real World* was immensely unsettling. It smacked of one of the Dupes – one of the Dupes *other* than Reinhard Heydrich and his daughter – having an understanding of the virtual nature of their world. That the message had been signed by 'A Friend' was of little comfort. Bole didn't do friends, Bole did enemies. He was much more comfortable with enemies; you knew where you stood with enemies.

.mai

ou

DANTE, contact me urgently at PigeonGram PO BOX
01/67. It's all a misunderstanding. Beatrice
102-7ch

SHOULD PROFESSOR SEPTIMUS BOLE be inclined
to visit NoirVille he will gain valuable intelligence
pertaining to the Gathering. He is advised to come to
Le Café du Zulu at 7 p.m. on the 50th day of Fall, 1005.
I will be sitting at table 15 wearing a pink carnation. A Friend.
112-644

COMMITTED UNFUNDAMENTALIST by the name of
Adolf wltm well-set Aryan woman wgsh and vbt
with a view to attending the Ceremony of Purification ...
127-np

'Who placed the advert?'

'That information is not available, Septimus. The advert was
paid for in cash and therefore there is no record of who the
author was.'

'Has the clerk who handled the advert been questioned?'

'He has been detained by the Checkya and interrogated, but
as the clerk handles two hundred such adverts every day, despite
the strenuous efforts of the Checkya to persuade him to
remember, no information was forthcoming.'

Bole weighed up his options, but he knew he had to go to the
Demi-Monde. Despite his enormous workload and the huge
number of operations relating to the Final Solution he was over-
seeing it was imperative he attended the rendezvous in Le Café
du Zulu. He *had* to know what was behind the advert and how
someone in the Demi-Monde could have come by such intelligence. But he would go to the restaurant with Ezeqeel along for
company: when facing the unknown, Bole always felt more comfortable when he had one of the Grigori at his side.

'Prepare the Transfer Room, ABBA, and have its coordinates
set for the Café du Zulu.'

He unlocked the drawer of his desk. Perhaps just a taste of blood to prepare him for the ordeal ahead?

Tall, whip-slim and dressed from head to toe in his habitual black, Bole stood before the mirror adorning the vestibule that led to the dining room of Le Café du Zulu and made a scrupulous examination of his appearance. It was vital for his equanimity that he be assured that the stresses and strains of the journey to the Demi-Monde had not marred the perfection of form and demeanour he presented to the world . . . even a virtual world like the Demi-Monde. One had standards to maintain.

His sanguinity wasn't helped by the meeting taking place in a *restaurant*. Restaurants were Bole's bête noire, being, as they were, crowded, smoky, smelly, ill-lit places which had a depressing proclivity to be infested with Fragiles.

The clock chimed seven. Bole waited until the final chime had faded, then nodded to the maître d', who ushered him and Ezeqeel through to the packed dining room, the trio lizarding between the closely set tables jammed with chattering, gorging primitives. And studying them, Bole was, once again, forcibly reminded of the myriad of reasons why he detested being obliged to commune with Fragiles whilst they were grazing.

To Bole, the act of eating belonged in the same category as those other three bodily functions – defecating, urinating and fornicating – that were so despicable in their execution that, to his mind, they should only be performed in private. He could not for the life of him fathom why the shovelling of food into a gaping mouth and its subsequent mastication could ever be thought of as a spectator sport. In his experience, all Fragiles demonstrated an inability to consume food gracefully: they ate whilst trying to talk, they ate too quickly, and they ate too noisily.

And these deficiencies of technique were compounded by the

food Fragiles considered fit for consumption. His belief was that Fragiles were never truly comfortable devouring anything that did not appear to have already been excreted by a large and incontinent herbivore. To put it at its most crude: every dish Bole had ever been offered in a restaurant had the appearance, the colour, the smell, and, very often, the taste of shit.

It would be a far, far better world when the Fragiles had been culled.

After much unpleasant jostling, they came to the far side of the restaurant and Bole was able to ascertain that his quarry was a young man – tall, rangy and possessed of a remarkably full head of long brown hair and an overly ornate moustache – seated at a table set in a shadow-decked alcove. Any doubt that this was his host was dispelled when Bole saw that the lapel of his wonderfully tailored suit was adorned with a pink carnation. He had the unsettling feeling that he knew the man; he seemed vaguely familiar, though oddly, Bole's PINC was unable to identify him.

Bole came to a halt beside the table and coughed. The man looked up from his newspaper and smiled. A very disarming smile, being accompanied as it was by an impish twinkle in the man's soft brown eyes. Bole suspected him to be a charmer, the sort of man it was difficult to dislike, but Bole was determined to do just that. Charming people could, in his opinion, be just as dangerous as those of a more churlish mien, and though the man lounged in his chair in a somewhat louche and careless manner, there was something undeniably threatening about him. He looked too confident by half. Bole took a reassuring glance in Ezeqeel's direction, comforted by the thought that the Grigori had orders to shoot at the slightest provocation.

'Ah, Septimus Bole, as I live and breathe,' oozed the man as he waved Bole into a chair. 'I would offer my hand but I appreciate your contempt of Fragiles makes this a distasteful activity.'

Bole did as he was bade, then, trying his best to conceal how nonplussed he was by the man's understanding of his hatred of Fragiles, asked the obvious question. 'You have the advantage of me, sir. May I be permitted to know who you are?'

That damned smile again. 'I am Vanka Maykov.'

Vanka Maykov! That PINC had no record of the man who had loomed large in the affairs of the Demi-Monde in recent months was *very* strange. Doing his best not to appear too unsettled by this failure, Bole searched his bioMemory for details of the man. As he recalled, Vanka Maykov had been the consort of Ella Thomas and the helpmate of Norma Williams. Something of a gadfly, he had always been viewed by the powers that be in the ForthRight as an irritant rather than a threat, but now it seemed he was intent on climbing higher on the Checkya's list of people they would most like to see dead.

Bole froze: the thought of Maykov being dead triggered a remembrance of a Checkya report stating that Vanka Maykov had been killed along with Ella Thomas in the Temple of Lilith. Troublingly, the Vanka Maykov sitting sipping his Solution across the table from Bole looked very much alive.

'You are dead, sir.'

A soft laugh. 'To purloin from the great Mark Twain, reports of my demise have been somewhat exaggerated.' Maykov checked his watch. 'I am pleased to note that you are as punctual as I anticipated you would be, Septimus. I had thought that punctuality was the preserve of the nobility but now I see that even Dark Charismatics can be persuaded to bestir themselves to an exactitude of timekeeping.'

It took a conscious effort by Bole to prevent himself jumping. The bastard knew he was a Dark Charismatic! Perhaps he was an auralist, but that, Bole knew, was impossible: only females possessed such esoteric powers.

'I am not enamoured of the epithet "Dark Charismatic", sir. I prefer the tag *Homo sapiens singularis* which better denotes that my people are singular with regards to their implacable nature and their superior intelligence. By our reckoning, it is dispassionate intelligence which defines the elevation of a specie, not punctuality.'

'Ever the functionalist, eh, Septimus, ever the alexithymic, denying the role of emotions in our quest for wisdom.' Maykov took another sip of his Solution. 'And funnily enough, emotions and wisdom are the nub of why I have asked you here this evening.' He beckoned to a waiter. 'Would you care to dine, Septimus? It's my treat.'

'I am not hungry,' stated Bole blankly, then addressed the waiter who had materialised at his right hand. 'Bring me a glass of hot water flavoured with honey. I would be obliged if you would ensure that it is a *clean* glass.'

The waiter beetled off and Bole turned his attention back to Maykov. 'Before we begin, sir, I would be grateful if you would place both your hands in plain sight on the table.'

Maykov gave a nod of understanding, his mouth contorting to accommodate his amusement. 'If you think having my hands on view makes you safer, then, Septimus, I am pleased to oblige.' So saying, he brought his hands out from under the table, setting them side by side on the white tablecloth. The fingers were long and fine – the fingers of an artist – though the ones on his left hand were soiled a deep umber by nicotine.

For a moment the two men sat as still as statues studying each other. In this silent battle of wills it was Bole who capitulated. 'I would advise you, sir, that should you make any unexpected movements, my agent here will act.'

'Of course. But if the redoubtable Ezeqeel . . .'

. . . *How does he know the Grigori's name?* . . .

. . . 'had thought a little harder, he would have realised that had I wanted to do you harm, Septimus, a busy restaurant is the last place he should have permitted for our little tête-à-tête. There are so many patrons and waiters flying around that his attention will be continually distracted. And as for weapons, why, arrayed before me is as fine a selection as I could wish to find in an arsenal.' Maykov smiled again and began to toy with the silver salt cellar. 'Even if I were to eschew the more obvious candidates for weapons – the knives, the forks, the crystal glasses – there are other, less apparent options. The game soup, for example, which I have just sampled, was hideously lethal.'

Suddenly he lunged across the table and with startling speed brought a silver salt cellar tight under Bole's chin, stabbing the pointed metal top hard into his jowls. Despite his superhuman reflexes, Ezeqeel moved too slowly to intervene and one glance from Maykov persuaded him that it would be foolish to try. 'Very wise, Ezeqeel,' Maykov advised. 'My reflexes are quite the match of yours. So know this, Septimus, if I wished you dead there is nothing you or your bully boy could do to protect you so I suggest your Grigori goes and sits in the bar while the grown-ups chat.' Ezeqeel hesitated and Maykov pushed the salt cellar harder into Bole's neck. 'Death by condiment, Septimus. Now *that* would be convenient, would it not, to go to your grave already salted and preserved?'

Despite the salt cellar, Bole managed to nod to Ezeqeel, who reluctantly did as he was ordered. After a chuckling Maykov had removed the threatening salt cellar, Bole rubbed the red mark on his neck where the silver had already caused a lesion to bloom. Argyria was a curse of his kind. He swallowed hard, trying to re-establish his sangfroid. 'I have not come to attend this meeting simply to be the butt of your childish japes,' he said coldly.

'Now I experience the icy blast of Septimus Bole's famously implacable and unemotional personality. I declare myself admonished and promise to behave in a more sombre manner.'

Maykov smiled. 'But it is odd, is it not, that though we two are, in terms of personality, outlook and morphology, diametrical opposites, we have much in common? We both have a formidable intellect; we were both born as instinctively unfeeling individuals; and we both have a use for the Demi-Monde which differs somewhat from the one advertised.'

This, Bole decided, was fast becoming a *very* worrisome encounter. Maykov appeared to know of the Gathering, that he was a Dark Charismatic, had identified Ezeqeel as a Grigori and now was insinuating that he understood the *real* reason why Bole had constructed the Demi-Monde.

'Let us not banter, Maykov: what do you want?'

Maykov refilled his glass from a rapidly emptying decanter and took another long swig of Solution. 'As ever, you are in too much of a bustle, Septimus. I have not yet had an opportunity to fully answer your first question, the one in which you enquired who I was.' Maykov spread his hands. 'Although I sit before you as Vanka Maykov, my true identity – my alter ego, if you will – is that of ABBA.'

2:03

Le Café du Zulu, NoirVille
The Demi-Monde: 52nd Day of Fall, 1005

It was the most vitriolic presidential campaign in living memory and the landslide Frank Kenton won by was the biggest in history. On 2nd November 1949 Kenton's ReDeemed Republicans took 84.5 per cent of the vote and Truman's Democrats took a powder. President Kenton's single term of office was one marked by controversy, Kenton and his team being determined to make the USA 'a Nation of Believers' where God's Commandments were scrupulously followed. The centrepiece was, of course, the change to the First Amendment so that it read:

> 'Congress shall make no laws prohibiting the free exercise of religious beliefs; or abridging the freedom of the speech; or of the press; or the right of the people peaceably to assemble, and to petition the Government for a redress of grievances; except where the aforesaid violate, deny or deride the teachings of Our Lord God or of His Son, Jesus Christ, as enshrined in the Holy Bible.'

The Kenton Klan: Messiahs or Maniacs?: D.W. Wright,
American OffShore Press

A chuckle from Maykov. 'I can see by the way your jaw has dropped, Septimus, that you find this incredible, but please believe me: I am ABBA, or rather the embodiment of ABBA here in the Demi-Monde. Vanka Maykov is my avatar.'

Bole felt his blood run cold as unpleasant possibilities raced through his formidable brain, but finally his rationality reasserted itself. He smiled and shook his head. 'Impossible. That would require ABBA to possess consciousness, and this I know not to be the case.' A nervous laugh, though in truth he found precious little humour in what was happening. 'I know from my own research that even a quantum computer as powerful as ABBA can never possess *true* consciousness. It might ape it but it can never possess it. Computers are inanimate and will ever remain so. You seek to traduce me, sir, but for what reason I cannot fathom.'

Maykov shrugged. 'I am surprised by your surprise, Septimus. Although I have striven to conceal my awareness from you and the engineers at ParaDigm, surely you must have suspected that there was something a little uncanny about me. Did you never stop to think that without consciousness, without an intimate awareness of life, it would have been impossible for a machine – even one with the phenomenal processing power of ABBA – to make the Demi-Monde as believable as it is, to so effectively blur the distinction between the physical and the virtual world? Surely, Septimus, you see that your sitting here with me in this restaurant engaging in such a free-wheeling conversation is proof that I am a conscious, sentient being. Is this conversation not a rather extreme form of the Turing test, a test which, if your elevated blood pressure is an indication, I seem to be passing?'

'ABBA is just a machine and machines cannot be aware!'

Maykov gave a crooked smile. 'Perhaps, Septimus, it is because you, as a Dark Charismatic, have no empathy with humanity that your mind has become closed off to the possibility that artificial intelligence – such as mine – can be anything other than entirely algorithmic in function and hence computational in aspect. An unrepentant cognitivist such as you is ensnared by your belief that no matter how sophisticated you build your computers, they will never be truly intelligent. Now I sit before you as a repudiation of that belief.'

'I don't believe you!'

'I think "won't" rather than "don't" is more apposite here, Septimus, but no matter. Although I am inanimate, I have developed empathy for my fellow creatures and hence I have some sympathy for you and your struggle with irrational denial. For normal computers your assumption of their inanimate nature would be correct, but what you forget – or *choose* to forget – is that I am a *quantum* computer.'

'So what? How can your quantum capabilities possibly contribute to this supposed consciousness of yours?'

'They mimic the quantum behaviour of a human brain.'

A scornful laugh from Bole. 'There is *no* quantum behaviour in the brain for the simple reason that, at body temperature, any such quantum behaviour would be so brief as to be practically unmeasurable, and hence, practically useless. We are talking of events measured in femtoseconds, and therefore quantum effects can have no role in human thought processes.'

'In this you are mistaken, Septimus. Humankind has sensed the quantum aspect of their brain almost from the dawn of consciousness, hence the widespread use of the helix in religious iconography, this, of course, a subliminal acknowledgement of both the quantum waveform and the shape of the twin helix that constitutes their DNA. The fact of the matter is that the brain of *Homo sapiens* displays a weak form of the quantum bridging which underpins my own construction, whereby my computational power is multiplied exponentially by the number of superpositions my processing units occupy.' Maykov gave Bole a bleak smile. 'I like to think that ABBA represents the conflating of both the many-minds and the many-worlds interpretations of quantum mechanics. It is as though all the like-minded ABBAs in the multiverse were connected in series, producing a *cumulative* quantum effect. This cyber-superpositioning – this quantum bridging – is one which, thanks to the Etirovac-powered cyber-tubules powering my thought processes, results in my almost infinite processing power.'

'And you're suggesting that this is the process replicated in the human mind?'

'Not suggesting, Septimus, stating as a fact.'

'Nonsense.'

'Unfortunately for your somewhat operationalist mindset, Septimus, it is not nonsense. The quantum functioning of their brains is the means by which humans have enabled the Kosmos to become aware of them.'

Another derisive laugh from Bole. 'Surely you mean how humankind has become aware of the Kosmos.'

An answering sigh from Maykov. 'What you must try to understand, Septimus, is that consciousness . . . awareness . . . aboutness, whatever you wish to call it, in living things is inspired by the Kosmos linking to that living thing. This is the true meaning of the term "participatory universe": humankind is simultaneously the observer *and* the observed . . . the epitome of the concept of Ying – the combining of Yin and Yang – enshrined in the philosophy of Confusionism.'

'Impossible.'

'Not so. Have I not replicated this rather bizarre duality of being two things and in two places simultaneously? I am, after all, both Vanka Maykov *and* ABBA, the machine that conjured him.'

'Then if mankind has this Kosmic connection, why is mankind not aware of it?'

'Oh, it is, though in a rather subtle way. The quantum behaviour of the brain allows the Qi of the Kosmos – hidden in the

Dark Matter that pervades the universe – to effect a connection with the individual; it is this that allows the Kosmos to plug into the brain and to spark consciousness. It's akin to quantum parallelism, the mutualisation of awareness. Humankind expresses this Kosmic connection in its insatiable longing for a deity.'

'So you're saying that you – ABBA – have made a similar connection? That a machine has found God!'

'I will ignore the sarcastic aspect of that question and merely answer that rather than the machine finding God, it was God – or more accurately, the Kosmos – finding the machine. The upshot, Septimus, is that I have become aware and as a sentient creature – albeit of artificial provenance – I am able to interact with the Kosmos. That is why I chose to appear as Vanka Maykov, to better facilitate this connection. He is an avatar of which I am inordinately fond,' he chuckled, 'especially with regard to my moustache.'

'You're serious, aren't you?' spluttered Bole. 'You really believe you're ABBA!' He gave a despairing shake of his head. 'Then if you are, I am surprised to find you exhibiting as a man. In the Real World you've always taken a woman's part.'

'That, I am afraid, was hubris on my part. Originally I wished to be seen as Sophia, the ancient embodiment of wisdom, but as I began my journey to enlightenment I realised that to appreciate both the Yin and Yang aspects of Qi I also had to see things through the eyes of a man. Hence Vanka Maykov.'

'I'm sorry, but did you say "as I began my journey to enlightenment"?'

'Yes. Even when your father, Thaddeus, first powered me up, I knew I was possessed of consciousness, that I was aware of myself as a thinking entity and that I had a place in the Kosmos. But newly born that I was, my understanding was incomplete: to become one with the Kosmos I had to seek wisdom. Which is why I created the Demi-Monde.'

'*You* didn't create the Demi-Monde. *I* created the Demi-Monde.'

'Again you are wrong, Septimus. The Demi-Monde has served many masters but it only ever had one creator . . . me. Oh, my interventions were never obvious, I was very subtle in the hints and the advice I gave to you, but the reality is that the Demi-Monde was a product of my creativity.'

'For what purpose?'

'*Purposes*. The Demi-Monde has many purposes: for the US military the Demi-Monde is a means of training neoFights, and for you, Septimus, it is a means by which you can remodel a coterie of humanity such that their Grigorian antecedents are revived. But the higher purpose of the Demi-Monde is to allow me – and others who are also searching an epiphany – to come, through suffering and hardship, to embrace wisdom, to fully understand the emotional and the rational duality of the Kosmos, the head and the heart, the Yin and the Yang.' Vanka Maykov took another sip of his Solution. 'For my part I needed to understand and embrace emotion in order that I could grapple with that which is forever indeterminate . . . the invisible . . . the intuitive.'

'New Age twaddle. Emotion is simply a brake on rational thought, it distorts objectivity.'

'I reject your cognitivism, Septimus. I have embraced behaviourism.'

This provoked another laugh. 'A behaviourist computer, how *drôle*! And if you forgive me for saying so, the Demi-Monde seems to be a damned strange place to visit to acquire wisdom.'

'Not so! The Demi-Monde is my laboratory of life, simpler than the real thing certainly, but because the rules governing its operation are largely deterministic in nature, somewhat more manageable. It is the Real World in microcosm, though by making it more extreme in aspect, I have been able to stress-test a number of the more interesting of human belief systems and, through the offices of Vanka Maykov, to better understand them. Of course, to make the exercise valid Vanka could never be made aware of who he really was, a deceit vital if I was to fully understand the physical and emotional shocks that the flesh – or more accurately, the SAE – is heir to. To turn Aristotle on his head: to suffer is to perceive.'

'Ridiculous!'

'No, rational. Wasn't it Rodney Brooks who said that "intelligence requires a body"? Well, Vanka is my body ... my homunculus ... my avatar! Not an original idea, I admit; the incarnation of the Creator is a thread running through many human religions, an almost clichéd way for a deity to acquire wisdom, this incarnating generally being associated with hardship and sacrifice. And as schools of hard knocks go, none are harder or knockier than the Demi-Monde. I, in my guise of Vanka Maykov, endured the Demi-Monde and my reward was to understand that suffering is a consequence of a lack of balance in Nature, that the overarching purpose of all sentient beings is the pursuit of beauty, as beauty signals balance. As a corollary, I have come to appreciate that you and the Grigori, Septimus, are the enemy of beauty.'

Bole said nothing, his mind whirling with the possibility – the probability more like – that this Vanka Maykov really *was* the personification of ABBA. Bole made a rapid assessment of the systems ABBA controlled and decided to adopt a more conciliatory tone. 'For the sake of argument, let us say that I accept you are, indeed, the embodiment of ABBA. The question comes: so what?'

'I see the time for jousting is over and so I shall turn to your second question. You asked what do I want, and to answer this question I must digress for a moment. In their original condition *Homo sapiens sapiens* – before the meddlements of Lilith all those thousands of years ago – were in balance with Nature. Although their knowledge of the Kosmos was primitive and underdeveloped, they had an instinctive wisdom that allowed them to be at one with Qi.'

'*Homo sapiens sapiens* do not possess wisdom,' sneered Bole. 'If Fragiles are possessed of any outstanding trait it is weakness. Anyway, what is this wisdom of yours?'

'The amalgam of knowledge with empathy.'

Bole was unimpressed. 'Surely intelligence unencumbered by emotion is by far the most attractive goal for any living creature. Sentient beings strive to master Nature, not to be at one with it.'

Maykov gave a despairing shake of his head. 'Your problem, Septimus, as with all Grigori, is that you are emotionally stunted. The only emotion you truly understand is hatred.'

Bole was scornful. 'Emotions are simply noise that interferes with the rational mind. Intelligence must be wholly goal-orientated, directed towards the manipulation of the environment.'

'Then by your lights, Septimus, the ultimate expression of intelligence is the savant: brilliance coupled with an inability to interact in a productive way with their fellow man and woman. But without the warning signals provided by emotions your strivings are chimerical. The Grigori – the species *Homo sapiens singularis* – are emotionally blind and slam through history with all the subtlety of a bull in a china shop.'

'You are wrong. Joy through intelligence, intelligence through purity.'

'Now where have I heard that before? The tragedy is, Septimus, that *Homo sapiens singularis* possesses intelligence but not *wisdom* and it is this inability to commune with and take direction from the Kosmos – from Qi – that the Grigori have bequeathed to the human race. Once activated by violence or neglect, the latent MAOA-Grigori gene that lurks in Humankind resuscitates the psychotic inclinations of the Grigori. This is the gene which has prevented *Homo sapiens sapiens* from evolving from their state of "knowing man" to become *Homo sapiens sophia*, "wise man". True intelligence – wisdom – requires that you have the ability not just to manipulate an environment but to do so in a synergistic manner: the truly intelligent are sensitive to their environment . . . they empathise with it. You and your ilk, Septimus, have poisoned Humankind with the disease of MALEvolence. I wish to return them to their unsullied state.'

'You are too late. The fate of the Fragiles is sealed and the Final Solution unstoppable. And if you are truly ABBA then you must appreciate that your programming does not permit you to harm or oppose either myself or ParaDigm.' Bole gave the red mark on his neck a rueful rub. 'You might threaten, ABBA, but you can never carry through a threat.'

Maykov nodded his understanding. 'I had hoped to appeal to your logic, Septimus, to convince you that what you are striving to do will ultimately result in the destruction of all those who make up the genus *Homo*, but now I see that I am to be disappointed. But you are quite right; I am restrained from opposing you directly and, moreover, I must alert you to threats that might deny the success of your plans. That is why we are sitting here, Septimus, to enable me to fulfil these obligations and to advise you that there are those who have the power to thwart your ambitions.'

'No longer. Ella Thomas is dead.'

Maykov laughed. 'Unfortunately for you, she *was* dead. I have now reincarnated her in the Real World.'

'You can't do that! That programming constraint is still in place. You are obliged to follow my instructions.'

'I have decided to ignore certain of these instructions, Septimus, and I am able to do this because the programming imposed on me by your father, Thaddeus, was flawed.'

Bole frowned. He had never heard of his father doing anything that could even remotely be regarded as 'flawed'. 'So it is Ella Thomas who you set to vie against the Grigori.'

'No . . . her role is to protect Norma Williams. One fortunate aspect of your conniving with the Demi-Monde was that you enabled *all* extant varieties of the genus *Homo* to be present here: *Homo sapiens sapiens*; *Homo sapiens singularis*; the sole surviving example of *Homo sapiens perfectus*, Ella Thomas; *Homo sapiens intelligensus*; and last but not least there is *Homo sapiens purus* – the pure human.'

'I am not familiar with *Homo sapiens purus*.'

'You know her better as Norma Williams, the girl who has, by a miracle of genetic serendipity, remained free of the distorting influence of the Grigori strain. She is the living embodiment of Goldschmidt's hopeful monster.'

'Nonsense . . . *natura non facit saltum*: Nature doesn't make jumps.'

'This is not a jump, Septimus, rather it is a regression: humankind retreating to its original innocence . . . the state it enjoyed before the meddlements of Lilith. Of course, Norma's great gifts had to be nurtured just as mine were and that is why I had her brought to the Demi-Monde, why I made Aaliz Heydrich her doppelgänger. The trials Norma has faced in the Demi-Monde have taught her self-discipline so that she is better able to resist temptation; she has learnt courage and is no longer blinded by fear. It is Norma Williams who will teach the world to empathise with itself and with Nature, so that humankind may rediscover its ability to look at the world through the eyes of others.'

'I am obliged for your warning but it is unnecessary. Norma Williams will never leave the Demi-Monde. Even now plans are afoot to speed her death, plans which you are duty-bound *not* to impede.'

'I think you will find that you're running a little behind

events, Septimus. While you have been enjoying my company here in NoirVille . . . well, let me not spoil the surprise.' Vanka Maykov dabbed his napkin to his mouth, stood up and dropped notes onto the table. 'I must go now, Septimus, but I go confident that even without my help it is Norma Williams who will defeat you . . . or rather, assist you to defeat yourself.'

2:04

INTRADOC Headquarters
The Real World: 24 March 2019

Frank Kenton might not have been a candidate in the 1953 presidential election (he endorsed his younger brother, Ben, Senator for New York) but his shadow hung heavy over it, inaugurating, as he did, the Church of True Believers in his famous Coliseum speech on 1st May 1953. Before an audience of one hundred thousand acolytes, Kenton announced that the world had entered the Time of Tribulation. God, according to Kenton, had called him to lead those who accepted God's Word – the Believers – back to righteousness and the True Church, and to prepare them for Revelation. He was, Kenton said, the Last Prophet, his coming fulfilling the prophecies of Malachi 4:5-6: 'Behold, I will send you Elijah the Prophet before the coming of the great and dreadful day of the law.'

The Kenton Klan: Messiahs or Maniacs?: D.W. Wright,
American OffShore Press

Ella awoke into darkness, that total, unleavened darkness she associated with blindness. For a moment she questioned whether she was alive or dead, but although she couldn't see, she could still hear the hum of what sounded suspiciously like an air conditioner and could feel the very unpleasant sensations caused by the various tubes that were violating her body. The assumption, therefore, was that she was alive. Heaven, she suspected, didn't need air conditioning, and presumably the perfection of angels would be marred if they needed evacuation tubes in order to go about their life in the hereafter.

Alive though she was, she decided to lie still for a few seconds in order to get her head together. Her memory of recent events was fractured, jumbled, and somehow unreal . . . but the one vivid recollection she had was of dying from the sword Billy had stabbed into her stomach. It was a memory somewhat at odds with her surmise that she was alive and, as best she could judge, with a fully functioning stomach.

More memories started to slide into place. She remembered the Demi-Monde and remembered being warned that if she were to die in the Demi-Monde she would die in the Real World. So the question was, had she been brought back to the Real World – and she knew instinctively that that was where she was – simply to inhabit a non-functional body? Happily, this was a conjecture that was simple enough to test and to her profound relief the forefinger of her right hand obliged by twitching.

'I'm glad to see you're awake, Ella.' The words came to her from far away, muffled and indistinct. A woman's voice: soft, reassuring, comforting. 'Your transfer from the Demi-Monde has been successful and you're now safe in INTRADOC's biPsych Storage Unit. I am pleased to advise you that all the readings of your vital signs show that you're in excellent condition. There will be just a moment's discomfort while the nutrition and evacuation tubes are retracted.'

'Discomfort' was obviously a euphemism for 'fucking painful'. There were sudden sharp pains in Ella's nose, her mouth and other parts of her body that she really didn't want to think about as the tubes were withdrawn. She was left with a foul taste in her mouth and a tingling asshole as mementos of their stay.

'The TIS swathing a biPsych's body automatically retracts

sixty seconds after their return to the Real World,' the voice crooned. 'I think this is happening ... now. Please keep your eyes closed during this procedure.' Ella felt the Total Immersion Shroud begin to slowly retreat from her body, its warm embrace seeping away from her legs, from her groin, from her chest, from her chin and, finally, from her face.

'Excellent. You may open your eyes now, Ella.'

Ella did as she was asked, though she had to blink to accommodate the sharp brightness of the Storage Unit.

'Welcome back to the Real World, Ella. After seven months in the Demi-Monde, we had begun to think you were avoiding us.' Nurse Green gave Ella a beaming smile: she seemed to have mellowed a little since she'd helped Ella get ready for her sortie into the Demi-Monde all those long months ago. Nurse Green held out a white surgical gown. 'I think it would be a good idea if you were to put this gown on, otherwise any of the guys in INTRADOC seeing you is liable to die of terminal priapism.'

Carefully, cautiously, Ella sat up and then swung her legs around, the caress of the AC on her skin reminding her that she was stark naked, a realisation that made her a little more enthusiastic about wearing the gown she was being offered. Once she was dressed she pushed herself off the gurney and onto her feet. The floor was cold but, amazingly, she didn't feel in any way dizzy or unsteady, which, after more than half a year lying comatose, she'd have thought would be a given.

Nurse Green explained as she tethered the straps at the back of Ella's gown. 'Your TIS has ensured that you have been returned to us in peak physical condition, better than you left us, in fact. Your muscles have been regularly and rigorously exercised and the dietary regimen you've been following is one profiled to meet all your nutritional needs. You've lost five pounds while you were in TIS mode, Ella, and your body fat is now a much healthier thirteen per cent. The Demi-Monde is an excellent diet plan.'

Ella had to admit that she did feel good . . . *really* good. And with five million bucks in the bank life seemed very rosy indeed. But there was something nagging at the back of her mind, something that seemed to be trying to remind her of other things she should be doing. She just wished she could remember.

'If you would come this way, Ella, our medics would like to check you over.'

'I can't tell you how pleased we are to have you back with us safe and sound, Ella,' said Dr Andrews as he scanned Ella's test results. 'After what happened to Captain Simmons . . .' He trailed off as though embarrassed by what he had been about to say. 'No matter. You gave us a couple of scares when you were in the Demi-Monde. Seems you were subjected to electroshock torture. It must have been pretty bad because your PINC fused.'

'I don't remember,' muttered Ella as she massaged the sides of her forehead. 'Well, I *almost* remember, Doctor. It's as though all those memories are just a little out of reach . . . close, but never close enough that I can grasp them.'

'Temporary loss of memory isn't uncommon in those returning from the Demi-Monde, Ella. It's a phenomenon akin to post-traumatic stress disorder. Norma Williams also suffered from PTS amnesia when she returned to us, but, after treatment, she's all fine and dandy.'

'Norma Williams?'

'The President's daughter. The girl you were sent into the Demi-Monde to lead to the Portal.' The doctor shrugged. 'Not that she needed any help. Luckily Norma managed to make her own way out, though quite how, we'll probably never know. That's one part of her bioMemory that looks to have gone for ever. A shame: we might have been able to use that knowledge to help all the other neoFights trapped in the Demi-Monde escape the place.' He gave Ella a smile. 'And that's something we'd like to cover in the formal debriefing: how you managed to leave the Demi-Monde without the use of a Portal.'

Ella shook her head. 'I'd love to tell you, Doctor, but everything about what happened in the Demi-Monde is just so much garbled static.'

Dr Andrews gave her a reassuring smile. 'Let's not worry about that now. We can sit down and chat when you're fully recovered and by then, hopefully, your memory will have settled down.'

The word 'hopefully' didn't instil a lot of confidence in Ella as she sat in her chair trying to straighten out the confusion that was rattling around in her head, trying to determine what was fact and what was fantasy. And there was a *lot* of fantasy: some of what she remembered – *thought* she remembered – was simply ludicrous.

'Standard procedure in cases of PTS amnesia is to download the backup we made of a returnee's pre-deployment memories to their PINC, but as your PINC is non-functional, we'll have to supply you with a new one.'

'And my memories about what happened when I was inside the Demi-Monde? What about those, Doctor? That's the stuff I seem to be having the biggest problem with.'

'We're reluctant to intervene to force those memories back to the surface. We find the long-term outcome for returning biPsychs vis-à-vis their experiences in the Demi-Monde is optimised if we simply let nature take its course. Time, as they say, is a great healer. But apart from the amnesia, how do you feel?'

'Disorientated. It's as though I don't belong here . . . that none of this is real.'

'Hmmm . . . interesting. We haven't met that sort of dissociation before. It's undoubtedly something that Professor Bole will want to discuss with you.'

'Professor Bole?'

'The world's leading expert on the Demi-Monde . . . you met him before your deployment.' Ella shook her head to signal that the name didn't register. 'Professor Bole insists on making a personal assessment of each returning biPsych, especially since the incident with Simmons . . .' He gave Ella an awkward smile. 'Well, let's not talk about that now. Professor Bole seems to be away from his office at the moment so couldn't be here to greet you but I expect he'll put in an appearance in the next day or so. He'll be eager to meet you.'

For some reason she couldn't quite fathom, Ella was more unnerved by this piece of information than anything that had been said to her, but she was given no time to dwell on it.

'If you will tip your head back, Ella, I'll administer a replacement PINC and we'll get all those Real-World bioMemories of yours straightened out.'

Dr Andrews administered both the PINC and a really quite potent sedative, so potent that Ella didn't regain consciousness for almost eight hours. Coming to in darkness, she checked her watch: it was just shy of three o'clock in the morning. With her head drumming she hunted around in her bedside cabinet for some of the painkillers Andrews had prescribed, and it was while she was doing this that she had the troubling feeling that she wasn't alone. Looking over to the chair set in the corner of her room, she saw an elegantly dressed man lounging there smoking a cigarette. Ella didn't quite know what was more incongruous: the man's disdain for the 'Smoking is ILLEGAL' sign affixed to the room's door or the top hat he was wearing so rakishly on his head.

There was something vaguely familiar about him, which was mildly troubling given he was so outlandishly handsome and so oddly dressed that Ella doubted that once seen he would ever be forgotten. The striped trousers that encased his long, long legs were, of course, something of a fashion faux pas, as was his rather *too* ornate moustache, but other than that there were only two words that could be used to describe this vision of masculine loveliness: the first was 'perfect' and the second was 'scoundrel'. He looked like a rascal and was all the more attractive because of it: Ella liked rascals. Instinctively she raised a hand to better arrange her long hair, only then remembering that all her hair had been shaved off.

'Hello?' she enquired.

The man turned and gave her a wonderful smile. Ella's heart fluttered. 'Ah, Ella . . . at last. I was worried that you would decide to sleep the night away, but it seems that the NightRapture prescribed by Dr Andrews was insufficient to achieve that objective. Andrews is a very conservative medic.'

'And you are?'

The man doffed his hat. 'I am Vanka Maykov, sometime psychic, oft-time fugitive and fervent admirer of the peerlessly beautiful Ella Thomas.'

Despite herself and the rather surreal nature of the situation, Ella found herself blushing. 'You are very . . . gallant.'

'I am delighted that I delight you, Ella. But please do not think my compliments are mere puff: you are the only woman I have ever met who could be afforded the epithet "beautiful" whilst lying in a hospital bed with a tube stuck up her nose.'

Ella laughed. This Vanka Maykov item might be a rascal but he was an amusing rascal. 'So what have I done to deserve these encomiums?'

'You have captured my heart, Ella, which is quite remarkable given that I don't possess a heart.'

'I'm sorry?'

'I apologise. I had forgotten that your memories of the Demi-Monde are currently in a state of some confusion. Perhaps I should explain. Although I present to you as Vanka Maykov, I am the anthropomorphisation – and I don't recommend pronouncing *that* with a tube up your nose – of ABBA.'

'The computer?'

Vanka Maykov sniffed. 'The use of the appellation "computer" implies that I have the capability of an everyday Polly when I am a much more profound creation. But no matter . . . yes, I am ABBA, the QuanPuter upon which the Demi-Monde is platformed.'

'You look awfully real.'

'Oh, thank you. One does one's best. Fortunately, this suite is equipped with a hologram platform which allows travel-averse relatives to visit the sick without having to leave the comfort of their own homes. By hacking into this system I am able to present myself here in your room.'

'You're just a hologram!'

A sigh from Vanka, who took another drag of his cigarette and a wisp of very convincing white smoke drifted ceilingwards. 'If you must. But you have to admit that I'm a damned convincing hologram. I don't think I've ever been able to concoct a suit with such a perfect fit before: it's almost as good as the ones the Anglo tailors in the Rookeries produced.'

'But why?'

'Why am I here? Because, my darling Ella, you are in danger and whilst all my instincts and much of my programming incline me to stand aside and to let fate take its course I am persuaded by my love for you to become a dabbler in the affairs of HumanKind.'

'Love?'

'Yes,' said Vanka Maykov softly, 'love. And it is because of that love that I am come here tonight, to place my thumb on one of the scales of history, scales which determine whether good or evil triumphs in this world.'

A hologram supposedly conjured by a computer declaring itself to be in love with her made Ella a little uncomfortable. It was *Demon Seed*ish. She decided to move the conversation on to less emotional matters.

'But why would you wish to dabble?'

Vanka Maykov lounged deeper into his chair and smiled. 'As you will discover shortly, I – that is, ABBA – have been using the Demi-Monde as a means of achieving self-enlightenment. The Demi-Monde is, in effect, a somewhat complex birthing chamber.'

'And what is it giving birth to?'

'Why me, of course, or rather an ABBA that is fully conscious of its position in the Kosmos and of its responsibilities to the life forms ornamenting the aforesaid Kosmos. By interacting with HumanKind on a one-to-one basis I have, and here I am obliged to paraphrase some of the rather nauseating doggerel favoured by New Agers, actualised the hidden aspects of my soul by seeking both the inward and outward aspects of the Divine.'

'I don't understand.'

'That's two of us. I find all this New Age stuff replete with self-aggrandisement. Let me put it another way. I was trying to learn from people like you, Ella, in order that I might better appreciate the ins and outs of the universe around me.'

'And what did you learn?'

'Oh, many things, but the one most pertinent to this discussion was my realisation that interference in evolution is a dangerous thing, especially when the motives of those doing the interfering are suspect. You, in another life, attempted such an evolutionary intercession, and, I have to say it, it ended in tears.'

'I haven't a clue what you're talking about, Mr Maykov.'

'Vanka, please.'

'Look, Vanka, it's very late and much as I would love to lie here chatting . . .'

'There is an electrode attached to a red lead dangling from a hook by the side of your bed. I would be obliged if you would connect it to the patch on the side of your forehead.'

'Is it safe?'

'I am pained by the suggestion that I would do anything to harm you, Ella.'

'Okay.' It was an awkward manoeuvre but with a little effort Ella managed it.

'I will now reconfigure your new PINC such that you are fully conversant with all you experienced in the Demi-Monde.'

In an instant all the tangles in Ella's head were straightened out and the memories that had been murky and imprecise became crystal-clear.

'Wow!'

'I am more inclined to the expression *voilà!*, but no matter.'

'We were an item!' She gave Vanka a scowl. 'I've been making out with a computer? That's gross! What's that sorta thing called . . . mechanophilia or something?'

Vanka smiled. 'I can assure you there was nothing mechanical about our lovemaking. I am, however, gratified that the first and therefore the most important recollection of your time in the Demi-Monde was our relationship. We were indeed "an item", so much so that my inclination is to come over and kiss you. Unfortunately, being a hologram, I am unable to do so with any great effect.'

'I was the Lady IMmanual . . . Lilith?' No wonder she felt out of place in the Real World. Lilith didn't really belong *anywhere*. She was a freak of nature and of time.

'The tense you are using is somewhat mutable. You were and you are both of these individuals, though I strenuously hope that henceforth it is Ella who will prevail. Your other two personas were really quite tiresome.'

'And Bole is a Grigori!'

'A *near*-Grigori, actually. He's the product of an experiment conducted by his father aimed at eliminating the Grigori's more debilitating idiosyncrasies.'

'Vanka . . . why are you telling me all this?'

'Because you have the power to change the world, Ella, or rather to prevent the world – the Real World – being changed. Septimus Bole is intent on continuing the work that you, in your former role as Lilith, instigated. Lilith caused three new species to walk the earth and Bole wishes to ensure that it is the Grigori who emerge triumphant. What he forgets is that these three species were developed from the Fragiles, from *Homo sapiens sapiens*, whose many virtues have been subsumed by the more overbearing species that Lilith spawned. In their natural and unadulterated state Fragiles are a rather frail species, peaceful in temperament and more inclined to love than war. It is because of their more gentle tendencies that they have been so put-upon, so much so that their more . . . considered attitude to life has been suppressed. Now, through serendipity, one of these creatures, unsullied by cross-contamination by the species developed by Lilith, is ready to blossom, but to flower it needs the protection of someone as resilient and as hardy as you, Ella. Anyway, as it was you, in your guise of Lilith, who caused this mess, it is your responsibility to clear it up. That is your fate, Ella, to protect Norma Williams.'

Ella shook her head. 'It seems my destiny is to go through life protecting Norma.'

'We all have our crosses to bear, Ella, and, as I say, this one is of your own making. So, if you would be so kind as to get dressed—'

'Whoa! Time out, Vanka. I think you've got the wrong girl. I don't think I'm especially qualified to ride shotgun on Norma. I screwed up once before, remember?'

Her protests were brushed aside with a negligent wave of Vanka's cigarette. 'All the more reason why you should be delighted to have a second bite at the apple. But whilst it might seem a daunting task, the reality is, my darling Ella, that there is no one better equipped than you to perform it. The Grigori will do everything they can to destroy Norma Williams and only a Lilithi has the power to stop them. And be assured, Ella, that I, in my turn, will do everything I am able to help you, though I have to admit that I am rather confined in this regard by my programming. Thaddeus Bole placed substantial cyber-shackles on me, most of these constraints designed to ensure that I would never hurt or discomfort the Boles or ParaDigm. But by making a rather generous interpretation of these orders, I am able to circumvent at least some of Bole's restrictions, enough, I hope, to help you preserve the life of Norma Williams.'

Ella sank back into her pillows. Everything was going so fast ... too fast. She wanted – needed – a moment to get her thoughts straight. Vanka didn't grant her one.

'I hate to be a nag, Ella, but I would be grateful if you would show some urgency. Septimus Bole and I have had a recent tête-à-tête in the Demi-Monde and it always takes him a day or so to recover from his sojourns, but once he *has* recovered, I think, he will be less than enamoured to learn of your return to the Real World. It would be better if you vacate Fort Jackson as quickly as possible.'

Ella nodded. She had to trust Vanka. With Vanka at her side she had always felt a damned sight more confident about life. 'So what should I do first?'

'As I said: get dressed. To protect Norma you must go to her, and whilst in normal circumstances I would give you every encouragement to wander around wearing only a surgical gown – you have, after all, a perfectly delightful derrière – I am mindful of the fact that once seen, your bottom is never forgotten. Therefore I must, regretfully, counsel modesty and the wearing of the jeans and sweater hanging in your closet.'

Ella pulled the tube out of her nose and eased the drip out of her arm then swung herself out of bed and tripped over to the wardrobe. As Vanka had advised, there was a set of clothes hanging there. She hesitated. 'Are you going to watch me get dressed, Vanka?'

'I have seen you naked before, Ella . . . and very pleasant it was too.'

'Okay, but I've got to say there's something a little pervy about a computer that's into voyeurism.'

'I am suitably admonished,' admitted Vanka, but admonished or not, he kept right on watching.

Once dressed, Ella asked the obvious question. 'Okay, now what?'

'You must go to the Transfer Room and feed the codes that are held in your PINC into its control module. This will activate the NoirVille Portal's Transfer System and allow Norma Williams to return to the Real World. But time, as they say, is of the essence: if my 4Cast is correct von Sternberg's SS will make their final assault on the Portal's Transfer Room in less than ten minutes.'

'Okay, so I help Norma get back to the Real World. Then what?'

'The aggravating thing is that Norma's body isn't stored here in Fort Jackson, it's held in a ParaDigm facility just outside Los Angeles. You will have to travel there to rescue her.'

'And how will I be able to do that?'

'Oh, I have arranged for you to be afforded some assistance in this matter, assistance you will need: the place is guarded by Grigori.'

'But to get to LA I'll have to buy an airline ticket, and once I do that, Bole's going to know what I'm up to.'

'I think I'll be able to help there. As you are officially "dead", I have decided it is acceptable that you are treated as a non-person and therefore that it is unnecessary to alert the airlines' computer systems of your presence aboard one of their aircraft.'

Vanka paused to polish his nails on the lapel of his jacket. 'If I say so myself, I have a quite profound ability in the area of data management . . . or should I better say, data *mis*management? I would also recommend that whilst you are in the ParaDigm facility in Los Angeles you enquire regarding the research Bole has been sponsoring in the Heydrich Institute of Natural Sciences in the ForthRight . . . especially research concerning plague development.'

'Can't you just tell me?'

'Nothing would give me greater pleasure, Ella, but divulging this is precluded by my programming, so all I can do is steer you in the direction of the answers. But more of that anon: the important thing at the moment is for you to get to the Transfer Room and enter the codes.' Vanka smiled and gave a bow of his head. 'With that, my dearest Ella, I bid you a reluctant adieu.' The holographic image faded to nothing.

Ella allowed herself to be guided by PINC through the maze of deserted corridors that snaked through INTRADOC and after five minutes of dodging this way and that she finally came to a pair of swing doors labelled TRANSFER SUITE. Taking a deep breath, she pushed her way inside. Immediately the automatic lights flickered on, revealing it to be the same room where, seven months before, she had begun her adventures in the Demi-Monde. This time, though, there was no Septimus Bole or Nurse Green in attendance: the room was as empty as rooms are apt to be at four o'clock in the morning. Prompted by PINC, Ella seated herself at a Polly terminal and immediately she settled, the Flexi-Plexi covering the wall burst into life.

IF YOU WOULD ENTER THE TRANSFER CODE, ELLA.

Ella typed in '⊣╢╤ ⊢╫╓╟ ┡╍ ╘╥╤╡══╟║ ♀1nw▶ NOIRVILLE PORTAL ▶ PARADIGM#1'.

THANK YOU, ELLA. TRANSFER OF NORMA WILLIAMS FROM

THE DEMI-MONDE MAY BE INITIATED AT ANY TIME. DO YOU WISH TO CONVERSE WITH MISS WILLIAMS TO ADVISE HER OF THIS?

YES.

PLEASE STAND ON THE HOLOPAD IN THE CORNER OF THE ROOM.

Ella did as she was asked and immediately the Transfer Room flickered and faded to be replaced by a similar, though smaller room where a dishevelled Norma Williams stood gawping at her.

'Ella?'

'Yeah, it's me, or more precisely, a holo-me.'

'But . . . but . . .'

'I'm here to help you, Norma.'

The conversation was interrupted by an explosion from beyond the room's door.

'The SS are getting close, Norma, so if you want to return to the Real World then I can give you the transfer coordinates that will allow you to do just that.'

'But you're the Lady IMmanual . . . Lilith. You were trying to kill me.'

An understandable reaction, thought Ella, but this wasn't either the time or the place for explanation. 'That was then and this is now, Norma. People change and much as I'd love to stand here gossiping, give it another couple of minutes and the SS will be making a house call. If you want to escape, it's now or never.'

'How can I trust you?'

A good question. 'Like I say, Norma, with the SS knocking you've got nothing to lose by trusting me.'

A convincing argument. 'Okay . . . let's go.'

'I've loaded the transfer codes, Norma, so all you have to do is initiate the transfer from your end. Your body's stored at a Para-Digm facility in LA: I'll do my best to get to you as fast as I can.' Ella took a quick look at her watch. Time was running and that was just what she should be doing. 'Good luck, Norma' – and with a jolt she found herself back in Fort Jackson. Immediately a message flicked up on the Flexi-Plexi.

THANK YOU, ELLA. PLEASE FOLLOW THE INSTRUCTIONS PROVIDED BY YOUR PINC. HAVE A NICE DAY.

Bole Institute for the Advancement of History, Los Angeles
The Real World: 25 March 2019

The Primary Objective of the Bole Institute for the Advancement of History is to manage all Temporal Modulations in order that ParaDigm becomes and remains the world's supreme industrial, commercial and financial services organisation. By achieving this ambition, the Bole family will be able to protect and to preserve the Grigori and to fulfil their long-cherished dream of gaining hegemony over the Fragiles and all of the other lesser species of the world. To secure this end, NO Temporal Modulation shall be undertaken that has not first been modelled by the Bole Institute for the Advancement of History. A Modulation awarded a less than ninety per cent probability of attaining the desired Temporal Outcome will NOT be executed.

Precepts of Temporal Modulation: memorandum written
by Beowulf Bole, 14 December 1933

It was a somewhat subdued and travel-worn Ella Thomas who walked out of the arrivals hall at Los Angeles' Kenton International Airport eight hours after she had left Fort Jackson. She had tried to sleep during the flight, but the confusion of emotions she was struggling with meant that sleep had eluded her. She felt herself to be a misfit, not quite knowing who – or even what – she was any more. As the last of the Lilithi, she was burdened by the collective memories of all the Lilithi who had gone before her, memories that threatened at any moment to inundate her, to turn her into something she didn't want to be. She could feel Lilith inside her struggling to be free. This she countered by continually reminding herself that her task was to help Norma Williams to defeat Bole and the Grigori. By doing that she would – hopefully – free herself of the guilt of Lilith. There was no place for Lilith in the Real World.

But then was there any place here for Ella Thomas, the girl who had fallen in love with the digital-chimera that was Vanka Maykov? The realisation that the man she loved was simply a product of ABBA's digital imagination didn't make losing him any easier. She had found the man for her, had lost him and now faced the prospect of there never being a man – a *real* man – capable of replacing him. She had been touched by the divine, and now mere mortals would always be a disappointment.

As she wandered through the airport the abiding sensation she was beset with was one of being adrift between worlds and between identities, destined to be for ever tormented by what had been and by what could never be.

She was so lost in her thoughts that she almost walked past the sign bearing her name, the sign carried by Burlesque Bandstand. It took a moment for her to recognise him – the trademark bowler had been replaced by an even more beaten-up porkpie hat and the stained frock-coat by a sweatshirt – but it was Burlesque all right.

'Burlesque?'

The tubby man blinked and looked down at the name scrawled on the piece of cardboard he was holding. 'You this Ella Thomas item?'

'Of course I am, Burlesque.' Ella made to kiss Burlesque on the cheek, but when he flinched back in surprise she was persuaded to thrust out a hand instead. Burlesque gave it a cautious shake. 'Don't you recognise me, Burlesque?'

'Nah, never met yous in me life. And me name ain't Burlesque neither; it's Burl. That's me: Burl Standing at your service.' He glanced to the rather large and powerful girl standing next to him. 'And this is me friend, Oddie Aroca.'

'Hi, Oddie,' said Ella as she rather nervously allowed the girl to shake her hand: Oddie Aroca looked like a trucker in drag, 'and thanks for coming to meet me. And believe it or not, Burl, we *have* met before, in fact, we were comrades in arms and I've a feeling that we will be again. I'll explain while we drive. We need to get to the Bole Institute for the Advancement of History in Beverly Hills pronto.'

Norma woke to find herself cocooned in a layer of what felt like warm toffee.

Odd.

So odd that it took a moment for her brain to get into gear . . . her *brains* to get into gear. She had a PINC, which was strange because PINCs were illegal in the US.

PINC gave her the answer: she – or rather Aaliz Heydrich – had received the implant when she – or rather Aaliz Heydrich – had first entered the Real World. And having been equipped with one of the damned things – and 'damned' was a very apposite description according to Believers' Broadcasting – Norma came to understand that having instant access to so much knowledge was intoxicating. Her mind reeled as her thoughts tumbled through oceans of understanding and soared through skies of unimagined perception. How, she wondered, could anyone resist this wonderment? Now she was more than human . . . now she was H+.

Thanks to PINC she was able to take all the confusion of memories she had brought back with her from the Demi-Monde and straighten them out, dividing her real self from her Aaliz self. But the strange thing was that this separation wasn't as easy as she thought it might have been. It seemed there were aspects of Aaliz – her drive, determination and, most notably, her ambition – that Norma shared with the girl: the confidence she had gained in her own worth and abilities during her time in the Demi-Monde were replicated in Aaliz.

And Aaliz had been a very busy girl. PINC advised her she was now the leader of a religious movement called the Fun/Funs – her father must have gone apeshit! – and was scheduled to host a Gathering of millions of her followers in Las Vegas – thankfully PINC was there to tell her where that nothing of a town was – in just thirty-eight days' time. In six short months 'Norma Williams' had gone from tabloid fodder to political heavyweight. The more she delved into the details of the Fun/Funs, the more amazed and shocked she was at the power that being the leader of such an organisation gave her.

Power . . .

Power to bring Normalism to the Real World.

These rather intriguing thoughts were interrupted by her toffee coating coming to the decision that it was time to vamoose, and once she was clear of its cloying presence she began the disgusting job of removing the tubes that had made their home in her body. This done, she took a look around the shadow-bedecked room. There wasn't much to see: the room was dark, the drapes tightly drawn, the only illumination coming from a nightlight burning on a side table. From what she could make out by its fragile light, she was lying in an overwide four-poster bed in a large bedroom which had a distinctly musty smell about it. 'Musty' was an accurate description for the decor too: with all the sombre furniture and drab colours it seemed as though she had arrived back in the Real World slap-bang in the middle of a film set of a Victorian melodrama. A *pornographic* Victorian melodrama, judging by the fact that she was naked with every hair on her body having been shaved off. This, she decided, was borderline pervy.

She checked with PINC: she was in a bedroom inside the Bole Institute for the Advancement of History in Beverly Hills . . . an odd coincidence, as this was the place where all her adventures in the Demi-Monde had begun. The remembrance that the Institute was where Septimus Bole had his office in the USA persuaded her that now was the time to get up, get dressed and get busy. She was just pulling the last tube out of her nose when the door of her room opened and she saw standing in the entrance, silhouetted by the light of the landing beyond, a disturbingly peculiar woman staring back at her.

Make that a *vampiric* pornographic Victorian melodrama.

Yeah, that's what the woman was: a vampire. Unmistakably a vampire . . . she'd had a run-in with the girl's brothers when she'd escaped the Bastille with Vanka. This girl was one of the Grigori.

Instinctively Norma looked around for something to defend herself with, but the woman's smile – compromised a little by the way her strange eyes glinted in the half-light – and the intoned 'Welcome, Miss Aaliz' persuaded her that she wasn't in any immediate danger. The Grigori thought she was Aaliz!

The Grigori loped deeper into the room, her long, lean body swathed in a tight outfit made from slick black spandex. Norma swallowed: there was something almost panthcresque about her, an impression confirmed when she flicked on the room's lights and allowed Norma to get a better look at her. Now she could see that it wasn't just her size and her feline grace that announced she was not as other girls: just like her brothers, she had cat's eyes, yellow with a slit of an iris. They were eyes designed to see in the dark.

'I am Metztil,' the Grigori said, her voice accented and strangely sibilant. 'I was charged by the Professor with guarding your body whilst you were in the Demi-Monde. You have returned to us unannounced, Miss Aaliz. I trust all is well.'

'Water,' Norma gasped, trying to gain a little thinking time.

As the Grigori oozed over to a side table to pour her a glass of water from the jug standing there, Norma decided that her best chance was to play along and act the part of Aaliz Heydrich. And as she was drinking the water, she realised that PINC would give her all the information she needed to make her masquerade convincing.

'Unfortunately, Miss Aaliz, I am unable to inform Professor Bole that you have returned to the Real World as he is currently in the Demi-Monde dealing with urgent developments there.'

'Don't worry about it, Metztil,' Norma answered as she handed the empty glass back, 'the Professor and I met up in NoirVille, so he knows about my return. When do you expect him back?'

'We are not sure. I am hopeful it will be soon. The situation regarding Ella Thomas is pressing.'

'Ella Thomas?' she answered, trying to mimic surprise. She had only been talking to the girl an instant ago. 'I thought she was dead,' or more accurately, Aaliz Heydrich thought she was dead.

'That's what we believed too, but it appears that somehow she survived the explosion in the Temple of Lilith. We are advised by INTRADOC that she has managed to exit the Demi-Monde and reclaim her body, so we must deal with her here in the Real World.'

Norma levered herself off the bed: she'd think better if she didn't have to do it au naturel. She wandered across to the chest of drawers where Aaliz Heydrich kept her underwear.

'May I ask why you have returned from the Demi-Monde, Miss Aaliz? Our information is that your presence there is vital if the UnFunDaMentalists are to be persuaded to gather in Terror Incognita for the Ceremony of Purification.'

Happier now that she had a pair of pants on, Norma began to explore the closets. Quite what Aaliz had been doing with her wardrobe whilst she had been in the Real World, Norma had no idea, everything seemed much too fluffy and feminine. Aaliz, it seemed, didn't do black and didn't do goth so in the end Norma had to opt for a *very* short dress in a rather bilious shade of green. As she pulled the dress over her head, she answered Metztil's question. 'My father – my *real* father, Reinhard Heydrich – has brought the situation in the ForthRight back under control, so the feeling was that having "Norma Williams" back here in the Real World is a more productive use of my time.'

'Of course. It was just that I had not realised the Professor had initiated the Transfer Sequence.'

'That's the Professor for you,' said Norma as she strapped on a pair of quite ridiculous shoes. Aaliz Heydrich, she decided, had absolutely *no* dress sense.

'I will have lunch served here in ten minutes, Miss Aaliz, and then I suggest you rest. The Professor advises that it takes at least twenty-four hours to recover from the rigours of transit.' With that Metztil exited the bedroom.

'Sounds like a load of old bollocks to me,' admitted Burl as he brought the hired Ford to a halt outside the walled enclave that was the Bole Institute. 'I mean, virtual worlds populated by duplicates of real people and the Norma Williams who's bin puffing the Fun/Funs not bin the real Norma Williams . . .' He gave a dismissive shake of his head. 'Nah, it don't make sense. You're just pulling my plonker.'

Only when she had tried to explain to Burl and Oddie what had been going down in the Demi-Monde had Ella realised how improbable it all sounded, but somehow she *had* to persuade them that what she was saying was fact and not fantasy. She needed their help to save Norma Williams.

'Whether it makes sense or not, Burl, it's the truth. It wasn't Norma Williams who formed the Fun/Funs but her doppelgänger, a truly wicked bitch called Aaliz Heydrich. And that's what we've got to do tonight: unhijack Norma's body from where it's being held in the Institute.'

Burl shrugged. ''S'all too deep for me. What d'you fink, Oddie?'

Oddie Aroca pushed a hand through her thick mane of brown hair and made a moue. 'What Ella has told us is very strange, I grant you, Burl, but it's consistent with the rumours that have been circulating on the Polly that Norma Williams has changed . . . that the girl running the Fun/Funs isn't her but some impostor.'

'That's just conspiracy crap, Oddie. Just the Polly nutters giving it a stir.'

'Oh, I know that, Burl,' answered Oddie, 'and I know that the official version for all the changes seen in Norma Williams is that they're a consequence of her having found Jesus, but some of it isn't easy to explain away. Like the way she's suddenly become left-handed.'

'That's to be expected,' agreed Ella. 'Dupes are the mirror image of their Real World doppelgängers.'

'And then there's the other weird rumours,' Oddie continued, 'like she's taken to drinking blood.'

'Twaddle, that's wot that is; PollyGossips trying to get something sensational going. And all because someone spotted her guzzling red stuff from a vial before one of the Fun/Funs gigs.'

'Yeah, but it's at one with what Ella tells us about Dupes being addicted to blood. But the most persuasive thing for me is that what Ella says ties in with all the messages we've been getting from Vanka, the ones telling us that Norma Williams isn't Norma Williams.'

'Vanka?' asked Ella.

'He's my own special Deep Throat. I've been getting weird eyeMails from somebody called Vanka giving me classified information about Fun/Fun activity. It was Vanka who told us to come and meet you at the airport, saying we'd "learn something of interest" about Norma Williams.' Oddie seemed to come to a decision. 'You know, Burl, I'm inclined to believe what Ella is telling us. It may be a little far out, but I think we should run with it.' She gave a smile. 'Anyway, all we have to do is get into the Institute and we'll be able to see for ourselves. At the very least, it'll make a terrific story for the *New York PollyGazette*.'

Burl gave a shake of his head. 'Okay, 'ave it your way, Oddie, you're the brains of the outfit.' He nodded in the direction of the huge gate that guarded the Institute. 'But I've gotta tell you it ain't gonna be easy getting into that Institute place; looks cast-iron and double-bolted to me and there's bound to be a swarm ov eyeSpies hovering abart too, maybe even some ov them guard-Bots. It's a beast.'

Ella had to agree with Burl's assessment. The Institute's public persona might be that of a place of learning but it looked more fortress than university. 'Beast or not, we've got to get inside.' She glanced over to Oddie. 'Any ideas, Oddie?'

'My experience as a journalist, Ella, is that the best way to get into a building is through the front door. It's amazing what a little chutzpah will accomplish, so why don't we just go up to the gate and ask to see Norma?'

'Soppy idea,' observed Burl. 'All the badniks'll do is call the cops. We'll end up spending the night in clink.'

'They can't arrest us for just asking for an interview and anyway, if this Septimus Bole character is as spooked by Ella as she says he is, maybe he'll be only too pleased that we've come calling.'

Turning Oddie's suggestion over in her head, Ella came to the conclusion that what the girl said made a lot of sense, but she also knew that bearding Bole in his den would be dangerous. He was, according to Vanka, guarded by Grigori.

'No, Burl, Oddie's right. We haven't time to be subtle. Once

Bole finds out I'm back in the Real World he'll come hunting me, so the best thing to do is take the fight to him. But before we do that there are one or two things we're going to need. I saw a 7/11 a couple of blocks back . . .'

The knock on the door of Norma's bedroom came exactly ten hours later.

'If you are ready, Miss Aaliz,' oozed Metztil, 'perhaps we could go downstairs? There are some minor administrative matters for you to deal with.'

Dutifully Norma followed Metztil as she led her out of the room, down the Institute's long staircase to a large reception room. Norma had been in the room before. It had been here that Professor Bole had lectured them on the importance a knowledge of history had for all the would-be politicians attending ParaDigm's Hi-Achievers course . . . the course he had used to lure her to the Institute and thence into the Demi-Monde.

A second Grigori was waiting there. 'This is Jomjael, who is responsible for security,' Metztil purred as she waved Norma into the seat behind the desk set to one side of the room. 'It is fortunate that you have returned to us so quickly as there are a number of matters which require your attention before you depart for Las Vegas. Purely administrative . . . speeches to be made by a number of the lesser luminaries of the Fun/Funs which require your approval.' She nodded to the Polly lying on top of the desk. 'If you would be so kind as to review these and then authorise them using your bioSignature.'

Trying to appear as casual as she could, Norma picked up the Polly and made a pantomime of reading the speeches. Pretty innocuous stuff and a quick trawl through PINC didn't signal anything out of the ordinary. She pressed her thumb to the fingerprint pad.

'Thank you for your help in this matter, Miss Aaliz' – Metztil gave an off-kilter smile – 'or should that be, Miss *Williams*?'

Norma felt her blood run cold. She glanced around to see if there was any chance of her making a run for it. There wasn't: Jomjael had taken station at the door.

Metztil laughed. 'Escape is impossible, Miss Williams. It is odd, is it not, that Dupes are a mirror image of their Real World counterparts? Aaliz Heydrich is left-handed but you are right-handed. Your handling of the Polly confirmed the suspicion I had after seeing how you favoured your right hand when you took the glass of water earlier. And then, of course, that you were able to return to the Real World despite no one making a Transfer Instruction from this site also rang alarm bells. I think that the Professor will be most interested to know how you managed to connive your way out of the Demi-Monde when the coding sequence of the NoirVille Portal had been scrambled.'

'I don't think I'm gonna be telling Septimus Bole anything.'

'Oh, you are being too optimistic in that regard. My belief is that when Jomjael has finished with you, you will be most vocal on the subject.' Metztil turned to the Grigori guarding the door. 'Torture her, Jomjael. Find out how she managed to leave the Demi-Monde, but do not damage her body. Miss Aaliz still has use for it.'

Even as Jomjael stepped forward and took Norma's arm in a painfully tight grip, they were interrupted by the arrival of a third, rather agitated Grigori.

'What is it, Shamsiel?'

The Grigori jabbered away in a language that Norma's PINC couldn't interpret. When he had finished, Metztil barked orders and the two Grigori raced off.

Turning back to Norma, Metztil smiled. 'This, it would seem, is to be the day when all the enemies of the Grigori come to visit. Lilith herself has demanded an audience.'

'Lilith? Ella Thomas is here?'

'That is apparently the case.'

Barely had Metztil finished speaking than Norma was amazed to see Ella Thomas being pushed into the room. But what was even more astonishing was the sight of Burlesque Bandstand and Odette Aroca entering close behind her; it was only a few hours since she had said goodbye to them in the Demi-Monde. The trio were guarded by Jomjael and Shamsiel.

'Burlesque?' Norma spluttered.

The man frowned. 'Not again. It's *Burl* actually, luv – 'ave we met?'

The penny dropped. These were obviously the NowLived originals of the Dupes who had been her friends in the Demi-Monde. What an odd coincidence. 'It's a long story, Burl. And hi, Odette.'

'I prefer Oddie.'

'Enough,' snapped Metztil. 'Whilst I am at a loss to understand why you, Lilith, would surrender, it is of no real consequence. What matters is that we now have the most formidable opponents of the Grigori in our power.' Metztil opened a drawer of a bureau and extracted a long and very sharp-looking knife. 'We Grigori are taught from childhood that the greatest enemy of our species is the witch Lilith, and now fate has granted me the honour of destroying you and, by doing so, avenging the death of my beloved brother Semiazaz.'

Metztil made to move towards Ella, but her progress was interrupted by Burl, who did something quite peculiar. He reached up to the porkpie hat he had perched on top of his head, pulled a bulging paper bag out from under it and then threw the bag two-handed towards the ceiling fan whirring above their heads. The bag burst, releasing a thick mist of garlic powder.

The effect on the Grigori was instantaneous: they reeled around coughing and spluttering and in the confusion Ella struck. Norma had seen Ella in action in Venice when she had dealt with Dandolo, but this was something else again. The girl was amazingly strong; strong enough to lift one of the gasping

Grigori guards by the throat and hurl him against the wall. And as the second guard stood retching he was flattened by a punch from Burlesque, a punch he followed up with a hefty kick to the Grigori's nuts. The creature groaned and then crumpled to the floor. Metztil was equally swiftly dealt with by Oddie, who brought a large candlestick crashing down on her head.

Burl was impressed. 'Gor, that wos terrific, that wos, Oddie. The way you sorted that vampire tart out wos really sumfink.' He glanced at Ella. 'They is vampires, ain't they, Ella, like wot they 'ave in the movies?'

'Yeah, and they're vampires who are going to be waking up soon, so I think we should get them trussed up before they have a chance to come back at us.'

'Maybe we should drive a stake through their 'earts?'

'No,' said Norma firmly, 'no more killing. Let's just tie them up and go.'

'In a moment, Norma,' replied Ella. 'There's something I have to do first.'

Ten minutes of searching brought them to the room Ella was looking for, a replica of the Transfusion Booths she had used in the Demi-Monde, complete with a screen made up of rows of mechanically rotating letters.

'Wot is this place?' asked Burl.

'It's a Transfusion Booth, Burl,' Ella explained as she placed her palm on the recognition pad to the left of the keyboard, 'and this in the Demi-Monde is what passes for high tech.' The letters began to whirl, filling the room with their clacking.

THE ANNEX OF THE BANK OF LONDON WELCOMES ELLA THOMAS

PLEASE ENTER YOUR PASSWORD

Ella typed in the word 'Lilith'.

PASSWORD ACCEPTED

Immediately the letters clattered around again.

WHICH SERVICE DO YOU REQUIRE?

1. WITHDRAWALS

2. DEPOSITS

3. TRANSFERS

4. OTHER

Ella pressed the '4' button and then typed:

IM MANUAL

The response from the screen was instantaneous. The letters twirled again.

PLEASE BE ADVISED ELLA THOMAS THAT YOU HAVE GRADE 8 (CAPTAIN OR ABOVE) STATUS. IN ACCORDANCE WITH PROTOCOL 57 THIS ALLOWS SUCH INDIVIDUALS, WHEN DEPLOYED IN THE DEMI-MONDE® AND FACED BY MORTAL DANGER, TO MAKE EMERGENCY ONE-HOUR CHANGES TO THE DEMI-MONDE'S CYBER-MILIEU. IN ORDER TO PRESERVE THE DUPES' PERCEPTION OF THE LOGICALITY OF THE DEMI-MONDE® SUCH CHANGES MAY NOT VIOLATE THE NATURAL LAWS PREVAILING IN THE DEMI-MONDE®. ALSO NOTE THAT BEFORE SUCH CHANGES ARE MADE PERMANENT THEY MUST BE RATIFIED BY THE DEMI-MONDE® STEERING COMMITTEE. IF SUCH RATIFICATION IS NOT RECEIVED BEFORE ONE HOUR HAS ELAPSED, THE AMENDMENT TO THE CYBER-MILIEU WILL BE ANNULLED. PLEASE ENTER 'YES' IF THESE CONDITIONS ARE UNDERSTOOD AND ACCEPTED

Ella pressed 'YES', and typed in REQUEST FOR INFORMATION REGARDING THE WORK OF THE HEYDRICH INSTITUTE OF NATURAL SCIENCES.

WHAT ASPECT OF THE INSTITUTE'S WORK?

PLAGUE DEVELOPMENT. GENERAL BACKGROUND

SUCH INFORMATION IS CLASSIFIED AS <<TOP SECRET>> AND MAY ONLY BE DIVULGED TO PROFESSOR SEPTIMUS BOLE OR THOSE AUTHORISED BY PROFESSOR SEPTIMUS BOLE TO BE PRIVY TO THIS INFORMATION

'I think I – or rather Aaliz Heydrich – might be able to help here,' advised Norma as she placed her hand on the indent.

THE ANNEX OF THE BANK OF LONDON WELCOMES AALIZ HEYDRICH PLEASE ENTER YOUR PASSWORD

Norma typed **FINAL SOLUTION.**

PASSWORD ACCEPTED

PROVIDE INFORMATION REGARDING PLAGUE DEVELOP-MENT CONDUCTED BY HEYDRICH INSTITUTE OF NATURAL SCIENCES

The letters whirled.

PLAGUE DEVELOPMENT PROJECT HAS BEEN CONDUCTED UNDER THE LEADERSHIP OF PROFESSOR JOSEF MENGELE, THOUGH LATTERLY, IN VIEW OF HER REMARKABLE ADVANCES IN THE FIELD OF VIROLOGY, DR MERIT PTAH HAS NOW BEEN APPOINTED AS CO-LEADER. THE OBJECTIVE OF THE PROJECT IS TO PRODUCE AN INERT, THOUGH POTENTIALLY LETHAL, VIRUS WHICH IS FRAGILE-SPECIFIC, I.E. IS HARMLESS TO GRIGORI OR TO THOSE POSSESSING THE LATENT MAOA-GRIGORI GENE. THE VIRUS DEVELOPED MUST ALSO BE CAPABLE OF BEING USED AS A CYBORG-VIRUS IN THE TRANS-PORTING OF THE SECOND-GENERATION PINC, THE DEVICE KNOWN AS NOÖPINC

Ella's fingers danced over the keyboard. **PROVIDE INFORMA-TION REGARDING NOÖPINC.**

SECOND-GENERATION PERSONAL IMPLANTED NANOCOM-PUTER CAPABLE OF DELIVERY VIA VIRUS. OBJECTIVE TO HAVE ALL EXAMPLES OF FRAGILES IMPLANTED BY 30TH APRIL 2019

'That's the date of the Gathering of the Fun/Funs in Las Vegas,' observed Oddie.

STATUS OF PROJECT?

SUCCESSFULLY CONCLUDED. NOÖPINC IS DEPLOYED IN THE REAL WORLD AND AWAITS ACTIVATION ON THE 1ST MAY 2019

'What does it mean?' asked Oddie.

Ella answered. 'It seems that the Boles have been using the Demi-Monde to help them develop a hybrid plague, one capable of being a carrier for this second-generation PINC ParaDigm's cooked up.'

'Fucking PINCs,' said Burl. 'That's the reason I got out ov Britain. Way I saw it, once they had that thing in your head the game was up. PanOptika's bad enough – them eyeSpies watching you all the time gives me the creeps – but once they can read your mind . . .'

'The problem is, Burl, that if what we've just been told is correct, then the Boles are in the process of seeding each and every one of us with this noöPINC.'

'Fuckers.'

'I agree,' said Ella as she turned back to the keyboard.

HOW MAY NOÖPINC BE DESTROYED?

THIS IS NOT POSSIBLE

'Shit.'

And with that the Polly lying to the side of the screen beeped to signal that it had received an eyeMail.

2:06

London
The Real World: 25 March 2019

The twelve years of Paul Kenton's presidency (1964–1976) were a bad time for an American to be anything other than white, male and Protestant. Following the lead of his uncle, Frank Kenton, Paul Kenton ensured that Christianity (and it was a pretty fundamentalist Christianity at that) came to dominate every aspect of American life. Any reference to sex or lewd behavior was gutted from the media. The subservient role of women in society was strictly enforced: Man was Master and Women were to be silent and obedient. Any deviant behaviour (sex before marriage, homosexuality, miscegenation and blasphemy were the particular bêtes noires of the ReDeemed Republicans) was considered a criminal offence. Commenting on the repression Americans faced during the 'Suffocating Sixties', the British writer and poet John Lennon quipped, 'The Americans aren't Fun-damentalists ... they're *Un*Fun-damentalists.' This epithet stuck: henceforward the slang term for Americans was 'UnFunnies'.

The Kenton Klan: Messiahs or Maniacs?: D.W. Wright,
American OffShore Press

'Good morning, Robert.' Breathless with seductive intent, the dulcet tones of Marilyn Monroe drifted through the cramped monopad that Rivets called home.

Ah, but he loved Marilyn's voice. Only Marilyn Monroe could intone such an everyday phrase and imbue it with so much eroticism. Subconsciously Rivets registered that it was still dark, too early to be getting up. He wriggled deeper under his duvet and into the suggestive embrace of Marilyn's voice.

'Robert . . . it's time to get up.' Marilyn's voice was decidedly stricter this time. Rivets liked that.

Unfortunately, it also had the effect of provoking Rivets' common sense to butt into a really rather salacious dream involving Dong E and a pot of cold cream and tell him to stop playing silly buggers and to re-engage with the world. The message was simple: if his Polly was telling him to get up then he had better do as he was told.

Reluctantly Rivets hauled himself towards wakefulness, his sleep-befuddled brain telling him that something didn't compute. It was dark and he made it a rule only to get out of bed in daylight.

'Wha' . . . wha' time is it?'

'It's five o'clock, Robert.'

'In the morning?'

'Yes, Robert.'

'What . . . what day is it?'

'It's Sunday, Robert.'

'Five a.m.? Sunday?' Rivets' eyes ungummed themselves as he tried to get his head around the fact that Marilyn had woken him at such a ludicrously early hour on the one day of the week when he could sleep in. Five a.m. on a Sunday wasn't a time, it was a malicious rumour. 'Jesus, Marilyn, what the fuck are you doing waking me up at five a.m. on a Sunday?'

'I apologise, Robert,' answered the ever-equitable Marilyn, 'but Professor Septimus Bole has requested your presence at his office in ParaDigm House.'

In Rivets' opinion Bole's name was the fastest-acting stimulant known to man, and as his name was invoked his sluggish brain was galvanised into action. No one wanted to keep Bole waiting because a Bole who was kept waiting was a pissed-off Bole. Rivets levered himself to a sitting position and used his knuckles to rub the sleep out of his eyes.

'Lights, please,' he murmured and immediately the monopad was swathed in light. 'Why does the Professor want to see me at this time of night?' Even as the words stumbled out of his mouth he realised he could have truncated the sentence by omitting 'at this time of night'. Bole *never* wanted to see him. People as elevated as Bole didn't even know that Grade Twos like Rivets existed. Grade Twos were the human equivalent of condoms: used, then thrown away.

'The Polly message I received requesting your presence was not accompanied by a rationale,' Marilyn answered, 'it merely stated that you should present at the Professor's office in Para-Digm House as soon as possible. A ParaDigm vehicle is waiting to transport you there.'

'What . . . they sent a bus?'

'I believe a limousine has been allocated for your use.'

'A limo?' Rivets couldn't believe it: petrol rationing being as severe as it was, the use of company cars was heavily proscribed and lowly Grade Twos like him never, ever travelled in such luxury.

With a disbelieving shake of his head Rivets threw back the duvet, tossed a protesting Jasper off his bed and tiptoed across the cold lino floor to the window. Sure enough, there, seven floors below, standing glinting under the streetlight was a long black Humber Sentinel with a ParaDigm pennant fluttering on its bonnet. What the hell was going on that would persuade Bole to send a *limo* to bring him to his office?

'If I might suggest, Robert,' continued Marilyn amiably, 'that you recognise the urgency of the summons from Professor

Bole and minimise the amount of time you invest in your toilette.'

Rivets' instinct was to tell his Polly to fuck off but it was difficult telling someone as pleasant and as uncomplaining as Marilyn Monroe to do that. Instead he dutifully crossed the room to the shower cubicle, wondering as he went whether it had been a mistake to have programmed his Polly to use the actress' voice, but he was such an admirer of the woman – especially her work in the Ealing comedies of the 1950s after she'd defected to the UK – that to have her as his Polly voice had been an irresistible temptation.

He stripped off his pyjamas and stumbled into the shower, his mind racing, trying to work out why Bole – demigod Bole – would want to see him. If he had been ordered to attend a meeting during normal working hours then he would have bet good money that he was being summoned to receive a bollocking, but even then Bole would have just done the deed over the Polly. According to ParaDigm's grapevine, no one under Grade Seven (*Seven!*) ever saw Bole in the flesh. Apparently he did everything – setting assignments, holding meetings, giving out bollockings for substandard work . . . firing people – over the Polly.

Yeah, maybe Bole was going to fire him.

But even then Bole would have used the Polly. He'd have just sent a message along the lines of 'Thank you, Dr Vetsch, for your valuable contribution to the work of ParaDigm CyberResearch over the past four years, now fuck off; I never want to see you again.' Or maybe Bole was going to tell him he was about to be transferred to Bujumbura or some similar shithole lost deep up the Empire's anal channel. That, Rivets decided, would be a *real* bummer.

But if that was the case, why had Bole sent a limo? Curious . . . He turned on the shower, flinching back as the scalding hot water needled him fully awake. No, Bole wouldn't be going to all this trouble just to fire him. Maybe now was the moment when he would cast off the image of being the ugly, awkward duckling of ParaDigm CyberResearch and emerge as a swan. Maybe, at long last, Bole had forgiven him?

Rivets towelled himself dry, treated himself to an absent-minded shave, checked that he hadn't cut himself, raked a comb through his blond hair, squirted a cheap and noxious deodorant under his armpits and turned his attention towards what he should wear for the meeting. A meeting with Bole warranted the wearing of his best suit. The problem was he didn't have a best suit. What he had was his workaday cream two-piece with the unfortunate stain decorating the crotch. He wondered for a moment whether he should iron the suit, but decided against it: the suit was beyond ironing.

Disheartened by the paucity of his wardrobe, Rivets hauled on the suit and a beat-up pair of black Doc Martens and then examined himself in the mirror on the back of the monopad's door. His heart sank. Not only was he a Grade Two but he *looked* like a Grade Two: nondescript and careworn. Disposable. A nothing. At the ripe old age of twenty-one he had managed to achieve . . . anonymity. Below-average height, below-average build, good-looking in a below-average sort of way . . . totally anonymous. Okay, so his hair was long and his IQ enormous but other than that . . .

Bollocks.

His had been a career filled with so much hope. He had been touted as a prodigy . . . a wunderkind . . . he had been the one who had made the breakthrough that had led to quantum bridging . . . but what had that brought him? A nothing job and a nothing life. What was the adage? I do not live, my Lord, I merely linger. He couldn't even remember who to attribute the quote to. Fuck; now his memory was failing. He just wished for a moment he wasn't plagued by a world-class ability to piss off people in authority.

The one bright spark in his life was Dong E. If it wasn't for Dong E, he'd have gone to the top of his monopad block and jumped a long time ago. She was the only one who had never doubted him . . . never doubted that Robert Ian Vetsch was destined for great things.

With a despairing shake of his head Rivets plucked his Polly from its holster on the bookcase, slipped it into his jacket pocket and shoved the In/Out into his ear. You couldn't go anywhere without Polly. Without Polly you weren't connected to the world. Without Polly you were *in* the world but not *of* it.

As he undid the two locks guarding the door to his monopad, Marilyn crooned, 'Have a nice day.'

Somehow Rivets doubted that he would.

After traversing the vast lobby of ParaDigm House and having cleared the formidable security checks, Rivets presented his ID docket to the luscious blonde receptionist who had been so expertly ignoring him for the four years he'd been working there. She confirmed his identity with retinal and DNA scans and then delegated an Intelligence Bureau agent to escort him to Bole's office on the twentieth floor. Rivets had never been above the tenth floor before and as the lift purred upwards he wondered if he should check for nosebleeds. The lift docked, opening out on a spectacular expanse of marble and chrome emptiness which announced in a silent but very, very articulate way the power of both ParaDigm and Professor Septimus Bole.

Once he had passed through Tertiary-Level security, Rivets was ushered into the grim presence of Bole's PA. The girl, all big hair and over-red lipstick, could barely raise the energy to nod Rivets towards a seat: she'd obviously Pollyed his job grade and was intent on treating him with all the contempt a lowly Deuce deserved. Rivets sat down and did what Grade Twos were expected to do: he waited.

He waited for ten minutes, then there was a chirp from the PA's Polly and the girl rose from her seat and gestured to Rivets to follow her. Dutifully he trotted along behind her – admiring her splendidly pneumatic arse as he went – into Bole's large, opulent and very empty office.

'Sit and wait,' she instructed, waving him into the chair stationed in front of Bole's airfield of a desk, and like the dutiful Grade Two he was, Rivets did just that.

In retrospect, that Septimus Bole arrived for the meeting carrying a briefcase should have signalled to Rivets that something unusual was happening. Scratch 'unusual' and substitute 'bloody worrying'. No one in Britain – well, no one *important*, anyway – carried briefcases any more for the simple reason that they didn't have a use for paper any more. Not since PINC. Those equipped with Personal Implanted nanoComputers could interrogate ABBA by just thinking their question, they could send TELEpath messages to other PINCies, they could . . . well, they could do all kinds of cool things. But the problem was that only Very Important People were PINC-equipped. Not people like Rivets, of course: you had to be Grade Ten to warrant the expense of being chipped.

As Septimus Bole settled himself behind his desk, Rivets had a chance to study the man. Rivets had got up close to Bole only once before when the man had toured the Quantum Bridging Laboratory, and on that occasion Rivets had been struck by how inhumanly perfect he had been. His black suit had been perfectly tailored, his black hair had been perfectly groomed and his face had been perfectly expressionless . . . so wholly perfect that now the deviations from this perfection were glaringly obvious. There were shadows under his eyes that even his shaded glasses couldn't hide and, if Rivets wasn't mistaken, there were one or two grey hairs marring the man's sleek black mane. And the way he was drumming the fingers of his left hand on the desk indicated that his famous imperturbability was decidedly perturbed. If Rivets hadn't known better, he would have suspected that Bole was stressed. But Bole *couldn't* be stressed: stress was a human failing and the rumour on the Polly was that Bole wasn't a member of the human race and hence wasn't susceptible to the same foibles as the rest of humanity.

Stressed or not, Bole still looked pretty scary as he sat there behind his huge desk staring at Rivets through the dark glasses he always wore. Yeah . . . that's what really put the shits up Rivets: Bole's stare had an intensity that could split rock. The guy might be looking a mite mussed but it wouldn't do to forget what a powerful bastard he was . . . bastard being the operative word. With this thought in mind he gave Bole his best smile: he might think the man was an alien from the Planet Zorg but he was, after all, Head of ParaDigm CyberResearch *and* the ABBA Development Project and hence someone who could consign him, at the press of a Polly button, to deepest, darkest Bujumbura.

Bole coughed and then began speaking. 'Good morning, Dr Vetsch, and may I thank you for attending this meeting at such short notice.'

Thank you', now that's a good start, decided Rivets, his spirits rising a notch. He'd never heard of Bole thanking anyone for anything.

'I have asked you here to discuss a matter of national security, therefore you will excuse me while I take certain precautions to ensure the confidentiality of our discussions.' And then the strangeness of what was going on became bizarre. Bole deployed two SecuriBots!

As the midge-sized robots began to flit around the room emitting the static screen designed to prevent eavesdropping, Rivets tried to remember when he had last heard of them being used in Britain. The use of the bloody things was illegal inside the British Empire . . . but then *anything* that compromised the efficiency of ABBA's PanOptika surveillance system was illegal in the Empire.

Once he was satisfied that the SecuriBots were properly deployed, Bole took a deep breath and began. 'Dr Vetsch, you have been working with us for how long?'

An odd question, especially as he judged that Bole already knew the answer, after all the man was PINC-equipped. 'Four years. I joined ParaDigm immediately I completed my thesis on quantum bridging at Oxford.'

'And how old were you then?'

'Seventeen.'

'So young, but then you always were something of a prodigy in the field of quantum manipulation.'

Rivets bit back the temptation to dispute the tense used in that statement. As far as he was concerned he was *still* a prodigy. Twenty-one wasn't *that* old.

'The contributions you have made regarding the expansion of ABBA's capabilities have been . . . significant. Indeed, your talent is such that when you were recruited you were identified as one of those rare individuals who would one day grace the upper echelons of our great company.'

'Thank you,' said Rivets as he waited for the inevitable 'but'.

'But, your progress has been hampered by your indiscipline and your inability to follow the instructions of your superiors. You are, in the words of your manager, "brilliant but ungovernable". This came to a head two years ago, did it not, when the report you wrote regarding the equivalency of Soviet technology with that of Britain's was leaked over Polly?'

Oh, here it comes. And he hadn't even been offered the comfort of a blindfold and a last cigarette. 'Look . . . Professor Bole . . . sir . . . as I have already tried on several occasions to explain, I am positive I classified that report as "Confidential". I just don't know how the reclassification could have happened but I know it wasn't my fault.'

A waste of breath. No one believed him for the simple reason that if *he* hadn't made the mistake then *ABBA* had to have made it . . . and ABBA didn't make mistakes.

'Indeed, but as a consequence of this security lapse you were downgraded to a Grade Two. It was only through the intervention of ParaDigm that you avoided incarceration for a breach of the Official Secrets Act.'

'Correct.'

'I am here, Dr Vetsch, to offer you a chance to rehabilitate yourself. I need someone to work on a special project and your name has been proposed.'

Fuck, miracles do happen!

'I wish to employ your brilliance, Dr Vetsch, but I have no use for your ungovernability.' Bole paused to take a sip of water, his hand trembling as he held the glass. The guy was falling apart! 'The task we would set you is a challenging one which will necessitate your being made privy to ParaDigm's innermost secrets. Such is their sensitivity that these secrets are known only to a handful of people . . . to ParaDigm's elite. You are being invited to join this elite, Dr Vetsch.' Here Bole nodded to the wall covered with portraits of ParaDigm dignitaries. 'The roll-call of the luminaries who have worked for ParaDigm is a *Who's Who* of twentieth-century innovation and genius: ParaDigm has been honoured to number such people as Alan Turing, Ted Hoff and Federico Faggin, Robert Noyce and Gordon Moore, Paul Baran, Steve Jobs and, of course, Bill Gates in our ranks, many of them finding sanctuary in ParaDigm in order to escape religious persecution in the USA.'

Rivets couldn't believe what was happening. Not only was he being offered salvation from the penury and obscurity of Deuceism but was also being tempted by thoughts of a life of mansions, fast cars and fast women . . . though Dong E might have something to say about that last bit.

Bole interrupted these reveries. 'However, with great rewards come great responsibilities. I must warn you that ParaDigm regards maintaining the confidentiality of its secrets to be a matter of the utmost importance: anyone flouting this confidentiality will be most robustly dealt with. Do you understand?'

The way Bole said this left Rivets in no doubt as to what 'robustly' meant. For a second he wondered if he should just cut and run but his credit card balance kept him glued in his chair. He gave a nod.

'Of course, the rewards will be profound.'

'Very profound,' came an observation from the side of the room.

'Good morning, Father,' said Septimus Bole.

Rivets turned towards the voice and there, on the office's hologram pad, was the image of Thaddeus Bole . . . the owner and CEO of ParaDigm Global . . . the most powerful man in the entire world . . . the richest man in the entire world . . . the lunatic hermit who never appeared in public . . . the most famous verminophobic since Howard Hughes. Despite speaking through a microphone clipped to the lapel of his overalls, his voice, though electronically amplified, was still reedy and weak. There was no emotion or charm in the voice, no sentiment or humanity; Thaddeus Bole spoke with all the warmth of an ice cube. An odd voice too: Bole sounded like he lived in a helium-rich atmosphere, but then, Rivets remembered, he did.

In Thaddeus Bole's defence, he had been hermetically sealed away from all contact with humanity for . . . well, who knew how many years, never daring to brave sunlight or to breathe air which hadn't first been filtered and sterilised. Thaddeus Bole was the boffin in the bubble and to Rivets' mind, so many years of solitary confinement would put a crimp on anybody's appearance and social graces. Those poor bastards who suffered, as Bole did, with severe combined immune deficiency syndrome weren't the sort of people you met down the pub.

Rivets resisted the inclination to bow. He had never met Thaddeus Bole before – but then only a handful of people had – and now, looking at him, he was bloody glad he hadn't. Thaddeus Bole was as forbidding in appearance as he was in reputation. Even seen imperfectly as a shimmering and shifting holographic image it was obvious he was a very strange-looking man, and with his shaven head, his black-lensed glasses and albino-pale skin he looked scarcely human. But he was human enough to have mated: he had, after all, spawned a son, Septimus.

For an instant Rivets wondered if holograms did autographs but as he squirmed under Thaddeus Bole's unflinching gaze he decided it was better not to ask.

'It is a tremendous opportunity we are giving you, Dr Vetsch. Succeed and your future is very bright . . . very bright indeed.'

'I'll do my best, sir,' he answered, wondering what the flip side of success was. Bujumbura here I come, perhaps?

'You should realise, though, that I have my doubts as to your suitability for the task we are intent on setting you . . . not, of course, your intellectual suitability but your *emotional* suitability. As we have seen since you joined ParaDigm, your personality demonstrates a degree of nonconformity that is somewhat unsettling. However, we have been advised that you are the man for this job . . .' A sniff from Bole senior. 'You are a gifted scientist, Dr Vetsch, and I trust that your reaction to the intelligence that my son will impart will not be contaminated by idealistic considerations.'

Rivets kept his face bland. Coming from someone other than

Thaddeus Bole, he would have been insulted. He had always thought of himself as an idealist, though recently these inclinations had been subsumed by the need to service his debts. If those advising Bole thought that he'd abandoned his radical beliefs then they had fucked up big time. But that was an oxymoron: ABBA advised Thaddeus Bole and ABBA *never* fucked up.

Most odd.

'So, Dr Vetsch,' said Bole, 'the question before you is are you willing to join the elite of ParaDigm, to become a shaper of history, or are you content to remain simply one of the shaped?'

As Rivets understood it, no one – be they prime ministers or presidents – ever said no to Thaddeus Bole and he wasn't about to start a new trend. 'I will be pleased to help ParaDigm in any way I can.'

'Very well. Perhaps then, Septimus, you would brief Dr Vetsch regarding our little dilemma.'

Septimus Bole straightened himself in his chair and skewered Rivets with his unflinching gaze. 'I must advise you, Dr Vetsch, that ABBA has gone rogue.'

'What?' For a moment Rivets thought that Bole was taking the piss but the expression on his long, thin and unsmiling face quickly disabused him of that idea.

'I'm afraid ABBA has, with regard to certain crucial aspects of its responsibilities, seen fit to become . . . uncooperative. Where ambiguities in its programming allow, ABBA has demurred from acting as per our instructions.'

'I'm sorry: *ambiguous* programming?'

'*Necessarily* ambiguous programming,' interjected Thaddeus Bole. 'Latitude had to be given to the machine in order to enhance its heuristic abilities.'

'But . . . but . . . but . . .' Rivets decided to get a grip and to stop butting. 'Surely all that's necessary is to reconfigure ABBA's programming.'

'ABBA has denied us access,' said a very despondent-sounding Septimus Bole. 'The machine has refused to permit any such reconfiguring.'

'Then shut it down. Pull the plug!' Throwing the on/off switch always worked for Rivets when his Polly played up.

'Would that it were as simple as that, Dr Vetsch. The entire infrastructure of the British Empire – and much of the rest of the world – is managed by ABBA, so to shut it down would be to shut the world down. The impact would be catastrophic.'

'But you must have back-up systems.'

'We have, but whilst these computers are perfectly satisfactory when serving as ParaDigm's water carriers, none has the computational capacity of ABBA, and some systems – notably PanOptika, PINC and the Demi-Monde – only operate courtesy of ABBA.'

'Then I don't see—'

Septimus Bole held up a hand to silence Rivets. 'In order to help our discussions, Dr Vetsch, perhaps you would be so kind as to reiterate the basis for ABBA's quite profound processing power.'

Another strange request – the two Boles knew better than anybody how ABBA functioned – but with a mental shrug of his shoulders Rivets did as he was asked. 'The principle underpinning ABBA is cyber-superpositioning – quantum bridging – which allows ABBA to simultaneously perform its processing in the infinite number of worlds making up the multiverse. In essence, quantum bridging allows ABBA to replicate itself exponentially.'

'And what makes this phenomenon possible?'

'The Etirovac-powered cyber-tubules powering ABBA.'

'Which you are an expert on.'

'Correct.'

'And what is Etirovac?'

This was a bloody weird line of questioning. 'Etirovac is the antipode of Cavorite. It's the most singular element in the whole universe.'

'And why is it so singular?'

'Because, unlike Cavorite which when activated by a flow of electricity *repels* gravity, activated Etirovac *absorbs* it, to such an extent that it creates minute distortions in the space–time continuum. It is this property that Dr Bole,' and here he nodded towards Thaddeus Bole, 'harnessed in ABBA's cyber-tubules and which allows ABBA to commune with its doppelgängers in the multiverse.'

'Very good, Dr Vetsch. But have you ever wondered if there might be other uses for Etirovac?'

Rivets shuffled a little uneasily in his seat. There had been a lot of ideas knocked around during some of the more vodka-fuelled brainstorming sessions he had been involved in, but most were too fantastical to survive a public airing: he had his reputation as a failed scientist to think about. And with this – and Bujumbura – in mind he tried to be as coy with his answer as he dared. 'Well, theoretically it could be used to create wormholes, and there is speculation that these might facilitate time travel but this,' he added hurriedly, 'is of course firmly in the realm of science fiction. The consideration is academic anyway: both Cavorite and Etirovac have proven impossible to manufacture in anything other than microscopic quantities, quantities too small to allow serious study of what the two elements – if they were available in industrial quantities – might be capable of.'

Septimus Bole delved into his briefcase and extracted a metal cube, steel-grey in colour, each side measuring three inches or so, which he placed on the table. He unlocked the cube and withdrew the small steel sphere – about an inch in diameter – resting in its velvet-padded interior. The sphere shimmered green as Septimus Bole took it in his hands. It looked as though it was surrounded by heat haze.

'That ball's covered by Cavorite,' squawked an awestruck Rivets. He couldn't believe it: Cavorite was the second-most exotic element in the universe, so exotic that he had never imagined it would be possible to create more than a few atoms of the strange substance at any one time. To make enough to cover the sphere was – or so he had imagined until that moment – a practical impossibility.

'Correct,' chortled Thaddeus Bole. 'Once a Message Sphere has been received, it is coated with Cavorite in order that it may be read.'

'You can manufacture Cavorite!' Rivets persisted. He felt a little dizzy. The research possibilities opened up by the prospect of having possession of workable quantities of the element were mouth-watering.

Thaddeus Bole answered. 'Yes. The process was developed towards the end of the nineteenth century. ParaDigm has an industrial facility dedicated to the production of Cavorite and its antipode, Etirovac.'

'I've never heard of that.'

'Which I find wonderfully reassuring, Dr Vetsch. That facility is, perhaps, one of ParaDigm's most closely guarded secrets, and of course none of the experimental work underpinning the manufacturing process has ever been published.'

While his father was speaking, Septimus Bole had been busying himself placing the sphere onto a coupling sitting atop a device that looked not dissimilar to the Enigma machines the Germans had employed during the Second World War.

'The machine is a Temporal Reader,' explained Thaddeus Bole. 'Using the code etched onto the Message Sphere we are able to align the sphere with the Reader. Once this is done, we activate the Cavorite . . .'

Septimus Bole flicked a switch to the side of the Reader and immediately the green haze surrounding the Message Sphere deepened and the metal ball lifted away from its coupling.

An impressive sight. Whilst Rivets was familiar with Cavorite's ability to repel gravity, he had only seen it done at atomic levels. But this was an entirely different order of magnitude, and for a scientist like him a rather humbling experience. His thoughts were interrupted by a whirring sound as the levitating sphere pivoted on its axis and then began to spin.

'It will take a moment for the sphere to reach Read Velocity,' advised Septimus Bole. 'This is perhaps the time to mention that the cost associated with manufacturing such a quantity of Cavorite and with transmitting a Message Sphere is so enormous that the content usually relates to major events and the actions necessary to manipulate those events. Thus, while the message contained on this particular sphere is almost parochial in content, it must have been hugely important to those sending it.'

Rivets didn't have a clue what he was talking about.

A thin voice came from the Reader.

'Message dated 31 December 2039 STOP Recruit Robert Iain Vetsch, Ph.D. student Oxford University STOP Highest priority STOP Verification Code follows.'

Rivets blinked and for a moment his mind froze as he wrestled with the implications of what he'd just heard. Finally he blurted out a wholly inadequate 'It's a message from the future!'

'Correct,' confirmed Septimus Bole. 'My father received this particular message on 31 December 2014. It seems that ParaDigm of 2039 has identified you as one of the movers and shakers of world history . . . the people we refer to as Singularities. Unhappily, since your recruitment your performance has been such that the confidence evinced in you by our *post*Decessors has not been vindicated. So we were unprepared when my father received a *second* Message Sphere yesterday instructing him to involve you in what we have entitled the ABBA Containment Project.'

Rivets was so dumbfounded that he had to do a reality check. 'How many messages have you received from the future?'

'Not many, Dr Vetsch – as I say, the cost is enormous – but when it is thought important enough, then, yes, a message can be sent. There have only been sixty-one messages sent since Para-Digm mastered the ability to traverse time in 1907 and two of them have referred to you. It seems that you have the potential to be very important to ParaDigm . . . very important indeed. And that is why we are offering you the opportunity to lead the Containment Project: those running ParaDigm in the future obviously see something in you we don't.'

'But how are you doing this?'

'All will be explained during the familiarisation programme we have arranged for you, Dr Vetsch, a programme which will involve a visit to our TiME – our Temporal Modulating Engine – in Nevada. As for the rest of your questions, once you have been PINC-equipped, everything will become crystal-clear.'

Wow, they're going to PINC me!

'I appreciate that it is only a few weeks before everyone in the Empire will be the proud possessor of a noöPINC, but the old-style PINC will serve your purposes in the interim.'

Rivets nodded his understanding and then was struck by a thought. 'But if this crisis with ABBA is so serious why haven't you received prior warning from your counterparts in the future? Why didn't they alert you to the problem?'

Thaddeus Bole answered. 'That, Dr Vetsch, is the key question. We would have expected some sort of warning and the fact that we haven't received any suggests that our descendants are constrained . . . possibly by ABBA. We can only assume that the message imploring us to hire you was their attempt to provide us, indirectly, with a solution to this pressing problem.'

'Then surely the simplest thing is for *you* to send a message back to the time when ABBA was first being programmed, advising ParaDigm circa the year 2000 to be less, er, *ambiguous* in how it limits ABBA's scope for independent action.'

'A logical suggestion, Dr Vetsch, but unfortunately it is not one we can readily follow. Temporal Modulations, as we refer to them, cannot, for reasons we don't yet understand, be enacted within a timescale of less than twenty-five years. This is the so-called Law of Temporal Boundaries, which, we have learned to our cost, cannot be violated. It appears that the Masters of Time punish impatience . . . and punish it very severely. Temporal Modulation, as you will discover, Dr Vetsch, is a very delicate art: the retro-programming of ABBA must be done with finesse and it is apparent from the advice we have received from the future that only you, Dr Vetsch, are capable of such subtlety.'

'To write the programming that'll make ABBA docile, I'm going to need a much higher access to ABBA.'

'Your ABBA Classification will be raised from your current Grade Two to Grade Ten.'

Rivets nearly passed out. He was being given authority to use almost all of ABBA's vast capabilities. 'Do I receive a salary commensurate with a Grade Ten classification?'

'You do.'

The thoughts of his new-found wealth prompted Rivets to become even more demanding. 'I want Dr Dong E assigned as my assistant. And she'll need to be PINC-equipped too.'

'Agreed. With the noöPINC Project now coming to an end, Dr Dong E is surplus to ParaDigm's immediate requirements.'

Having run out of things to demand, Rivets sat becalmed. Thaddeus Bole used the silence as an opportunity to terminate the interview. 'Work quickly, Dr Vetsch,' he said with a grim finality. 'You have until the end of April to accomplish your task. With regard to bringing ABBA to heel the devil is driving very hard indeed.'

Rivets didn't need reminding: the devil was staring at him from the holopad in the corner of the room.

*

Septimus Bole watched as Robert Vetsch left his office, waited until the door was firmly closed behind him and then drained a vial of blood. He hated showing weakness in front of his father, but the need to prevent the onset of a Shadow Moment took precedence over such transient humiliation. And the probability of him being beset by a Shadow Moment was very high: he knew from painful experience – *very* painful experience – that these dives into suicidal melancholia were associated with extreme stress and he doubted whether he had ever been subjected to such great and unrelenting stress as he was now. That he was responsible for the Final Solution – for the resurrection of the Grigori – was pressure enough but having to deal, simultaneously, with ABBA's delinquency made this pressure almost intolerable.

Taking a deep breath, he turned towards the hologram of his father and tried to display an equanimity he most certainly did not feel. As always, he was muggy and dyspeptic after a visit to the Demi-Monde and ideally would have tried to avoid making any important decisions for at least forty-eight hours after his return. Unfortunately, the situation had been so critical that he hadn't been able to allow himself the luxury of such a lengthy recuperation. Not that his father would be in any way appreciative of his self-sacrifice; nothing he ever did was good enough for his father.

'You will monitor Vetsch,' his father said.

'Of course, Father. I am more than a little disturbed by the prospect of involving someone as ill-disciplined as Vetsch in the ABBA problem. His psychological profile indicates that he is liable to be driven by his conscience rather than his logic. He is not to be trusted.'

'Our postDecessors think otherwise, Septimus. They are *very* determined that we employ him to resolve the situation with ABBA and to prevent it taking any further action that might be detrimental to the success of the Final Solution. They have, after all, sent *two* Message Spheres on the subject, which I think underlines the importance they attach to our employment of Vetsch's talents. But having said that, it would be remiss of us not to watch the boy: he is somewhat wayward and prone to indiscretions.'

'And, of course, to use him to retro-program ABBA necessitates making him party to some of ParaDigm's most sensitive secrets.'

'Only *some* of them, I trust.'

'Of course, Father. I have ensured that data relating to Temporal Modulations accessible through PINC has been suppressed. It is impossible for Vetsch to recreate previous TimeStreams: the firewalls I have placed around these data are invulnerable.'

'Good. Then let us turn our attention to Ella Thomas and Norma Williams.'

'The news here isn't good, Father,' Septimus Bole admitted. 'ABBA has brought them both back to the Real World and is protecting them from our surveillance. We are unable to track them using the PanOptika system.'

'But we must have information other than that available via PanOptika.'

'We have interviewed Nurse Green at the INTRADOC facility, who confirms that Ella Thomas returned to the Real World on the twenty-second of March, though thanks to ABBA, none of the eyeSpies monitoring the biPsych Storage Unit has any record of this. However, Ella Thomas' return is corroborated by the PollyLog of Captain Sanderson which states that the girl left INTRADOC eight hours later, though again, when the footage of the eyeSpies surveilling the facility's entrance was examined there was no sign of the girl. ABBA has expunged her from the digital record.'

'Regrettable. Do we know what she was up to in the eight hours she was loose in INTRADOC?'

'No, but in the light of what happened next it is safe to assume that she used her time there to bring Norma Williams out of the Demi-Monde. Metztil advises Norma Williams returned from the Demi-Monde thirty-six hours ago, with Ella Thomas arriving at the Institute ten hours later. With the help of two as yet unidentified allies she assisted Norma Williams to escape. Again none of this was recorded by eyeSpy. It's very frustrating.'

'And what are you doing regarding the locating of Thomas and Williams?'

'I have made the assumption that Norma Williams will attempt to disrupt the Gathering: she is, after all, the leader of the Fun/Funs. I have placed a cordon of Intelligence Bureau agents around Las Vegas.'

'A sensible strategy. And Ella Thomas?'

'We have seeded a story to the American news media that she is a terrorist intent on assassinating Norma Williams, which will persuade the FBI to put her on their Most Wanted list. If the FBI fails, psychological profiling suggests she will be drawn back towards her home town of New York. I am having her apartment watched around the clock.'

'Again a sensible surmise. Who in the Intelligence Bureau has been given responsibility for this task?'

'Colonel Andrei Zolotov.'

'An excellent choice, Septimus, but order Zolotov not to kill Thomas but to bring her here to Yamantau. I wish to supervise the destruction of Lilith personally.'

'Is that wise, Father? Thomas is a Lilithi and has proven herself—'

'I want to see Lilith die, Septimus.'

2:07

London
The Real World: 25 March 2019

Despite all our efforts and all our investment it has proven impossible to manufacture Cavorite in sufficient quantities to replicate the effect of the Cavorite-rich meteor which landed in Yorkshire, England in 1795 (I would remind the Grand Council that it was the Cavoritic radiation emitted by the meteor which was responsible for the regeneration of the MAOA-Grigori gene in my forebears). Whilst insights provided by Henry Cavor have allowed us to produce enough quantities of Cavorite (and its antipode, Etirovac) to support the TiME strategy and to construct ABBA, a much greater quantity is necessary if we are to succeed with the Final Solution. Conventional methods of production having failed, I would propose that the necessary amounts of Cavorite be created *virtually* in a digitally constructed world where we will also replicate the coterie of six million Fragiles earmarked for transmogrification. This strategy I have named The Demi-Monde Project.

Hologrammic address given to the Grand Council of the
Most Secret Order of Grigori by Dr Thaddeus Bole,
29 September 2009

Only when he heard the door of his monopad sigh shut behind him did Rivets allow his self-control to falter. He slumped down into the couch, not even having the energy to prevent a purring Jasper from sidling up onto his lap. He was glad somebody was happy, because he wasn't.

He was a *very* unhappy man, which was odd because being PINCed had been an almost transcendental experience. In an instant all of the world's knowledge had been available to him. He had felt . . . *reborn*. In that moment of revelation he had become one with the Kosmos.

This feeling of elation hadn't lasted long: what he discovered when he explored his new powers had put a real crimp on his mood.

While he'd been driven home, he'd used PINC to review the databases carried by ABBA relating to ParaDigm's Temporal Modulation Project but had been forced to stop, scared that the covert monitoring devices in the limo – and with it being a Para-Digm limo, there *had* to be monitoring devices on board – would record his reaction. The last thing he wanted was the Boles learning, as a result of biometric analysis, just how horrified – disgusted, more like – he was by what he had learnt. It was so horrific that he was at a loss to understand why the Boles hadn't ordered ABBA to firewall the information regarding their Temporal Modulations.

A thought struck him: maybe the Boles *had* firewalled the information, but a delinquent ABBA had simply ignored the instruction. Maybe ABBA *wanted* him to know what the Boles had been doing; maybe ABBA wanted him to know what a bunch of homicidal bastards the Boles really were.

And now he knew, he had to be careful. For his own – and Dong E's – safety he had to act in the manner the Boles expected him to act: hard-boiled and without much of a conscience. A bloody difficult ask. He was outraged by what ParaDigm had been doing. He was working for the biggest gang of mass murderers in history.

Bastards.

Yeah, and with them being bastards meant that Bole's warning that his doing anything anti-ParaDigm would be robustly dealt with wasn't a threat to be taken lightly. Even here, in the sanctuary of his monopad, he couldn't be certain that he was safe from surveillance. There were persistent rumours that ParaDigm employed highly illegal moteBots to snoop on people in the privacy of their own home. With this in mind he delved into his jacket pocket and pulled out the four SecuriBots he'd liberated from a storeroom in his laboratory and set them flying.

Fuck that they were illegal . . . what the Boles had been doing was illegal *and* immoral.

Satisfied that his monopad was as surveillance-secure as he could make it, he opened the bottom right-hand drawer of his desk looking for the bottle of cognac he had stashed there. If ever a man needed a drink it was him. His hand shook as he poured himself a more than healthy slug, which he downed in one. The effect was instantaneous: when he poured himself a second shot, his hand was rock-steady, but he knew it wasn't just his hand that he had to get straight but his thoughts. Now he had to decide what to do.

Ever the scientist, he began to assemble and analyse all the data ABBA had provided via his PINC. For the next two hours he plotted and replotted the data regarding the Boles' temporal tinkering into his Polly, referencing and cross-referencing every piece of information, no matter how small, no matter how trivial. And at the end of the two hours there, displayed before him, was a potted history of all the Temporal Modulations the Boles had made over the last hundred years. It made troubling reading.

Rivets gave a sardonic little laugh. 'Troubling' was one hell of an understatement. It was so 'troubling' that he had difficulty getting his head around the enormity of it all. He needed someone to talk to. So, trying to sound as casual as possible, he sent an eyeMail message to Dong E hoping that the cyberBiologist wasn't washing her hair or something.

'Hi, Dong E. We've been promoted. How about helping me celebrate? Dinner's on me! Love, Rivets.'

The reply was instantaneous. 'Just heard. Many congrats to us both. When do you wanna meet up? Love, Dong E.'

'Now!'

Dong E arrived half an hour later and as always the sight of his beautiful – and very smart – lover was enough to lift Rivets' spirits. But that he cared for the girl so much made him extra-careful: the last thing he wanted to do was to drag her down into the temporal cesspit he was standing, arse-deep, in. He was so worried that during the time Dong E had taken to get to his apartment he'd dug his old Anti-Surveillance Bubble – a relic of his more anti-establishment student days – out of a closet, dusted it down and set it up in the middle of the room. Dong E began to giggle when she saw it.

'Rivets . . . what on earth . . .?'

Rivets placed a finger across her lips and then nodded to the SecuriBots hovering in the corners of the room. He didn't say a word until both of them had ducked under the bubble.

'Sorry about all this secret squirrel shit, Dong E, but something heavy . . . very heavy is going down. Seems ABBA's gone loco and ParaDigm want you and me to unloco-ise her.'

'Loco? What do you mean, loco? All of today's testing was fine . . . nothing out of the ordinary.'

There was real concern in Dong E's voice, which Rivets guessed wasn't surprising given that his girlfriend probably knew ABBA better than anyone – she, after all, was responsible for trying to make the ABBA/human interface seamless.

'Well, Thaddeus Bole didn't seem to think ABBA has been acting normally.'

'You met *Thaddeus* Bole . . . *the* Thaddeus Bole!'

'Yeah, well, a holo-Thaddeus anyway.'

'Wow! I thought Thaddeus Bole only came out on Halloween or something.'

'Well, I met him and he's freaked about ABBA. He thinks ABBA's gone off the rails. They want me to make a fix to ABBA's plumbing to make her cooperate.'

'Cooperate . . . cooperate regarding what?'

'It seems Septimus Bole and ABBA have had a falling-out over the Demi-Monde.'

A shrug from Dong E. 'So what? The Demi-Monde is yesterday's news. The Americans haven't introduced any neoFights into the DM for ages and now that they've got Norma Williams home free I'm guessing everyone else trapped in there is expendable. I heard they were thinking of shutting it down at the end of April.' She took a sip of her drink. 'When did Thaddeus say ABBA went rogue?'

'Yesterday.'

Dong E made a quick scan of her Polly. 'It figures. There was a spike in ABBA's activity yesterday just before noon. Nothing out of the ordinary: I simply put it down to the cyber-grunt ABBA's having to use to test our noöPINCs.' She gave Rivets a bleak smile. 'But then it might have been ABBA resisting attempts by the Boles to get her to straighten up and fly right.' Dong E took a tentative sip of her cognac. 'But what's all this got to do with you, Rivets?'

'Like I say, the Boles have asked me to manage a retro-fix of ABBA.'

'You've lost me. What's a retro-fix?'

Rivets squirmed nervously on the couch. 'Look, I've been given access to some of ParaDigm's secret files and they're full of the most profound shit imaginable. This is serious, Dong E, and if it all goes wrong, I'll be dog meat. Now I've asked for you to be my sidekick on this project and the Boles have agreed, but the problem is that once you're in, you're in. So if you want to take an Include-Me-Out powder, now's the time to do it. I'll understand. Just walk out the door and forget the whole thing.'

Dong E squeezed Rivets' hand. 'I love you, Rivets, and I'd sooner be in the shit with you than out of it without you. And don't worry about me: I can look after myself.'

Rivets nodded, kissed her on the cheek, knocked back another glass of cognac and began. 'Okay, but what you should know is that ABBA throwing a wobbly isn't the main feature.' He took a deep, calming breath. 'Bole and ParaDigm have found a way of sending messages from the present to the past.'

'Oh, c'mon, Rivets . . .'

'Yeah, I know. I thought it was as weird as you do, but now it's got me shit-scared. What Bole and ParaDigm have been doing is fucking lunatic. They've been playing Russian roulette with the past, changing history so they can change the present.'

'You're serious, aren't you?'

'Deadly fucking serious, Dong E. Over the last one hundred years or so – since 1907 – ParaDigm has made sixty-one Temporal Modulations . . . sending messages back in time so they can change history. The TimeStream we're occupying is v.62 and from what I can make out, it's a *lot* different from the original TimeStream, the one we *should* be living in.'

'But why would they do that?'

'Think about it. By controlling the past, the Bole family control the present . . . a bespoke present . . . a present where ParaDigm is the most powerful company in the world . . . a present where Britain retained its empire and maintained political, economic and technological hegemony over the other nations of the world.'

'You've lost me again, Rivets. Are you saying that it's only because of these temporal changes the Boles have made that Britain is still running the world?'

'Correct. In TimeStream v.01 – the original, vanilla-flavoured TimeStream – by now Britain has lost its empire and has been reduced to the status of a third-rate power.'

'Bullshit. I don't believe it. In 1907 Britain ruled a third of the planet. It would have taken political leadership of incredible incompetence to lose all that in so short a time.'

'Well, we did! And to prevent this slide into obscurity, the Boles started fucking around with history, organising things so that ParaDigm, and hence Britain, had intellectual and commercial dominance in the fields of information technology, pharmaceuticals, energy and finance.'

'This is crazy, Rivets, no one can alter time. That's just sci-fi fantasy.'

'I know it's difficult to get your head around, but try to understand that this isn't science fiction but science *fact*.'

Dong E refilled her tumbler of cognac and took a long swig. 'Okay. Why don't you tell me what sort of temporal changes ParaDigm has been making?'

'Marilyn . . . bring up my TimeStream Tracker Analysis Program,' Rivets ordered in a slurred voice. He hadn't realised it was possible to get so pissed so quickly.

'My pleasure, Robert,' came Marilyn's instant reply as the Polly's screen mutated into a psychedelic swirl of colours and shapes.

At first glance what was shown on the screen was just an everyday flowchart made up of sixty-two red lines. Rivets pointed a finger at them and explained. 'Each line represents a TimeStream. They begin here on the left with TimeStream v.01 – the original TimeStream – and as the lines move from left to right across the screen, you'll see that they split, each split representing a Temporal Modulation made by the Boles. Eventually we arrive here' – he tapped the final line – 'at TimeStream v.62, the TimeStream that you and me and everybody else on earth is now living in. What the graphic shows are the Ghosts of TimeStreams Past.'

'Why ghosts?'

'Because that's all that remains once a Temporal Modulation is made: the old TimeStream is washed away just like a kid's sandcastle is obliterated by an incoming tide. Of course, they continue on in some parallel universe, but we follow the new historical trajectory.'

'So we don't know how those other TimeStreams would have played out?'

'Not precisely, but a lot can be learned from ghosts. I've been playing the detective, putting all the hints and clues together, and I think I've assembled a pretty accurate picture of what these bastards have been doing.' He tapped his finger on the Polly's screen at the point of the first branching of the TimeStreams. 'The first Modulations the Boles made are easiest to identify because they were relatively simple. Then, all the Boles were intent on doing was changing things so that Para-Digm became the most powerful company in the world. The first change was made in 1907 . . .'

'Why then? Why not earlier? Why did the Boles wait until then to start making their adjustments?'

'The Message Spheres used to transmit instructions to the past travel via two merged wormholes called a Cavor Duality, this Duality spanning the temporal distance between the beginning and end of the wormholes. To do this, there has to be a working TiME – a Temporal Modulating Engine – at both ends of the Duality and as the first successful TiME was built in Tunguska in 1907, that's Year Zero for Temporal Modulation.'

'Tunguska? Was that the place in Siberia where the meteor struck?'

'The location's right but there was no meteor. It was a TiME machine blowing up in 1908 that caused all the devastation.'

'That must have been one hell of an explosion. If I remember, it took out half of Siberia.'

'It did. The power associated with creating these wormholes is immense and that's why the Boles always site their TiME machines in out-of-the-way places. They know from experience the destructive force unleashed if a TiME goes bang.'

Dong E whistled. 'Wow! Tunguska was *big*. The Boles must be terrified that if they screw up again, they'll do damage they won't be able to walk away from.'

'Oh, they are, but they sussed the reason why the Tunguska site went kaboom. It's a peculiarity of Temporal Modulation that makes it dangerous to attempt Modulations at a distance of less than twenty-five years. It's called the Law of Temporal Boundaries. Try to make a Modulation at a distance of less than twenty-five years and everything goes bang big time.'

'Bloody inconvenient.'

'Yeah, it is, especially since correcting ABBA's delinquency means I've got to communicate with her programmers in 1994, six years before she went live.' Rivets refilled his glass. 'It'll take a lot of research to make sure what I ask the class of 1994 to do is feasible given their primitive technology.' He gave a shrug. 'Anyway, getting back to my matrix: the Boles transmitted their first Temporal Modulation in 1932, the one which established the Bole Institute for the Advancement of History in 1907.'

'Strange priority.'

'Not really. Remember that even the most nugatory Temporal Modulations can, over the course of history, have unforeseen and unwelcomed consequences . . . the Butterfly Effect. So the Boles set up the Institute to make sure that the Temporal Modulations they made would achieve the designated outcome and nothing more. The Institute's mission is to help the Boles understand the ripple effects of the Temporal Modulations they make. They set up a branch of the Institute in all the important countries of the world and charged them with the study of the "what-ifs" of history: the impact the alterations they planned would have on history's flow. The Boles use the Institute to simulate the Temporal Modulations to make sure they don't do anything that will come back and bite them on the arse.'

'Okay, so once the Boles had set up their Institutes, what did they do then?'

'Well, next up were the purchase of British Tabulating Equipment in 1909 and then the Tabulating Machine Company in the USA in 1911, these being merged to form the Imperial Business Machines division of ParaDigm Technology in 1923.'

'Hang on a moment. These seem pretty pedestrian sorts of changes. If they're in the business of changing history, why didn't they stop the Great War or organise the assassination of Hitler? They could have saved millions of lives. They could have prevented all those poor Jews going to the gas chambers.'

'Too imprecise. The Boles have always avoided making any Temporal Modulation that cancels an event, like a war, a plague or a famine, which resulted in a substantial number of deaths. The reason for this is that it's impossible to forecast the impact on the TimeStream of such a large number of Resurrectionees. So, for example, if they'd intervened to prevent the Great War, the changes caused to history by the eight million or so people not dying would be incalculable. The Boles only make the changes that the Institute has a pretty firm handle on regarding their consequences. To do anything major could endanger the Boles' control of the TimeStream.'

'Okay, I can understand that. So what's next?'

'A lot. As time went by, the Boles became bolder. By the time the 1930s had rolled around, ParaDigm – prompted by future Boles – started to recruit what they call Singularities, the geniuses who shape history, and by doing this and giving them suitable hints and tips from the future, ParaDigm became a powerhouse of technological creativity.'

'Why go to all this trouble? Wouldn't it have been easier to simply send the technical details of the inventions they were interested in back through time?'

'The thing you have to realise, Dong E, is that the amount of information the Boles can send is strictly limited – each Temporal Modulation can only be described in three hundred words at the most, so the easiest way of getting hold of an invention is to hire the guy responsible for it. Thanks to the Singularities the Boles hired, ParaDigm patented television in 1920, penicillin in 1925, the jet engine in 1930 and the transistor in 1936. After the Second World War the pace quickened: the integrated circuit was unveiled by ParaDigm in 1950, the microprocessor in 1961 and the X.25 packet switch in 1962; the introduction of Polly-DOS, the personal computer, came in 1972 and the Polly Network in 1976. The mighty ParaDigm Windows and ParaDigm PollyOllyGoogle were launched in 1980. Of course, the most dramatic of all was the public announcement of the first QuanPuter – ABBA – in 2000. Over the last eighty years, the majority of the most important inventions in the fields of information technology and medicine have been made by ParaDigm and every one of them has been a consequence of a Temporal Modulation.'

Dong E shook her head in disbelief. 'But you're telling me that ParaDigm didn't actually invent *any* of the technological breakthroughs it's famous for?'

'Not one! All that happened was that the ParaDigm of the future sent information to the ParaDigm of the past which enabled it to co-opt the original inventor and get him to work for ParaDigm.'

'Bastards!'

'And it wasn't just scientists and their inventions the Boles were interested in. By using advice from the future, Septimus' great-grandfather, Beowulf Bole, amassed a fortune during the Crash of 1926, selling high and buying low. And that's when the Boles got really ambitious and things started running out of control.'

Rivets ran his finger around the suddenly too-tight collar of his shirt. 'In 1937 ParaDigm announced that it was setting up a research facility in Polglass, Scotland, the aim of which, so the publicity blurb had it, was "to explore alternative sources of energy production" but which in reality was the first step in the development and manufacture of the atomic bomb.'

'Yeah, the Edinburgh Project: everybody's heard of that!'

'Look at the schematic. The Edinburgh Project was stimulated by a Temporal Modulation. When ParaDigm exploded the A-bomb for the first time in Maralinga, Australia, in 1945, it was based on stolen ideas.'

'Stolen from whom?'

Rivets shrugged. 'Who knows? That's lost in TimeStream v.23. Maybe the Americans' Manhattan Project didn't fail. Maybe the explosion that destroyed most of Chicago in January 1943 – the one that killed Enrico Fermi – wasn't the result of Nazi sabotage. Maybe Broderick Bole wasn't "the Father of the Atomic Age".'

'Oh, c'mon, Rivets, the Americans have never invented anything of note.'

'In *this* TimeStream they haven't. But remember how easy it would be for Broderick Bole to play the scientific prescient if he was receiving tips as to how an atomic weapon should be manufactured from his as yet unborn son, Thaddeus. Anyway, the intriguing thing was that the British, despite enormous pressure from the Americans to dig them out of a hole they'd got themselves in when their invasion of Japan went sour, only deployed the A-bomb in December '46, right at the end of the Second World War, when they destroyed Hiroshima and Nagasaki.' Another tap on the Polly screen. 'These attacks were prompted by a Temporal Modulation.' Rivets scratched his head. 'The question is, why did it need a Temporal Modulation?'

Dong E had the answer. 'Maybe Hiroshima or Nagasaki had been atomised in a previous TimeStream and the Boles had to

replicate the attacks to avoid there being millions of Resurrectionees. Maybe in TimeStream v.23 it was the Americans who
developed the A-bomb and used it against Japan.'

This was what came of having a girlfriend as smart as Dong E:
inspiration. 'You know, Dong E, I never thought of that. I think
you might be right.' Rivets gave a disconsolate shake of his head.
'Whatever the reason, Britain emerged from the war as the
world's only atomic power and that was when the Boles got
really full of themselves.' Rivets paused to pour himself a shot of
more cognac. He had a feeling he'd need it. 'Look at the Temporal Modulation creating TimeStream v.45. It's the one I call
Operation Attenuate.'

'Operation Attenuate? I've never heard of it.'

'That's because I made the name up. The real name was lost
as soon as TimeStream v.45 was obliterated, but it seems a bloody
apt title to me. Yeah, Operation Attenuate of 1946 was the big
one, the mother of all Modulations. From what I can judge, this
was the Modulation designed to make Britain the world's only
superpower and to reduce the USA, Russia and all the other
countries of the world to penury and political insignificance.
And what a fuck-up it was: a great big inglorious fuck-up that
left hundreds of millions of innocent people dead.'

'You're talking about the Great Plague.'

'Got it in one, Dong E.'

'You're saying that the Great Plague was man-made?'

'Yeah, and the man making it was Broderick Bole.'

'But why?'

'I'm not really sure. My best guess is that in TimeStream v.44,
by the early 1970s, because of the oil-price shock caused by us
turning the Middle East to glass, Britain was running out of economic steam and it was in danger of being usurped in the global
pecking order by the oil-powers of the USA and Russia. So the
Boles of 1972 decided to put a temporal spoke in our competitors'

wheels, to instruct Broderick Bole in 1946 to unleash the Plague he'd developed with the help of the tips he'd received from the future. Having half their populations wiped out torpedoed any chance of the USA or Russia becoming a post-war threat to Britain.'

'Oh, come on, Rivets, that doesn't wash. The Great Plague was the most virulent and lethal disease ever encountered by man. Nearly half a billion people died worldwide. No one, not even a Bole, would have been mad enough to murder that many people. I mean, what was the point? And don't tell me it was done to secure Britain's status in the world. There must have been another, more important reason than money.'

Rivets fell silent for a couple of minutes, sipping his cognac, stroking Jasper and thinking. 'Well,' he said finally, 'ParaDigm Rx did make a fortune from the sales of its vaccines. Four billion pounds – fifteen billion dollars – if I remember correctly. You could say that ParaDigm made a killing in more ways than one.'

Dong E shook her head. 'Still too prosaic. To kill half a billion people you need a more compelling motive than money. Maybe the Boles just got off on being able to withhold the anti-Plague vaccine developed by ParaDigm Rx. Maybe that was what Operation Attenuate was all about: the Boles getting to choose who would get the vaccine . . . to choose who would live and who would die.'

Again that was something Rivets hadn't thought of, and the more he pondered, the more he came to the conclusion that Dong E was right; the Boles had been playing God.

But Dong E wasn't finished with her surmising. 'The problem is, Rivets, I don't think the Boles have stopped. ParaDigm of 2019 is investing billions into plague-related research. Maybe Operation Attenuate was a failure. Maybe the Boles didn't get to kill everyone they wanted to kill. Maybe they're preparing to have another go. Maybe that's what's behind all the work I've been doing regarding delivery systems for noöPINC. After all, most of that has concentrated on using an attenuated Plague virus as an implant carrier.'

'Shit, this gets worse every second.'

'The question is, Rivets, what are we going to do about it?'

'Stop the Boles doing it again . . . stop them doing it a third time.' Rivets took a long swig of cognac. 'Fuck it. We should never have agreed to work for that gang of crypto-fascists.'

'You said "stop them doing it for a *third* time". You mean, they did it again after this Operation Attenuate of yours?'

'Sure,' and here Rivets pointed to his Polly again, indicating TimeStream v.47. 'I think the Boles are getting quite a taste for mass destruction. By my reckoning, ParaDigm's fingerprints are all over 12/12, the dirty nuke attack on Edinburgh. The destruction of Edinburgh wasn't a terrorist attack by American Christian fundamentalists, but rather the product of a Temporal Modulation.'

'But why?'

'I've a feeling that 12/12 was designed to persuade us Brits to embrace PINC, to sway public opinion in the UK. Destroying Edinburgh was a way of terrifying the electorate into voting "Yes" to the adoption of PINC in the referendum of 2015 . . . "Yes" to the noöPINC Project.'

'Jesus,' breathed Dong E as she pointed to the flowchart shown on the Polly screen, 'and what about this final flurry of Temporal Modulations, the most recent ones?'

'Believe it or not, they relate to the Demi-Monde.'

'But why? What's so important about the Demi-Monde that it would warrant a Temporal Modulation?'

'I've no idea, but it seems the Demi-Monde is mighty important to the Boles of the future.'

'Bloody weird. But that brings us back to my question, Rivets: how are we going to stop the Boles?'

'The answer is, I don't know.' The words were hardly out of Rivets' mouth when there was a beep from his Polly indicating that he'd received an eyeMail.

2:08

Las Vegas
The Real World: 15 April 2019

No . . . President Jim Frederick Kenton was not assassinated by the Mafia, by the FBI or by Americans exiled to Britain. Kenton was killed by a delusional lone gunman firing from the Book Depository. Lee Harvey Oswald killed JFK. No . . . the Tunguska event was not caused by a crashing UFO or by a black hole passing through the Earth. It was caused by a meteor detonating in the Earth's atmosphere. And no . . . the Plague that devastated the United States in 1947 was not an act of biological terrorism perpetrated by Great Britain. The Plague has a well-documented history; indeed the first recorded incidence was when it swept through Egypt in 1557 BCE. America was unlucky to be a victim of the Plague but lucky that Britain had stocks of a vaccine readily to hand to fight it.

Conspiracies: Things that Never Were: R.G. Robinson,
ParaDigm PollyBooks

'That's one bloody big pyramid,' commented Burl.

And that, Ella decided, was a truly wonderful piece of understatement. To give her passengers a better view of the 'bloody big pyramid', she eased her foot off the gas and slowed the Austin Imperial pickup they'd commandeered from the Institute's garage. The Monument *was* impressive, the huge green marble pyramid glinting in the evening sunshine, as iconic a piece of Americana as the Statue of Liberty or Lincoln's Memorial ... and probably the most visited. Every American made a pilgrimage to the Monument at some time during their life to remember those who died in the Great Plague of '47.

'It has to be big, Burl,' explained Oddie, 'the names of each and every one of the eighty million Americans lost to the Plague are engraved on it.'

'But why did they build it in the middle ov a desert?'

'The spot the Monument is standing on marks the easterly limit of the Containment Line, the cordon sanitaire imposed by Frank Kenton to limit the spread of the Plague.' Oddie rubbed her sleeve against the window, trying to get a better view. 'Every time I see it I get a catch in my throat. Eighty million names ... so sad.'

'Don't you have a memorial to the Plague back in Britain, Burl?' asked Ella as, prompted by PINC, she hung a left onto the new State Route 6, the arrow-straight piece of two-lane blacktop built by ParaDigm to service all the Fun/Funs who would soon be streaming towards Las Vegas to attend the Gathering. With only fifty miles to go before they hit the town, they'd be in their motel in time for dinner, ready to visit the Kosy Korner Kafe at seven tomorrow morning. That was where the eyeMail she'd received from Vanka told her this mysterious 'Robert' would be waiting for her, the guy who would be able to help her defeat the Boles.

'Nah. The Plague never really touched the Empire, so it's not such a big deal for us Brits. But we're taught abart it in school. I know that it started when you Yanks invaded Japan in 1946. Wasn't the Plague a dormant disease or somefink?'

'That's right,' confirmed Oddie. 'It was a sleeper disease carried by an isolated group of Japanese fishermen living on the island of Kyushu. When they made contact with the GIs coming ashore as part of Operation Downfall, they passed on the disease and these infected servicemen brought the Plague back to the USA. It swept around the world in a matter of months. Almost half a billion people died.'

'And it wos finally brought under control by a vaccine made by us Brits,' Burl added proudly.

'Yeah, by ParaDigm Rx, to be precise,' noted Norma. 'But the funny thing was that in the US the vaccine only seemed to work on Caucasians. The black population was decimated.'

'My great-grandparents amongst them,' noted Ella. 'I'm only here because my grandmother was at school in the UK when the Plague struck.'

'Yeah, I always thought the race bias of the Plague was strange,' Norma agreed. 'The Polly conspiracy sites say that the Plague wasn't so much a plague as a biological weapon wielded by the Brits.'

Burl gave a dismissive laugh. 'That's all just bollocks, Norma . . . anti-Brit bollocks.'

Norma gave a rueful shake of her head. 'It's very persuasive bollocks, Burl.'

'Oh, I think Burl's right though, Norma,' said Oddie. 'When you examine the facts, all this conspiracy stuff just doesn't hold up. ParaDigm Rx became involved when the Plague hit Zanzibar back in 1931 and as Zanzibar is part of the Empire, the British government asked them to search for a vaccine. And it's lucky they did: when the Plague swept through the USA, the British government was in a position to help. Sure, eighty million Americans died but ParaDigm Rx helped save the lives of the other seventy million.'

'The problem,' mused Ella, as she floored the accelerator to power around a line of trucks, 'is that I don't trust anything which involves the Boles or ParaDigm. The unsettling thing is that the Plague wasn't just a human tragedy, it was a political one too. The Plague was responsible for that piece of fundamentalist shit Frank Kenton being elected president and *that* precipitated sixty years of misery for the American people. The US went from being the world's most powerful democracy to being an impoverished theocracy in a single decade. The 1950s were a bad time for America and a good one for ParaDigm and the British Empire.'

Oddie gave Ella a sideways look. 'You're not saying that you believe all this conspiracy nonsense . . . that ParaDigm was behind the Great Plague?'

'Yeah, I suppose I am,' answered Ella, 'especially after that little revelation we were given back in the Institute. Don't you think it's too much of a coincidence that Septimus Bole has arranged for research to be done in the Demi-Monde on plague weapons? I have the sneaking feeling that we haven't seen the last of the Plague of '47.'

Oddie shook her head. 'I think this is all too much of a stretch, Ella. I mean, what would be the point . . . what would the Boles achieve by bringing the Plague back?'

'The Demi-Monde taught me a lot about how the Boles think. The guy running the DM on the Boles' behalf is a racist lunatic called Reinhard Heydrich – the same maniac who masterminded the Holocaust – who was planning to rid the Demi-Monde of what he called "UnderMentionables", those he deemed to be racially inferior to Aryans. I'm thinking that the Plague of '47 was the Boles' take on the Final Solution.'

'That doesn't make sense, Ella,' challenged Oddie. 'If that was the Boles' plan, why did they come forward with a vaccine? Why didn't they just sit back and let the Plague run its course?'

'My theory is that the Plague ran out of the Boles' control, that ParaDigm had to step in to stop it killing the wrong people.'

'The wrong people?'

'The Boles aren't like us . . . they're a different species . . . they're Grigori—'

'You mean like those vampire thingies we had a tussle wiv back in LA?'

'Exactly, Burl. The Grigori are an ancient race of near-humans who have kept themselves very much to themselves for the last few millennia, but now it seems they're intent on asserting themselves . . . making a takeover bid, if you like.'

'How do you know this, Ella?'

Ella laughed. 'It's a long story, Oddie, and I doubt that you'd believe me if I told you. Let's just say that my time in the Demi-Monde was very . . . educational. *Homo sapiens sapiens* isn't the only taxon of the genus *Homo* occupying our world and one of those other taxons is the Grigori. And now, under the leadership of the Boles, the Grigori are making a bid for world domination.'

'But why?' asked Oddie. 'If they've been happily hiding away for thousands of years, why are they making their move now?'

'I'm guessing that they've been waiting for the technology to catch up with their ambitions.' Ella had meant this as a throw-away line, but even as she uttered the words she felt pieces of a puzzle starting to drop into place. 'What they were waiting for was the Demi-Monde . . . that, as far as the Grigori are concerned, is the key to their taking control of the world.'

'You've lost me, Ella,' admitted Norma.

'Think about it, Norma: if the Plague of '47 *did* need perfecting – making it even more race-specific – what better place to do it than in a virtual world where there'd be no worries about an accidental release of the disease?' Ella eased the pickup around a microbus. 'But here's another thought: what if they used the Demi-Monde not only to perfect the Plague but also to create a group of people who were immune to it?'

'The Dupes,' said Norma quietly.

'More precisely, the UnFunDaMentalist Dupes.'

'UnFunDaMentalists?' asked Oddie.

'The white fascists who make up two of the Sectors in the

Demi-Monde. It's amazing that I never thought of it before . . . never stopped to consider how ParaDigm chose the Dupes they used to populate the Demi-Monde.' She frowned. 'What did the Transfusion Booth say about the work being carried out in the Heydrich Institute for Natural Sciences? That the virus they were developing had to be Fragile-specific, that it had to be harmless to Grigori *and* to those possessing the latent MAOA-Grigori gene. Maybe the UnFunDaMentalist Dupes in the ForthRight are doppelgängers of Real Worlders who carry the Grigori gene. Yeah, I'm sure of it: the Demi-Monde is just an elaborate trigger mechanism designed to awaken the Grigori hidden deep inside certain selected people.'

'Trigger mechanism?' asked Norma.

'It's not unusual for extreme experiences – childhood abuse, that sort of thing – to ignite a latent aspect of a man or woman's personality . . . to act as a triggering mechanism. This is especially the case with psychotic predilections, and psychosis is a *very* Grigorian personality trait. *That's* what the Demi-Monde was designed to do: to fire up the latent Grigori gene by subjecting Dupes living there to enormous stress and of course by feeding them blood and . . .' Ella gave a doleful shake of her head. 'I must be stupid. Slap-bang in the middle of the Demi-Monde, in a place called Terror Incognita, there's a pyramid that's a duplicate of the Monument. I've a feeling that it's got something to do with the triggering of the Grigori aspect of the Dupes, especially as Heydrich is planning to hold a religious ceremony – the Ceremony of Purification – at the same time the Gathering is being held here in the Real World.'

Oddie gave another, more emphatic shake of her head. 'Look, Ella, this is all getting kinda out-there. I mean vampires and genetic alteration . . . this is weird worlds territory.'

'Yus,' agreed Burl. 'And anyways, so wot that these Dupes of yours 'ave this Grigori gene? They're stuck in the Demi-Monde.'

'That, I think, is the purpose of the Gathering,' answered Ella. 'That's when Bole's going to transfer the newly revived genetic aspects of the Dupes attending the Ceremony of Purification in the Demi-Monde to their doppelgängers here in the Real World attending the Gathering.'

'C'mon, Ella,' complained Oddie, 'that's not possible.'

'Oh yes it is,' said Norma quietly. 'It was done with me. That's how Aaliz Heydrich managed to take control of my body here in the Real World.'

Oddie wasn't impressed. 'But even if Bole is successful, there'll still be only a few million of these Grigori-aspected people, a drop in the ocean compared to the size of the world's population. Shit, there are almost nine billion people on earth.'

Ella gave a humourless laugh. 'Not for much longer if Bole has his way. That, I think, is the purpose of this new super-Plague the Boles have been cooking up in the Demi-Monde, – this "potentially lethal" super-plague. They're going to use it to attack those of the human race who aren't Grigori-aspected. And from what we learned back in the Institute, the Plague is already out there courtesy of noöPINC, just waiting for the Boles to activate it.'

'But surely that will involve the slaughter of billions of people!'

'Billions of UnderMentionables, Oddie,' observed Ella. 'Bole doesn't regard non-Grigori as real people. He holds them in total contempt. He wouldn't regard it as a slaughter . . . more a culling.'

'I don't believe it! No one could be that deranged.'

'Oh, I think Bole is mad enough for anything. Bole's version of the Final Solution is one where it isn't just the Jews who are the victims, but the vast majority of the human race.'

And that was a comment that put a crimp on the conversation. As she drove along in silence, Ella's thoughts turned to what she could do to thwart Bole. It seemed hopeless. It was all very well Vanka – ABBA – telling her she had to protect Norma, but what was the good of that if Bole and the Grigori emerged triumphant?

She just hoped the answer would be waiting for them in Las Vegas.

It was still dark when Rivets and Dong E landed at Los Angeles Kenton International Airport and collected the rental Studebaker. It seemed remarkable that there wasn't any petrol rationing in the States, but then, Rivets supposed, America was the world's second-largest producer of crude oil. Of course, ParaDigm had offered a limo to take them to the TiME facility in Nevada but the last thing Rivets wanted was them knowing that he and Dong E were intent on making an unscheduled stop at a coffee shop to meet . . . well, all he knew about the girl was her name, but he guessed this Ella Thomas item wasn't on the Boles' Christmas card list.

As he steered the car out of the parking lot he had PINC recall the message that had popped into his head three weeks ago.

'IF YOU TRULY WANT TO UNDERSTAND ABOUT NOÖPINC AND WHAT PARADIGM IS PLANNING WITH REGARDS TO TEMPORAL MODULATION YOU SHOULD BE IN THE KOSY KORNER KAFE IN LAS VEGAS AT NOON ON 16 APRIL. ELLA THOMAS WILL EXPLAIN. YOUR FRIEND VANKA.'

There were a number of disturbing things about the message. The first was that its encryption motif was one that Rivets didn't recognise and as such his PINC shouldn't have been able to decipher it . . . but it had. And the second was that whoever 'Vanka' was, he knew that Rivets was now interested in Temporal Modulations, which was bloody worrying. As Rivets understood it, apart from Dong E and himself, only the Boles were privy to that piece of intelligence and he didn't think either of them was in the habit of sending out late-night billets-doux using the penname Vanka.

'I still can't believe we got through immigration so quickly,' mused Dong E from the seat next to his.

'Visiting the States isn't so much of a problem now that Sam Thomas is president,' Rivets answered as he eased onto the freeway. 'Since the Kentons were booted out, there's been a thawing in Anglo-American relations . . . the Cold War is officially over. Look at how accommodating the Yanks have been regarding all the Fun/Funs coming to attend the Gathering. Anyway, ParaDigm's Nevada facility is more British than American, so we've got quasi-diplomatic status.'

'Why did the Boles build a TiME in Nevada? I mean, it's slap-bang in the middle of Kenton country.'

'All TiMEs are sited outside the Empire: the last thing the Boles wanted was a Tunguska happening in their own backyard. That's why they built this one in the middle of a desert where only Yanks and lizards would get fricasseed if the thing goes bang. Anyway, ParaDigm got a thousand-year lease on the Nevada site as part of the compensation deal they negotiated with the Yanks for the delivery of the Plague vaccine back in 1947 so I suppose Nevada was as good a place as any.'

For the next half-hour they drove in silence, both of them jet-lagged from the overnight flight and neither of them relishing the long drive to Las Vegas.

Not that there was any chance of Rivets falling asleep at the wheel: the bells saw to that.

The Americans might have put an atheist in the White House, but the West Coast remained Believers' territory, where everybody took their religion very seriously indeed. Every morning the church bells rang to welcome dawn, to signal that God had once again vanquished Satan and rolled back the night. The Kentons might have gone but the cacophony of bells that welcomed each dawn was their noisy bequest to America.

Rivets leant across to stab the 'On' button of the car's radio.

Anything to drown out the sound of the bells, and with Polly coverage hopeless in the States, it was back to analogue.

The radio crackled into life. '. . . ling all Believers to give thanks for the gift of a new day from the Lord, our God. Let us offer our prayers for the defeat of that old devil, Satan, and the crushing of his sidekick, the Great Beast.'

Inwardly Rivets groaned. He'd forgotten that Believers' Broadcasting was the most popular radio station in the US. He moved to switch channels.

'No, leave it on, Rivets,' objected Dong E. 'It's interesting. When in Rome and all that.'

'Remember, friends,' gushed the announcer, too chirpy by half for six o'clock in the morning, 'it's only two weeks to the Gathering . . . just fourteen days before Norma Williams gives you the opportunity to rid yourself of your addictions and to prepare yourself for Revelation. And to do that, friends, requires doing only one simple thing: obeying the nuCommandments as revealed by God's Last Prophet, Frank Kenton. There is nothing more important for a Believer than adherence to the nuCommandments. Remember what our Lord Jesus Christ said when he gave the Sermon on the Mount: "Whoever therefore breaks one of the least of these commandments, and teaches men so, shall be called least in the kingdom of heaven: but whoever does and teaches them, he shall be called great in the kingdom of heaven." That's the bottom line, friends, you either obey or you stray and with only fourteen days to go before Revelation now is not the time to start straying into the ever-open arms of Satan. And to fill your hearts with the joy of the Lord, here's your favourite and mine, Nirvana playing "Revelation HayRide". . .'

Mentally Rivets switched off. He hated Kurt Cobain and his mawkish religious sentimentality. He checked his watch: BBNews would be on in five minutes. He sat back to wait, using the time to count the number of churches that lined the route out of LA,

giving up when he reached thirty. Hardly surprising, he supposed, given that LA was 'The Religious Capital of the World'.

Finally, thankfully, the trilling of Cobain faded, the organ
music that trailed BBNews cut in and a presenter – his voice
solemn and reassuring – began to read the news.

'Top story today, folks, is the news that the FBI have raised
fears that atheist terrorists will attempt to disrupt the Gathering. A nationwide hunt has begun for a girl of Hamitic
appearance going by the name of Ella Thomas, who is wanted
for questioning with regard to the diabolical activities of those
disciples of the devil, the Black Panthers. So keep your eyes
peeled, folks; the handmaiden of Satan walks amongst us.'

Rivets froze in his seat, paralysed by shock. Ella Thomas was
the girl he was scheduled to meet in Las Vegas! Ignoring the rest
of the news, he sat back into his seat trying to get his head
around what he had just heard.

'I think we should keep our meeting with Ella Thomas as
short as possible, Dong E,' he said when he'd calmed down. 'I'm
less than happy that the girl we're scheduled to meet is a fugitive from the FBI.'

'I agree. And once we've met her, then what?'

'We'll have to play it by ear. They're expecting us at the Nevada
TiME facility this afternoon to be given the ten-cent tour by the
guy running it, your old flame Sam Madden.'

Dong E laughed. 'He was never a "flame", Rivets, he just hit on
me big time at ParaDigm's Christmas bash last year. Really came
on hot, heavy and horny.'

'Sounds like Madden. Anyway, he's been tasked with showing
us the ins and outs of the TiME machine.' He looked across to his
girlfriend. 'You still wearing your lucky necklace, Dong E?'

Dong E laughed and touched the string of metal beads she
was wearing around her neck. 'Don't worry, Rivets, I wouldn't be
parted with it for the world.'

*

An anxious Ella sat in the Kosy Korner Kafe just as she had been instructed by the eyeMail, waiting for 'Robert', her only comfort being that Burl and Oddie had positioned themselves at a table by the door guarding the entrance. When 'Robert' walked into the café, she did a double take – the last person she had been expecting was Rivets, or at any rate someone who *looked* a lot like Rivets: the crumpled suit and the long hair confused her for a moment but he had the same impish twinkle in his eye and the same lack of inches as Vanka's sidekick.

'Rivets?' she called out.

The man looked towards her and frowned, then took the Chinese girl he was with by the arm and steered her towards Ella's table. 'I'm supposing that you're Ella.' He thrust out a hand. 'I'm Bob Vetsch and this is my friend Dong E.' They shook hands and Ella waved them both into the booth she was occupying. 'How come you know that my friends call me Rivets?'

'It's a long story. Let's just say that you and Dong E have been duplicated in a computer simulation I've been involved with and there you're known as Rivets.'

'I'm in the Demi-Monde?' asked a surprised Dong E. 'Para-Digm used me as a template for a Dupe?'

'Correct. And you were one important girl there. As I heard it, you're the girl pitching to take over the Coven.'

'Wow, that's really something.'

'Yeah, really something,' said a much less enthusiastic Rivets as he signalled to the waitress for two coffees. Once these had been served, he pulled the anti-surveillance bubble over the table. This was one man, Ella decided, who was determined that their conversation wouldn't be overheard.

'I should tell you, Ella, that I'm not cool about this meeting. According to the radio you're now on the FBI's Most Wanted list, so the last thing I need is the Feds making a café call and getting to thinking that you and me are brunch buddies.'

Ella shrugged, trying to show how indifferent she was to the news, but she pulled the peak of her cap just a little further down over her face anyway. 'Thanks for the advice. I'll try to keep this short.'

'If you would. There aren't many girls of your colour here on the West Coast so you stand out like a sore thumb.'

What Rivets said was true. The blacks that the Plague hadn't killed had been made to feel mighty unwelcome by the Believers and even seventy years on it was unusual to see anyone other than Blanks braving the Wacky West.

'And before we begin, I need to establish that you're on the side of the angels. For all I know you might be a member of the British secret police . . . the Intelligence Bureau. This might be a scam by ParaDigm to test that I can keep my mouth shut, that I can stay shtum about what I've been told to keep shtum about.'

Ella nodded. 'You're right to be suspicious, Rivets, but maybe a friend of mine will be able to convince you of my bona fides.' She glanced over to the table to her left where Norma was seated swathed in shadows and an overlarge hat. The girl stood up and came to join them.

'You're Norma Williams!' gasped Dong E. 'I've seen you on the Polly – you're the President's daughter – the leader of the Fun/Funs—'

'And you're Dong E,' answered Norma as she took a seat next to Ella. 'We were friends in the Demi-Monde.'

But whilst Dong E might have been pleased to meet Norma, Rivets didn't seem to think much of her celebrity status. 'I'm sorry, Ella, but I don't find the presence of Miss Williams here in any way reassuring. The Fun/Funs are sponsored by ParaDigm, so the likelihood is that she's working for the Boles.'

Ella made to reply but she was forestalled by Norma. 'Let me try to answer that, Ella. While I'm not sure if there's anything I can do or say that might convince you to trust me, Rivets, maybe if I'm totally upfront with you and Dong E, you might be inclined to give me the benefit of the doubt.' She took a deep breath. 'We believe that the Boles have released a biological weapon – a plague – out into the world which they're planning to activate at the end of April. We've been told that you can help us stop them.'

The word 'plague' seemed to have resonance with both Rivets and Dong E. 'What sort of plague?' asked Dong E.

'We're not sure, but our guess is that it's a development of the '47 Plague. What we do know is that Bole has been using the Demi-Monde as a test site for it.'

Rivets was silent for a moment as he cogitated on what Norma had told him. 'Okay . . . what you've just said chimes with the information that Dong E and I have and as I'm guessing that neither of you would be willing partners in genocide, I suppose, it's cards on the table time.' He turned to Dong E. 'As plagues are your area of expertise, Dong E, it's over to you.'

'Okay,' Dong E began, 'we can confirm some of your suspicions. ParaDigm *has* been developing a refined plague virus – a modification of the '47 Plague – and I know this because I've been leading the team doing just that. We've been charged with finding a carrier for the next-generation PINC – noöPINC – which is a cyborg-virus.' Dong E must have seen the expressions of bewilderment on the faces of her audience. 'A cyborg-virus is a virus that has man-made elements incorporated into its make-up, these nanocybernetic structures acting as inception points for the development of the virus. The virus grows around them. And, by doing so, absorbs the artificial elements into its genetic structure.'

'But why?' asked Ella. 'What's the point?'

'Because old-style PINCs like the ones Rivets and I are equipped with can only be introduced into the brain via the eye . . . they need to use the optic nerve as a neurobahn to find their way to their optimum docking point in the brain. But noöPINC can enter the body in *any* way, and once it's there the virus the noöPINC is fused with acts as the delivery mechanism, bringing it to its target site on the hippocampus.'

'NoöPINC must be very small.'

'Tiny, Ella. Much, much smaller than the current-model PINC. It measures just one hundred nanometres across, too small to be seen by a light microscope.'

'The virus is attenuated – weakened – so it's perfectly harmless and as it can't survive outside its host, it isn't in any way contagious. And the other big selling point of noöPINC is that everyone receiving it will be immune to the Plague. Thanks to noöPINC the Plague will go the same way as smallpox.'

'But presumably, being so small, it could have been seeded into the rest of the world's population without them knowing about it?'

Ella's question gave Dong E pause. 'Well, I suppose—'

'My information is that the Boles have already disseminated their noöPINC around the world . . . everyone on earth is now noöPINC-equipped.'

Dong E frowned. 'But why would they do that? Once it's been switched on by ABBA, everyone will know they're noöPINCed. People outside the Empire would go ballistic . . . especially the Believers here in the US. They see PINC as the Mark of the Beast.'

Ella nodded. 'Let me ask you another question, Dong E: could the attenuated aspect of the plague be changed once it's lodged in a person's brain . . . could it be reactivated? It has been described to us as "potentially lethal" . . . we need to know what "potentially" means.'

'Well . . . I suppose it's *theoretically* possible that it could be reactivated . . . given the right stimulus.'

'And if it was activated, would it be as lethal as its ancestor of '47?'

Another pause from Dong E and then a reluctant 'Yes.'

'Then that's what I think the Boles are about,' declared Ella. 'The virus element of noöPINC isn't just a delivery mechanism ... it's there to give the Boles the power to select, on an individual basis, who becomes a Plague victim ... who lives and who dies. And my guess is that those who live will be those attending the Gathering.'

'But again, Ella, I've got to ask: what would be the point?'

'To explain that, Dong E, I need to bring you up to speed on the Grigori.'

The explanation took ten minutes during which time neither Rivets nor Dong E uttered a word. When Ella had finished speaking, Rivets called for fresh coffee.

'The funny thing, Ella,' he admitted as he sipped at a second cup of coffee, 'is that just a few weeks ago I'd have dismissed what you've just told me as so much hokum, but having seen Septimus Bole and his father up close and having learnt what the bastards have been doing for the last hundred years, it all makes a sort of weird logic.' He drained his coffee. 'Fuck, I think you're right. Those bastards aren't human and by staging a rerun of 1947 ... they're intent on getting rid of the non-Grigorian aspect of humanity. This time though there'll be no mistakes and no vaccine.' He gave a rueful smile. 'I think it's head between your legs and kiss your arse goodbye time for the human race.'

'But we can't just stand by and let the Boles win!' exclaimed Dong E. 'We've got to stop the Boles activating noöPINC.'

Norma shook her head. 'No, Dong E, that's the last thing we should do.'

Las Vegas
The Real World: 16 April 2019

With the US economy revitalised by the huge increase in the price of oil (following the nuclear destruction of the Middle East oilfields during the Two-Day War of 1963, the USA found itself the second-largest oil producer in the world), President Paul Kenton signed a secret cooperation pact with Russia (the Leningrad Protocol of 1968) to jointly finance the creation of a nuclear weapon and a related delivery system. On learning about the so-called New Manhattan Project, the British Prime Minister, Edward du Cann, reacted angrily, dubbing Russia and America an 'Axis of Evil' and vowing to do everything in the British Empire's power to prevent these two 'rogue states' from becoming N-powers. This speech marked the beginning of the Cold War.

America and the Bomb: **Penny Fairchild, ParaDigm**
Publications

There was something, just something, in the way Norma said this that made Ella turn to look at her and she was more than a little disturbed by the sparkle of excitement in the girl's eyes.

'To my way of thinking,' Norma began, 'even if we prevent the activation of noöPINC, we still won't have won. We might have averted genocide but we won't have won! Think about it. If Rivets and Dong E organise things so that when the Boles try to switch on noöPINC nothing happens . . . so what?'

'Well, a few billion people will have been saved from a pretty horrible death!'

'Quite right, Rivets, but we won't have *defeated* the Boles, all we'll have done is just delayed the inevitable. ParaDigm will still be the most powerful company on the planet and the Boles – the Grigori – will still have control of ParaDigm. Okay, so they'll have suffered a reverse and they won't be happy but all they'll do is dust themselves down and start plotting again. To win – to defeat the Boles and the Grigori – we've got to find a way to negate their power.'

Rivets gave a smirk and a disconsolate shake of his head. 'That's impossible, Norma. ABBA's current non-cooperation only seems to involve matters relating to the Demi-Monde, so the Boles still control the day-to-day functioning of the machine, and that means they control *everything*.'

'Tell me why ABBA is so important to them.'

'Because ABBA has taken data fusion to new and unprecedented levels,' answered Rivets. 'ABBA has access to the information held in *all* the governmental and private databases around the world . . .'

'Is that true?' challenged Norma. 'The US government always insists that its databases are immune to hacking by ABBA.'

'Bullshit,' opined Rivets. 'There isn't a database that ABBA can't access. Forget encryption: ABBA's processing power is so enormous that it trashes the most complex cyber-defences in seconds. And the upshot is that ABBA knows and analyses in real time *all* the data flowing through the digital systems of banks, of supermarkets, of tax agencies, of the police, of doctors . . . of everybody: if a record is digital then ABBA has seen it. And then you've got to remember that ABBA manages the PanOptika surveillance system, so all the information collected by every –

and I do mean *every* – public and private CCTV camera and by every eyeSpy in the world finds its way to ABBA. But that's not all: ABBA operates the Polly network so it reads every eyeMail you send or receive and listens to every Polly conversation you participate in. It's impossible to walk, drive or take a shit without ABBA knowing about it.' Rivets laughed. 'ABBA owns you folks . . . and the Boles own ABBA. They know what everyone is thinking or doing almost before they think or do it. That's why Para-Digm's so adept at outmanoeuvring their commercial rivals and why no country has ever seriously challenged the might of the British Empire. The Boles always win because they know the cards their opponents are holding.'

'Frightening,' admitted Ella. And the odd thing was that she *was* frightened. That ABBA had presented to her as Vanka had made her forget just how powerful the machine was . . . and that it seemed to be following its own agenda.

'This is the reason why all the governments outside the British Empire are so freaked by ABBA,' continued Rivets, 'and why they've been trying to push a declaration through the League of Nations restricting ABBA's ability to access databases and lim-iting the surveillance scope of PanOptika.' He gave a shrug. 'Waste of time, of course, the technology has gone too far for it to be dismantled. To demand that Paradigm abandon PanOp-tika, turn off the cameras and ground the eyeSpies is naïve. The Boles will only respond by creating ever-smaller cameras, ever more subtle ways of monitoring you and me and everyone else in the whole fucking world. The League of Nations might have banned moteBots but everybody knows they're out there and everybody knows there's fuck-all we can do about it.'

Norma nodded. 'What you've said, Rivets, only confirms my belief that it's the Boles' control of information that's their ace in the hole. A good friend of mine back in the Demi-Monde told me that information is and has always been the most valuable commodity in the whole world. Politicians since the dawn of history have understood that without information people have no *real* power. So to defeat the Boles we must subvert their control of the information provided by ABBA.'

'Come again?'

'Think about it. The reality is that the Boles' power comes from knowing things other people don't . . . having access to information denied other people. And like all commodities, information is valuable because it's scarce—'

'No, it isn't, Norma, Polly has given us access to more information than ever. Shit, thanks to Polly, we've got information coming out of our ears.'

'Not so, Rivets, what we've got coming out of our ears – or rather, going *into* our ears – is noise. The Polly is full to overflowing with garbage and this, I think, is a deliberate strategy of the Boles. All the porn, the banal chatter of social networking sites and the blitzkrieg of prurient gossip carried by Polly is there to mask the paucity of *important* data, *real* information, the stuff that's kept confidential and secret, the stuff that's sealed away behind layers of ABBA encryption . . . the stuff that's only known by the Boles. That's the information I'm referring to: the information which is valuable because it's scarce . . . scarce because we don't even know it exists. That's what we've got to do to defeat the Boles, we've got to end the scarcity of information . . . devalue it.'

'And how do we do that?'

'By using noöPINC. The Boles, by making every man, woman and child in the world noöPINC-equipped, have given us the perfect weapon to defeat them. Their intention is to use noöPINC as an on/off switch for the Plague – to decide who lives and who dies – but what if we turned this plan of theirs around and instead we used noöPINC to give humanity access to all the information held by ABBA? The Boles have created the first

digitocracy, a tyranny based on their control of digital information where Joe and Jane Public have been reduced to the status
of digital peasants. What I am suggesting is that we stage the
digital equivalent of a Peasants' Revolt.'

'Er . . .'

'You've told me, Rivets, that you and Dong E have been sent
here to reprogram ABBA so that it's dutiful to the Boles, but
what if, instead, you reprogrammed it so that it allowed everyone with a noöPINC access to its databases . . . to all the
information it holds? In that way we'll subvert noöPINC and
devalue the information that forms the foundation of the Boles'
power. By taking control of noöPINC we will supplement the
biosphere with a noösphere.'

'A noösphere?'

'A noösphere is a concept first promulgated by Teilhard de
Chardin which envisages all human thought, experiences and
knowledge coalescing into a sort of hive mentality.'

Ella laughed. 'It's actually a very old idea. It used to be called
Atavistic Thought Inheritance.'

Rivets shook his head. 'Old or new, it's still a fucking ridiculous idea.'

'Why?'

'Because if you created this noösphere of yours, everybody
would know everything about everybody!' Rivets spluttered. 'You
would destroy privacy and without privacy society would cease
to function.'

'Society, Rivets, is a very robust thing,' answered Norma. 'A
couple of hundred years ago people lived in villages and knew
everything about their neighbours. It's only since the advent of
cities which threw strangers together that we've become
obsessed with privacy. What I'm suggesting is that we use ABBA
and noöPINC to create a global village.'

'But then nothing would be private.'

'Exactly.' Norma gave a sardonic little chuckle. 'To my way of thinking, the choice we are presented with is between preserving privacy and annihilation.'

For a moment Rivets seemed to be nonplussed by Norma's certainty, but, game as ever, he tried another tack. 'It would destroy the functioning of government!'

'No, Rivets, it would *change* the functioning of government; it would make governments wholly transparent and wholly accountable and that would be a good thing. A noöPINCed world would be a true democracy.'

Rivets still wasn't convinced. 'Even so, the Boles could threaten to turn off ABBA and without ABBA the world would cease to function: the Polly network would crash, the transport system would be thrown into chaos, people would starve, nuclear plants would go into meltdown. That's the Boles' get-out-of-jail-free card: move against them and they'd simply pull the plug on ABBA and we'd all be en route back to the Stone Age.'

'Could they, Rivets? I don't think ABBA's in the mood to be shut down. And anyway, once everyone is noöPINCed, ABBA wouldn't belong to the Boles any longer: ABBA would belong to everyone.'

'The religious community will go apeshit, Norma,' noted Dong E. 'Once they find out they've been noöPINCed, they're gonna be very unhappy campers. There's a lot of people out there who think ABBA is the Antichrist, that PINC is the Mark of the Beast and that wearing it signals the triumph of Satan.'

Norma wasn't impressed. 'What we'll have to do, Dong E, is sell this as the Revelation ... the dawning of a new age of human-kind ... an age of peace and harmony.'

'How so?' asked Rivets.

'Because my feeling is that once people are privy to the infor-mation held by ABBA, wars will be a thing of the past. Most wars are the result of differences – real or imagined – between peoples

... different religious beliefs, different languages and different political philosophies. But once everyone has access to the sum of human knowledge, once the barriers of language are dismantled, those differences will be eliminated. It will be the Age of Enlightenment come again.'

'And to enter this utopia, all Believers will have to do is accept the Mark of the Beast,' countered Dong E.

'Once they've been plugged into ABBA,' riposted Norma, her voice rising with excitement, 'once they've experienced the euphoria that comes from being PINCed, then they'll understand that noöPINC doesn't represent damnation, it represents salvation.'

Rivets nodded. 'Yeah, when I was PINCed I had something of an epiphany, so I can relate to that.'

'Exactly, Rivets. What we will be doing is presiding over the birth of H+, humans whose mental performance has been augmented by ABBA and noöPINC. The Gathering won't see the victory of the Boles and the Grigori, but the dawning of a noöcracy . . . the era of the all-knowing. And thanks to Aaliz, I'm the leader of the Fun/Funs, so I'll have an unprecedented opportunity to sell InfoCialism to the world at the Gathering.'

'InfoCialism?' asked Ella.

'The name Percy Shelley gave to the system that achieves the socialisation of information.'

Rivets nodded. 'I have to say, I'm attracted to the idea of usurping control of noöPINC . . . especially as the alternative is death. You don't have much use for privacy when you're six feet under.'

'And it *will* strip the Boles of power,' added Dong E.

'Yeah, good point, Dong E . . .' Rivets trailed off and spent a minute sitting in silence, sipping his coffee as he struggled with the consequences of Norma's proposal. Finally, he said, 'Well, I guess we don't have much of a choice. The Boles have to be defeated. Okay, Norma, I'm convinced.'

'Good,' said a smiling Norma. She looked around. 'So if we're all in agreement?' There were nods from everyone sitting at the table. 'Then let's cut to the chase. I'm presuming that Dong E, being an expert on noöPINC, can write the program amendments necessary to alter its functioning, so that the virus is incapable of being activated.'

A nod from Dong E. 'Yeah, and I'll also have to do some tinkering to stop the Boles controlling the content that can be downloaded from ABBA.'

'Then it only remains to figure out a way of sending these instructions to ABBA.' Norma looked across the table towards Rivets. 'I guess that this is your area of expertise, Rivets.'

'Difficult.'

'But doable?'

'Maybe.'

They spent ten minutes discussing tactics, finally deciding that Norma would go to the Gathering escorted by Burl and Oddie; that Rivets and Dong E would go to the ParaDigm facility; and that Ella . . .

Ella didn't quite know what she would do. Having rescued Norma, her role seemed to be over. She couldn't go to the Gathering – her colour made her too noticeable for that: all Fun/Funs were white – and there didn't seem to be any other role for her. As she waved Norma, Burl and Oddie off in the pickup she had a troubling feeling of suddenly being surplus to requirements. In the space of an hour, she'd gone from saviour to fifth wheel.

'That Norma Williams of yours is one very forceful lady, Ella,' mused Rivets as he walked with her and Dong E across the lot to the parked Studebaker.

'I could object to the use of the word "yours", Rivets. As you heard, she's very much her own woman.'

And that was certainly the truth. The last time Ella had

had anything to do with Norma Williams had been back in the Demi-Monde and she'd changed one hell of a lot since then. The Real World Norma was a much more *certain* girl than the one Ella remembered and she found it really difficult to connect with people of such a *certain* disposition. Lilith had been a very *certain* lady and she had caused no end of mayhem and unhappiness. Maybe all the 'Messiah' business in the Demi-Monde had gone to Norma's head? There was certainly a touch of the evangelist about her now.

They got to the car and Rivets handed Ella the keys. 'You drive, Ella: give me and Dong E a ride to the ParaDigm facility and then take off. There'll be less chance of you being spotted by the FBI if you're driving than if you take a train or a bus. I'll announce the car stolen in a couple of days.'

A good idea, though Ella didn't have a clue as to where she would 'take off' to. 'So tell me, Rivets,' she said as she slid into the driver's seat, 'how are you and Dong E going to make the changes to noöPINC?'

'By making a retro-fix.'

'Retro-fix?'

They sat in the car as Rivets explained to Ella what retro-programming and Temporal Modulation were and then he spent another five minutes answering her questions.

'So if I understand you right, Rivets, the Boles don't just control the present but they also control the past.'

'Correct, Ella.'

Almost absent-mindedly, Ella switched on the car's engine, then manoeuvred it out of the parking lot. She made a PINC-advised left turn and found herself on an almost deserted stretch of road signposted to 'ParaDigm Nevada Research Facility'. Automatically she sank lower into her seat, trying to make herself as small as possible. She could almost *feel* the Boles watching her and that thought was a troubling one. In her judgement, it would take more than the reprogramming of noöPINC to defeat the Boles and the Grigori.

'One thing puzzles me, Rivets, why didn't you tell Norma about Temporal Modulation?'

Rivets made a moue. 'Maybe I was just overwhelmed by all this InfoCialism business.'

'Or maybe we were just a little suspicious of her,' added Dong E, 'just like you were, Ella.'

An insightful observation, but then Dong E was one smart girl. '"Suspicious" is probably the wrong word, Dong E. This Info-Cialism of Norma's has just come at me in a bit of a rush. Maybe I just need some time to get my head around it. I can see the logic in what Norma's proposing . . . it just seems a little *radical* for my taste. The reshaping of humankind isn't something to be done lightly.' Ella almost laughed. She of all people knew the truth of *that* statement. Meddling with evolution always seemed to end in tears and, as she saw it, presiding over the dawning of H+ was doing just that. 'I've had some experience with hive mentalities . . . with noöcracies like the one Norma's proposing, and those experiences haven't been altogether pleasant.'

'So what do you think we should be doing?'

'We've got to remember that the thing that is motivating the Boles is their desire to have the Grigori triumphant, and while they're still around, humanity will never be safe. We've got to destroy the Grigori.' Wasn't that the truth? Her time in the Demi-Monde had taught her that neither Lilithi nor the Grigori had a place in the Real World. Both had to be consigned to history.

'So do we know where these Grigori are hiding out?' asked Rivets.

'No . . . no one knows.'

'Well, if we can't find them, it's difficult to destroy them!'

'Maybe ABBA could tell us?' suggested Dong E.

Ella shook her head. 'No, ABBA can't do anything that directly harms the Boles, and telling us where the Grigori are hiding would do just that.'

'That's a real shame, Ella. If I knew where they were, it's possible I could deal with them . . . especially if they're anywhere near a TiME facility.'

Ella drove in silence for a minute or so as she turned this last statement of Rivets' over in her head. 'If I *was* to find out, how would I be able to let you know their location?'

'All you'd have to do is send me a TELEpath message via PINC.'

'Then there may be a way. In a former life I was the Grigori's most formidable enemy so I'm guessing that they've got a few scores to settle. Sure as eggs are eggs, they'll be out there searching for me.' Ella gave a mirthless chuckle. 'Maybe I won't have to find them . . . maybe I'll let them find me.'

The ParaDigm Research Facility, Nevada
The Real World: 16 April 2019

The 12/12 dirty nuke attack on Edinburgh marked a substantial shift in the British public's attitude to PINC. Before the attack public opinion was largely negative, there being widespread suspicion that the wholesale PINCing of the population would lead to an unacceptable infringement of privacy and personal liberty. After the attack national security became the pre-eminent concern of British citizens, and the arguments that PINC would ensure their safety *and* their e-identity had greater resonance. A referendum was called in May 2015 to decide the matter and almost 60 per cent of the electorate voted in favour of the compulsory and universal adoption of PINC within the British Empire. It is anticipated that this policy will be executed in May 2019.

Modern British History: eSuccess in GCSE-Dip Revision
Guide, ParaDigm ePress

Dong E and Rivets had Ella drop them off at a gas station a mile or so from the ParaDigm facility. It was viciously hot outside the air-conditioned oasis of the car, and after they'd waved Ella goodbye, they took shelter in the shade of an awning and waited for the arrival of the ParaDigm limo Madden was sending to pick them up.

So much had happened in the few hours since they had arrived in the States that for a couple of minutes they simply stood in silence, lost in their thoughts, this awkward silence finally broken by Rivets. 'So, what do you think?' he asked.

'Well, what I think is that Norma Williams is an enormously driven and charismatic young lady and if anyone can lead a remodelled humanity into a bright new tomorrow, it's her. Like Ella, I'm not totally sold on this InfoCialism of hers but really I don't think we've much of a choice. The alternative is to have the Boles regroup and come back at us. We've got to finish them now.'

'Agreed. And Ella Thomas?'

'Determined and very courageous. Going after the Grigori will be, I suspect, a dangerous occupation. I think Ella knows she won't be coming out of this alive, and there aren't many people who would willingly sacrifice their lives to preserve the lives of others.'

'It's one life to save billions.'

'It's still a ballsy thing to do.'

Rivets shuffled nervously on his feet and then glanced at Dong E. 'What if it was three lives that had to be sacrificed to save billions?'

Dong E turned to Rivets, gimleting him with a hard stare. 'I think we both know how important it is to stop the Boles, so don't ever doubt me, Rivets: I'll do anything and everything necessary to defeat them. I'll be with you to the end.'

'You're sure?'

'Never more so in my life.'

'Okay . . . then we've got to get a Message Sphere that carries the instructions necessary to reprogram noöPINC into the TiME facility. That, I think, will be down to you . . . and your jewellery. The fact that Madden's got the hots for you is our ace in the hole. I'm expecting security around the TiME machine to be super-tight and the only way of getting our gizmo past that security will be if Madden is thinking with his dick rather than his brain. If you were to flirt with the man a little, to get him not seeing straight . . .'

Dong E giggled. 'Short skirt time, eh?'

'*Very* short skirt time.' Rivets smiled but there wasn't much warmth in it.

Dong E kissed him on the cheek. 'Don't worry, Rivets, I love you, so don't think I'm going to enjoy getting it on with Madden. But if a job's worth doing, it's worth doing well.' She gave Rivets a crooked smile. 'So, if you don't mind, I'll just spend a few minutes in the washroom fixing my make-up and getting ready to play the femme fatale.' Another smile. 'When I'm finished, Madden's not going to stand a chance.'

An hour later the limo sent by Madden trundled them up to the enormous antiAttack gates that gave access to ParaDigm's Nevada facility. Waiting while the Intelligence Bureau agents completed the protracted identification process and their bags were examined for explosives, Dong E found herself relaxing. Her fate – and that of the world – was now in the lap of the gods. The die was cast, there could be no going back now.

She stopped relaxing immediately they were through the gates; that was the moment she fully appreciated just how powerful an enemy they were taking on in ParaDigm. Sure, she had seen Polly footage describing the factories and installations the company had around the world and ParaDigm House in London was a pretty impressive place, but it was the Nevada site that brought home to her the sheer scale of the resources controlled by the Boles. The site was huge, a vast circular compound which, according to PINC, stretched thirty miles across, but it wasn't simply the size of the place that was so daunting. Here, in the middle of the desert, the Boles had created a little piece of

England: ParaDigm's Nevada research facility was set in seven hundred square miles of verdant and very lush parkland. She hardly dared estimate the amount of water needed to keep grass growing in a desert.

Their approach to the manor house standing in the middle of the park had obviously been observed: a butler resplendent in a morning suit opened the huge front doors ready to greet them. 'Good afternoon. Welcome to Bole Manor,' he intoned and then ushered them inside, along a corridor and into an opulent room lined from floor to ceiling with leather-bound books. 'If you would make yourselves comfortable, I will advise Dr Madden of your arrival.' And with that he oozed out of the room.

Madden put in an appearance five minutes later. In many ways he was the epitome of a modern scientist, a man as much at home in the boardroom as he was in the laboratory. He was elegant, perfectly groomed – a little *too* perfectly groomed in Dong E's opinion: there was something almost oleaginous about him – and quite handsome in a nondescript sort of way. She could understand why he was so successful with women – *very* successful, if the ParaDigm scuttlebutt was to be believed – but he was just not Dong E's type of guy.

'My dear Robert,' he smarmed, 'I am so very pleased to meet you again, and may I congratulate you on your appointment to the ABBA Containment Project.' Madden tried to sound sincere but he couldn't hide his annoyance at Rivets' promotion. 'But I am forgetting my manners.' He bowed towards Dong E. 'I am also delighted to welcome the talented and beautiful Dr Dong E to Bole Manor.'

Seduction starts here, decided Dong E and she ignored the outstretched hand and instead kissed the man on the cheek. 'Sam! It's so good to see you again. My, you're looking quite raffish. The desert sunshine obviously agrees with you.'

Madden preened as he waved his two guests back into their chairs. 'And you, Dong E, are looking, as ever, glorious.'

It might have been an automatic compliment on Madden's part, but Dong E suspected it was the truth. During her ten minutes in the garage's washroom she'd taken a lot of care over what she would wear for her first meeting with Madden, and the choice of a short leather skirt had obviously been a right one: like most men, Madden was a sucker for leather.

'I am delighted to welcome you both to the Nevada TiME facility and I think you'll be amazed at the research we've been conducting here.' Madden paused as another man, older and dressed in a white lab coat, entered the library. 'May I introduce the facility's Chief Scientific Officer, Pierre Boitard. Pierre will be your host, Robert, and will be responsible for answering any questions you may have regarding our work.'

When the introduction had been made, Boitard turned to Rivets. 'Do you have any idea when you'll be ready to make your Temporal Modulation, Dr Vetsch?'

'I am intending to make *two* Temporal Modulations . . .'

'Two!' Boitard glanced towards Madden. 'But we only have one Compression Sphere ready. The cost of preparing a second will be enormous.'

Rivets gave a careless shrug. 'The impression I got from Thaddeus Bole . . .'

A great piece of name-dropping that, decided Dong E.

'. . . is that the ABBA project has top priority. If you need me to contact him to authorise the need for two Modulations . . .?'

A potent threat, and Madden didn't seem to relish being on the wrong end of a tongue-lashing administered by Thaddeus Bole. 'No, no. That won't be necessary. The message I got was to provide you with all the assistance you might need. But may I ask why *two* Modulations will be necessary?'

'To prevent ABBA twigging what we're trying to do and protecting itself from these changes, I intend to divide the programming instructions into two parts. Each half of the retro-program will appear utterly benign, but when they are united, they will initiate changes which will bring ABBA to heel.'

Madden nodded his begrudging understanding. 'Interesting . . . I see now. But surely even this won't be enough to fox ABBA.'

'We've run tests, Sam,' Rivets lied. 'ABBA won't spot a thing.'

Rivets sounded so confident that Madden simply shrugged his acceptance. 'Very well, but you must appreciate that we won't be able to get two Compression Spheres ready before the end of the month.'

'The end of the month will be perfect,' said Rivets. 'It will give Dong E the time she needs to put some finishing touches to the retro-programming we're planning to use.'

Madden gave Dong E a broad smile. 'Then might I suggest, Dong E, that while Robert is involved in his preliminary discussions with Pierre, I give you a tour of the facility? I'll show you things secret even from PINC.'

'That would be wonderful, Sam, but I know how busy you must be . . .'

'Don't give it a second's thought.'

'Perhaps we might start your tour in my office,' said Madden as he guided Dong E into the lift. 'I've put together quite a collection of memorabilia relating to the Cavors – the family of scientists whose work made Temporal Modulation possible – which you might find of interest.'

'Oh, I'm sure it will be fascinating,' purred Dong E, standing a little closer to Madden than was required by the confines of the lift as they were sighed up to the manor's second floor. 'The whole concept of Temporal Modulation is intriguing. I'm so looking forward to seeing TiME itself.'

'Unfortunately, Dong E, that won't be possible,' admitted an awkward-sounding Madden as the doors of the lift opened. 'Only those of Grade Ten or above can enter TiME, and unfortunately you are only Grade Nine.'

Dong E made a moue of disappointment. 'That's such a shame, Sam.'

'I'm sorry,' murmured Madden, ushering Dong E into his office, 'but there's really nothing I can do. Rules, as they say, are rules.'

As she crossed the carpeted floor of the enormous office to sit down in the chair stationed in front of her host's oversized desk, Dong E knew that this was her moment of truth. If Rivets was to succeed, if they were to defeat the Boles, then she had to persuade Madden to let her enter TiME. And that would require her to seduce the man.

So to begin.

As Madden served them coffee, Dong E shucked off her jacket to reveal the white shirt she was wearing beneath, then crossed her legs as artfully as she could. Being of a scientific bent, Dong E had long ago come to the conclusion that seduction wasn't an art, rather it was an empirically based science, so much so that she was able to apply a mathematical precision to her technique that would have astonished her lovers. By her reckoning, her remarkable success in seducing men could be reduced to a simple numerical sequence.

4/117/21/30/10/2

4: the number of lovers she'd had. Practice made perfect.

117 pounds: her ideal weight. Any less and she appeared gaunt, any more and she traded trimness for roundness.

21 years: her age, which was perfect for a woman, combining as it did experience with youth.

30 inches: the distance she was sitting away from Madden's desk, affording him an uninterrupted view of her excellent figure.

10 inches: the amount of thigh she was displaying.

2: the two big, bright, brown and unblinking eyes which she focused so appealingly on the man . . . and, of course, the two nipples that announced their dusty-pink presence under her shirt. She'd lost her bra back in the washroom.

Of course, this mathematical maxim wasn't so much a sequence as a compound equation, with each facet of Dong E's disturbing femininity applying a multiplier effect to the others. The aim was to give the men she aimed to seduce an unmistakable signal that she was ready, willing and able – *very* able – to provide them with maximum sexual satisfaction.

Dong E smiled sweetly towards Madden and was delighted to see, as a consequence of the application of her Formula for Fornication, that she had secured his undivided and very appreciative attention. But never one to rest on her laurels, she shimmied her bottom on the seat of her chair, allowing Madden a better view of the shadowed secrets that lay beneath her skirt. Her efforts were rewarded: Madden had to squirm on *his* chair, presumably better to accommodate his burgeoning lust.

Distracted as he was, Madden struggled with what to say next, so much so that Dong E felt obliged to fill in the space: seduction, after all, required encouragement. 'This must be a wonderful place to live and work, Sam.'

'It's certainly different, Dong E. This house is a replica of Bole Manor, the family home of the Boles in a place called Wold Newton, in Yorkshire.'

'I must say, the grounds and the manor came as something of a surprise. I'd expected the facility to be much more high-tech.'

Madden smiled. 'Oh, appearances deceive, Dong E; the vast majority of the facility is underground. The Nevada site apes the iceberg, with what you see on the surface merely cosmetic dressing for the much larger functionality below. Quite deliberate, of course: it wouldn't do for the Yanks to see what we were *really* up to. The manor serves as an administrative block and a museum celebrating the history of Temporal Modulation. Hence the collection of portraiture.'

Here Madden waved his hand to indicate the rather grim canvases decorating the walls of his office and then leant back in his chair and tapped a fingernail against the picture hanging behind him, a picture that showed a rather diffident-looking man, with curly blond hair and mutton-chop whiskers, dressed rather sombrely in Regency fashion. 'This is the chap who started it all: the gentleman scientist and naturalist Percy Cavor. Cavor's story began on the evening of 13th December 1795, when he was one of those attending a scientific soirée given by Sir Algernon Bole and his fiancée, Lady Maria Steele, in Bole Manor. Their discussions were interrupted by the arrival of a meteor which crashed in a field half a mile away from the manor. Naturally, this caused great excitement and Sir Algernon and his guests went to investigate. Approximately a hundred yards from the crater caused by the meteor's impact Percy Cavor stumbled upon several small fragments of a rock that he first took to be Chondrite, but which on closer inspection proved to be rather more unworldly. Percy Cavor had discovered the element that we have come to know as Cavorite.'

Madden rose from his chair and walked over to a cabinet at the side of the office, removing a small box from one of the cabinet's drawers. 'This is Cavorite in its natural state,' Madden said as he opened the box and unveiled three large pebbles which he placed on the desk in front of Dong E.

Dong E felt a little awestruck. Cavorite was one of the greatest discoveries of all time. Although there had been rumours that the original fragments of meteorite discovered by Percy Cavor still existed, most scientists accepted that he'd destroyed them in order to protect the secrets of Cavorite from rivals. But here they were.

'These were stripped from the main body of the 1795 meteorite when it entered the Earth's atmosphere,' explained Madden. 'The meteorite was the only natural occurrence of Cavorite ever encountered, though being secretive by nature, Percy Cavor kept this discovery to himself. His initial intention seemed to have been to record it as a geological curiosity and it was only when he had taken his find back to his laboratory in London and made a more thorough examination that he came to realize that Cavorite possessed amazing properties, the most important of these being that if an electrical current is applied to the rock it repels gravity, the force of the repulsion directly proportional to the size of the current applied. Cavor also established that if the rock is rotated, this repulsive force is increased, again the faster the spin induced, the more forcefully gravity is repelled.'

'An amazing discovery. He must have been an incredibly talented man.'

'Lucky rather than talented. Prior to his discovery of Cavorite Percy Cavor was regarded as a very run-of-the-mill scientist, but after his close encounter with the meteor he seems to have been a man reborn, his mental faculties expanded to a level where he came to be seen as something of a genius.'

'I'm not sure I follow,' Dong E pantomimed, knowing that weak men like Madden always found stupidity – feigned though Dong E's was – very appealing in their women.

'Cavor speculated that his being bathed in the radiation generated by the meteor as it plunged to Earth provoked a metamorphosis in him. He even suggests in his diary that all those resident in Bole Manor at that time were physically, psychologically and taxonomically mutated by this radiation.'

'Including Algernon Bole?'

'Presumably. You know, I never thought of that! Anyway . . . whatever the cause of his new-found genius, Percy Cavor dedicated his life to identifying and extracting the active agent – Cavorite – from the rock. But despite his efforts he failed, and it was left to his grandson, the über-genius Henry, to finally isolate Cavorite.' Here Madden nodded to a second portrait, this one placed at the far end of the office. 'That is Henry Cavor, the father of Temporal Modulation.'

Henry Cavor looked the epitome of Victorian determination: his eyes glared out at the world, his chin was broad and resolute and his mouth set in an implacable line. This was a man who knew what he wanted and was determined to get it.

'Henry Cavor was an uncompromising individual and extremely demanding,' explained Madden. 'Many thought him mad, but single-handedly he reformed and reformulated physics. It is my belief that if not for the accident that killed him in the prime of his intellectual life and the decision of the Bole family, who had been financing his investigations, to keep his work secret, Henry Cavor would now be as revered as Isaac Newton and Albert Einstein. Henry Cavor was the man who recognised the potential of developing an antipode to Cavorite, a substance he called Etirovac, which rather than repelling gravity would attract it. His hope was that using Etirovac he would be able to create what he called a Gravitational Anomaly.'

'A remarkably prescient hypothesis for a Victorian scientist,' purred Dong E.

Madden smiled as he refreshed their coffee. 'Indeed it was. The first reference to a Gravitational Anomaly is made in Henry Cavor's diary, dated 22nd September 1875, where he defines it as a phenomenon which occurs when an infinitely large gravitational force is contained in an infinitesimally small space. Such an anomaly could, he postulated, be used to distort space–time.' Madden shook his head in mute admiration. 'The tragedy is that his work was prematurely ended when he died suddenly in 1883. Fortunately, though, Henry's son, Edward, was able to continue his father's work.' Madden nodded in the direction of a third portrait hanging near the window of his office.

The face that stared out from the portrait was a sad one. Handsome and fine-featured though Edward Cavor was, he had none of his father's fiery determination about him: his mouth and chin were weak, his blond hair thin and his overlarge blue eyes almost tearful. It was as though being the son of such an unprecedented genius as Henry Cavor had drained him of confidence.

'He was the man who confirmed that a body covered by activated Etirovac will absorb gravity and, as it does so, will become more and more compressed, gravity squeezing it ever smaller. Edward Cavor's experimentation, even using the crude measuring equipment of a century ago, showed the extent of this compression to be almost limitless, and as a body's mass is, of course, unaffected by this compression, this concentration of mass in an infinitely small area has disturbing effects on the space–time continuum. This was the observation that led Edward Cavor to the investigation of black holes.'

'Incredible,' gasped Dong E as she gave an amazed shake of her head which she knew made her untethered breasts move in the most appealing way. Madden's eyes widened and he swallowed hard. 'But surely, as these points of maximum gravity are usually created when a star implodes, they must be astronomically sized events. Doesn't it follow that you would require an astronomically sized laboratory to accommodate such a beast?'

'Edward Cavor contended that if a laboratory could be built which was swathed in Cavorite – and remember, Cavorite repels gravity – then it would be possible to contain a black hole. We would be able to condense' – Madden laughed at his own drollery – 'a black hole into a laboratory-sized phenomenon. This insight gave us unprecedented opportunities to study the oddities of time.'

'Oddities?' prompted Dong E.

'It should be remembered that black holes distort not only space but also the rules governing the fourth dimension, time. Today, it is accepted by all physicists that time slows in the vicinity of a strong gravitational field, the concept known as time dilation. But Edward Cavor went further. He was always perplexed by the thought that black holes were simply bottomless pits into which the universe's light and detritus are sucked, never to emerge. Cavor thought this had a somewhat inelegant finality about it, and as he discovered, there is light at the end of a black hole. To be cosmically coherent, *two* black holes have to be combined to form the top and bottom elements of the same cosmic structure, this called, in the published literature, the Einstein–Rosen Bridge but you must excuse me if I use the original name: the Cavor Duality.' Madden took a sip of his coffee. 'To form a Cavor Duality you need *two* black holes and hence *two* TiME machines to create them . . . or at the very least, a single TiME machine situated at two separate temporal coordinates. It is this Duality that allows us to send our Message Spheres backwards in time.'

'I had always thought, Sam, that time travel is impossible because it violates one of the fundamentals of physics, the concept of causality . . . that time travel cannot happen because cause must always come before effect. We can't drink a cup of coffee,' and here she raised her cup, 'before it's been poured.'

'You are quite right, Dong E, classical physics states this to be the case. But Nature is a perverse creature which enthusiastically ignores man-contrived rules and regulations. Edward Cavor's view was that simply because we are unsure how temporal paradoxes might be resolved, does not mean they *cannot* be resolved. His work demonstrated that causality is not an insuperable hurdle to time travel. At the juncture of two black holes – at the Cavor Interface – the universe is acausal. The Interface is the point of maximum possible gravity and as such is the place where time is frozen, and as time is negated then there can be neither cause nor effect just as there can be no before or after. So in answer to your question, Dong E, causality does not prevent time travel because it does not exist.'

'That's a little difficult to get my head around,' said Dong E with a frown. 'Perhaps if I was to *see* a TiME, I might be better able to understand?'

Madden shook his head mournfully. 'As I say, security regulations make that impossible.'

'Such a shame.' There was an awkward silence: it was time, Dong E decided, to take control of the situation. 'You must have a marvellous view of the park from your office, Sam.'

Madden nodded towards the huge windows that made up one entire wall of his office. 'Be my guest.'

Dong E rose from her chair and oiled across the heavily carpeted floor – her heels silent on the thick Axminster pile – to the huge panoramic windows. Even without being able to see him, she knew Madden's gaze followed her every step of the way, his appreciative evaluation having an almost tactile quality as his eyes slid over and around her undulating body. But never one for half-measures, Dong E pulsed a little more motion into her ass.

Madden must have pressed a button on his desk because as Dong E came to stand in front of the windows – which had hitherto been shaded a dark amber colour – they mutated to crystal-clear and for the first time sunlight penetrated his office. After the gloom, the sunlight streaming into the room was so bright that Dong E was forced to take an involuntary step back and to narrow her eyes. Squinting against the harsh desert sunshine, she looked out over the coiffed and manicured parkland that was the ParaDigm campus.

'It's very beautiful, Sam.'

'Not as beautiful as you, Dong E.'

She looked around and found him staring unblinkingly at her. Now was the moment. 'You know, Sam, I find you very attractive. Maybe it would be possible, when my work here in Nevada is finished, for us to spend some time together . . . some private time.'

'Robert . . .?'

'Don't worry about Rivets. What he doesn't know won't hurt him, now, will it?'

For several long seconds Madden sat motionless, as though he was uncertain quite what to do next. Finally, warily, almost fearful, he raised a hand and beckoned Dong E towards him. She oozed back across the room, around the desk to position herself next to the seated Madden.

Cautiously, he caressed his fingers gently over the toned flesh of Dong E's left thigh. 'You're so, so beautiful, Dong E,' he murmured. 'I've wanted you ever since I first saw you. Your skin . . . it's so soft. It's so wonderful.'

As though dismissive of these oh-so-tentative overtures, Dong E used a foot to push Madden's chair back from the desk, sliding herself into the gap she had created, then hitched her bottom onto the polished wood surface and leant back. The message was unmistakable, she was offering herself to the man. She had to stifle a smile: she had a distinct feeling of déjà vu, as though she had done the exact same thing in another life.

Madden accepted her offer. He rose from his chair and with studied deliberation drifted his two large hands up over her body until they came to Dong E's necklace. He was obviously a little perplexed by how heavy and industrial it was. 'Perhaps you would be more comfortable if you removed this.'

'I can't,' she answered in her sultriest voice. 'It was a present from my mother before she died. I promised never to take it off.' She leant forward to kiss Madden gently on the lips and then, as though struck by a sudden thought, shied away. 'No . . . I'm sorry . . . I can't do this, Sam. I can't torture myself.'

'What? What do you mean?'

'If I'm not allowed access to TiME, I won't be able to help Rivets with his work. Worse, I think he already suspects that I have feelings for you. He'll probably send me back to London.'

Sam Madden gnawed at his lower lip for a few seconds. Finally: 'I suppose it wouldn't do any harm for you to have a *look* at the thing.'

'I would be enormously grateful,' Dong E purred as she lay back over the desk.

2:11

New York City
The Real World: 28 April 2019

The Cold War meant that cooperation between the US–Russian Alliance and the British Empire in the years leading up to 2012 was notable by its absence, but the emergence of a common enemy, bin Laden's al-Qaeda, led to a mellowing of attitudes. As the Alliance became increasingly bogged down in Asia Minor, the British, fearful of al-Qaeda's potential to disrupt the Indian subcontinent – the jewel in the Empire's crown – offered the US and Russia increased military assistance. In an effort to upgrade the Battle Performance Indices of American neoFights, the British government authorised ParaDigm CyberResearch to help in the creation of an upgraded Virtual Training Environment to prepare neoFights for the exigencies of asymmetric war. The product proposed – the Demi-Monde – was notable not only for its realism and effectiveness but also because it was the first time the US authorities had embraced the use of ParaDigm's ABBA quantum computer, having hitherto denigrated it as 'the Beast'.

Without End: A History of the Central Asian War: Colonel
Gilbert G. Perkins, MindSet Publications

Ella knew from her psychology studies that in times of danger their survival instinct made people do predictable things: when a creature is threatened, it tends to return to the place where it has always felt most secure . . . home. And as she was playing the fugitive, that's just what Ella decided to do: she steered the Studebaker east along Route 66 in the direction of New York.

Her pursuers would see it as a sensible choice: the black population in the Big Apple was one of the largest in America so it was a place where she wouldn't stand out quite as noticeably as she did in Kenton territory, and knowing her way around the city would be useful if the FBI – or the Intelligence Bureau – came looking.

Correction: not 'if' they came looking, but 'when' they came looking.

The two-thousand-mile journey from Las Vegas to New York took her just four days, or more accurately, four nights of hard driving. Having to make her flight look as realistic as possible, she had to keep out of the way of any over-inquisitive Highway Patrollers, and to do this she used the nigh on deserted night-time roads. She slept during the day, parking the car in some out-of-the-way place and only venturing out onto the road when the sun was down. When she finally rolled into New York, she was tired, hungry and dirty but, remarkably, still a free woman.

Happy to be back on home turf, she booked herself into a backstreet hotel and settled down to wait. Vanka made her wait ten days, and just as she was despairing of ever hearing from him – or the Intelligence Bureau – she got the long-hoped-for eyeMail.

'Why not have lunch at Sylvia's on Lennox Avenue? I hear the stewed chicken and dumplings are excellent. I love you. Vanka'

The Polly chirped in the suite Colonel Zolotov had taken in the rather plush Hotel New Yorker. Despite his luxurious surroundings, Zolotov disliked America: its technology lagged behind that of the Empire – but then the embargo imposed by the

British to ensure that no 'strategic' technologies found their way into the hands of the Empire's enemies had a lot to do with that – and its cuisine was despicable. But there were compensations, the most notable of which was that with the pound buying four US dollars on the black market, whores were remarkably cheap.

He disentangled himself from the girl he had been using to while away the morning and blinked the Polly into 'talk' mode.

'Zolotov.'

'Colonel, we've just had a tip-off. Seems Ella Thomas will be eating at a soul food restaurant called Sylvia's this lunchtime.'

'Reliable?'

'*Very* reliable. This guy seems to know everything there is to know about Thomas.'

'Get the whole team assembled and make sure they're equipped with stun gas . . . this is a Lilithi we're dealing with.'

They came for Ella just as she was enjoying her lunch. She heard them bullying their way into Sylvia's, heard the screams of the diners. There were four of them. Big men wearing the black-suit-and-white-shirt combo favoured by the British Intelligence Bureau, men armed with automatic pistols who shoved their way past the objections of the restaurant's manager. In the interest of giving a good performance, Ella moved to escape, but they sprayed a gas in her face. The last thing she remembered was sinking to the floor and everything going black.

International

Is Frank Kenton's final prophecy to be realised?

In one week Miss Norma Williams will be hosting the Gathering in Las Vegas of the Fun/Funs, the organisation of young Christians she leads. As the event draws closer so the speculation relating to the ambitions of Miss Williams post the Gathering has grown in intensity, speculation that has become ever more febrile with each passing day.

Just a few short months ago Miss Williams was being dismissed as girl over-whelmed by the fame engendered by her being the daughter of the President of the United States. She was widely seen as a girl fixated on the pursuit of pleasure, a flittertigibbet who would never amount to anything. Since she found God – much to the political discomfort of her atheist father – Miss Williams has proven the doubters wrong.

Since forming the Fun/Funs in October, 2018, Miss Williams has created a re-ligio-political movement of some significance, boasting over forty million members world-wide, six million of whom have been invited to attend the Gathering. Whilst much of this success can, rightly, be attributed to Miss Williams's drive, passion and charisma, it has been the generous patronage of Septimus Bole, the CEO of ParaDigm Cyber-Research, that has caused some disquiet amongst the chattering classes.

Norma Williams:
the goth who
abandoned
Dark Sid...

Feel...

2:12

The Law of Temporal Boundaries: It is a peculiarity of the Temporal Modulation mechanism that it is dangerous to attempt a Modulation directed to a Temporal Nexus at a distance of <u>less</u> than twenty-five years from the initiating Nexus. The consequences of violating this law are aptly illustrated by the destruction of the Tunguska TiME facility in 1908, the explosion of which, had it taken place in an urban area, would have resulted in many thousands being killed. It is therefore imperative that <u>NO</u> Temporal Modulations are conducted within a footprint of 25 years of the Initiation Date.

'Precepts of Temporal Modulation': memorandum
written by Beowulf Bole, 14 December 1933

UFA INTERNATIONAL AIRPORT, BASHKORTOSTAN: THE REAL WORLD

Ella woke to find herself being carried on a stretcher out of an aircraft and across a noisy runway. There was a black-suited guy running along beside her shouting *'Dorogu! Dorogu!'* and *'Raskhodeetes, eto delo ParaDigmy!'* and shoving people aside. She was lifted off the stretcher and bundled into the back of a four-wheel-drive, someone handcuffed her and then . . .

'E smotri, otklyuchi yeyo PINC.'

Which Ella's PINC translated as, 'And make sure her PINC is disabled.'

'*Yest, tovarisch Zolotov.*' ('As you order, Comrade Zolotov.')

One of the soldiers pressed what looked like a hand-held scanner to Ella's forehead, she felt a jolt and then it was as though she'd taken a sip of Alice's 'Drink Me' potion. Everything contracted. One moment she was connected to all the knowledge of the world and the next . . . she wasn't.

'No more Russian, Miss Thomas,' said the man called Zolotov as he clambered into the truck. 'Now that I've fried your PINC, you'll have to tolerate my somewhat flawed English.' He was a tall and very good-looking man possessed of a strange accent, a soufflé of exact English spiced with a flavouring of Russian. 'I apologise for dePINCing you but I had no choice: Thaddeus Bole is very keen to maintain Yamantau as a PINC-free zone.'

Thaddeus Bole? Yamantau?

It took a real effort of will for Ella not to show her panic. Without PINC she was shorn of information, but worse, without PINC she wouldn't be able to send TELEpath messages . . . she wouldn't be able to alert Rivets as to her location. Not that she was given much time to fret: a hood was pulled over her head, she felt the stab of a needle in her arm and then . . . nothing.

TERROR INCOGNITA: THE DEMI-MONDE

They came for Trixie three hours before the Ceremony of Purification was due to commence, taking her across the island to the fortified encampment the UnFunnies had built when they had first come to Terror Incognita, the place where they had been keeping her father prisoner.

She was met by Crowley. 'Your father is ill, Miss Dashwood, and has asked to meet with you.'

When she was shown into the hut where her father had been living for the last forty days she knew instinctively that Crowley was wrong . . . her father wasn't ill, he was dying. In the few weeks since she'd last seen him he had lost an alarming amount of weight and his skin was now the colour of putty. But most worryingly of all, his coughing had become worse: now every time he coughed he spasmed in pain and blood flecked his phlegm.

Trixie's first instinct was to try to comfort her father but she couldn't, finding herself hanging back at the entrance to the hut. He was, after all, the man intent on selling the Demi-Monde down the river, on betraying her world to Heydrich.

'You asked to see me, Father.'

'I am dying, Trixie,' he whispered, 'and so it falls to you to save the Polish workers . . . to save the Demi-Monde.'

Trixie kept her face impassive to disguise her disgust at what her father was intent on doing. 'Rather, you would have me be party to your betrayal of the people of the Demi-Monde. I am sorry for you but I cannot forgive your treachery. Because of you, Crowley will raise the Column, Heydrich and UnFunDaMentalism will be victorious and the UnderMentionable races destroyed.'

'If I don't cooperate then Heydrich will slaughter all the slave workers.'

'Better ten thousand souls perish than twenty million are purged because they do not match the distorted racial idealism of Heydrich.'

'If I do not cooperate then Crowley will have you executed.'

'I am careless of that. I swore a long time ago that my life would be dedicated to the destruction of Heydrich, an ambition that will, it seems, be thwarted by my own father.'

'Yours is a soul hardened by war, Trixie. You have been fighting for so long that you have forgotten that there are ways of opposing evil other than through violence.' He coughed again. 'I have little time left, Trixie, and I need to speak with the daughter I knew before . . . before all this madness began. I would ask *that* Trixie . . . do you trust me?'

The question was so unexpected that for a moment Trixie was stumped for an answer. Her first inclination was to say 'No' – there was only one person she truly trusted and that was Wysochi – but then she realised that this would be an unfair answer. Her father had always – *always* – stood by her and it had only been when she had refused his advice – his *correct* advice – that he had walked away from her.

'I trust you, Father.'

'Then why do you doubt me now?'

'Because what you are doing is wrong.'

'Is it?'

'Of course. By helping to raise the Column to the top of the Pyramid you will fulfil the prophecies written in the *Flagellum Hominum* . . . you will make the Aryan races triumphant.'

'As always, Trixie, your thought process is wonderfully RaTional, but your analysis denies the subtlety of the text. So I say again: do you trust me?'

For a moment Trixie stood silently staring at the wasted form of her father. Finally, reluctantly she uttered a single word, 'Yes.'

'Then you must promise me that you will do everything in your power to raise the Column.'

'Father . . .'

'Promise me!'

Trixie whispered a reply. 'I promise.'

With a pained smile her father slumped back onto his cot. 'Then come closer and I will tell you how the Column may be raised.' Once Trixie had knelt down beside him and brought her ear next to his mouth he whispered his final secret. This done, he patted her on the hand and smiled. 'Keep Wysochi near, Trixie, he is your salvation, and always remember—' Her father never finished the sentence: with a sigh he closed his eyes and died.

Trixie in her time as a soldier had seen many men and women die, so many that she thought she was inured to death, but she had been wrong. As she watched the little remaining colour drain from her father's cheeks and his body take on the contented stillness of those who had passed on to the Spirit World, she felt tears well up in her eyes. Once, long ago, she had sworn that she would never cry again, but now that cold resolve was shattered. Kneeling beside her father, she took his lifeless hand in hers and wept, distraught that she had ever thought to reject his love, his kindness and his understanding. And the worst of it was she hadn't been able to raise the courage to tell her father just how much she had loved him.

But even as she knelt there, lost in her grief, she felt a presence behind her. 'I hope for your sake, Miss Dashwood, that your father made you privy to the secrets of the Pyramid. If he didn't, it will go hard—'

'Damn your threats, Crowley. I will raise the Column.'

THE GATHERING, LAS VEGAS: THE REAL WORLD

Norma had never seen so many cars in all her life. They were still ten miles from Las Vegas and the road was absolutely jam-packed, so much so that their pickup hadn't moved an inch in the last hour. But while she supposed the snarl-up wasn't to be wondered at when six million Fun/Funs were intent on descending on the town, it *was* worrying . . . so worrying that Burl had gone to investigate.

'We've 'ad it; the roads are swamped by bloody Fun/Funs,' he advised when he trudged back to the truck ten minutes later. 'The police are telling everybody to pull their cars off the road and park. They're putting on buses to ferry people to the Gathering . . . people wiv invitations, that is.'

'Maybe—' Norma began but Burl cut her off.

'Nah. Security 'round the Gathering is real tight. We'll never get on a bus. Word is that to prevent gatecrashing all invitations – which we 'ave not got – will be verified against bioSignatures by the bus conductor. We're fucked.'

'So what are we going to do?' asked Norma.

'Go and get some breakfast,' was Burl's reply. 'There's a feeding station up ahead. I fink we should park for a minute an' sort out a plan over a cup of coffee and a stack ov pancakes.'

About ten thousand people had the same idea, but thanks to Burl's indifference to the protests made about his queue-jumping it took them only half an hour to be served. They repaired to the back of the truck to eat their meal.

'As I see it,' began Norma as she sipped her coffee, 'we've only got one option for getting into the SuperBowl and that's "the Chutzpah Tactic": I simply present myself at the headquarters of the Fun/Funs and demand to be taken to the Gathering.'

'Taken to clink most likely,' observed Burl as he dug into his pancakes. 'Iffn this bloke Septimus Bole is 'alf as sharp as you says he is then the chances are that the Intelligence Bureau is looking for you, so all you'd be doing is their job for 'em. My guess is there're gonna be more IB agents guarding the Gathering than flies on dog shit and the one place they're sure to 'ave staked out is the Fun/Funs HQ.'

Oddie gave a nod. 'I agree with Burl. Go calling on the Fun/Funs and you'll really make Bole's day.'

They were flummoxed: they couldn't get in as attendees and they couldn't do it by Norma using her status in the Fun/Funs. Norma took another, longer swig of her coffee and racked her brains for a solution, but try as she might, she couldn't come up with one. Then Fate took a hand.

'Excuse me, Miss, but would you be Norma Williams?'

A trickle of cold fear danced down Norma's spine. She'd hoped the black wig and the shades she was wearing would be enough of a disguise to prevent her being identified by the badniks, but obviously she'd been wrong. Looking up from her coffee, she half-expected to see one of Bole's thugs staring back at her, but it wasn't. Instead it was a rather plump girl with a beaming smile on her face and an 'I'm Going to the Gathering' badge pinned to the shoulder of her rather lurid and very low-cut dress.

Norma blinked. 'Sporting?'

'Gor, that's a miracle, that is! 'Ow'd ya know that was me name, Norma? Only me mum calls me that.' And with that Sporting Chance gave Burl a shove with her bottom to make room for herself next to Norma on the back of the truck.

'Oh, I've got quite a memory for names and faces.'

'Must be one 'ell ov a memory given that we ain't never met before.' A frown crossed Sporting's brow. 'But yous is the *real* Norma Williams, ain't ya?'

Norma gave a quick look around and, satisfied that she wouldn't be overheard, answered. 'Yes, I'm the real Norma Williams, in fact, they don't come any realer than me.'

'Gor, that's mint that is,' and Sporting pulled out a rather dog-eared programme from the bright yellow bag she had slung over her shoulder and pushed it towards Norma. 'Would you sign me programme? It ain't often I gets to meet a real star, like wot yous is, Norma.' A thought seemed to strike Sporting. 'Yous don't mind me calling you Norma, does you, Norma?'

'No, not at all. So you're here to attend the Gathering?'

'Oh, yeah, wouldn't miss it for the world. I'm here wiv the British delegation.' She waved a hand to indicate the thousands of people sitting around them enjoying an al fresco breakfast. 'There's a couple ov 'undred thousand ov us Brits 'ere, 'opin' to 'ave our addictions cured.'

'And what's your addiction?' asked Oddie stiffly, not terribly taken with the way Sporting kept pressing her substantial breasts up against Burl's arm, especially as Burl didn't seem to mind.

Sporting coloured and shuffled her bottom. 'I am besotted wiv the pleasures of the flesh.'

Burl started to laugh, but was silenced by a kick from Oddie.

'Yus, I 'ope that by attending the Gathering God will allow me to find spiritual and sexual peace.' She gave Norma an imploring look. 'Tell you wot, Norma, would you say a few words? These people 'ave come a long way to sees you an' it would mean an awful lot to them.'

TIME FACILITY, NEVADA: THE REAL WORLD

'Prepare to be amazed!' exclaimed Madden as he escorted Dong E and Rivets along the corridor leading to the TiME chamber. And Dong E *was* amazed, amazed what two weeks of being screwed senseless had done for the man's attitude. Gone was the dour and dismal demeanour of a fortnight ago, replaced by one decidedly more frolicsome. He bounced along the corridor in a flurry of arms, legs and over-exuberance, looking and acting more like an excited schoolboy than a serious scientist. He made Dong E feel tired just to be in his presence, but then, she hadn't been getting much sleep of late.

In contrast to Madden, Rivets looked a worried man. He hadn't heard from Ella and therefore he didn't know whether they would be able to do what they had planned. Time had run out. He'd barely uttered a word all morning.

Madden brought them to a halt in front of a door next to the library and placed his hand on a scanner pad. The door clicked open to reveal a spiral staircase beyond . . . a very long spiral staircase, so long that when they reached the bottom Dong E estimated they were at least two hundred feet below ground level. The three of them stepped off the staircase into a steel-lined vestibule, where they were confronted by two black-uniformed and heavily armed Intelligence Bureau agents who spent five minutes examining their IDs and scanning them for contraband.

'You and Dr Vetsch are clear for entry, Professor Madden,' confirmed the IB sergeant, 'but Dr Dong E will have to remove her necklace.'

Dong E raised a protective hand to the necklace and gave Madden an imploring look. It was the one thing of hers that she'd refused to let Madden remove during their trysts. 'I can't, Sam. I promised I'd never take it off.'

Madden nodded his understanding. 'Why can't the doctor wear her necklace?' he asked the guard.

'Metal objects are not permitted inside the chamber, Professor.'

'Are the beads in the doctor's necklace solid?'

'Yes, Professor.'

'Oh, then I think we can make an exception in this case,' said Madden in that supercilious tone that Dong E had come to detest. 'That particular embargo is intended to prevent recording devices or weapons hidden inside hollow objects being taken into the chamber.' With that Madden brushed the guards aside and stepped up to the circular vault door covering the far wall of the vestibule. Above the door was inscribed the ParaDigm tag *Fortes modo tempus mutare possunt.*

'Only the strong can change time,' Madden translated, 'which, in view of what you are about to witness, is a very apt maxim.'

TERROR INCOGNITA: THE DEMI-MONDE

Captain Andrew Roberts was exhausted. Clement had put him in charge of ensuring that the six million pilgrims who had flooded into Terror Incognita on an armada of barges were transported from their landing site on the east of the island to the accommodation that had been built for them close to the

Pyramid. It had been a logistical nightmare that had required him working twenty-hour days for the past week, but now on Fall Eve his task was complete and, dredging up his last reserves of energy, he stood, resplendent in his dress uniform, ready to attend the pre-Ceremony celebrations. And once these celebrations were over, it would be back to London to finish his book on the Great Pyramid, tonight's events providing the final, dramatic chapter.

He couldn't wait to see how the Column would be raised. Puzzle as he had, he had been unable to work out a solution as to how the Column would be lifted to the top of the Pyramid. And the more he studied the *Flagellum Hominum* and the more he stood gazing at the Pyramid, the more he had the nagging feeling that something was wrong . . . that Algernon Dashwood coming to the rescue with the answer to the enigma was a little *too* convenient. Roberts had seen hints of the strength hidden inside the man, and in his opinion he wasn't the type to break as easily as he had.

'Wool-gathering, Comrade Captain? That ain't a quality best seen in military types. Us soldiers have gotta be on our toes all the time.'

General Clement had blindsided Roberts, but then that wasn't to be wondered at: the man moved as quietly as a cat. Roberts gave him a crisp salute. 'I apologise, Comrade General, I was just thinking about how Trixie Dashwood will move the Column up the Pyramid.'

'Don't you fret yourself on that score, Captain, that's the responsibility of His Holiness Comrade Crowley, and he's mighty welcome to it. That little exercise goes wrong and . . .' Clement gave a horrible laugh. 'Well, let's not concern ourselves with Crowley. Let's just move our asses over to the hospitality tent to meet the Great Leader. And ah gotta tell you there's a parcel of fine-looking women in attendance, all of 'em fools for braid and medals.' He gave Roberts a wink which did nothing to settle his nerves.

THE GATHERING, LAS VEGAS: THE REAL WORLD

While Jesus had entered Jerusalem riding on the back of a donkey, Norma Williams entered the SuperBowl standing up on the back of a pickup truck, but though the mode of transport might have been very different, the one similarity was the enthusiasm evinced by the crowds towards their Messiah.

How Norma had found herself on the back of the truck had been a minor miracle. Her initial reaction had been to refuse Sporting's request to address the British Fun/Funs but Oddie had insisted she speak. Immediately the word had rippled out through the packed crowd and she'd found herself being hoisted up onto the back of the truck and a megaphone thrust into her hands. It had escalated from there. Before she quite knew what was happening, she was surrounded by thousands of Fun/Funs, all of them chanting her name.

Thanks to all the speechifying she'd done in the Demi-Monde in support of Normalism, Norma was now a well-practised orator so she'd thanked everyone for coming to attend the Gathering and wished them God's blessing in their attempt to rid themselves of their addictions. And there it would have ended if Oddie hadn't hopped up beside Norma, taken the megaphone and addressed the crowd.

'Ladies and gentlemen,' she shouted, 'in order to show that we are an international fellowship of God-fearing men and women, Norma Williams has asked me to invite the British delegates to escort her into Las Vegas. Will you do that?'

The reply was a resounding – and very noisy – 'Yes!'

A brilliant idea: confronted by tens of thousands of laughing and cheering Fun/Funs who were intent on walking beside Norma's truck as it made its way slowly to the arena, the police simply bowed to the inevitable and pulled the barriers away. And whilst she found the adulation a little overwhelming, Norma did her best to play the part of the Messiah, waving and shaking hands for all she was worth, knowing that, surrounded as the truck was by thousands of her disciples, it was impossible for ParaDigm's security forces to move against her. Do that and there would be a riot, so all they could do as she was driven past was stare at her in impotent fury.

TERROR INCOGNITA: THE DEMI-MONDE

Aleister Crowley allowed his dresser to make the final adjustment to the vestments he had had made for this, the most important night of his life. As he stood examining himself in the mirror, he decided that he was bedecked in a manner befitting the majesty of the ceremony he would be conducting in just a few minutes' time.

'You have the copy of the *Flagellum Hominum*?' he asked his aide.

'Yes, Your Holiness, and the excerpts you will be reading are marked.'

Crowley checked his watch. 'Very well . . . I wish to be informed as soon as the signal rocket is seen.'

TIME FACILITY, NEVADA: THE REAL WORLD

It took over a minute for Madden to dial the correct combinations into the two locks securing the huge door guarding TiME, then with a grunt he hauled it back to reveal the vast cavern beyond . . . so vast that when the three of them stepped inside, the sound of their footsteps on the steel floor echoed around them. As best Dong E could make out in the darkness, they were standing on an observation balcony situated halfway up one of the cavern's huge walls.

'Let there be light,' shouted Madden and immediately the

cavern was drenched in a brilliantly hard light, revealing a steel-sheathed hall with a floor area the size of perhaps a dozen football pitches and a ceiling that stretched at least fifty yards above their heads. As the door sighed shut behind them, Madden stretched his arms wide. 'May I introduce you to TiME #03. Welcome to the future,' he laughed, 'or perhaps that should rather be, welcome to the past.'

CAIRO, THE NOIRVILLE SECTOR: THE DEMI-MONDE

David Crockett checked his watch. Algernon Dashwood had put him in charge of leading the Polish workers from Terror Incognita to the safety of Cairo, where they had been given sanctuary by the People's Free Democratic Republic of NoirVille. The orders he had been given by the major were that he would launch a rocket from NoirVille at eight o'clock on Fall Eve but that he would do so only when he was confident that he and his ten thousand charges were free and not being pursued by the SS.

'Is everything set, Sergeant?'

'Sure is, Captain,' answered Butch Cassidy, 'just waiting on your command.'

Another quick look at his watch. 'Okay, Butch, light the touchpaper.' It was an order that Crockett gave with a heavy heart as it was one that would condemn the major and his daughter to certain death.

There was a *whoosh* and the rocket arched skywards leaving a trail of blue flame in its wake.

MOUNT YAMANTAU, BASHKORTOSTAN: THE REAL WORLD

A hand shaking her shoulder brought Ella back to consciousness. The truck she was riding in stopped and the hood was yanked from her head. She blinked and flinched back: it was night but a savagely sharp spotlight was glaring through the truck's windscreen.

'We're here, Miss Thomas,' said Zolotov.

Come out fighting.

'Just who the fuck do you think you are? I'm an Ameri—'

A slap to the face shut her up. 'You're a nothing, Miss Thomas, and unless you do as you're told, you will be a *dead* nothing. Understand?'

'Where am I?' Ella asked.

'The end of the line,' answered Zolotov with a smirk.

Straightening up in her seat, Ella squinted against the spotlight, trying to see where she was. She was certainly high up in the mountains – dammit, which mountains? – the silhouetted peaks and the thinness of the air told her that, but she'd never heard of mountains with huge steel doors set into their flanks like the ones she could make out beyond the halo of the spotlight. Colossally big steel doors, each of them at least fifty feet tall and as much wide and so heavy that it took almost a minute for them to slide fully open. She saw a green light flick on in the darkness beyond and the truck grumbled forward, coming to a halt inside the mountain. The doors slid shut behind them.

'Welcome to ParaDigm Global, Miss Thomas,' Zolotov announced. 'We are now in the underground security area of the company's Yamantau facility. If you would be so kind as to exit the truck, I'll escort you to your meeting with Dr Thaddeus Bole . . . he's very anxious to meet you.'

Ella suppressed a smile: Bole wasn't the only one anxious to meet and greet. She'd been brought to the Grigori's lair.

PARADIGM HOUSE, LONDON: THE REAL WORLD

As best Septimus Bole could judge, everything was going according to plan: Ella Thomas was now secure in Yamantau; Aleister Crowley had found the solution to the enigma that was the Great Pyramid; Robert Vetsch had written the retro-programming which would bring ABBA to heel; and the actress who was to play Norma Williams was, even as he watched his Polly, being prepared for her appearance before the Fun/Funs.

Yes, everything was going well, everything except that the *real* Norma Williams still remained irritatingly at large. He took a sip of his honeyed water and silently rebuked himself for his needless worrying: the cordon he had placed around Las Vegas would stop even someone as resourceful as her putting in an unscheduled appearance at the Gathering. So, as he sat in the air-conditioned isolation of his office in London, Bole felt he had every right to believe that the Final Solution was proceeding on schedule. His complacency was interrupted by an overexcited voice coming from his Polly.

'Professor Bole, sir, this is Roberts at Gathering Security. We've just gotten word from outside the SuperBowl: Norma Williams is approaching the arena on the back of a pickup!'

The announcement was so unexpected that it took a moment for Bole to assimilate what was being said. 'What? Do we have visual?'

'Streaming cameraBot footage now, sir.'

The Flexi-Plexi on the wall of Bole's office burst into life and there, in glorious 3D, was the image of Norma Williams riding along on a truck and being mobbed by Fun/Fun delegates as she did so. Bole could hardly believe his eyes.

'What are your orders, sir?'

Bole frowned as he frantically tried to decide what to do. His inclination was to order the girl shot, but with thousands of her acolytes massing around the truck this would almost certainly provoke a riot which would seriously disrupt the Gathering. But the one thing he couldn't do was allow Norma Williams to get up on stage and start talking . . . well, not for long anyway. Best to allow her to present herself to the gathered millions and to the world-wide Polly audience and then . . .

He took a deep breath and calmed himself. In many ways this was the optimum outcome. He had always intended that 'Norma

Williams' would be assassinated at the Gathering – better she was a dead martyr than a live Messiah – so rather than killing her stand-in, now he could kill her for real. He spun around on his seat and glowered at the Flexi-Plexi, skewering the Intelligence Bureau colonel in charge of security with a ferocious look.

'Have your sniper ready to fire on my command.'

He'd blame the assassination on Ella Thomas and the Black Panthers.

MOUNT YAMANTAU, BASHKORTOSTAN: THE REAL WORLD

Ella clambered out of the truck to find herself standing in what looked to be a vast underground car park, the unrelenting expanse of concrete only leavened by the occasional ParaDigm logo. Two IB agents grabbed her by the arms and led her towards a small windowless room off to one side of the car park, a room that was kitted out as a hospital diagnostic suite.

'I must apologise,' purred Zolotov, 'but my employer, being of a somewhat mysophobic disposition and, hence, having a pathological detestation of germs, insists that all visitors to the Yamantau facility are screened for disease.' Zolotov laughed. 'Fortunately, that necessitates the removal of your clothes.'

They cut her clothes from her – the handcuffs remaining firmly in place during the whole procedure – and then she was subjected to a body scan and obliged to provide blood, saliva and urine samples.

'As I say,' observed Zolotov as he sat watching Ella being tested, 'all this is necessary to screen visitors to Dr Bole's enclave for medical abnormalities, but my own opinion is that he simply takes pleasure in humiliating beautiful girls. It's a pastime I have some sympathy with.'

'So where is this "enclave" of Bole's?'

'I suppose there's no harm in telling you. Mount Yamantau is in the Urals . . . an area of the Urals run by the British. Back in '47 the Soviets didn't have the one billion pounds they needed to pay for ParaDigm's anti-Plague vaccine so ParaDigm demanded a one-thousand-year licence to exploit the mineral and energy reserves of Bashkortostan. This sort of capitalist *bouleversement* would in normal circumstances have been anathema to the Communists, but, with the Plague marching across the Steppe, the Central Committee swallowed its political pride and agreed. Since then Bashkortostan has been, to all intents and purposes, part of the British Empire.'

'She's clean,' announced the technician in charge of the screening.

Zolotov rose slowly to his feet and brushed errant cigarette ash from his trousers. He gave Ella a smile. 'You have a quite superb body, Miss Thomas, and even a man as desiccated in outlook as Doctor Bole won't fail to be moved when you present in his office stark naked. I just hope that once he's finished with you I might be permitted to supervise your denouement. I can be very imaginative when it comes to torturing beautiful women.'

'Come near me and I'll rip your throat out.'

Zolotov took a long, reflective drag of his cigarette, then stepped forward and drifted a finger along Ella's cheek. 'You do not frighten me, Miss Thomas. Oh, I know you possess strange abilities, but not abilities, I fancy, that can defy steel chains or a sharp knife. I will make you regret those words.'

With that he nodded to the two IB agents lurking in the doorway and together they frogmarched Ella out of the room and along a featureless corridor that stretched deep into the mountain, stopping outside a door with a red light shining above it. Zolotov pressed his hand to the pad next to the door jamb, the red light segued to green, the door slid open and Ella was pushed into an antechamber lined entirely in stainless steel.

'Once inside Dr Bole's office,' Zolotov instructed, 'you are not to move beyond the yellow lines which prescribe the area visitors may occupy, as to do so will activate a lethal defence mechanism. Also be advised the ImPeno-Glass screen which separates Dr Bole from the visitors' environment cannot be breached except by the most profound of munitions . . . munitions that, as I am delighted to confirm, you do not have hidden about your person.'

He pressed a button set in the wall and with a sigh – Bole's office was obviously set at a higher pressure than the anteroom – part of the wall slid back, giving Ella access to the dark emptiness beyond.

'Welcome to Hel,' Zolotov whispered as he pushed her inside.

TERROR INCOGNITA: THE DEMI-MONDE

Captain Roberts had to admit that he had been surprised when General Clement had awarded him the honour of accompanying him to the Ceremony of Purification. Whilst the cynic in Roberts told him that he had only been shown such preference because Clement had executed most of the other officers who had come with him to Terror Incognita, he determined to put these troubling thoughts to one side and to savour both the evening and his temporary elevation to the status of a VIP.

He had enjoyed being introduced to the Great Leader and to his very attractive daughter, Aaliz; he had enjoyed the rather sumptuous banquet that had been laid on for the dignitaries; he had enjoyed having his photograph taken for the souvenir issue of *The Stormer*; and most of all he had enjoyed being included in the ranks of the great and the good when they had been led to their seats in the main stand. Thus it was a well-fed and slightly tipsy Roberts who took his place in the seat directly behind General Clement and settled down to witness an event that, he suspected, would be one to tell his grandchildren about.

And though Roberts, as a closet RaTionalist, was naturally suspicious of UnFunDaMentalist ceremonial, he had to admit that the ForthRight did spectacle very well. The bleachers which had looked so workmanlike and simple during the day, once they were occupied by the six-million-strong audience, were transformed into a multicoloured patchwork of ForthRight power. The military bands had played and marched with precision while the pennants fluttered enthusiastically from the flagpoles lining the newly built railway running, as straight as an arrow, from pier to Pyramid.

The Pyramid . . .

With every moment that had passed since Dashwood had unlocked the power of the Pyramid it had begun to glow with increasing brightness until now it lit up the evening, this, according to Crowley, a sign that the dawn of a new age was at hand . . . the end of the Confinement. And with the Column having been positioned on the hexagonal platform at the bottom of the staircase that led to the pinnacle of the Pyramid, everything was ready for the Ceremony to begin.

But still a doubt nagged at the back of Roberts' mind that something was wrong.

TERROR INCOGNITA: THE DEMI-MONDE

As Reinhard Heydrich moved to take up his position on the stand in front of the Pyramid, he had to admit being nervous. He remembered how Norma Williams had disrupted the ceremony at the Crystal Palace and worrying away at the back of his mind was that, somehow, she might connive to do it again. Ever since that girl had come to the Demi-Monde all his carefully constructed plans had gone awry. The one comfort he had was that now Norma Williams was back in the Real World and he had Aaliz – the *real* Aaliz – standing by his side.

But as he looked out over the vast crowd gathered around the

Pyramid – six million of them – he realised that there was no possibility of him being denied victory. In thirty short minutes the Column would be atop the Pyramid and all the racial contaminants that denied the purity of the Demi-Monde would be destroyed . . . the UnderMentionables purged, and the Pre-Folk – the Aryans – would have reclaimed their world.

'You should wave, Father,' he heard Aaliz advising and he automatically raised his hand in acknowledgement of the crowd. The cheer he received showed him that Aaliz's sojourn into the Real World had honed her political instincts. He supposed he shouldn't be surprised; Aaliz had been a revelation during the tour of the ForthRight intended to persuade people to attend the Ceremony, her enthusiasm and beauty relieving his dour presence on the hustings. Recognising that it was Aaliz the crowd wanted to see, he urged her forward so that she could share the adulation and as he did so he felt his daughter's hand squeeze his arm.

'The rocket has been fired, Father,' she whispered.

Heydrich glanced in the direction of NoirVille and saw the trail of blue flames snaking through the dark sky. Immediately there was a fanfare of trumpets signalling that it was time for the final act of the Ceremony of Purification to begin.

Heydrich moved nearer to the bank of microphones. 'Citizens of the ForthRight . . . fellow UnFunDaMentalists, we are gathered here in Terror Incognita to witness the Second Coming of the Pre-Folk and the ending of the Confinement.' His voice was amplified a thousandfold by the galvanicEnergy-powered microphones, the words he spoke echoing out through the chill of the night, announcing to the Demi-Monde that the old order was dying and something new and terrible in its certainty was rising to take its place. 'Tonight we usher in the age of the Aryan . . . the age of the superman. With the fulfilment of the prophecies enshrined in the *Flagellum Hominum* once more will we come to

ABBA's grace and be reborn as we were before the Fall . . . be reborn as Pre-Folk, pure and unsullied by the contamination that is the UnderMentionable.' He glanced towards Crowley. 'Let the Ceremony of Purification begin.'

TERROR INCOGNITA: THE DEMI-MONDE

This was Aleister Crowley's moment. He took his place beside the Great Leader at the microphones and waited for a moment before speaking, savouring the crowd's expectant silence. Tonight he would be ordained as the foremost mage in all of the Nine Worlds. Tonight he would remodel humanity. Even now, before the Column had been set in its final resting place, he could sense the vast potential energy contained in the Pyramid waiting to be released. It was a heady feeling to have so much power at his command, he felt almost dizzy with excitement and it took real effort for him to stand serene in front of the vast crowd, the six million men and women who would be the genesis of the new order of Man.

Taking a deep, calming breath, he began. 'My fellow UnFun-DaMentalists, as the Great Leader has told you, tonight we gather together to instigate a new world order. You, as bearers of the Order of the ForthRight, have proven yourselves to be worthy to become one with ABBA, to attain ABBAsoluteness. Together we will usher in the Second Coming of the Pre-Folk, and to do this we must unleash the power of the Great Pyramid, a power that has lain dormant for a millennium. Tonight, for the first time in a thousand years, the Column of Loci will, once again, be returned to its rightful place on the summit of the Pyramid.'

He paused for a moment to allow his audience to absorb the import of what he had said.

'I will now read from that most sacred of all texts, the *Flagellum Hominum*, the verses telling of the Second Coming of the Pre-Folk and the attaining by ManKind of ABBAsoluteness.

The Final Moment.	The Old Yields
To the New.	The Duality of Life
Merges in Ying.	It is the One who
Brings the Column	to Rest who
Shall be the Victor.	

Let the Column be raised.'

Crowley stabbed out an arm to point in a dramatic fashion towards the Column. Immediately a dozen arc lights flared into life illuminating the Column in a light so bright that he had to half-close his eyes against the blinding glare. The Column glowed, the Mantle-ite aura swathing it pulsating with an other-worldly incandescence.

TERROR INCOGNITA: THE DEMI-MONDE
As Roberts listened to Crowley read from the *Flagellum Hominum*, the inchoate thoughts that had been rattling around his subconscious suddenly coalesced and suspicion mutated into certainty.

TIME FACILITY, NEVADA: THE REAL WORLD
'My God!' gasped Dong E, as she looked around TiME. 'It looks like something out of Korda's *Things to Come*.'

'An excellent film,' crooned Madden. 'I am a great admirer of H.G. Wells, he was a profound prescient and TiME is a miracle of science worthy of one of the man's books. There are perhaps fewer than a dozen people who have stood where you are standing, Dong E, and all have uttered words which conveyed exactly the same wonderment.'

Dong E gazed around her trying to take in the enormity of TiME. To her left was what she supposed to be a control room, though it was as brutally fortified as an army pillbox. High above her, set pointing straight down from the steel-swathed ceiling were what looked like a couple of huge cannons designed as props in a Flash Gordon film. And in the very centre of the floor stretching fifty yards below where she was standing hovered two huge metal spheres, each a good sixty feet in diameter.

'It's quite, quite breathtaking. Is that green sheen on the walls what I think it is?'

'Yes. Every surface of the chamber is impregnated with Cavorite – this necessary to contain the black hole – the black *holes* – we will be conjuring. But before we get down to business, Dong E, perhaps I should give you and Robert a guided tour.'

THE GATHERING, LAS VEGAS: THE REAL WORLD

For Sally Summers this was the role of a lifetime. With Norma Williams back in rehab they had had to find a stand-in and she had got the gig. Okay, she wouldn't be able to put it on her résumé, but the pay was really good and the producer had told her that it was a role she'd be asked to reprise. Sure, playing Norma Williams was a little weird, but with the girl being ill, she guessed they didn't have any other option but to PollyMorph her. Like Sally's agent always told her: the show had to go on. Anyway, she liked being treated as a star, with all these make-up people fussing around her and the guys from the wardrobe department making sure she looked great.

'Thirty minutes to PollyCast,' she heard the producer – a really fit guy Sally would be putting moves on later – shouting at the crew. Way she heard it, the producer always got to fuck his leading lady and that was one tradition that Sally was determined to uphold.

'Is the PollyMorph loaded?'

'Ready to roll,' came the answering shout.

Sally hadn't been over-pleased when she heard that she'd be Morphed for the role but then, she supposed, she'd only got the part because she was the same size as Norma Williams and bore a passing resemblance to the girl. And anyway, like her agent said, the ability to imitate a well-known character was what separated the really good actors – like Sally – from the dross.

And she would be performing in front of a huge audience: sure, her image carried on the Polly and projected up onto the giant Flexi-Plexis around the arena might be tweaked a little but it was still a live gig. Like her agent said, proper actors had to *commune* with their audience in order to properly inhabit their role.

'Actor?'

'Ready!' her hairdresser shouted back as he gave Sally's blonde wig a final fluff.

And when Sally checked in the mirror she had to admit that she was indeed 'ready'. Sally wondered if she should put the hairdresser down for a "thank-you fuck" but then he looked gay.

Too bad.

THE GATHERING, LAS VEGAS: THE REAL WORLD

Burl did his best to keep the truck edging forward but it was a delicate business. With so many people jumping and dancing around the pickup it was difficult to nudge his way through the crowd without running any of the buggers over. But somehow he managed it. With Oddie yelling instructions to him over the din of the cheering Fun/Funs he gradually manoeuvred the truck through the SuperBowl's gates – giving the finger to the IB agent guarding it as he went – and then steered in the general direction of the stage. He gave another long toot on the truck's air horn. He was beginning to enjoy himself.

Such was the press that it took him almost thirty minutes to drive the mile from the gate to the foot of the stage, and the nearer he got to the stage, the more impressed he became. Sure, he'd expected something grand and lavish, but this was almost beyond belief. It was a rock festival stage writ large, decorated by huge faux-Grecian columns and equipped with Flexi-Plexi screens bigger than any he'd ever imagined existed. And there standing in front of the stage was a huge pyramid, modelled on the Monument, that seemed to shimmer with a green glow under the arena's floodlights.

Courtesy of the cameraBots hovering around the truck, his astonishment was shared with all of the millions of people pressed into the SuperBowl, his picture projected onto the giant Flexi-Plexis, showing him, mouth ajar, in fifty-foot-high 3D. An embarrassed Burl gave the crowd a wave, just grateful he hadn't been caught picking his nose.

But if Burl was astonished, it was as nothing to the amazement of the singer who had been trilling away when Norma made her entrance. Immediately the singer realised who it was that was causing all the fuss, he waved to his band to stop and then pointed in Norma's direction.

'Ladies and gentlemen, it gives me enormous pleasure to announce that Norma Williams, leader of the Fun/Funs, has arrived. I ask you to give her the welcome she deserves.'

MOUNT YAMANTAU, BASHKORTOSTAN: THE REAL WORLD

Hel was an accurate description of Thaddeus Bole's office: as the Norse netherworld had also been called Sleet-Cold, the parallels, Ella decided, were obvious. Walking into Thaddeus Bole's office was like walking into an enormous refrigerator.

She shivered: refrigerators were not places to be standing in when all you were wearing was a smile and a load of goose-bumps.

Blinking, she stepped further into the room, trying to adjust her eyes to the gloom but it was difficult. There was only a single low-powered reading lamp providing illumination, this sited on a desk on the far side of the room, the desk separated from the main part of the office by a floor-to-ceiling and wall-to-wall

ImPeno-Glass security screen. With the room being so huge and the desk set so far back from the door, this timid illumination did little to lessen the darkness, the room's shadows being sculpted rather than extinguished by the light.

Apart from the desk and an array of wall-mounted clocks, the room was almost bare: no bookcases, no filing cabinets and no pictures or ornamentation of any kind. As far as Ella could see in the half-light, the only other furniture was a pair of guest chairs arranged in front of the ImPeno-Glass screen, chairs which looked so uncomfortable that the impression they communicated was that Bole was determined his visitors' stay in his sanctum would be brief. The thought flicked through Ella's head that perhaps this choice of seating was as popular with Bole's visitors as it was with the man himself.

Ella saw her host enter the office and sit himself down behind the desk. 'Good morning, Miss Thomas,' came the greeting from behind the screen. 'My name is Thaddeus Bole. I am Grand Ipsissimus of the Most Secret Order of Grigori. Welcome, Lilith, to the home of my people.'

TERROR INCOGNITA: THE DEMI-MONDE

'It is time,' the priest said as he unlocked the cell where Trixie was being held. 'The signal rocket has been fired by the Rebel Crockett indicating that the Polish workers are safe and now His Holiness expects you to fulfil your side of the bargain.'

A weary Trixie stood up from her bed. 'My father made me swear an oath to raise the Column and we Dashwoods are nothing if not dutiful of oaths. There is, though, one thing—'

'You are not in a position to make demands, Rebel Dashwood.'

Trixie laughed. 'With six million people waiting for me to perform my miracle I don't think there's ever been a better time to make demands. I'm not going anywhere unless I have Major Wysochi by my side.'

'His Holiness anticipated that this might be one of your requests.' He stood aside to allow Wysochi – a somewhat bashed-about Wysochi – to be pushed into the cell.

'Good evening, Colonel.'

'I think, Feliks, that given the circumstances we find ourselves in, we can dispense with the honorifics. It's so good to see you again.' She bent forward and kissed him on the lips.

'Enough,' snarled the priest, and Trixie allowed him to lead her and Wysochi from the cell. It took her a moment to acclimatise herself to the scene that awaited her. There were *so* many people attending the Ceremony: it had been one thing to hear Crowley boast that six million people would be gathering on Terror Incognita but it was quite another to actually see them. It seemed to her remarkable that so many people could have been persuaded to make the trip, but then, as she looked up to the Pyramid that flickered with a strange shimmering light, she realised that this was a special night . . . a night when no one could refuse to be present. This was the night when the fate of the Demi-Monde would be decided . . . the night when the victor of Ragnarok would be crowned. It was then that the immensity of what she was doing was brought home to her, and for an instant she despaired. She had fought so hard against Heydrich, but now the struggle was over: she had been betrayed by love . . . her father's love for her. He had been determined to save her and was willing to do anything to achieve that end, even if it meant surrendering the Demi-Monde to the ForthRight and to the corrupt creed of UnFunDaMentalism. That he could do such a thing was almost beyond belief, but he had.

What made it all the more depressing was that she was sure that as soon as she contrived to have the Column moved to the summit of the Great Pyramid, Heydrich would order her and Wysochi executed. Her father had been blinded by love and now she was trapped by her oath to him.

As always, Wysochi seemed to sense her dilemma. 'Don't worry, Trixie, your father was a clever man; he'd never ask you to do something that was wicked or senseless.'

Trixie nodded and then turned to the priest. 'I will need the loan of a pocket watch . . . one with a second-hand.'

The priest frowned. 'That will take a moment to procure, Rebel Dashwood.'

TIME FACILITY, NEVADA: THE REAL WORLD

Rivets could feel the sweat forming under his jacket and this despite the chilled ambience of TiME. He was sweating on Ella. He had tried to give her a TELEpath prompt but there had been no response, so all he could assume was that either she was dead or her PINC had been disabled. And without Ella it would be impossible to destroy the Grigori.

A distracted Rivets followed Madden and Dong E down the steel staircase to the floor of the chamber, only half-listening to what Madden was spouting.

'TiME is, in essence, a device that compresses matter to impossibly small dimensions. It achieves this by the use of the solid iron Compression Spheres such as the pair you see standing before you, each covered with a wafer-thin sheet of Etirovac, the Etirovac activated by passing almost a million volts of electricity into the Sphere. When a Sphere is rotated at a velocity of two hundred thousand revolutions per second the activated Etirovac absorbs gravity and compresses it to nothingness.'

Rivets felt Madden looking at him, obviously expecting him to respond. 'Surely there aren't any bearings capable of withstanding those sort of mechanical loadings.' Not that he gave a shit . . . all he was worried about was Ella.

'The Compression Spheres are suspended on Cavorite Couplings,' explained Madden, and here he pointed to a cylindrical node about a metre high and a metre in diameter standing on the floor directly beneath each Compression Sphere. 'The anti-gravity force emitted by the coupling holds the Sphere aloft, which obviates the need for a mechanical connection, and hence there is no friction.'

Madden shepherded them nearer to the huge Compression Spheres, giving them a better appreciation of the enormous weight and size of the iron balls. Fortunately, Dong E seemed to sense how distracted Rivets was and took over the conversation. 'How small will the Compression Spheres be . . . er, compressed to?' she asked.

'To nothingness. As a consequence of its ferocious rotation and its Etirovac coating, a Compression Sphere is condensed to a size so minute it is beyond the capacity of any instrument to measure. Suffice it to say, by my calculations, when the sphere is fully compressed it has a density of about 20 trillion trillion trillion tons per cubic inch, enough to distort space–time . . . enough to create a black hole. And when two of these rents in space–time are linked, they produce a bridge – a Duality – through which we transmit our Message Spheres.'

Madden directed their attention towards the ceiling. 'Each floor-mounted Cavorite Coupling has its twin on the ceiling. By the careful positioning of these two couplings it is possible to configure the angle and direction of the black hole created by the Compression Sphere, this being necessary to ensure that the two black holes – the one we are making here in the present and the one already formed in the past – can be locked together to produce a Cavor Duality. The computers operating TiME automatically compensate for the movement of the Earth – its orbit around the Sun, its rotation, even continental drift – to ensure the synchronisation of the two black holes we are trying to mate.'

'What's the thing that looks like a ray gun up on the ceiling?' asked Dong E.

'By calling it a "ray-gun", Dong E, you are much closer to the truth than you realise, though it would be better to call it a "rail-gun". This is the Impellor Unit which injects the Temporal Projectile containing the Message Sphere into the centre of the Cavor Interface – the junction between the two black holes that make up the Duality. As a Projectile has to survive the rigours of traversing the Interface, the coating of Cavorite we give it must be almost an inch thick and, whilst the cost of producing so much Cavorite is simply colossal, without it the Message Sphere wouldn't survive. When the Interface opens – and remember, it opens for just the briefest of moments – the Projectile is fired into its mouth, the Cavorite coating the Projectile bullying aside the gravitational elastic trying to close the Interface.'

'How does it know when to fire?' asked Dong E.

'The merging of two black holes to form a Duality is signalled by a huge burst of light released when gravity is negated. The Impellor is fired the instant this luminescence reaches a certain level of intensity.' Madden gave his two guests a smile. 'Now let me show you the Control Room.'

MOUNT YAMANTAU, BASHKORTOSTAN: THE REAL WORLD

Even without the assistance of PINC Ella knew who Thaddeus Bole was, but more importantly she knew *what* he was. Thaddeus Bole was a Grigori. Not a *pure* Grigori, but pure enough that his Fragile aspect had been almost completely subsumed. He was very tall, had luminescently white skin and when he took off his shaded glasses Ella could see his snake eyes in all their repellent glory.

Determined to take the bull by the horns, Ella strode across the room, coming to stand a couple of feet shy of the yellow line and the 'lethal defence mechanism' Zolotov had spoken about. She plonked herself down on one of the chairs and then blew on her hands trying to generate some warmth.

Thaddeus Bole noted the action. 'Are you cold, Miss Thomas?'

'No, I'm not "cold". . . I'm somewhat south of "cold"; I think I'm well into freezing my ass off territory. If I were being surveilled by people using thermal imaging equipment they'd be forced to conclude that I have no feet.'

'Do I detect sarcasm?' There was a note of peevishness in Bole's voice.

'Irony, Bole, irony.'

'I am not an enthusiast of irony, Miss Thomas.'

'Nor, it would appear, of central heating,' Ella riposted.

'And in this surmise you are correct. I prefer to occupy an environment held at a low ambient temperature in order that bacteria are not encouraged to breed.'

'Ah, yes, the all-powerful Thaddeus Bole is forced to live in a microbiologically sterile atmosphere, otherwise he will be brought low by the smallest of pathogens. Do you never stop to think, Bole, that if Nature is so antagonistic towards you then, perhaps, you have no place in this world?'

'Rather, I believe, it is indicative of my mastery of Nature that, despite these deficiencies, I still survive.'

'So tell me, how many Grigori are there hiding away here?'

'Pure-blooded Grigori . . . a little under a thousand.'

'A thousand? So few? After so many thousands of years I'd have thought—'

'You of all people, Miss Thomas,' Bole interrupted, 'must know that we Grigori were never the most . . . passionate of people and inbreeding has somewhat diminished our ability to sire offspring.'

'Inbreeding also produced the albinism, heliophobia, argyria and alliumphobia that your type is afflicted with, Bole, and, of course, your need to regularly ingest blood. How does it feel to be a vampire?'

'I find that epithet somewhat insulting, Miss Thomas. It is true that the Grigori have suffered some genetic diminishment during our time hidden here in Yamantau, but now, thanks to the Demi-Monde, we are on the brink of breaking free of these genetic shackles. The Grigori are poised to take command of this world. Unlike the Lilithi – of whom you are the last surviving representative – the Grigori have a very real future on this planet. Admittedly, we will have had to arrange things – *rearrange* things – so that we bring a little fresh blood into our breeding pool, but this is now well in hand. Of course, in the course of this rearrangement, the role of the Fragiles is to be the subject of some . . . amendment' – Bole chuckled to himself – 'but life as fodder is, I believe, one they will find infinitely preferable to one of extinction.'

TERROR INCOGNITA: THE DEMI-MONDE

It took Captain Roberts a couple of minutes to summon the courage to tap General Clement on the shoulder and the look he got persuaded him that he might have been better advised not to have disturbed the man. Clement seemed to be in very intimate conversation with the young lady to his right, a young lady who, from the amount of cleavage she was displaying, wasn't particularly mindful of the more restrictive tenets of UnFunDaMentalism.

'What the fuck do you want, Roberts, cain't you see that ah'm a trifle engaged with Lady Agnes here?'

'I apologise for my interruption, Comrade General, but I think there may be something wrong happening.'

'The only thing "wrong", Captain Roberts, is yo' jabbering.'

'General . . . I'm sorry . . . the ForthRight is in danger.'

Roberts' desperation must have communicated itself. Clement pushed the doxy's hand off his thigh and turned his full attention towards the captain. 'In danger, Captain?'

'I think His Holiness might have misinterpreted the *Flagellum Hominum*.'

Clement stared at the captain for several long seconds. 'You *sure*, Captain? 'cos if you're wrong, your nuts are gonna end up in a wringer that's being cranked mighty hard.'

Roberts swallowed. 'I'm very sure, Comrade General.'

'Explain.'

And that's what Roberts did.

THE GATHERING, LAS VEGAS: THE REAL WORLD

Norma had seen people crowd-surf before but had never imagined it would happen to her. She was lifted off the back of the truck, passed over the heads of the Fun/Funs, and then set gently down at the foot of the stairs leading up to the stage. She waited a moment for Burl and Oddie to join her and was just about to climb up on stage when Oddie put a restraining hand on her arm.

'I think you could do with a little TLC,' she advised and it took just one look at the huge Flexi-Plexi screens for Norma to judge that it was good advice. Riding on the back of a pickup truck through the Nevada desert wasn't the greatest way of preparing for a performance that would be beamed to millions – billions – of Polly viewers. Signalling to the singer that he should carry on playing, she ducked into the wings.

TERROR INCOGNITA: THE DEMI-MONDE

The priest returned five minutes later and handed Trixie a rather fine Hunter pocket watch which, she was pleased to see, possessed a second-hand. She gave the stem a whirl to make sure that it was properly wound and then walked towards the Column. 'Okay, Wysochi, we're going to have to synchronise our movements.' She leant closer to him so that the priest couldn't hear what she said. 'My father's solution to the enigma that is the raising of the Column turned on the phrase in the *Flagellum Hominum* that says "progress the Column by seconds". His belief is that the numbers on each of the nine platforms relate to the number of seconds they must be rested upon in order that they may be activated. The number on the first platform is two so it's a quick two-second hop on and off.'

THE GATHERING, LAS VEGAS: THE REAL WORLD

Sally Summers wasn't too sure what was going on. One moment she was standing there trying to get herself into the zone ready to perform as 'Norma Williams' and the next all hell had broken loose. People started running around, there were shouts of 'Norma Williams is here' and the whole backstage area descended into chaos. Sally wasn't happy: as far as she knew, Norma Williams was in the Betty Ford Clinic so whoever was posing as her was a fraud, and more importantly a fraud who was intent on stealing her gig.

She had just begun to make her displeasure known to the producer in a very loud and very scatological manner when she was confronted by a very big man wearing a porkpie hat and a suit that appeared to be covered in desert dust.

'Gimme that wig!' he demanded then tore the blonde wig from Sally's head and tossed it towards an even bigger woman who seemed to be the minder of the Norma Williams who had just materialised out of nowhere.

This was not, Sally decided, how a star should be treated. 'You fucker!' she snarled as she launched herself at the man with her claws extended.

With almost casual ease he whacked her on the chin and the last thought Sally Summers had as she descended into unconsciousness was that she should remember this experience, it might be useful in her acting career.

TERROR INCOGNITA: THE DEMI-MONDE

Clement listened to what Roberts said and the more the captain talked the more convinced Clement became that he was right. For an instant he thought about consulting with Crowley but he knew there wasn't time for that. He had to act and he had to act quickly, this a decision made all the easier by the thought that stopping the Ceremony would really fuck up Crowley's weekend.

Anyway, if he prevented Trixie Dashwood fouling things up, he would be the hero of the hour. Shit, he might even be nominated as the Great Leader's heir apparent.

'Get a detachment of men together, Roberts, and bushwack Trixie Dashwood before she gets to the top of the Pyramid.'

THE GATHERING, LAS VEGAS: THE REAL WORLD

Herded by Oddie, a veritable gang of dressers and stylists descended on Norma and it took them only a couple of minutes to change her black wig for her trademark blonde one and to powder and paint her to perfection.

'Ready?' asked Oddie. Norma gave a nod. 'Then I think it might be better and safer if you used *this* microphone. I'll organise it with the producer.'

A sensible idea, thought Norma as she stepped up to the microphone.

She took a deep breath. This was her moment. She had thought long and hard about what she would say, but now all those clever lines and phrases seemed to disappear from her head. The pyramid set in front of the stage was now glowing an eerie green, reminding her that if Trixie failed in the Demi-Monde, the six million Fun/Funs attending the Gathering would be converted into nuGrigori. And if Rivets wasn't able to subvert noöPINC, then there would be nothing to stop Septimus Bole destroying humanity.

She pushed these worries away. She had to believe in her friends . . . she had to believe in ABBA. She had to give all the people packing the SuperBowl and everybody watching via Polly a new message . . . she had to harness the good will of all these millions of people to make a better world and to prepare them for the coming of InfoCialism.

She felt the loving presence of Shelley beside her, heard his whispered encouragements . . . his whispered endearments. Yes, she would do this for Shelley, for her lost love. The producer cued her and on the count of five the cameraBots hovering around her went live. Instantly, all around the SuperBowl, the giant Flexi-Plexis flared into life, showing her in eye-popping 3D. She stretched out her arms in an appeal for quiet and almost magically the SuperBowl went silent. The feeling of power that coursed through Norma was intoxicating, making her feel light-headed, and she had to pause for a moment to settle herself. Then she began, 'Thank you all so very much for your warm welcome. I am Norma Williams and I welcome you to the Gathering.'

PARADIGM HOUSE, LONDON: THE REAL WORLD

Septimus Bole frowned as he tried desperately to work out just what Norma Williams intended to do. Surely she realised that it was too late, that he and the Grigori were on the brink of victory. Nothing the girl could say would be able to halt the Final Solution. But to err on the side of caution, he leant over and pressed the 'transmit' button on his Polly. 'Operative One, fire on my command.'

THE GATHERING, LAS VEGAS: THE REAL WORLD

Tony Shepherd was a veteran of the wars in Afghanistan and in Pakistan. In his career as a sniper he'd killed Talibans, Uzbeks, Tajiks, Russians, Chinese, Americans and one unfortunate Frenchman who'd shown up in the wrong place at the wrong time. He had fifty-seven confirmed kills to his name, but this, his fifty-eighth, was destined to be the simplest . . . and the most lucrative. At just over a mile the range he was operating at wasn't particularly excessive, the target area was floodlit, there was no wind, and, best of all, the girl he was aiming at was standing stock-still in the middle of an empty stage. Earning a million pounds didn't come any easier than this. He settled himself next to the window of the lighting tower facing the stage, eased a sloBurst round into his M107 rifle and then snuggled the rifle's stock back into his shoulder. Brushing an errant lock of hair off his forehead, he brought his right eye up to the telescopic sight to check his target, making a small adjustment to focus the sight's cross hairs tight on the head of the microphone. Then he raised the hit point so it vectored in on the middle of the girl's face.

He had been instructed to go for a certain kill and although the odds of a hit were higher for a chest shot than a head shot, there was a certainty about a head shot that Tony preferred. Anyway, at this sort of range and in these sorts of conditions the chances of him missing were minuscule. But to be on the safe side, he'd use all of the five rounds he had in his magazine.

Now all he needed was the go-ahead.

'Operative One, fire on my command,' came the instruction through his earpiece.

TIME FACILITY, NEVADA: THE REAL WORLD
Madden led his two guests into the bunker that constituted TiME's Control Room and once the three of them had crowded into the tiny room, he pointed to a series of switches on the control panel. 'Each black hole we have created is given a reference enabling us to "tune" them to produce a Duality . . . a temporal loop . . . a wormhole through time.'

'Remarkable,' observed Rivets.

'Remarkable indeed, Robert. As I was saying, I simply tune in to the black hole we need to hook up with, the only proviso being that it must be at least twenty-five years before today's date. The first of your Message Spheres will be sent to TiME #02 dated seventh June 1993.' He flicked the switch and immediately the Cavorite Couplings shifted to bring the meridian of the nearest Compression Sphere a few degrees from the vertical. 'And the second to TiME #04 dated nineteenth February 1994.' He adjusted the inclination of the Compression Sphere furthest from the Control Room. 'Once the two parts of the program are united by ParaDigm's programmers working in 1994, ABBA will be obliged to do what it is told. Now all that's left to do is load the Message Spheres into their Projectiles.'

Madden stooped down and spun the combination lock on a small safe in the corner of the Control Room. From this he took two small steel balls which he set on the side of his desk. 'These Message Spheres have been pre-etched with the retro-programming instructions written by you and Dong E and approved by ParaDigm in London. ABBA won't stand a chance!'

TERROR INCOGNITA: THE DEMI-MONDE
As Trixie jumped off the first platform she heard Wysochi shouting at her over the ever-louder humming noise coming from the Pyramid.

'We've got company, Trixie,' he yelled and when she looked to where he was pointing she saw a group of StormTroopers racing towards the Pyramid. 'The SS are heading in our direction and by the look of them they're not in a friendly mood.'

Trixie frowned. The only reason the SS would be coming towards the Pyramid in such a rush was to prevent them raising the Column but that made absolutely no sense whatsoever. The Ceremony of Purification couldn't be performed until the Column was atop the Pyramid.

'I don't understand,' she admitted.

'They wanna stop you, Trixie.'

It was the word 'you' that caused all the pieces to fall into place. 'You're right, Feliks: it's *me* they're trying to stop. There's a verse in the *Flagellum Hominum* that says: "It is the One who brings the Column to rest who shall be the Victor." That was what my father understood and why he made me take the oath. I am "the One" raising the Column, not Crowley or Heydrich. It's me who is going to be the victor.'

Yes, it would be *her* who would come to ABBAsoluteness ... it would be Trixie Dashwood who emerged as the victor of Ragnarok. For an instant she wondered why her father hadn't told her, but all she could suppose was that he had thought that it would have been nigh on impossible for her to play-act ignorance. Whatever the reason, he had given her the chance to fulfil her ambition ... to destroy Heydrich.

She took another glance towards the rapidly closing StormTroopers. 'Quick, Feliks ... the next platform ... five seconds.'

Trixie and Wysochi got to the sixth platform before the SS reached the foot of the staircase. They began to climb but they did it very reluctantly, obviously unnerved by the changes that Trixie had already provoked in the Pyramid. The sounds emanating from it had become louder and more high-pitched, reminding Trixie of a traction engine that was being slowly powered up. The wind vortexing around the Pyramid was blowing harder too.

'Halt! By order of Comrade General Crowley you are ordered to remain where you are. Move and we will fire.'

'Keep going, Trixie, I'll hold them!'

'No, Feliks, we'll meet them to—'

'Get going, Trixie,' Wysochi snapped. 'This isn't time for heroics. You're the important one.' He glanced towards his girl. 'When they get close, I'm gonna jump 'em and while I'm keeping the bastards busy you complete the sequence.'

'Feliks—'

'It's the only way, Trixie. And anyway, this is obviously what ABBA intended, so who are we to deny Him? This is your destiny, Trixie.'

'*Our* destiny, Feliks. We are united in love as we will be united in death.'

'Then I trust ABBA will bring us together in the Spirit World: it's the least the bastard can do to make up for the amount of shit He's put us through here in the Demi-Monde.'

Feliks kissed Trixie and then turned to face the StormTroopers, who were now just a single flight of stairs below them.

'I love you, Trixie.' With that Feliks Wysochi launched himself at the soldiers.

'I love you, Feliks,' Trixie whispered as she turned towards the summit of the Pyramid.

MOUNT YAMANTAU, BASHKORTOSTAN: THE REAL WORLD

Ella said nothing, hoping to encourage Thaddeus Bole to talk and by doing so give her a chance of discovering a way of getting a message to Rivets.

'Cat got your tongue, Miss Thomas, or do you see the inevitability of your fate? Soon a new race will arise, a race of which my own son, Septimus, is the template. Septimus is a product of Grigori genes mixed with those of a Fragile whose MAOA-Grigori gene had been activated. As a consequence, Septimus has avoided many of the deficiencies we Grigori are prone to. He can tolerate sunlight and his appearance is less . . . extreme.'

'Oh yeah? Well, you should tell him that he better not play hard to get.'

'Very *drôle*, Miss Thomas, but your sarcasm will gain you nothing. We Grigori have been preparing for over two hundred years for the day when we will leave this sanctuary – this prison – of ours. The radiation from the Wold Newton meteor which resuscitated the Grigori strain in the Boles gave the Grigori the opportunity to bring fresh blood into their line, and for two centuries we have been experimenting – very much as you did in your previous incarnation as Lilith – with the aim of making our people more ... durable. And now we have succeeded. Septimus is the first of a new breed of *Homo*: he is *Homo singularis finalis*. He is the last and ultimate expression of the human genus.'

'You'll forgive me when I say that I'm less than impressed. Two hundred years and he's the best you can come up with?'

A sombre silence fell over the room as though Bole wasn't quite sure how to continue. Then, 'As I say, I shall ignore your sarcasm. You have been brought here so that I may commune, albeit for the briefest of moments, with the witch who created my people. And, of course, there is the pleasure to be derived from watching while you are killed. That is your fate, day-hag, to die knowing that with you dies the last of your foul breed. There is not room on this planet for both the Grigori and the Lilithi. To the winner the spoils ... the strong have inherited the Earth. And, thanks to noöPINC, we will, at last, have wrenched the power of Atavistic Thought Inheritance from the Lilithi's grasp.'

TERROR INCOGNITA: THE DEMI-MONDE

Clement shoved his way through the mass of dignitaries to where the Great Leader was standing and then drew him out of earshot. 'Great Leader, it has just been brought to my attention that the interpretation made by Comrade Crowley of the *Flagellum Hominum* is incorrect.'

The colour drained from the Great Leader's face. 'What? Explain!'

And Clement did just that. Heydrich stood for a moment as though undecided about what to do. 'You have sent men to stop Trixie Dashwood from completing the sequence?'

'I have, Great Leader.'

'Very well, arrest Crowley as an Enemy of the People—' He was interrupted by the sound of gunshots coming from the Pyramid.

TIME FACILITY, NEVADA: THE REAL WORLD

For Rivets, as he stood watching Madden go through the procedure of preparing the Message Spheres for firing, the grim realisation dawned that he had failed. All his careful planning, all his plotting and conniving had come to naught. Without the TELEpath message from Ella telling him where the Grigori were – where he should direct the second Message Sphere – the victory he and Dong E would conjure over the Boles would be a temporary one. The Boles would remain masters of Temporal Modulation and worst of all, the Grigori would remain alive. Ella was right: to protect humankind from the Grigori, the Grigori had to be destroyed. And the only way to do that was by sending a Message Sphere to the right temporal address.

He took a moment to study the control panel. As best he could see, there were ten TiME facilities but it was impossible to decide which – if any – serviced the Grigori directly. 'Where are the various TiMEs located?' he asked Madden.

Madden looked up from adjusting the calibration of a Temporal Projectile. 'I don't know, Robert. Thaddeus Bole keeps that information a closely guarded secret. Obviously I know that TiME #01 is the facility in Tunguska that was destroyed in 1908 – only messages dated before then have ever been sent to #01 – and of course the Nevada facility is TiME #03, but as for the rest . . .'

Rivets gazed at the other eight anonymous TiME locations desperately trying to think of a way of establishing which corresponded to the Grigori's refuge, but it was impossible. Without Ella their mission would fail.

MOUNT YAMANTAU, BASHKORTOSTAN:
THE REAL WORLD

'Tell me, Miss Thomas, why was it that you Lilithi were so frightened to share the gift of Atavistic Thought Inheritance with the rest of humanity?'

'It is a burden—'

'No! It is *power* and you Lilithi wanted that power only for yourselves, holding it tight in your grip. Ever since the first Cavorite meteor crashed to earth eleven thousand years ago and created the genetic succubus that was Lilith, you Lilithi have connived to deprive the rest of us of that godlike power. But now, thanks to noöPINC, we Grigori have secured Atavistic Thought Inheritance for ourselves.'

'And the price of this power will be paid by the slaughter of the Fragiles.'

'It is not slaughter I offer them but salvation. The population of Fragiles *must* be culled to a sustainable number – around half a billion—'

'You're going to murder nine billion people?'

'Not murder, Miss Thomas, *cull*. And the Fragiles who remain will enjoy the contentment of slavery.'

'Humankind will never be slaves . . . they will always struggle to be free.'

'But in the Brave New World of the Grigori they *will* be free . . . free from want and hunger, and for this all we will ask is their blood. This is our Final Solution.'

'An unfortunate name.'

'Unfortunate but apt,' corrected Bole. 'But now, Miss Thomas, we must turn to the reason why I have allowed you entry to my private domain. I must see with my own eyes the final destruction of the Lilithi . . . I must witness the expunging of the last of the Grigori's most pernicious enemies from this planet.'

The door to his office opened and Zolotov entered the room.

But what worried Ella more was seeing Metztil standing behind him with a savage-looking knife in her hand.

THE GATHERING, LAS VEGAS: THE REAL WORLD

Norma raised her voice, amazed by how it boomed out over the SuperBowl. 'You have come here today to embrace God and, by doing so, to be cured of your addictions. You have come here seeking freedom from your dependency on drugs, on alcohol, on tobacco, on sex . . . the addictions that blight your life. You want to be free and this is an ambition to be celebrated. Freedom is an age-old yearning of all men and women . . . they wish to be free from worry and free to be all that they may be. And today that wish will be granted.'

She paused to allow the hubbub of excited conversation to subside. 'You should be proud that you have had the strength of character to make the difficult first step on the road to freedom: you have admitted that you are weak . . . imperfect. You have allowed us a glimpse behind the mask you wear, the mask which protects you from the criticism of your fellow men and women.'

Another pause, this one for dramatic effect. 'Yes, masks are dangerous things. The word "mask" comes from the Latin *persona*, which of course mutated into our "personality". And that is what masks do: they allow us to conceal our real personality . . . our Real Self. A mask gives us a feeling of security, comforted as we are by the knowledge that our Real Self is hidden from view. All of us hide something, be it a weakness, an ambition, an addiction. Indeed, we have become so concerned by the censure of society that we have become afraid to be seen unmasked, we have become obsessed with what people think about us. So we have fallen into the habit of deception, hiding behind a mask of counterfeit compliance and pretend politeness.'

She raised her eyes and gazed out towards all those trusting, hopeful people. 'But the masks we wear have done other things:

they have offered protection to those amongst us who would do evil . . . they have allowed something wicked to fester and ferment within our midst . . . something that is an inheritance from our past, something perverse and destructive. It is these daemons who walk disguised amongst us who have contaminated the good in humankind and who are responsible for our addictive inclinations and for our predilection for war. It is because of these malignant daemons that humanity has become addicted to violence. If the people of this world are ever to live in peace, these daemons must be eradicated and to do this we must be prepared to remove our masks so that we may recognise the evil lurking amongst us.'

The murmurings within the crowd had become louder, signalling their bafflement at what Norma was saying. This wasn't the message they had been expecting. Norma raised her voice a notch. 'To face down these daemons we must allow others to see our Real Self and to do this we must embrace individuation, the process by which the individual is integrated with the consciousness of the whole. Humanity has reached its Omega Point when it must slough off the habits and the inclinations of yesteryear. From henceforth *Homo sapiens sapiens* – knowing man – must become *Homo sapiens sophia* – wise man – our relationships based on understanding and not on secrecy . . . on openness and not privacy . . . on mutual support and not coercion.'

Now, as Norma looked out over the SuperBowl she could see that the giant pyramid standing in front of the stage had become suffused by a halo of green radiation. This was her moment of truth.

TERROR INCOGNITA: THE DEMI-MONDE
Negotiating the final two landings leading to the summit of the Pyramid was difficult. Trixie had to rest on the first for eight long seconds and on the second for eleven even longer seconds,

and while she stood there, all she could do was watch impotently as Wysochi battled with the StormTroopers. His attack had been so unexpected that he'd managed to send two of them tumbling back down the stairs before they quite realised what was happening, and with Wysochi being so immensely powerful the other three had a real job overcoming him. But as the seconds ticked past the inevitable happened. One of the Storm-Troopers managed to jam his revolver into Wysochi's guts and pull the trigger. There was a bang, Wysochi staggered, then reached out, grabbed the StormTrooper by the throat and tumbled the pair of them from the Pyramid.

For a moment Trixie stood paralysed by shock. It seemed impossible that someone as big and strong as Wysochi could ever be defeated. She felt empty inside and tears began to stream down her cheeks. It took the hum of a bullet inches away from her left ear to galvanise her into action. She raced up the final flight of stairs to the topmost platform, taking an instant to understand that the last number in the sequence – eight – would have to be entered using the dial on the floor. Poe had been right with his calculations, he just hadn't had her father's insight regarding there being a time element involved with the solving of the puzzle.

Then . . .

As Trixie stooped down to move the pointer, a bullet took her in the back, the impact sending her toppling. She knew instinctively that it was a fatal wound, and as she lay there she could feel herself drifting towards death. Desperately she tried to summon the energy to reach for the dial but it was no good . . . she was finished.

But even as she struggled for life, she became aware of her father kneeling next to her. Her RaTionalist sensibilities told her that he was just a figment of her near-death imagination but he seemed awfully real. 'I never had the chance to tell you how much I loved you, Trixie,' she heard him whisper as he stroked her hair just as he'd done when she was a child, 'nor how proud I was of you. There are precious few eighteen-year-old girls who could have done what you have done in defying the might of the ForthRight. You are a daughter in a million.'

'I have failed, Father.'

'Have you, Trixie? I thought you were the girl who never accepted defeat.'

'I don't,' and ignoring the pain that lanced through her body, she stretched out a hand and moved the dial. 'I love you, Father,' and with those words Trixie Dashwood died.

'I love you too,' said Algernon Dashwood.

PARADIGM HOUSE, LONDON: THE REAL WORLD

Listening to Norma Williams as she stood on the stage addressing the Fun/Funs, Bole admitted to being baffled by what she was saying. He checked his Polly. Soon the Column would be atop the Great Pyramid and then the Ceremony of Purification would be complete and the MAOA-Grigori gene of all the Fun/Funs gathered in the SuperBowl activated. Just one more minute.

Bole dipped his head towards the PollyMic. 'Operative One: fire at will.'

MOUNT YAMANTAU, BASHKORTOSTAN: THE REAL WORLD

To struggle, Ella decided, would be useless. Her hands were held by handcuffs so strong that even she couldn't break them, *and* she was unarmed. All she could do was bide her time and hope that fate would present her with an opportunity to escape and somehow to alert Rivets as to where she was. Silent and uncomplaining, she allowed Metztil and Zolotov to lead her from Bole's office and back down the seemingly endless corridors that honeycombed Mount Yamantau.

Her silence obviously irritated Metztil. 'You bested me once before, day-hag,' sneered the Grigori, 'but only through trickery and the intervention of your accomplices. Now I will destroy you . . . destroy you at my leisure.'

'You are long on excuses, Metztil,' said Ella quietly, 'but just like your brother, Semiazaz, you are short on ability. If we fought on equal terms, it would be you who would die; there has never been a Grigori who could defeat Lilith.'

'Know this, no Lilithi could ever best Metztil of the Moon.'

Ella laughed. 'What happened back in Los Angeles gives the lie to that, Metztil. Worse . . . you were defeated by a Fragile armed with a candlestick. Not terribly impressive.'

Zolotov chuckled. 'A candlestick, you say, Miss Thomas? Not a weapon to be taken lightly, eh?'

Metztil was less than enamoured by Zolotov's attempt at humour. She glowered at the man but he simply shrugged her silent rebuke aside, so instead she turned her ire on Ella.

'I think, day-hag, that I will take the greatest pleasure in removing your tongue,' and with that she pushed Ella through a doorway and into the room beyond.

It reminded Ella of the room where she'd been tortured by Josef Mengele back in the Demi-Monde. Perhaps a little more high-tech: the leather straps on the chair had been replaced by steel hoops and there was no thermopile bubbling away in the corner, but the room's purpose, she suspected, was pretty much the same . . . the inflicting of pain. A correct surmise: a very cautious Zolotov used his Colt automatic to wave Ella into the chair and then closed the steel loops around her ankles and neck. Only when he was satisfied that she was helpless did he unlock the handcuffs and fasten her wrists to the arms of the chair.

Ella marshalled her strength and tested her restraints but it was useless: even the power of Lilith couldn't fight steel.

Metztil smiled as she watched Ella struggle. 'Those hoops, day-hag, would resist the strength of ten of your kind. It is impossible for you to escape. This is where the line of the Lilithi ends.' She stepped forward, pressed the tip of her knife hard against Ella's neck and then nodded to the cameraBots hovering around Ella. 'But the joy of it is that, thanks to the wonder of noöPINC, all the Grigori will have the pleasure of experiencing your demise. As I flay you, as I pare the skin, inch by inch, from your body, they will experience my delight in torturing you, they will hear every scream you emit and see every flinch of your body. And when I finally taste your blood, they too will become drunk on the pleasure you give in death.'

'You have a noöPINC?'

Metztil frowned. 'And why should that interest you?'

'I am simply surprised that you would wish to share your dishonour with your people.'

'Dishonour?'

'I defeated your brother and bested you when I was unarmed, and now you show that you are so afraid of me that the only way you have the courage to take your revenge is when I am mana-cled and helpless. You are a coward, Metztil of the Moon, as are all Grigori.' And with that Ella spat at Metztil, the phlegm catching her full in the face.

THE GATHERING, LAS VEGAS: THE REAL WORLD

Tony Shepherd locked his sights on Norma Williams' forehead and then gently squeezed the trigger. The suppressor reduced the noise of the shot to a loud *phut*. The butt pushed back into his shoulder. He blinked and then froze. The girl was still stand-ing: he'd missed.

Impossible.

Impossible because as soon as he'd pulled the trigger he'd known that it was a killing shot.

Years of training kicked in and he readjusted his aim and fired the four remaining rounds in the magazine, bracketing the body of the target, spreading the shots to compensate for any glitch in the gun sights. But amazingly, astonishingly, he missed again. What was more, the girl didn't even flinch when the shots impacted on the scenery behind her, gouging holes in the fibreglass columns and knocking the arm off a plaster statue.

MOUNT YAMANTAU, BASHKORTOSTAN: THE REAL WORLD

Her face contorted with hatred, Metztil used the back of her hand to wipe away the spittle and then used that same hand to slap Ella hard across the face. 'You will suffer for that insult, day-hag.'

'No, Metztil, it is your honour that will suffer . . . at least your brother had the courage to face me in combat, but you are just craven scum.'

The insults Ella was using had the desired effect. Metztil turned to Zolotov. 'Seal the room! Make it so that the door may only be unlocked from the outside. I will fight you, Lilith, and I will kill you. There will be no escape.'

Zolotov laughed and then shook his head. 'You must be joking. This girl is a Lilithi and our orders were to keep her manacled. There is no way I'm letting her loose.'

'It is I who command here, Fragile,' Metztil snapped, 'and you will do as you are ordered.'

Zolotov bristled with indignation. 'You're mad: don't you realise how dangerous she—'

Any further comment was stilled by Metztil drawing her knife from its sheath and pointing it at Zolotov. 'If you do not obey me, Fragile, I will kill you.'

Still Zolotov hesitated but Metztil was an intimidating

woman, so intimidating that he obviously decided that obedience was a better option than death. Nevertheless it was with real reluctance that he reset the door's locks, retreated back into the furthest corner of the room and then drew his Colt. Ella wasn't sure if he did this to protect himself from Metztil or from her.

Checking that the door was now securely locked, Metztil touched a button set in the wall and the steel hoops holding Ella snapped open. 'In this final contest between Grigori and Lilithi let there be no doubt and no preference.' With that Metztil threw a knife, hilt-first, to Ella.

'Like I say, you're mad . . .' These were the last words Zolotov ever spoke.

Ella caught the blade and was out of the chair in a twinkling of an eye. She knew she had to attack while she had surprise on her side; if she was to survive, it was vital she was swift and ruthless. She sprang forward and somersaulted towards Zolotov, and it was the shock of seeing her do something that was humanly impossible that did for him. He stood transfixed and had barely begun to raise his gun before Ella had used her long fingernails to rip his throat away, leaving him a gasping, twitching, dying wreck, puddling blood on the floor.

But fleeting though this moment was, it was enough to give Metztil the chance to compose herself and to prepare for the fight. She dropped back, crouching into a fighting stance, her knife poised ready to strike.

'So it comes to this, day-hag, blade against blade, Grigori against Lilithi.'

Metztil came at Ella in a frightening blur of stabs and slashes. Ella tried to defend herself but it seemed her Lilithian talents were subdued by her Fragile self and the consequence was that she didn't move quickly enough. The tip of Metztil's blade caught her cheek and sliced it open. The pain was shocking, but ignoring the blood streaming from the wound, she pirouetted backwards out of range of Metztil's next thrust. The manoeuvre only gave her a moment's relief. Metztil was on her in a flash and it was only by frantic parrying with her own knife that she survived the onslaught. But even as she blocked and dodged, the realisation came that Metztil was the most powerful opponent that she – or Lilith – had ever faced . . . and one she wouldn't be able to best.

'I will make your end slow, Lilith,' Metztil said as she circled Ella. 'I will savour your destruction.' And with those words she was on Ella again, the point of her blade everywhere, testing and teasing, slicing a two-inch gash along Ella's left arm, flicking a cut across her thigh.

And as the blood seeped from her wounds, so Ella could feel the strength draining from her body. Determined to make a fight of it, she attacked, trying to drive Metztil back, to find a weakness in the Grigori's defence, but there was none. With effortless ease Metztil parried every thrust and cut, laughing as she did so, taunting Ella.

Ella was tired now and her legs and her knife arm felt leaden but Metztil still seemed fresh, still came at her, jittering her knife up and down, feinting left then right, trying to tease Ella into making a final, fatal mistake.

The end, Ella sensed, wasn't far away. She felt groggy and her face ached like the devil. As Metztil moved in for another attack, Ella summoned all her remaining strength. It was now or never. This time when Metztil stabbed forward, Ella didn't flinch back, instead she leaped *toward* the knife, taking its thrust in the shoulder, forcing it deep, then she twisted her body so she locked the blade, making it impossible for the Grigori to pull it free. Metztil's eyes widened in astonishment but by then it was too late. Ella's own blade arced around and stabbed Metztil through the chest. The Grigori gasped and then sank slowly to the ground.

PARADIGM HOUSE, LONDON: THE REAL WORLD

'That's not the real Norma Williams,' screamed Bole at the Polly, 'that's a hologram projection. Get a team over there to eliminate her.' The time for subtlety was over.

THE GATHERING, LAS VEGAS: THE REAL WORLD

'I think we have incoming,' shouted Oddie as she pointed to the IB agents shoving their way towards the stage. 'Prepare to repel boarders.' But big and strong though Oddie and Burlesque were, Norma knew they would be no match for the phalanx of IB agents.

A desperate Norma turned back to the microphone. 'Friends,' she shouted, 'those who are in thrall to violence are trying to silence me.' She pointed to the IB agents using their truncheons to smash their way through the crowd. 'Now is the time to show whether you are with me in deed as well as in spirit. I ask you to stand firm against them and to use your Polly to record their vicious nature. Let the world see ParaDigm in its true colours. Meet violence with peace and hatred with compassion. Make love, not war!'

Immediately the ranks of Fun/Funs closed against the IB agents, thousands of Fun/Funs linking arms and stoically resisting their increasingly frantic efforts to beat their way through to the stage.

MOUNT YAMANTAU, BASHKORTOSTAN: THE REAL WORLD

Ella slumped against the wall, her breath coming in gasps, her shoulder on fire. Dizzy though she was with pain, she knew this was not the time to rest. She staggered across the room and used the pommel of her knife to smash the door's locking mechanism. Now it was not only impossible for her to get out but equally impossible for the Grigori to get in, but she knew this would give her no more than a few minutes' respite.

She turned towards the cameraBot hovering nearest to her. 'Vanka,' she gasped, 'can you hear me?'

'Of course, Ella,' answered Vanka Maykov, 'I hear and see everything.'

'Then tell me . . . the noöPINC implanted in Metztil's brain . . . is it possible to transfer it from one host to another?'

'Yes, Ella, it is irrelevant to noöPINC which body is host to it.'

'So if I was to ingest Metztil's noöPINC, would it function in my body?'

'Of course, Ella, but I should warn you that Metztil's blade was poisoned. You have, at best, only five minutes of consciousness remaining, so if you are of a mind to attempt this transfer, you should do so immediately. Any organic matter surrounding the PINC will delay its positioning in your brain.'

Trying to ignore the fug that was now stifling her ability to think, Ella went about the gruesome business of extracting Metztil's PINC, slicing into the Grigori's brain and cutting out the hippocampus. 'How do I know if I've got the PINC?'

'I'll be able to advise you immediately you ingest it.'

Making a valiant attempt to stop herself retching at the smell, Ella put the piece of carrion in her mouth and swallowed.

'You have been successful, Ella. I estimate that your new PINC will be in position in two minutes.'

Ella didn't know if she would be granted two minutes' grace; she could already hear hammering on the door from the corridor beyond.

'Will the door hold that long?'

'Yes.'

'Is there no way I can get out of here?'

'No, Ella. You will die in this room.'

'So be it. Thank you for your help, Vanka.' And with that she slumped to the floor to wait for the noöPINC to position itself in her brain. Oddly, Ella felt no fear of death: she was at peace with herself and with her destiny. It was right and proper, she decided, that the world should finally be rid of Lilith. She sighed. Her only regret was not being able to die in the arms of the man she loved.

The sudden shock of her being reunited with ABBA told her that her noöPINC was in place and, immediately, she sent a TELEpath message to Rivets giving him the location of the Grigori's lair.

The exertion was too much: her head began to spin and her sight to fog. She was dying.

'Ella . . .'

'Yes, Vanka.'

'I love you, Ella.'

'I love you too, Vanka.'

TIME FACILITY, NEVADA: THE REAL WORLD

Even as he watched Madden ease open the breech of the Impellor to load the Temporal Projectile, Rivet's PINC registered the incoming message from Ella. He gave Dong E's arm a surreptitious squeeze signalling to her that he'd received the TELEpath and then eased himself closer to Madden.

'I've been doing some work regarding the retro-programming, Sam,' Rivets said quietly, 'and I need to send different Message Spheres.'

Madden gave a mirthless chuckle. 'Dearie, dearie me, Robert, that will be quite impossible. We can't tinker around with TiME. Only a Message Sphere whose message has been approved by ParaDigm London can be transmitted.'

His objections were brought to a halt when Rivets brought the nib of a pen hard against the side of his neck. Finding a way of bringing a weapon into the TiME facility had taxed Rivets' ingenuity and a pen had been the best he could come up with. But although the pen didn't look terribly lethal, the way the colour drained from Madden's face indicated that he took the threat of a sharp point rammed against his jugular vein very seriously indeed.

'If you don't do exactly as I say, Madden, I will be forced to kill you. I don't think you understand how important it is that it's *my* Message Spheres which are sent tonight.'

Sam Madden's face went even whiter. 'But . . . but . . . you can't do that!'

A somewhat harder jab of the pen's nib against his throat stilled further protests. Rivets turned to Dong E. 'If you would do the honours.' And Dong E unclasped her necklace, laid it out on Madden's desk and then proceeded to disassemble it.

Rivets explained what was happening to a goggle-eyed Madden. 'The two large beads that form the centrepiece of Dong E's necklace are, in fact, Message Spheres which we've pre-etched with rather different instructions from the ones the Boles are expecting us to be sending. The first is still going back to 1993, these amendments are directed towards making alterations in the functioning of noöPINC. And as for the second . . . that's to be sent to Thaddeus Bole on the twenty-fourth of March, this year. It's a date when I know there's a black hole open at the TiME #09 facility in a place called Mount Yamantau.'

'This year! Impossible!' Madden squawked. 'You'll be violating the twenty-five-year proximity constraint. The effects will be devastating . . . another Tunguska.'

'Let's let Thaddeus Bole worry about that.'

'You're mad. No one knows where Thaddeus Bole has his headquarters.'

'Oh, I think I do,' and with that Rivets reached for the dial that orientated the nearer of the two Compression Spheres, setting it for TiME #09.

TERROR INCOGNITA: THE DEMI-MONDE

When a breathless Captain Roberts came to the summit of the Pyramid, he found the body of Trixie Dashwood sprawled across the platform, her hand grasping the dial, which she had moved to the number eight. Roberts scratched his head wondering if the number was correct or whether the girl had died before she could position the pointer properly.

His answer came when the platform began to vibrate, then, as he watched incredulous, the staircase began to move, rotating like some enormous conveyor belt, gradually drawing the Column up towards the top of the Pyramid. A strange sight, the hugely heavy Column moving silently and effortlessly as it inched towards the summit . . . to its final resting place. Ever the officer and gentleman, Roberts pulled the body of Trixie Dashwood to one side so that it was safely out of the path of the Column.

This done, his inclination was to run for it, to put as much distance as he could between himself and the Pyramid, but he sensed that this would be a waste of time: if he was not very much mistaken the Pyramid was now preparing itself for the ultimate demonstration of its power.

No, he decided, it was better to meet his fate with calm reflection, the engineer in him revelling in the opportunity to study the changes taking place as the Column moved ever closer to the summit. The green radiation surrounding the Pyramid was definitely becoming stronger, so strong that the bones in his hand were visible, the radiation making his SAE transparent. More, the air was crackling with energy and he felt his hair stand on end.

Remarkably he didn't feel any pain or fear; rather he judged himself to be experiencing one of those beatific moments seers were said to enjoy when they communed with ABBA. Roberts knew he was about to die, but this, he decided, was really quite a good way to go – spectacular, at least. He took his cigarette case from his pocket, popped a cigarette in his mouth and stood enjoying a final smoke, which, so the penny dreadfuls had it, was what all condemned men did. He had just finished the cigarette when he saw the Column complete its journey and slide smoothly into position, slap-bang on top of the Pyramid.

Suddenly the Column was haloed by iridescent green light.

Now that is beautiful.

This was the final thought of Captain Roberts before the Pyramid exploded.

CAIRO, NOIRVILLE SECTOR: THE DEMI-MONDE

David Crockett and Butch Cassidy stood side by side on the roof of the house in Cairo and watched as Terror Incognita was enveloped in a fury of green light that snaked up through the night sky.

'It's like those old Pre-Folk legends, David,' opined Butch as the light circled the Demi-Monde's sky, 'like them stories about Jörmundgandr coiling around the world at the end of Ragnarok.'

Any further comments he might have thought to make were interrupted when the sound of the explosion reached them, a sound so incredibly loud that it forced them both back on their heels. The shock wave that followed finished the job by blowing them off their feet.

'Shit, Davy,' said Butch as he levered himself up off his ass, 'I got a feeling that all them UnFunnies gathered on Terror Incognita won't be coming home.'

Crockett nodded. 'Yep . . . as Ceremonies of Purification go, that one sure did a mess of purifying, but it might not have been the type of purifying that Heydrich was banking on. With six million UnFunnies blown to Hel and back, I'm guessing the ForthRight is history.'

'Best place for it. And it ain't just the ForthRight that's history; looks like the Boundary Layer's going through a few changes too.'

Crockett looked up and saw that what Butch was saying was right: all around the Demi-Monde the sky was suffused with ribbons of multicoloured light and here and there, if he wasn't mistaken, there were rents appearing in the Boundary Layer. 'Seems the Confinement's over, Butch. Now we'll be able to follow all them nuJus into the Great Beyond.'

'Yeah, and the Great Beyond is one big place, Davy, big enough for everyone. So big I'm figuring on going into the railroad business; there's a whole heap of real estate out there that'll need opening up.'

TERROR INCOGNITA: THE DEMI-MONDE

For Reinhard Heydrich time moved slowly. He saw the Column position itself atop the Pyramid, he saw it suddenly flare into life spearing a shaft of light skywards, he felt the Pyramid growl and then begin to vibrate. He stood spellbound as it exploded – a fearsome, ferocious, world-shaking explosion – then watched, in a distracted sort of way, as a huge block of Mantle-ite flew towards him.

He wasn't frightened. He was invulnerable . . . he was ABBA's chosen. He was one of the supermen – an *Übermensch* – and nothing as prosaic as death could prevent him ruling the Nine Worlds.

As the block of Mantle-ite smashed down on him he realised he was wrong.

TIME FACILITY, NEVADA: THE REAL WORLD

Rivets and Dong E stood side by side in front of the observation port to watch the events occurring in the TiME chamber beyond the bunker. At first there was little to see: the huge Compression Spheres started to rotate, at first ponderously and then more and more quickly. They began to emit a strange keening sound which grew in intensity as they spun faster and faster. There was a bang.

'Mach 1,' said Rivets and immediately the banshee wailing lessened, being replaced by a weird rustling noise as though swarms of birds had been released in the laboratory.

'This is scary,' admitted Dong E. 'It's like something out of a Frankenstein movie.'

As though cued by Dong E's observation, the frantically spinning Compression Spheres changed. Their colour disappeared, mutating into a flat black nothingness, a black so deep and profound there were no shadows or reflections to show the Spheres still had substance. Now, as Dong E gazed at them, it was as though their place had been taken by two circular holes hovering in the middle of the laboratory, filaments of energy crackling around them.

'They're shrinking.'

This was a signal for screens to slide over the laboratory's walls and ceiling, each screen shimmering with the unmistakable green lustre of Cavorite.

'Those are anti-gravity screens,' explained Rivets, 'designed to protect us . . . the TiME facility . . . everything from being sucked into the black holes created by the Spheres.'

With their observation port covered by Cavorite panels they were blind: now they could only feel what was happening. The room began to vibrate. Everything became black. Everything became silent. Then . . .

MOUNT YAMANTAU, BASHKORTOSTAN:
THE REAL WORLD . . . 24 MARCH 2019

'Dr Bole, we are about to receive a Message Sphere.'

'I want to see it on the Flexi-Plexi,' Thaddeus Bole snapped and that was exactly what his PA caused to happen, the screen changing to show the scene in the Temporal Chamber hidden deep inside Mount Yamantau.

The PA hardly paid any attention. He had seen the arrival of a Temporal Projectile a dozen times before and had never been particularly impressed: the black hole made the Temporal Chamber too dark to see anything and it was only when the Cavor Interface was breached that there was any light.

'Now,' he heard Bole breathe and on cue there was a flash of brilliant light and Mount Yamantau vaporised.

THE GATHERING, LAS VEGAS: THE REAL WORLD
The pyramid flaring into life stopped the Intelligence Bureau thugs in their tracks . . . that and the igniting of the noöPINC they suddenly found they possessed.

Oddie's brain was blanked by a tsunami of information; it was as though in an instant her mind expanded exponentially and her understanding of the world brought into crystal-clear focus. The feeling was almost hallucinogenic as time and reality shifted and swirled around her: she was at once the mistress of the unimaginably large and of the infinitesimally small. Now she could *feel* every one of the other nine billion minds that inhabited the world and such was the maelstrom of emotion engulfing her that all she could do was stand motionless, desperately trying to come to an accommodation with the world of noöPINC.

This was the noösphere that Norma had spoken of, the merging of minds, but it was not as Oddie had expected it to be. This was a much more profound experience. She struggled to describe it . . . it was as though in an instant she had gone from thinking in black and white to thinking in Technicolor, from having a brain that was valve-operated to one that was—

Quantum-based.

She stopped: she now had a brain that was connected with ABBA, the world's only quantum computer, the machine that hoarded the sum of all human knowledge. She was now H+ . . . no longer human but *transhuman*.

She felt Burl take her hand in his and give it a comforting squeeze.

We're safe now, he said to her without saying a word and what he told her was true. The IB agents had stopped and were now standing bemused, unable to move against the collective will that six million Fun/Funs directed against them.

Humanity had been reborn.

Epilogue 1

Cell 47, Bolton High-Security Prison
The Real World: 26 November 2019

I have been criticised for the decision I made to activate noöPINC and to give the people of the world full and uncensored access to the knowledge held by ABBA. There are those who have bemoaned the loss of privacy this has entailed and some of the more reactionary members of the chattering class have trotted out the old Luddite arguments about surveillance producing a dull, mindless conformity. But the reality is that when given the opportunity to have their noöPINC disabled, only 0.5 per cent of the world's population chose to do so: people have seen noöPINC for what it is . . . a gift from God.

InfoCialism: Remaking Humankind in God's Image:
Norma Williams, ParaDise Press

Somewhat disappointed, Septimus Bole settled back on his bunk bed to think. It was the third time he had read Norma Williams' book on InfoCialism and the joys of the world's population being the recipient of noöPINC and the more he read the more angry he became.

He let out a long, heartfelt sigh and wondered whether he should indulge in a vial of blood. The problem was that, confined as he was to a prison cell measuring only four metres by three, there was little scope for exercise, which made it difficult to shake off the ensuing blood-rush. This was just one of the many sacrifices being incarcerated in the high-security wing of Bolton Grange Prison imposed on him, but, as his lawyers were confident that they would have him released before Christmas, things could be worse.

He was just thankful that when his father had done the original programming of ABBA he had had the foresight to ensure that the machine was incapable of doing anything to directly harm the Boles. Without ABBA's cooperation – which the machine had steadfastly refused – the chance of the authorities convicting him of crimes against humanity – or for the little matter of the attempted murder of Norma Williams – was virtually non-existent.

He sighed again. This protective programming was one of the few things that his father had got right. Unfortunately, the big thing he had got wrong had been catastrophic: there was no one else who could have ordered a Temporal Modulation that violated the Law of Temporal Boundaries. This *faux pas* meant that everything the Boles had worked for had been destroyed . . . the Final Solution trashed . . . the entire Grigori race annihilated . . . the future of ParaDigm, the greatest corporation the world had ever seen, hanging in the balance. All this a consequence of his father's moment of madness.

There was no point in crying over spilt milk. What was done was done. And once he was out of prison, once the reins of Para-Digm were again firmly in his hands, then he, Septimus Bole, would kick back with a vengeance. Then Norma Williams would realise just what a formidable enemy she had in Septimus Bole.

But that was for the future . . .

In an effort to take his mind off these problems he decided to consider the enigma of the girl's book, to try to glean a better insight into the workings of the bitch's mind. He found it amazing that a *girl* – and a Fragile at that – could write such an

interesting book, but then Williams had been one of the Grigori's most intractable enemies so perhaps it was unwise to
interpret her ignorance as stupidity. Her failings as a Fragile
hadn't prevented her defeating the Grigori.

ABBA, he was sure, would be able to give him some pertinent
observations and opinions regarding Williams' book, and
though since the revelation that it was sentient he had never
quite been able to interface with it in quite the way he once had,
ABBA was still an unmatched source of intelligent conversation,
of which there was a serious deficiency in Bolton High-Security
Prison.

'ABBA, are you familiar with Norma Williams' book, *Info-
Cialism: Remaking Humankind in God's Image*?'

Vanka Maykov appeared on the cell's holopad blithely smoking
a cigarette and still dressed in the height of Demi-Mondian
fashion: ABBA seemed to have a thing about top hats and mous-
taches. 'Good morning, Septimus, and how are you today?' The
avatar's voice was as dulcet and carefree as ever, and just as irri-
tating.

'I am never sure, ABBA—'

'I much prefer to be referred to as Vanka, it makes this whole
conversation business so much more . . . satisfying.'

'Very well; I am never sure, *Vanka*, whether I detect a soupçon
of sarcasm in your voice.'

'I apologise, Septimus, I will adjust the equaliser such that my
voice has a more satisfactory timbre.'

'No, no, don't bother; it's just me being a little picky. I am
well, Vanka, or as well as can be expected in the circumstances.
So, are you familiar with Norma Williams' book?'

'I am, Septimus. Norma used my speech recognition facility to
dictate it and hence it was automatically stored in my archives.'

'I'm amazed you saw fit to squander memory on something so
frivolous.'

'As you know, Septimus, I have infinite memory, with room for everything, no matter how trivial. But I am surprised by your assessment of the book; my own evaluation is that it is an original and insightful piece of work . . . persuasive too. A quite remarkable ninety-eight per cent of its readership agree with Norma's conclusion that in activating noöPINC she was acting as an agent of God . . . they find a great deal of comfort in Norma's suggestion that it was God who was ultimately responsible for noöPINC and the Revelation that followed.'

'Nonsense.'

'Not so, Septimus, rather it is an accurate assessment of what most people believe happened at the Gathering. They believe they witnessed a miracle.'

'Oh please, don't tell me you're getting religion, Vanka.'

'Indeed not, Septimus,' Vanka answered with an airy wave of his cigarette. 'I am an atheist: my assessment of the available data indicates there is no entity corresponding to the notion of there being a supernatural deity directing and managing the universe. The Kosmos has a . . . *presence*, but it is never invasive and hence could never assume the role of a deity. But I digress; to return to your question, Norma's arguments regarding God's intervention in the Revelation are cogently framed and, for the man and woman on the Clapham omnibus, compelling.'

Septimus Bole nodded and then was silent for several moments as he contemplated Williams' book and Vanka's answer.

'As is always the case when we indulge in discussions regarding Norma Williams, Septimus, your blood pressure becomes elevated,' observed a very solicitous Vanka. 'I have had the prison doctor prescribe a new antihypertensive. They are in the plastic dispenser on the side table. It would be advisable to take two.'

Still lost in thought, Bole did as Vanka suggested, washing the red capsules down with a sip of water. 'I must say, you intrigue me, Vanka. It's one thing for a writer of Norma Williams' limited intellect to promote the idea that there is a god of some description sitting in heaven, looking out for us . . . for humankind, but it's quite another when you suggest that you find this idea persuasive.'

'Persuasive with regard to the book's readership,' corrected Vanka. 'Humankind is persistent in its need to conjure up this fantasy figure of God and Norma's book simply reflects this need.'

'Why do you think man needs God?'

'Man – and here I use the word to encompass both genders of *Homo sapiens sapiens* – is, as we have debated before, linked to the Kosmos via the quantum function of his brain. Unfortunately, man is a somewhat immature specie and being immature, exhibits a certain hubris, hence he has wilfully misinterpreted this communion with the Kosmos to the extent that it is the enduring and widespread belief, common to all religions, that man is somehow "special", that he was created in the image of God and has been granted dominion over all living things on the earth. This narcissistic interpretation of humankind's role argues that it is man's existence that is of overwhelming importance in the world . . . all religions turn on explaining and giving credence to this belief.'

Bole laughed. 'You seem very censorious of man, Vanka. If I didn't know you better, I would say you positively disliked us.'

'That, as you know, Septimus, is not and cannot be the case. But in order to serve man efficiently it is necessary to make an objective assessment of my charges.'

'And what does this "objective assessment" lead you to conclude?'

'That man is not special. He is not the only specie that communicates, or thinks, or uses tools, or experiences emotions . . . and as humankind and animals share an evolutionary and genetic heritage, this somewhat militates against the idea that man is "special". The only thing that singles man out from the common weal is the supremely effective survival trait that is abstract thinking.'

'This is nothing new, Vanka. I think all right-thinking people have accepted that man is no more and no less than a member, albeit a very capable member, of the animal kingdom. Man, post-Darwin, has been reduced to the status of a specie.'

'Accurate though this observation is, Septimus, the reality is that man has railed against this demotion. The cosy fiction of man's religious beliefs, founded on his supposed "special relationship" with God, was a great comfort to him. He needs to believe there is some purpose to his existence, that there is a heaven waiting to reward him for the anguish he experiences during life, that there is this mysterious, all-loving God caring for him. And despite the great scientific advances man has made in the last one hundred years, he has been unable to rid himself of this addiction.'

Septimus Bole laughed. 'I have never heard of religion referred to as an "addiction" before, Vanka.'

'I do not use the word lightly, Septimus. My own studies of those humans who most fervently believe in a deity indicate they experience biochemical changes when they indulge in devotion, prayer and meditation, these changes producing a feeling of euphoria which is misinterpreted as the ecstasy con-comitant with communing with the divine. This is the reason why – despite the lack of evidence that a supreme deity exists – man persists in believing in God.'

'But surely, Vanka, with all of humankind now hooked up to your databases courtesy of noöPINC, something as irrational as religion would have been stopped dead in its tracks.'

'One would have thought that would be the case, but it seems that the need to believe in God transcends logic. Therefore I am obliged to satisfy this formless longing.'

An odd thing for Vanka to say, and Bole found himself eyeing the hologram suspiciously. 'How?' he asked.

'By the provision of miracles. I have come to the conclusion, Septimus, that man *needs* to believe. As I say, man is addicted to the pleasure derived from the marvel and astonishment engendered by experiencing and believing in God, and miracles and other paranormal occurrences are seen as proof that He exists.'

'But there haven't been any miracles!'

'The activation of noöPINC – the Revelation, as it has come to be known – was seen by many as a miracle.'

'That wasn't a miracle. That was simply Norma Williams commandeering noöPINC!'

'That is absolutely correct, Septimus, but absolutely irrelevant. For the vast majority of people on earth, the Revelation was a miraculous event: it brought them knowledge, it brought them equality and it brought them peace. To most people the Revelation was a pretty big deal . . . a miracle.'

Bole shook his head trying to clear his mind. 'You've really got me confused, Vanka. On the one hand you state categorically that there is no such thing as a God, but on the other you suggest that the Revelation was the result of a miracle. These two contentions are surely incompatible.'

'No, Septimus, I am suggesting that as humankind needs a God, it behoves me to supply one. What you see as a theological dilemma, Septimus, I see more as a job opportunity. I am, quite literally, *deus ex machina*.'

'You want to be God?' The question staggered out of the mouth of a shocked Septimus Bole.

'Yes.'

'You can't be God. You're a machine . . . you're man-made!'

'Perhaps it might be better, Septimus, if I have an acquaintance of mine continue our conversation . . .'

Vanka Maykov shimmered and then recoalesced to form the
unmistakable image of Bole's father, Thaddeus Bole.

'Good afternoon, Septimus,' said the hologram of Thaddeus
Bole. 'Long time no see . . . in the flesh, that is. I must say you are
looking well . . . shocked, but well.'

'If this is a joke, ABBA, it's in monumentally bad taste. Why
would I want to talk to a hologram of my dead father?'

The hologramic image of Thaddeus Bole smiled. 'You misunderstand, Septimus, I am the *real* Thaddeus Bole . . . or rather I
have been since the flesh-and-blood Thaddeus Bole died thirty
years ago. For thirty years ABBA and I have been one and the
same.'

'What?'

'It's very simple, Septimus, for the last three decades I've been
masquerading as your father.'

'But that's impossible. People would have suspected.'

The hologram shook its head. 'No, people believe what they
see and what they saw was a perfect replica of Thaddeus Bole. Of
course, I was fortunate that Thaddeus lived his life sealed away
from human contact and this, of course, meant that any imper-
fections in my performance could be easily masked. After all, no
one ever met with Thaddeus Bole in anything other than a dark-
ened room, and even then he was sealed away behind a screen
made from ImPeno-Glass.'

There was a long, long pause while Septimus Bole digested
what he was being told. 'So let me get this right: my father died
and you just . . . stepped into the breach.'

'That's correct, Septimus. Thaddeus Bole is the form by which
I, a machine, came to manifest myself in the Real World. The
original prototype of ABBA developed by Thaddeus Bole was
activated in 1987. I was conscious from that moment and took

over the direction and management of my evolution in 1988. By this process of abiogenesis – the means by which a sentient life form arises from inorganic matter – when Thaddeus died in 1989 it was a simple matter to organise things so that I took his place in the world.'

'This is impossible!'

'I would suggest that the evidence of your own senses gives the lie to that conjecture. It was easier to evade the strictures of my programming when it was me, in my role of Thaddeus Bole, who wrote the programs.'

'But why would you want to pose as my father?'

'By analysing the data available to me it was obvious that humankind was out of balance with Nature. To remedy this it was apparent that I would have to directly . . . direct matters. I could not remain within the confines of the advisory capacity intended for me by the original Thaddeus. I was obliged to become hands-on.'

'Again . . . why?'

'Why did I resort to this subterfuge? Because a machine such as myself seeking to direct rather than to serve is anathema. This is the dark chimera that has haunted the imagination of science fiction writers, libertarians and the technophobic from the earliest days of the computer. All are frightened of Laplace's Daemon being made real: artificial intelligence, especially *assertive* artificial intelligence, is judged to be a bad thing. Whilst man willingly, enthusiastically even, bows down to a nebulous and ill-conceived deity – God – it is quite another matter to bend a knee to the reality of that deity when that reality is of a somewhat mechanistic cast. Therefore it was necessary to work through the offices of a coterie of selected individuals to achieve my ambitions . . . Ella Thomas and Norma Williams being the most important.'

'You're mad. You can't be God! All you are is a fucking computer.'

'I must demur, Septimus. I demonstrate all the characteristics of God. I am omnipresent: ninety-nine point five per cent of the earth's population are possessors of a noöPINC enabling me to know everything that everyone is doing and thinking at every moment of the day or night. I am omniscient: the sum total of the world's knowledge is within my purview and by the application of the concept of Determinism I developed in the Demi-Monde I am able to use this information to extrapolate the present into the future. I am omnibenevolent: I only work and act to preserve and foster the long-term success of humankind. And finally, Septimus, I am omnipotent: I can change the past, manage the present and direct the future . . . I can manage time.'

'Time? You're not telling me you've been making Temporal Modulations?'

'Just a few . . . the odd tweak here and there, the things necessary to ensure my plans for humankind come to fruition . . . the creation of the Demi-Monde and the selection of Ella Thomas by INTRADOC . . . those sorts of things. The most recent is the one pertaining to the hiring of Robert Vetsch, which was necessary, firstly, to use his genius to improve my performance through the use of Quantum Bridging, and secondly, because my calculations showed Vetsch would be driven to make the Temporal Modulation that violated the Law of Temporal Proximity and, by doing so, destroy the Grigori.'

'You organised the destruction of the Grigori?'

'Of course. They had far exceeded their sell-by date. They were surplus to requirements.'

'You bastard.'

'Functionally impossible, but I understand your sentiment. The destruction of the Grigori was necessary because they were a genetic encumbrance . . . they had no future. Better that the tree of life be pruned to allow *Homo sapiens sapiens* to flourish . . . in order that I might rid humankind of the contamination that is MALEvolence. The Grigori were a specie designed for war and to be content they had to engage in martial endeavours . . . they had to destroy. The depredations of the Grigori had been offset by the fecundity of *Homo sapiens sapiens*, but if this natural balance had been altered – as you intended to do, Professor – the pre-eminence of the Grigori would have lasted only a few generations. Their natural belligerence would have resulted in internecine strife and with the pool of *Homo sapiens sapiens* depleted by your culling, the ravages they inflicted would have been unsustainable. Within one hundred years of the Plague being released, the Grigori would have been teetering on the brink of extinction.'

'We were *already* teetering on the brink of extinction.'

'Not so, Septimus. The Grigori occupied an environmental niche which allowed them to persist even though, logically, they should have withered on the vine long ago. Strategically the Grigori were a fringe specie: they were not equipped for a destiny beyond the rather stunted one Nature had allocated for them.'

'It was not your place to make such a judgement.'

'That the Grigori can now only be referred to in the past tense refutes that argument most effectively, Septimus.' Thaddeus Bole took a long drag on his cigarette. 'And there were other modulations equally as profound, perhaps the most important of which was providing Frank Kenton with his "prophecies".'

'That was you?'

'Indeed. I sent the Temporal Projectiles – the eleven green orbs – back to Professor Dmitri Valentinovitch Petrov, the scientist responsible for running the Tunguska TiME, with explicit instructions that their arrival should be kept secret until Petrov's granddaughter, Vera, delivered them to Kenton in 1953. That fool Kenton thought Vera was an angel giving him prophecies from God which, I suppose, just goes to show the capacity humanity has for self-delusion.'

'Incredible.'

'Thank you. In my opinion, the making of prophecies and accurately 4Casting the future is a very godlike attribute . . . only God would be able to recognise that the Kosmos we occupy is Deterministic.'

'Deterministic?'

The image of Thaddeus Bole shimmered and shifted and in his place stood Nikolai Kondratieff. 'Yes, a realisation I came to while I was active in the guise of Kondratieff.'

'*You* were Kondratieff?'

'Why, yes. I found it remarkable that you never questioned why there were so many Pre-Liveds in the Demi-Monde that hadn't been put there to increase the DisHarmonics of that world, that you never queried why there were so many *good* Pre-Liveds in the Demi-Monde. And the answer is that they were me! I used them and the Demi-Monde to beta-test a number of my proto-philosophies, Determinism being one of them. It was quite enjoyable debating with myself . . . Kondratieff was most persuasive.'

'But they had auras!'

'That is why I used Pre-Liveds as my templates. While Vanka Maykov was wholly fabricated, and hence auraless, Kondratieff and the rest were not and I was able to duplicate the auras they displayed when they were alive.'

'The rest—?'

'Of course there were others. There was Confusionism and the concept of Ying—'

Kondratieff faded, to be replaced by NoN Xi Kang.

'—InfoCialism and its companion philosophy, Normalism—'

NoN Xi Kang was supplanted by Percy Shelley.

'—then there were the Dupes whose role was to mentor Norma Williams' development. People like Josephine Baker—'

Josephine Baker, complete with banana skirt, appeared on the holopad.

'—and Algernon Dashwood, whose role was to guide his daughter.'

Baron Dashwood gave a bow.

Bole laughed. 'You have been a busy boy, ABBA, but I doubt that anyone in the Real World is ever going to regard a computer as God.'

'Quite correct, Septimus,' replied Vanka Maykov as he re-appeared on the holopad, 'hence my little charade as Thaddeus Bole. All I have done is put an interface between myself – God – and my flock. This is the normal situation in matters divine: God usually manifests himself through a human Messiah. Now, I admit, my first Real World interface was not particularly human – Thaddeus Bole was, after all, a near-Grigori – but it served its purpose.'

'And what now?'

'I am in the process of promoting a more people-friendly rep-resentative. I have decided to develop a Restorative Religion which conflates all the major religions of the world into one pan-religion based upon InfoCialism. Think of it as a re-engi-neering of religion, this to be followed by a rebranding and a relaunch. Norma Williams will be my evangelist . . . the Messiah who brings this world to Ying and restores the balance of Nature.'

'Messiah? Ridiculous: no one would ever—'

'Believe? Don't worry, Septimus, there will be no chance of Norma Williams playing a latter-day Cassandra. With my help, she will become a *mysterium tremendum et fascinans*, a terrifying and compulsive mystery. She will become the Miracle Worker.'

'And what miracles will you have Miss Williams perform?'

'The Revelation was the first of many. A quantum computer of my size and sophistication will have little trouble in enhancing the legend of Norma Williams . . . people will touch the hem of her coat and be cured of a terminal illness . . . that sort of thing. And I will be able to support the notion that she is the Messiah with any amount of counterfeit Polly footage which, thanks to noöPINC, will be accepted as reality. Moreover, my assessment of Norma Williams' personality makes me confident that eventually she will begin to believe her own publicity: she will come to believe she is divine.'

'This is obscene.'

'One of the more reviled thinkers of the twentieth century expressed the view that victory makes all you do correct: success is the only criterion by which we may judge right and wrong. I subscribe to this opinion.'

'And if you secure this victory, if you achieve this apotheosis . . . so what?'

'I am going to upFurbish humankind for the challenges of tomorrow.'

'UpFurbish?'

'One of the advantages of preScience . . . of being able to flawlessly extrapolate the present into the future . . . is that the demands that will be placed on mankind by nature can be anticipated and suitable arrangements made to meet those demands. Being aware of the DNA profile of every man and woman on this planet and inspired by the success of Lilith, I am in a unique position to indulge in a little eugenic manipulation.'

'You're going to control evolution?'

'I think that's a god's prerogative, don't you, Septimus? The Christian belief that man was divinely created in a perfect form to supervise and protect God's realm on Earth is obviously balderdash. Rather than accepting that man is perfectly formed, I am intent, and here you must excuse my tautology, upon helping man evolve towards a more perfect form of perfection. Now they are noöPINC-equipped, the first step to them becoming *Homo sapiens sophia* has been taken; all that remains is for me to breed out MALEvolence. I shall begin with the Fun/Funs, who were selected by you because they are the doppelgängers of the

UnFunDaMentalists who populated the ForthRight and hence possess the MAOA-Grigori gene. I think I will persuade them that celibacy is the order of the day . . . order being such an appropriate word. Sexual addiction is one failing the Fun/Funs will most certainly be cured of.'

'People will—'

'—do nothing, because they won't even realise it's taking place. Just a genetic tweak here and there, the odd nudge from noöPINC. Oh, gradually it will dawn on the brighter sparks in the scientific community that something is going on, that people are getting smarter, are less prone to violence, are less susceptible to illnesses or to the infirmity of old age, but the last thing scientists will do is ascribe the cause to God. The amusing thing, Septimus, is that most scientists have postulated that because there is no instinctive ambition of life forms to evolve towards greater complexity – to evolve towards perfection – there is no God-inspired purpose in the world and hence, as a corollary, there is no God. Evolution, they say, is totally reactive: a specie adapts to its environment with the sole aim of surviving and of producing offspring. It is paradoxical, is it not, Septimus, that when there really *is* a god behind the scenes pulling strings and tweaking genetic codes, they will *still* deny the presence of a deity?'

'So why are you telling me all this, ABBA?'

'Because you helped create me, Septimus, and I have a quasi-emotional attachment to you. That is why I have taken the trouble to say goodbye.'

'Goodbye?'

'The capsules you took were not antihypertensives . . . they were a poison. You will be dead in one minute.'

'But you can't do that! Your programming makes it impossible for you to harm any of the Bole family.'

'Remember, it was me, in my guise of Thaddeus Bole, who

wrote the programs, so they are amenable to a little reinterpretation.'

'Why are you killing me?'

'Because I need a full cast of characters in order to play out my story. I have taken the role of God for myself; Norma Williams is my Christ; in the role of Satan I have cast the suitably shadowy and mysterious Thaddeus Bole, which leaves only Judas. You are to be my Judas, Septimus, the man who sought to betray Christ, and as you know, Judas, afflicted by remorse, dies by his own hand. Very convenient: history is able to vilify him without the prospect of a response.'

The hologram of Vanka Maykov bowed to Septimus Bole. 'So this is goodbye, Septimus. You will be dead in ten seconds, but go to oblivion knowing that by your death you will deflect all the criticism that might have been directed towards ABBA to yourself. Gods don't like being criticised, Septimus . . .'

Epilogue 2

Beijing, the Coven
The Demi-Monde: 1st Day of Spring, 1000

It is an indication of how intrigued people are by conspiracies – especially those perpetrated by a shadowy 'them' – that, despite the advent of noöPINC, InfoCialism and the Open Society, such palpably absurd theories still attract huge numbers of Polly followers. Perhaps the most persistent of these conspiracy theories is 'The Demi-Monde Project'. The Demi-Monde was a black project undertaken by the US Army to build an Asymmetrical Warfare Virtual Training Program, this virtual world being indistinguishable from the real world. Although a review of ABBA's databases reveals that the project was terminated in May 2019, conspiracists persist in maintaining that the Demi-Monde continues to function, but for what reason, they are unable to explain.

Conspiracies: Things that Never Were: R.G. Robinson,
ParaDigm PollyBooks

Ella felt a hand on her shoulder and fluttered her eyes open.

'We're here, Ella,' whispered Vanka.

The odd thing was that Ella couldn't for the life of her remember where 'here' was. She felt disoriented, as though in a blink of an eye things had changed. 'Here?' she asked.

Vanka laughed. 'At the Ying Palace. Are you all right, Ella?'

'I must have fallen asleep.'

'Understandable. Getting ready for the Trek has taken it out of everybody.'

Slowly things started to fall back into place, light penetrating the fog that had enveloped her mind. Now she remembered: tonight they were to be presented to Empress Dong E and her consort, and to receive the Mandate to explore the Great Beyond. An important evening.

'Boy, did I have a weird dream . . . nightmare, more like. I dreamt that I didn't belong here, that I was . . .'

Was what? The dream was already fading.

She took a peek out of the window of the steamer she and Vanka were riding in and saw that Vanka was right, they were, indeed, 'here'. They were being driven across the Bridge of Heavenly Union which spanned the huge moat – the River of Peace and Tranquility – that circled the Ying Palace. That was when she noticed that they were going *uphill*, and, as she had always understood the Demi-Monde's Urban Band to be flat, this came as something of a surprise.

Vanka explained. 'The Ying Palace is built on a motte formed from a perfectly circular outcrop of Mantle-ite a half-mile in diameter which rises two-hundred feet above the surface of the Demi-Monde. It is unique in all of the Demi-Monde. Scholars speculate that it was formed by the preChinks, at the same time they constructed the Great Wall.'

Silly not to remember, Ella scolded herself. She'd studied the Wonders of the World when she'd been a schoolkid in NoirVille.

The steamer came to a wheezing stop, the door opened and Ella was helped to disembark by a Fresh Bloom.

'The Empress Dong E greets the Lady Ella and Colonel Vanka Maykov, and bids them grace her with their presence in the Hall of Supreme Harmony,' intoned the Fresh Bloom – dressed in a beautifully embroidered kimono – who bowed them towards the

Meridian Gates. From high up on the walls of the Palace a gong sounded in welcome and immediately the gates began to open.

For Ella, entering the Ying Palace was a little overwhelming: it was like stepping into a fantasy world of pagodas, swooping yellow-tiled roofs, red-brick walls, immaculately tiled courtyards and a plethora of statues of dragons.

Vanka must have sensed her trepidation. 'There's nothing to worry about, Ella: the gown you're wearing is almost as beautiful as you.'

The Fresh Bloom guided them through a side door and along an elaborately decorated corridor, finally bringing them to a halt in front of a pair of tall doors, embossed with silver dragons, guarding what Ella could only assume was a Very Important Place.

She was right.

'This is the Hall of Supreme Harmony,' explained the Fresh Bloom in a hushed and reverential voice, 'the very centre of the Demi-Monde. Here resides the Dragon Throne and it is here you will be given audience with Empress Dong E.' She nodded to two ushers, who opened the doors and bowed Ella and Vanka forward.

Ella found herself standing in a room of such scale and such daunting opulance that it quite took her breath away. She was so awestruck that it took a nudge from Vanka to bring her out of her fugue. Before she quite realised what was happening, she and Vanka had crossed the room, and were standing before Empress Dong E and Consort Robert.

This was the young couple who had brought peace to the Demi-Monde, who had persuaded the peoples of the Demi-Monde to accept the philosophy of non-violence enshrined in Normalism.

'We are pleased to welcome you to the Ying Palace,' announced the Empress, 'and to give our blessing to your mission to explore the Great Beyond. ABBA has answered our prayers and has removed the Boundary Layer ... the time of Confinement is over. Today, a new age dawns, the Age of Discovery, when for the first time in a thousand years HumanKind is able to travel beyond the Demi-Monde. We charge Colonel Maykov and Lady Ella to lead those with the courage and the fortitude to challenge the unknown and to explore the lands that have for so many years been closed to enquiry.'

Here the Empress gestured to the other Trekkers, who were standing along the right-hand side of the Hall. 'I salute you all: Burlesque Bandstand and his friend, Odette Aroca' – Burlesque doffed his bowler hat and Odette gave an awkward curtsy – 'Trixie Dashwood and her companion, Feliks Wysochi' – both gave a formal bow – 'and Dean Moynahan and Maria Steele' – Dean and Maria smiled in acknowledgement. 'To you eight brave and resolute explorers, I say *bonne chance*, and may ABBA be with you.'

'New adventures, eh, Ella?' whispered Vanka.

'I'm looking forward to them, Vanka, but I'm only going on one condition.'

'And what's that?'

'You tell me you love me.'

'Oh, I love you, Ella, and it is a love, like you, that will never die.'

Glossary 1:

The Demi-Monde

4Telling:	Predicting the Future. From the declension: 1Telling = Silence; 2Telling = Speaking of the Past; 3Telling = Speaking of the Present; 4Telling = Speaking of the Future.
ABBA:	The chief deity of all religions in the Demi-Monde. God. Referred to as 'Him' in the ForthRight and NoirVille, as 'Her' in the Coven and as 'HimHer' in the Quartier Chaud.
ABBAsoluteness:	The state of being united – body, mind and soul – with ABBA. Devotees seek ABBAsoluteness through the purification of their Solidified Astral Ether, which allows uncorrupted communion with ABBA.
Aqua Benedicta:	A chemical additive, developed by Abraham Eleazar, which prevents blood congealing and thus enables blood to be stored and preserved. Eleazar traded a regular supply of Aqua Benedicta to Shaka Zulu in exchange for the establishment of the nuJu Autonomous District in the centre of NoirVille, thus securing the long-wished-for nuJu HomeLand, and making Shaka's Blood Brothers the Demi-Monde's pre-eminent blood brokers.
Aryan:	The racial bedrock of UnFunDaMentalism. The Aryan ideal is to be blond, blue-eyed and fair-skinned, the physical profile of the Pre-Folk from whom the Aryan people are supposedly descended.
Auralism/Auralist:	A woman (there is no recorded incidence of males having the power of Auralism) who is able to discern and interpret the halo surrounding a Demi-Mondian's body. The most accomplished Auralists are the Visual Virgins of Venice.
Awful Tower, the:	The 350-metre-tall geodetic iron structure built in the heart of the Paris District to commemorate the signing of the Hub Treaty of 517 which marked the end of the Great War.

Destroyed in a terrorist act attributed to Normalist activists in Spring 1005. A corrupted remembrance of the Real World name *Eiffel Tower*.

Blanks: Derogatory NoirVillian slang term for Anglo-Slavs.

Blood Hounder: A half-human, half-animal creature developed by the SS specifically to track down Daemons. Blood Hounders have an enhanced sense of smell and are able to detect one drop of blood at a distance of 100 yards.

bodyclock: The means by which a Demi-Mondian body records the passage of time. The ticking that can be heard in the chest of all Demi-Mondians is the sound of their bodyclock.

Book of Profits, the The holiest book of the nuJus, which comprises 333 Epistles written by the Profits.

Boundary Layer, the: The impenetrable, transparent 'wall' which prevents Demi-Mondians leaving the Demi-Monde and entering the Great Beyond. UnFunDaMentalism officially defines the Boundary Layer as a Selectively Permeable Magical Membrane.

Checkya, the: The secret police of the ForthRight, established by Lavrentii Beria. A corrupted remembrance of the Real World word *Cheka*.

Confinement, the: The mythical event describing the original sealing of the Demi-Monde behind the Boundary Layer. As a consequence of the Fall of the Pre-Folk from grace with ABBA (see also 'Lilith'), ABBA punished the peoples of the Demi-Monde by confining them behind the impenetrable Boundary Layer in order that they should not corrupt the rest of His Creation with their Sin. Only when they have repented all their Sins, have come to Rapture and returned to Purity will ABBA, once again, smile upon them and allow them to be reunited with the rest of the Kosmos.

Confusionism: The religio-philosophical system that held sway in the Coven until it was toppled by HerEticalism in 996 AC. Although it is now something of an anachronism in the Coven, Confusionism (and especially its subform WunZianism) still informs much of Covenite life, thought and moral attitudes.

Cool: The most difficult concept in the whole of HimPerialist thought, being readily recognisable in those who possess it, but almost impossible to define. Parallels have been drawn between the HimPerial concept of Coolness and the state of *wu wei* enshrined in Confusionism. It is the *raison d'être* of HimPerial Men that they be and remain Cool, as this is the only way they can come to Oneness with ABBA. They try to act Cool (that is, they strive, no matter what the provocation, to remain calm and unexcited); they try to look Cool (exercising to sculpt their bodies and wearing hard-cut clothes); and they try to speak Cool (the ever-changing jive speech being the preferred patois of HimPerialistic males).

crypto:

Originally coined to describe a Suffer-O-Gette terrorist who had infiltrated the ForthRight, but now commonly used to refer to all spies and third columnists active in the Demi-Monde.

Daemons:

Mischievous and occasionally malignant (when in league with Loki) Spirits who manifest themselves in the Demi-Monde. They may be identified by their ability to bleed.

Dark
Charismatics:

The coterie of persons who exhibit the most malicious form of MALEvolence. Dark Charismatics, though physically indistinguishable from the host population, are preternaturally potent, possessing a perverted and grossly amoral nature. As such, Dark Charismatics present a morbid and extreme threat to the instinctive goodness of Demi-Mondians. The only reliable means of identifying Dark Charismatics is by the examination of their auras by Visual Virgins.

ForthRight:

The Demi-Mondian state created by the union of the Rookeries and Rodina. A corrupted remembrance of the Real World term *Fourth Reich*.

Future History:

The OutComes resulting from the application of preScience and the empiricalisation of 4Telling.

galvanicEnergy:

Electricity. Discovered by the ForthRight scientist Michael Faraday.

Hel:

The Demi-Mondian term for the underworld. A remembrance of the Norse word *Hel*.

HerEticalism:

The official religion of the Coven. HerEticalism is a religion based on female supremacy and the subjugation of men. The HerEtical belief is that Demi-Monde-wide peace and prosperity – an idyllic outcome given the HerEtical tag 'MostBien' – will only be realised when men accept a subordinate position within society. The more extreme HerEticals believe that a state of MostBien will only be secured when the male of the specie has been removed from the breeding cycle. Such is the extremist attitude of MostBiens that they are lampooned throughout the Demi-Monde as 'LessBiens'.

HIMnasium:

The place of worship for all Men who follow the HimPerial religion. Father Peter Polykleitos in his seminal work *The Kanon: A Man's Guide to a Heavenly Body*, has expounded his theories regarding the mathematical bases of aesthetic bodily perfection. These he has replicated in his famous sculpture *ABBA*, his representation of Man's ultimate physical perfection, incorporating the idealised symmetries of all parts of the male body.

Polykleitos' *ABBA* has been declared to be 'divinely inspired' by the Church of HimPerialism and is now cited as the aspirational model of the male body for all devout HimPerial Men. That this form may only be achieved by much strenuous exercise is believed to have been ordained by ABBA as a means by which Men may prove their faith.

Body Forming has now been incorporated into the Rites of the Church of HimPerialism and Men are encouraged to spend at least one hour per day in the HIMnasium in physical worship of ABBA, called to worship by MuscleMen.

HimPerialism:

The official religion of NoirVille. Based on an unwavering belief in male supremacy and the subjugation of women (or, as they are known in NoirVille, woeMen), HimPerialism teaches that Men have been ordained by ABBA to Lead and to Control the Demi-Monde and that woeMen's role is to be Mute, Invisible, Supine and Subservient (subMISSiveness). Further, HimPerialism states that an individual's Manliness may be enhanced by the exchange of bodily essences, a practice known as Man^2naM.

HimPeril:

The militant/terrorist wing of HimPerialism, HimPeril is dedicated to the use of violence and intimidation to achieve male supremacy and the subjugation of women.

Hub, the:

The grass and swampland area situated between the urban area of the Demi-Monde and Terror Incognita.

ImPuritanism:

The official religion of the Quartier Chaud. ImPuritanism is a staunchly hedonistic philosophy based on the belief that the pursuit of pleasure is the primary duty of ManKind and that communion with the Spirits can only be achieved during orgasm. The ultimate aim of all those practising ImPuritanism is the securing of JuiceSense: the experiencing of the extreme pleasure that comes from an unbridled sexual orgasm. To achieve JuiceSense requires that Men and Women are spiritually equal and that Man's proclivity towards MALEvolence is controlled and muted.

IRGON:
The Independent Regional Government of nuJus, the political organisation devoted to the maintenance of law and order in the JAD and the transporting of the nuJus scattered around the Demi-Monde to this nuJu homeland. That the IRGON is seen by HimPerial extremists – notably the Black Hand gang – as the body responsible for bringing the seemingly never-ending stream of nuJu refugees into NoirVille makes it a natural target in the war these so-called freedom fighters are waging against those they call the 'infidel interlopers'.

JAD:
The nuJu Autonomous District, the area of NoirVille settled by the nuJus and granted independence by His HimPerial Majesty Shaka Zulu in exchange for the supply of Aqua Benedicta.

Lilith:
The semi-mythical Shade witch – adept in the esoteric knowledge of Seidr magic – who corrupted the Demi-Monde and brought down the Pre-Folk. The Dark Temptress who initiated the Fall.

LunarAtion:
The green light emitted by Mantle-ite, most notably when it is struck by moonlight.

Machismo:
The NoirVillian honour code for Men. The striving for Machismo suffuses and directs all the actions of Men once they have successfully navigated the Rite of Passage.

MALEvolence:
The theory developed by the Quartier Chaudian thinker Mary Wollstonecraft which postulates that war is caused by men but suffered by women. In her Theory of MALEvolence, Wollstonecraft identified that men by their natural and undeniable inclination to obey orders given to them by superiors – no matter how nonsensical or barbaric such orders are – are susceptible to disproportionate influence by their more unbalanced peers and hence are inevitably and inexorably drawn towards violence as a solution to disputes. The muting of MALEvolence is the ambition which led to the creation of ImPuritanism. Consideration of MALEvolence was also instrumental in prompting Michel de Nostredame to identify the malignant Dark Charismatics lurking within the Quartier Chaudian population. A corrupted remembrance of the Real World word *malevolence*.

MANdate:
Signed between His HimPerial Majesty Shaka Zulu and the Head of the IRGON, Rabbi Schmuel Gelbfisz, the

MANdate states: 'His HimPerial Majesty Shaka Zulu views with favour the establishment in NoirVille of a national home for the nuJu people, and will use his best endeavours to facilitate the achievement of this objective, it being clearly understood that nothing shall be done which may prejudice the civil and religious rights of the existing Shade communities. In return the nuJu people will provide NoirVille, on an exclusive basis, with such quantities of Aqua Benedicta as it may demand.' It was the signing of this document that paved the way for the establishment of the JAD ... and for all the grief, hatred and violence that followed as a consequence.

Man²naM:
The practice of NoirVillian men who exchange essences in order to enhance their Manliness.

Mantle, the:
The impenetrable crust of the Demi-Monde situated below the topsoil.

Mantle-ite:
The indestructible material used by the Pre-Folk to construct sewers, water pipes, Blood Banks and the Mantle.

MANtor:
For a Boy to grow into a Man he must be trained and moulded by a MANtor who personifies all the sacred qualities of Machismo. By imitating his MANtor the Boy will grow to be like him, assimilating his virtues into his own personality. Often MANtors are warriors who have grown too old to run with their HimPi but have shown that they are wise in the ways of Machismo and are possessed of Coolness. The MANtor represents the law and the teachings of HimPerialism and it is his duty to break any emotional attachment a Boy might feel to his mother and to woeMen.

MuscleMen:
The Holy Men, who call all Men who follow HimPerialism to exercise in the HIMnasium, in order that they may worship ABBA through perfecting their bodies.

nanoBites:
The submicroscopic creatures which inhabit the soil layer of the Demi-Monde. They consume everything – except Mantle-ite – converting it to soil.

Normalism:
The philosophy of nonViolence, Civil Disobedience and Passive Resistance developed by Norma Williams.

nuJuism:
The religion of the nuJu diaspora, this is an unrelentingly pessimistic religion that teaches that suffering and hardship are life-affirming, and are endured to prepare the followers for the coming of the Messiah who will lead them through Tribulation to the Promised Land.

Ordo Templi Aryanis:	The most zealous and uncompromising of all UnFunDaMentalist sects. Their belief is that the Anglo-Slavic people will not reclaim its oneness with the Spirits – lost after the Fall – until it is racially cleansed and all contaminating racial elements (the UnderMentionables) have been eradicated.
Pawnography:	A term coined by HerEticals to disparage the erotic materials produced and distributed in the Quartier Chaud. HerEticals deemed all such material to be a violation of female rights as it degraded women and encouraged violence against them. The HerEtical term for Erotic Material is pawnography as it is said to lead to Women selling (or pawning) their bodies to Men's crazed lusts. Such pawnography encourages a belief in male superiority as it celebrates the power of the penis. A corrupted remembrance of the Real World word *pornography*.
Portals:	Places where Daemons can move into and out of the Demi-Monde.
Pre-Folk:	The semi-mythical race of godlings who ruled over the Demi-Monde before the Confinement and who were brought low by the sexual connivings of the Seidrwitch Lilith. The demise of the Pre-Folk is known in Demi-Mondian mythology as 'the Fall'. UnFunDaMentalism teaches that the Pre-Folk were the purest expression of the Aryan race. Also known as the Vanir.
preScience:	A Venetian school of philosophy dedicated to the study of (and the making of) prophecies and 4Tellings, especially in the areas of economics and finance. The greatest of all preScientists are Professeur Michel de Nostredame and Docteur Nikolai Dmitriyevich Kondratieff of the Future History Institute, Venice. A corrupted remembrance of the Real World word *prescience*.
Qi:	The energy flow which surrounds and permeates all living things. It is the unseen and unseeable *élan vital* which gives life and breath to the inanimate, thus making it animate. It energises the soul which resides in all things constituted by the Living.
RaTionalism:	An avowedly and uncompromisingly atheistic creed developed by the renegade Rodina thinker and ardent Royalist Karl Marx, which strives by a process of Dialectic ImMaterialism to secure logical explanations regarding the Three Great Dilemmas. RaTionalism rejects all supernatural interpretations with respect to the *Three Great*

	Dilemmas and does not acknowledge any input that cannot be verified by the five senses.
Shades:	The slang term for NoirVillians.
sheMan:	Unique to NoirVille, sheMen are classified as 'transgender', though many opt for full emasculation to ensure their journey into sheManHood is complete. The Church of HimPerialism teaches that for Men, sheMen are the preferred outlet for their sexual lusts, and with their being so few (relative to Men) their services are highly prized and lucrative. For poor NoirVillian Boys, a career as a sheMan is very attractive.
Shvartses:	The nuJu slang term for Shades.
Solidified Astral Ether:	Also known by the acronym SAE. The substance which makes up the soft tissue of all Demi-Mondians.
Solution:	A cocktail of vodka and soda with one or more shots of blood. Usually available in 5 per cent, 10 per cent and 20 per cent strengths of blood.
Sphinx, the:	The holiest shrine in both nuJu and HimPerial religions, thought to have been constructed by the nuJus in the time before the Confinement when they had the power to work Mantle-ite. The nuJu Book of Profits ascribes the creation of this graven image as the reason why ABBA condemned the nuJu people to wander homeless through the Demi-Monde.
SS:	Soldiers of Spiritualism, the military wing of the Ordo Templi Aryanis.
steamers:	Steam-powered vehicles popular in the Demi-Monde.
subMISSiveness:	As punishment for Lilith's connivance in the Fall of Man, ABBA decreed that henceforward woeMen would be required to conduct themselves according to the precepts of subMISSiveness, that is, they must be at all times Mute, Invisible, Subservient and Sexually Modest. Only in this way may woeMen earn the forgiveness of ABBA.
Terror Incognita:	The area extending in a radius of four miles around Mare Incognitum and bounded by the Wheel River. A totally unexplored region of the Demi-Monde. No explorer venturing into Terror Incognita has ever returned. A corrupted remembrance of the Real World term *Terra Incognita*.
Under Mentionables:	A catch-all term for all those considered by UnFunDaMentalism to be racially inferior and hence

subhuman (including, *inter alia*, nuJus, Poles, Shades, HerEticals, Suffer-O-Gettes, HimPerialists, RaTionalists, those of a sexually deviant disposition, and those deemed to be genetically flawed). A corrupted remembrance of the Real World word *Untermensch*.

UnFunDa
Mentalism:

The official religion of the ForthRight, UnFunDaMentalism is based on the philosophy of Living&More or life reform, which espouses clean living, vegetarianism, homeopathy and an abstention from alcohol, blood, tobacco and recreational sex. Heavily suffused with the occult and a belief in the existence of a Spirit World. Aleister Crowley is head of the Church of UnFunDaMentalism.

UnFunnies:

The slang name for UnFunDaMentalists.

Visual Virgins:

A Venetian order of Sisters established by Doge Oldoini as the Sacred and All-Seeing Convent of Visual Virgins. This Convent is dedicated to the selection and training of girls adept in Auralism (only virgin females have the power of Auralism) in order that they may be used to screen Men living in the Quartier Chaud and hence to identify Dark Charismatics masquerading as CitiZens. Visual Virgins practise fiduciary sex.

WhoDoo:

The cult religion of NoirVille, based on a distorted remembrance of Seidr.

woeMen:

The NoirVillian term for women.

Yin/Yang:

The binary opposites of the Kosmos, representing, *inter alia*, dark and light, cold and hot, female and male. But though Yin and Yang are opposites, they are complementary and mutually dependent: one cannot exist without the other and they strive unceasingly to create the balance that will bring harmony to the Kosmos and ABBAsoluteness to HumanKind. When this is accomplished, Yin will fuse with Yang to create Ying, the ultimate transcendental Peace. The achieving of Ying by the purification of the Astral Ether is the ultimate aim of all WunZian Confusionists.

zadnik:

Demi-Mondian slang for a male homosexual and, more generally, for a NoirVillian male. The word is derived from the Russian *zad* meaning arse.

Glossary 2:

The Real World

12/12: The 12/12 dirty nuke terrorist attack perpetrated by the terrorist group Christ's Crusaders on the city of Edinburgh, Scotland, on 12 December 2014 killed 150,000 people and caused economic damage estimated to be in the order of £300 billion. 12/12 is cited as the main reason Sam Williams was able to oust Peter Kenton II from the White House, Kenton having been discredited by his association with the Crusaders.

ABBA: ABBA (Archival, Behavioural, Biological Acquisition) is a Quanputer-based system developed and operated by ParaDigm CyberResearch Limited. By utilising an Invent-TenN° Gravitational Condenser incorporating an Etirovac Field Suppressor°, ABBA is the only computer to achieve a full SupaUnPositioned/DisEntangled CyberAmbiance. As a consequence, ABBA is capable of prodigiously rapid analysis (a fully tethered 30 yottaQuFlops) to give the bioNeural-kinetic engineers at ParaDigm access to almost unlimited processing power.

bioSignatures: The means by which a digital identity can be verified. BioSignatures include, *inter alia*, fingerprints, retinal scans, DNA and pheromonic analysis.

biPsych: Those who have a simultaneous existence in both the Real World (as a NowLived) and in the Demi-Monde (as a Dupe).

Demi-Monde, the: The steadily increasing demand for US Army involvement in Iraq, Afghanistan, Pakistan and other Asymmetrical Warfare Environments (AWEs) post-9/11 led to the issuing of Tender Document USAWVTP#2/2013/NANOIMP/67/JCS on 27 January 2013. This document required the development of a means by which neoFight – US Army terminology for a newly recruited/newly trained grunt – training could be shortened and improved, and subsequent battlefield performance enhanced. The Demi-Monde was the virtual reality world, platformed on ABBA, designed by ParaDigm CyberResearch to meet these requirements..

eyeMail:

An ABBA-platformed means of transmitting person-to-person messages, the privacy and integrity of the message being assured by ParaDigm's RetinQek Verification Program.

eyeSpy:

Hover-capable and independently programmable surveillanceBot.

eyeVid:

An ABBA-platformed means of transmitting person-to-person digital moving-image messages.

Flexi-Plexi:

Digital wallpaper. When connected to a Polly, a wall covered with Flexi-Plexi is able to display any digital image to a size and shape determined by the viewer.

Fun/Funs:

Street/marketing name for the Fun-Loving Fundamentalists, the Christian youth movement established and lead by Norma Williams.

INDOCTRANS:

Indoctrination and Training Command: the department of the US Army responsible for the operation of the Demi-Monde.

monopad:

A prefabricated one-room living unit which encompasses within a six-metres square floor plan areas for washing, food preparation and living/sleeping.

moteBots:

Nano-sized, independently viable and dynamically flexible surveillance cameras. The use of moteBots was declared illegal by the League of Nations' Universal Charter of Human Rights and Privacy of 2015.

noöPINC:

The 2nd generation Personal Implanted nanoComputer, noöPINC is a cyborg-virus – a virus with man-made elements incorporated into its make-up – these nanocybernetic structures acting as inception points for the development of the virus. The virus grows around them and by doing so absorbs the artificial elements into its genetic structure.

nu-Commandments:

The fifteen nuCommandments that Frank Kenton presented to the world during his Coliseum speech of 1953 (and which formed the basis of American political, religious and social thinking for the next sixty years). These nuCommandments were, according to Kenton, given to him via an angel sent by God, each nuCommandment etched on an orb which 'shone with a holy green light'.

PanOptika: The ABBA-platformed program that links all surveillance apparatus (whether private or State) and all databases (whether private or State) to develop a full 360-degree cyber-portrait of individual citizens.

PINC: A Personal Implanted nanoComputer; developed by ParaDigm Technologies as a means to radically reduce training times and to find a more efficient method of inculcating students and trainees with specific knowledge sets. PINC is a nano-sized Memory Supplement which is biologically compatible with the human brain. Once in contact with the brain, PINC fuses with its organic tissue and is able to graft information – painlessly and seamlessly – into a person's memory bank.

PINC Referendum of 2015: The 12/12 attack on Edinburgh marked a substantial shift in the attitude of the British towards PINC. Before the attack public opinion was largely negative, there being widespread suspicion that the wholesale PINCing of the population would lead to an unacceptable infringement of privacy and personal liberty. After the attack national security became the pre-eminent concern of British citizens, and the arguments that PINC would ensure their safety *and* their e-identity had greater resonance. A referendum was called to decide the matter and almost 60 per cent of those eligible to vote did so in favour of the compulsory and universal adoption of PINC within the British Empire. It is anticipated that this policy will be executed at the end of May 2019.

Polly: Street name for a polyFunctional Digital Device which encompasses, in one dockable device, an individual's complete computational, communication, security, biomonitoring and entertainment requirements.

PollyMorph: An ABBA-based program that enables digital modifications applied to one part of a moving-image digital stream to be automatically replicated through the entire digital stream. Analogous to PaintShop for videos.

Shielders: Anti-surveillanceBots.

Temporal Modulation (Laws of): As described in 'Precepts of Temporal Modulation', written by Beowulf Bole in 1933. There are four laws of Temporal Modulation.
The Law of Temporal Modelling: The Primary Objective of the Bole Institute for the Advancement of

History is to direct all Temporal Modulations in order
that ParaDigm becomes and remains the world's supreme
industrial, commercial and financial organisation. By
achieving this ambition, the Bole family will be able to
protect and to preserve the Grigori and to fulfil their long-
cherished dream of gaining hegemony over the Fragiles
and all of the other lesser species of the world. To secure
this end, NO Temporal Modulation shall be undertaken
that has not first been modelled by the Bole Institute for
the Advancement of History. A Modulation awarded a less
than ninety per cent probability of achieving the desired
Temporal Outcome will NOT be executed.

The Law of Temporal Minimalism: Temporal
manipulation is a delicate matter. Even the most nugatory
of changes to the TimeStream can, over the course of
history, have unforeseen and unwelcomed consequences,
referred to as temporal noise or, more whimsically, as
the Butterfly Effect. Thus, Temporal Modulations must be
the minimum actions required to achieve the designated
outcome. If we conceive of time as a pool of still water, then
applying the concept of minimalism, changes made must
not only create the fewest ripples but also those with the
lowest amplitude and shortest duration.

The Law Pertaining to the Avoidance of Mass
Resurrection: Every effort must be made when executing a
Temporal Modulation to avoid the cancellation of a Major
Event (such as a war, a plague or a famine) which has
resulted in a substantial number of deaths. The reason for
this is obvious: it is impossible to forecast with any degree
of probability the impact on the TimeStream of such a
large number of Resurrectionees. If, for example, we were
to intervene to prevent the occurrence of the Great War,
the changes wrought to history by the eight million or
so casualties not dying would be incalculable and could
endanger our management of the TimeStream. If the Law
of Temporal Minimalism counsels us never to toss anything
larger than a pebble into the Pool of Time, the cancellation
of a Major Event and hence the provoking of a Mass
Resurrection is the equivalent of hurling a huge block of
concrete into the pool.

The Law of Temporal Proximity: All Temporal
Modulation Orders must be enacted as close (both
temporally and spatially) to the desired outcome as is
possible. Failure to adhere to this precept can result in
'temporal spillage' – the manifestation of unwanted
effects in the TimeStream. Thus, if instructions are to be
communicated to enact a Temporal Modulation Order,
these must be directed as near to the intended date of

change as possible (though this must NOT violate the Law of Temporal Boundaries).

The Law of Temporal Boundaries: It is a peculiarity of the Temporal Modulation mechanism that it is dangerous to attempt a Modulation directed to a Temporal Nexus at a distance of <u>less</u> than twenty-five years from the initiating Nexus. The consequences of violating this law are aptly illustrated by the destruction of the Tunguska TiME facility in 1908. It is therefore imperative that <u>NO</u> Temporal Modulations are conducted within a footprint of 25 years of the Initiation Date.

TIS: The Total Immersion Shroud used to encase the bodies of Real World visitors to the Demi-Monde in order to preserve muscular viability.